THE GHOST AT BEAVERHEAD ROCK

Carol Buchanan

Carol Buchanan Books
Kalispell, Montana

Book Layout ©2013 BookDesignTemplates.com

Ordering Information:
For all sales inquiries, email Carol A. Buchanan at her website: http://carol-buchanan.com

The Ghost at Beaverhead Rock / Carol Buchanan. -- 1st ed.
ISBN 978-0-9864203-0-6

In Loving Memory of

Sylvia Murphy (1916-2015)

By asking questions, she improved my writing.

By her belief and encouragement, she inspired me.

A time to kill and a time to heal

—Ecclesiastes 3:3

Thank You To ...

Sue Greskowiak, of Artistic Barbering in Kalispell, MT, for her knowledge of the life of barber shops.

Robert Harrison, who described and mapped out the old stage route from Bannack to Beaverhead Rock.

William Levy, historian of the family, provided me with information about his 5-g grandfather, Lewis Hershfield, a banker in Virginia City in 1864.

Dr. Carrie Merrill, OB/GYN, guided me in the realism of Martha's difficult pregnancy.

Jess E. Owen, president of Authors of the Flathead, and author of the Summer King fantasy chronicles, led the group in our monthly "Open Readings" during the developmental phase of this novel.

Heidi M. Thomas, editor and author of the Cowgirl Dream novels based on her grandmother's dream to be a rodeo bronc rider, proved that writers need editors.

Especially, I want to thank Richard S. Wheeler, the great author of historical fiction set in the West, who has encouraged me since I first showed him God's Thunderbolt: The Vigilantes of Montana.

And as always, my computer guru, infrastructure manager, and indefatigable backup, Sir Richard (aka Dick Buchanan). Also my husband of 40 years.

Part I

~~1~~

Above all, Timothy must not see it. No sixteen-year-old boy should ever see it, least of all Timothy, who had buried a murdered friend last winter, and his murdered father in the summer. By the time they were found, each could only be identified by the things he carried: A borrowed pocket knife. A pilfered frying pan.

Boys his age did not grow calluses; their wounds went deep and scabbed over, festering underneath. This could break the scab.

Keep your wits about you, Daniel Stark told himself. He must prevent Timothy from seeing this. For the boy's sake and his own.

He had wanted no part of it. Exhausted after weeks' accumulated sleeplessness aboard jolting stagecoaches, he had wanted only to lie down on a bed, even having to share it, however old the straw in the mattress might be, as long as it did not move beneath him. But when the others approached him on the street after supper and reminded him of his duty, he'd been forced to go with them.

For several cold hours wrangling over the necessity of it, he'd held out only to have men change sides until he stood alone, worn down by their logic. They reminded him that the by-laws mandated a unanimous verdict. And so he'd conceded.

Waiting for Timothy on the porch of the Bannack Restaurant, he listened to the memory: their boots crunched over crusted snow, they swore in whispers to quiet their weeping burden as they climbed the hill. Dan's gaze followed their path into the darkness where the unseen gallows stood on a rise.

The mountains behind it had not yet emerged from darkness, though morning twilight lightened the sky through rents in the heavy cloud cover.

Down the street, a four-horse team pulled the stagecoach up to the Overland office. He and Timothy must be on it before light came.

Dan considered going back into the restaurant to hurry the boy, but he knew that would only make him even slower, sip the dregs of his coffee, sop up the last drop of syrup. Timothy had been contrary ever since they had met at Fort Hall, a three days' journey south. Dan had been patient, thinking Timothy grieved for his father.

But his patience with the boy's sullen attitude had thinned. Intending to go in and drag him out, Dan turned on his heel just as the restaurant door creaked on its hinges.

"Brrr." Timothy stamped his feet.

"Yes it is," Dan said. Pretending to enjoy the sky, he glanced up toward the rise behind the town. Ragged clouds sailed the night sky, moonlight silvering their edges, though darkness hid the gallows. Good. If they could board the stage quickly enough, Timothy would never see it. "The stage will be ready to leave in a few minutes. We'd better board."

Timothy ignored him.

Dan tried again. He pointed his chin toward the Overland office. The horses' breath steamed in the lamplight spilling from the windows. They stamped and shook themselves, rattled their harness. They wanted to run, to get warm.

"We'd better get a move on."

"What's the all-fired hurry? We got plenty of time." Timothy looked up, past the rise behind the town. "Look at that moon."

Through a parting in the clouds, the full moon shone bright and coldly indifferent to the man who had died on that rise a few hours ago. "We have to hurry." He quickened his pace. "Help me load my boxes."

"Them damn boxes. You been fussin' about them since we met up. What's in 'em? Gold?" His humorless laugh meant, No one ever brought gold into gold country; they took it out.

If he answered yes? What would Timothy say then? Accuse him of staying so long in New York just to make more money? The accusation would be true enough, as far as it went. "I want to get home. I've been away from your mother too long."

"Damn right you been away too long. You could've come home sooner. She pined for you. We expected you when they found Pap."

Dan let that pass. What did finding McDowell's body have to do with expecting him home? How could he have known that Timothy's father had not lit out for parts unknown? That was what so many rough men did when the Vigilantes hunted down the gang terrorizing the region. "Then let's not keep her waiting any longer." Praying Timothy would follow, he lengthened his stride.

Not hearing anyone behind him, Dan looked over his shoulder. Timothy stood gazing up at the sky as though in wonder. Had he never noticed moonlight on flying clouds before, the changing beauty of the sky?

Christ, if he saw it.

Walking back as fast as he dared, Dan gripped Timothy's elbow. "Come on. They'll leave without us."

"Hey! Let go of me." The boy wrenched free.

At the stage office, the driver came out, stretching his arms, rolling his shoulders to loosen them. A bullwhip trailed in long loops from one hand. He touched his hat-brim to a woman who wore a fur wrap. Wiping one hand on his trouser leg, he offered it to assist her stepping up into the coach. She said something that brought a smile to his face, and gave her hand to the man who followed her.

"They're loading. We have to go. Come on."

The wind shredded the clouds and the moon shone on the flatter ground in front of two small hills that plunged into a gully. On the gallows. On the hanged man whose head lolled toward his shoulder.

"Good God Almighty." Timothy leaped into a run uphill toward the thing. "We gotta cut him down."

Dan charged after him, close on his heels, yet not close enough to grab his coat, hold him back. He slipped on dead bunch grass under snow, jumped the sluice ditch, dashed between cabins on Bachelor's Row.

He caught Timothy several yards from the hanging corpse. Tackled him. They tumbled together onto the hard ground. "No, Tim, don't look." He lost what he meant to say as the corpse turned on its rope.

Its frozen eyeballs stared into his soul.

Timothy struggled free, stood up. "Christ, Dan'l, Christ." He turned away and vomited.

Rising, Dan laid his hand on Timothy's convulsing back. He should have prevented him from ever seeing this.

The corpse had no feet.

~~~

To Tim's way of thinking, the stagecoach driver should've waited until they'd buried the poor fella decent, and said a prayer over him. It would've been all right with the married couple sitting across from him and Dan'l. The coach had only them four as passengers. They wouldn't be inconveniencing nobody. In November people didn't travel to Virginia City, they left it, getting out before winter settled in. The driver wouldn't wreck the schedule, though, and Dan'l wouldn't hear of waiting two days for the next stage.

"I've been away from your mother too long as it is," he'd said.

Other men had come a-running, and said they'd take care of him.

The coach rode like a bucking horse, and too many other folks' hinder parts had squashed the seat padding. They kept the window leathers down on account of the cold, and that meant bad air and worse light. His mouth tasted like shit, and he wanted to puke again.

Walking back to the hotel last night after dinner, they'd met three men Dan'l knew. Tim would bet his last flake of gold dust they was part of this. They'd invited Dan'l to a meeting, but he knew it was an invitation Dan'l couldn't say no to. Right then, Tim had figured it was Vigilante business. But this?

The Vigilantes hadn't hung nobody for a couple months. Tim had thought that was all over. It should've been. They didn't need the Vigilantes to keep order now. This was a Territory, signed off by that bastard in the White House, and it had a governor. They'd had elections for a legislature a week ago. A Chief Justice had come in, and court was set to open in a month. A Yankee court, a mudsill court, but still. Better'n the miners' courts and the Vigilante tribunals they'd had up to now. Each county had its own sheriff and a deputy. The Vigilantes didn't have nothing to do.

So why'd they hang this poor fella?

Dan'l sat next to him, facing backward to give the preacher and his wife the whole seat facing front. He held his rifle propped between him and the coach wall, and the long box holding Mam's present between his knees. Tim extended his legs to brace his feet against the base of the opposite seat, where the couple sat.

The woman sniffed and touched a big handkerchief to her eyes and nose. Her husband comforted her, "My dear, his soul is with the Lord now. Our Lord is a God of infinite mercy."

"But he was so pitiful," she said. "What sort of monsters would hang a man who had no feet?" She wept again into her handkerchief.

What did Dan'l think of that? Tim wondered. What would happen if he said, Here's one of your monsters, sitting right here. Make Dan'l defend himself. Defend what they'd done. If he could defend it. He wished to hell Dan'l would say something, but he sat stone quiet, till Tim wanted to shout: Why'd y'all hang him? He couldn't have done nothing to nobody. He was dying of gangrene anyway.

Stretching his legs to ease a cramp in his foot, he accidentally touched the parson's leg. The man snapped, "I'll thank you to keep your boots to yourself."

Almost, Tim unloaded on him because who the hell cared about a little dirt when he'd seen what he'd seen just a bit ago? Mam had brought him up right, though, taught him to respect his elders, so he pulled his feet back. "Beg pardon. I had a cramp in my foot."

"Give thanks to God that you have feet." The wife blew her nose again.

"My young friend is not so foolish as to subject his feet to frostbite and gangrene." Dan'l talked like a book when he was angered.

"You, sir, are you utterly lacking in sympathy?"

The woman might've said more, but the man sitting on her other side spoke up: "My dear wife is quite correct. How could anyone hang a man in his condition? It's unconscionable. Our Lord said, 'Blessed are the merciful.' He meant us to have mercy on sinners because we are sinners ourselves."

No one said anything to that.

They jounced along for a bit, until the parson said, "You two went to cut him down? Am I right?"

"Yes," said Dan'l.

"I understand there was a note," the preacher said.

"Yes," Dan'l said. "It read, 'Rawley! He came back! He was warned!'"

"What does that mean?" asked the parson. "'Came back'? 'Warned'?"

"And how does that justify murdering the poor creature?" The woman asked. "Surely they could have pitied the poor man's condition."

Dan'l said nothing.

A dry axle squeaked; horses' iron-shod hooves hammered the rocky surface. Again the parson asked, "What did that mean?"

Fed up with Dan'l keeping quiet and pretending he hadn't been part of it, Tim demanded, "Yeah, what did it mean?" Dan'l was the Vigilante prosecutor, he was probably behind that infernal sentence to start with. "Why carry it out now? Whatever he was, he weren't no danger to nobody. Not in the shape he was in."

"Yes," the preacher said. "Couldn't they have had mercy on him?"

In his corner, Dan'l held onto that long box like his life was in it. A present for Mam, he'd told Tim when they met at Fort Hall, but he wouldn't say what it was. Just when Tim would've yelled at him, he broke his silence. His voice rasped like he had a catarrh or something. "When the Vigilantes banished Rawley last winter they made it clear that his life would be forfeit if he returned. He understood that. Hanging him now showed other criminals that they mean what they say."

The parson asked again, "Could they not have pitied his awful condition?"

The traces jangled, hooves clattered on the iron ground. The dry axle squeaked.

Dan'l said, "We are not in the business of showing mercy to the merciless."

~~~

At Rattlesnake Ranch, the coach stopped. While stable hands unhitched the tired horses and caught up a fresh team, the passengers left the coach to warm up inside the ranch building.

It was just as Dan remembered: the scorched fireplace set into the back wall, the same gray smell of meat simmering in a pot over the fire, the round-shouldered bartender's dark glare of hate for a Vigilante. He stood Martha's box against the wall and left the rifle slung on his shoulder.

The preacher pulled up a stool near the fireplace for his wife and stood between her and Timothy and Dan, as if shielding her from his evil influence. Preacher though he was, there was money somewhere in their makeup. He wore a wool coat with a fur collar, and the fur shawl around his wife's shoulders extended down in front like an apron to protect her lap and keep her warm when sitting in a coach. She warmed her hands in a beaver muff.

He wanted to say, If it hadn't been for us, you would not reach Virginia with your money. Or without it, depending on how disappointed the robbers were. He thought of one man running for his life when robbers found he was poor. A ball parted his hair as he fled.

No matter what they guessed, or thought they knew, he could say nothing. He had sworn an oath of secrecy last winter, to tell no one about their deliberations, the evidence, or the witnesses who told of threats, narrow escapes, robberies. The gang members who unburdened themselves before they met their Maker.

Green wood in the fireplace exploded. As Dan brushed sparks from his sleeve, Timothy hissed into his ear, "Why the hell did you do it?"

He chose his words for their neutrality: "Only another sixty miles to go. Then we're home." Home. The word thudded to the floor.

"I don't understand," Timothy insisted. "Why'd you do it?"

Hearing him, the woman let out a small scream.

"You were part of it?" demanded the preacher.

Dan ignored him. He could not attempt to justify himself to these people, but if Timothy would not let it go, he would explain as far as his oath allowed. To him alone. "Help me check on the freight." Collecting Martha's present, he shut the door on the cold warmth of the place. Seeing as how the Vigilantes had hanged the former owners, the bartender would complain of Vigilante injustice, call them stranglers.

Timothy caught up with him. Their boots crunched loud on the snow-crusted ground. In the lee of the building, at a corner where log ends stuck out in irregular lengths, they sheltered from the breeze.

Dan stared at the frozen ground. Why should he be compelled to explain that decision? To justify it when he found no justification in his own mind? He had voted to hang a crippled man, and he wanted to vomit.

"We freezing our asses for a reason?"

Looking up, he found Timothy scowling at him.

If only he could erase the decision and its consequences. He would have to tell Timothy what he could and pray for his understanding.

"Last winter, we did have mercy on Rawley. We were not sure about some of the evidence against him. There was an element of reasonable doubt about his role. He was not the strongest character nor very intelligent. We knew he passed on gossip about miners leaving with their gold. Robbery victims told us he was present during one robbery at gun point, maybe two. He never thought about another man's suffering, how he worked months in cold streams – you know about that. And then to have it all taken away. None of the gang ever thought about the families waiting at home."

"Yeah, I know." Timothy shifted about, squirmed a little. Was he thinking of the endless hours he'd crouched in Alder creek, or drove a sledgehammer to break rock for the gold?

"We also felt some men accused him for their own selfish reasons, but there were too many accounts of his complicity to let him go. He liked to be known as a tough man, to be around the roughs and the truly tough men."

He did not say, your father was one of that sort. Timothy McDowell knew it all too well.

"We voted to banish him on condition he would be shot on sight or hanged if he came back. If we'd had a jail, he would have been there still."

"There's a jail now," said Timothy.

"Yes, so I've heard." He did not have to say he'd learned that in the night. "When was it built?"

"Middle of July."

He walked a step or two into the wind to hide the extra moisture in his eyes. So much suffering could have been avoided if they'd had a jail then. He turned back.

"Without a jail, we could either hang Rawley or banish him." He had recommended banishment, and he had to pause, looking into his own inner darkness, seeing where that sentence had led. "Instead of going over the mountains to Lewiston, he stayed out of sight. Being afraid of death, he waited too long until the gangrene had taken his feet." Thinking of how Rawley had suffered, he had to stop to regain some control. "When he crawled into town, it was too late by weeks. The doctor said more amputation would not stop the gangrene."

He left unsaid: Once you cut a man's legs off, what else was left? The flesh above his knees was already streaked with infection.

After hours of wrangling, sickened by this haggling over which miserable end to give him, and knowing he could never prevail, he had voted with the others to carry out the sentence because all capital sentences had to be unanimous, according to the bylaws. They had voted then one by one: Aye. Bleak voices in candlelight tossed by cold drafts.

"Damn it, Dan'l, he couldn't have done no harm to anyone now. Like the fella said, he was dying anyways."

"I know. But consider this." The final argument he could not overcome: To carry out the sentence or not. "The roughs who made life hell a year ago equate mercy with weakness. They promised to get even, and they meant it. If we had spared Rawley out of pity, they would think we were weak. They swore vengeance and we believe them."

"You hung him so as not to look weak? Nobody could ever think you-all are weak."

"Because we do what we say. We carry out the sentences we pronounce." Hearing chains jingle and men swear, he peered around the logs. The lead team was almost hitched up.

"You could've let him be this time. He was dying anyways."

"In that meeting I learned that we are still the only wall between order and chaos. They told me last night, even with Territorial status we do not yet have a legal system, or codes of law, or adequate law enforcement. Can't you understand how weak that is?"

The stage driver shouted, "Movin' out, folks! Get in or stay here."

Timothy blocked Dan's way. "What I understand is, hanging a man with no feet was a devilish thing to do, and nothin' you say can change that."

"Would you be happier if we'd let him rot?"

Timothy wheeled and started toward the coach. Over his shoulder he said, "Far as I'm concerned, hanging a man with no feet is murder."

Martha's box slid from Dan's grasp, dropped back against the wall. When he picked it up, he had to fight to hold onto it with hands gone numb despite his leather fur-lined gloves. As he crossed the yard, a snow devil spun into his path and caught him into its dark center, a whirl of biting snow and howling wind, uncertain whether a step would take him forward or back, whether he stood or had fallen. When it cleared, he was at the coach, where one of the stable hands waited to shut the door. Unslinging the rifle, he carried the box and the long gun into the vehicle and took his seat.

~~2~~

The whip cracked, loud and sharper than a pistol shot. The horses sprang into a gallop, and the stagecoach lurched into speed. The coach canted a degree or two, then rocked hard to the side. The preacher's wife cried out, and Dan fell against Timothy, whose sharp elbow fended him off.

Startled, he realized they had driven most of the way to the next stage stop at Stone's Ranch while he had been lost in a kind of churning fog.

Opposite, Timothy sat with arms crossed over his chest, his hands tucked into his armpits; his hat brim hid his face above the tight line of his mouth.

Dan could grasp hold of no coherent train of thought. The snow devil had raked out his mind, leaving his ideas torn and floating before they settled into a random pile of torn scraps, two thoughts lying uppermost: Rawley's frozen glare and Timothy saying, 'murder.'

Had it been? Had he committed murder?

What would Martha think? She would learn of it, and being intelligent, she would know without being told that he had been involved. Timothy's accusation of murder was a scarlet letter on his coat that he would wear into Virginia City.

He was going home to a place he had never been.

Sometime later the stagecoach halted. The driver yelled down, "Stone's Ranch, folks. Just changin' the horses. Don't get out or you'll be left." Hooves clopped on the frozen ground, harnesses jangled. A stout whack followed by a man's curse: "Stand still, damn you." A minute later: "Good boy." The vehicle rocked as the driver climbed to his place. "Gee up there, you good-for-nothing cayuses." The bullwhip cracked. The stage jerked forward. The horses set out at a smart trot, across the long flat basin toward Beaverhead Rock.

Lost in his thoughts, Dan vaguely knew they splashed through a stream, then another, and a third.

The preacher asked, "Where are we?"

"Beaverhead Rock," Timothy answered.

Dan unhooked a corner of the leather curtain and looked out. Wind, rain, and melting snow had eroded deep vertical clefts in the limestone bluff looming out of the ground to rise a few hundred feet above the stream. Then the road turned, and Dan lost sight of it.

He hooked the curtain closed, restoring the cold gloom with its commonplace stink of foul breath and dirty underwear.

A frigid breath stinking of something at once rancid and sweet sighed along the back of his neck. Hitching his scarf up around his mouth and nose, he coughed. The odor stayed in his nostrils. He had smelled it before.

The sweetly sickening stench of a moldering corpse.

Breathing through his mouth, he tried to shut out the putrid odor. He peered at the minister and his wife. Sunk into their private thoughts, they seemed oblivious, wanting the ride over with, to reach their destination, to be warm again.

Just in case, he asked, "Do either of you smell something?"

"No," the parson answered for both of them.

Timothy shook his head.

In front of Dan, a shadow thickened, took the shape of a man standing knee-deep in the tatters of a restless mist that hid his lower legs. The head dropped sideways and downward in the broken-neck way of the hanged. Dan closed his eyes to shut out the apparition. When he opened them, it was still there.

I do not believe in ghosts. The shout stayed within the walls of his mind. *I am not a murderer.*

Would Martha – would she think him capable of murder?

He could tell her, I have never killed for profit or – God forbid – pleasure.

The Vigilantes had hanged those who had murdered about a hundred people for their gold. They had evidence. Without a court, or law enforcement, or laws to enforce, someone had to protect the citizens. Someone had to risk their lives, even their souls, to establish peace in Bannack and Alder Gulch.

Hanging Rawley was justice. He could have left the country.

Then what of Slade? Oh, God, Slade. If he had gone home when they told him to, he would still be alive.

No. His own choice had brought their fate on himself. And yet he could not squelch the guilt, the certainty that there had to have been a better way. If only they could have found it.

That smell. The shadow leaned against its wall of air. Dan's scalp crawled.

It could have been any of the twenty-odd men the Vigilantes had hanged. He had pulled a rope or two himself.

A whisper quiet as thought tickled his ear: *It didn't have to be this way.*

You made the wrong choices then, he told it.

The shadow, the form, vibrated. Had something disturbed it?

A draft, no doubt.

There is no such thing as a ghost. I am not a murderer. I will prove it.

~~3~~

Sometime after the coach began to cross the valley of the Stinking Water river, Dan realized the apparition had vanished.

Its stench, its shape – they were never there, he told himself. They'd been figments of his overwrought imagination, strained by exhaustion and the night's horror.

The coach rocked into a pothole, then over a stone, and the driver slowed the horses. Dan heard men shouting over hammers clanging on iron, hoofbeats, cattle lowing, and knew they were in Alder Gulch, but the noise was thinner than he expected. He unfastened the leather and peered out to see log cabins strung out against the dry, rocky hills. Yes, Alder Gulch. There were far fewer habitations than he'd expected, but it was the end of October – no, November, well into the season when men left to go home or elsewhere to winter in warmer places.

He buttoned the curtain.

Today was November first, the New Year's Day of the rest of his life. Soon he would be with Martha. How would she receive him? Uncertainty crept up his backbone, tightened his throat. He had promised to return before the ice covered the gold in Alder creek, but he'd been gone so long that she had sent Timothy to find him and bring him back. What would she think? He wanted to hold her. Love her.

He ached with wanting her.

She would ask, What kept you? Why did you not write? He could explain the need for more gold to repay Father's debt, how he'd been caught up in gold trading, the love of the risk.

But Harriet?

He could never explain Harriet, her blonde hair spread out on a rose-patterned carpet. Martha must never know about Harriet among red and yellow roses.

As the coach rolled out of Junction, the minister said, "I am the Reverend Asahel Hough, Pastor of the Methodist Church in Virginia City." He pronounced his name 'huff.' He introduced his wife, then held out his hand to Dan and Timothy in turn.

So he had decided to be a Christian, Dan thought, shaking the offered hand.

When he and Timothy had said their names and touched their hat brims to Mrs. Hough, the parson said, "We are not complete newcomers. We came to Virginia City in June as missionaries. We were in Bannack to invite people to the dedication of our new Methodist church. It's on the corner of Jackson and Cover Street, in Virginia City. You are both welcome to attend."

Mrs. Hough said to Dan, "You, sir, would be especially welcome. We would hope you would repent so that our Lord could ease your great burden of guilt and your soul would find rest in His mercy."

The coach slowed and lurched to a stop. The driver called down, "Just unloading the mail for Nevada City, folks. No need to get out."

Recovering, grateful for the poor light that hid his burning face, Dan said, "Thank you for your consideration, Mrs. Hough, but I do not repent. Considering everything, I would have to act as I did."

"May God have mercy on your soul," said Reverend Hough.

The coach moved out at a quick trot.

~~4~~

The passengers lapsed into the sort of silence that was louder than shouting. Dan braced himself for more lecturing for the good of his soul until hooves and wheels splashed through a small creek. Daylight creek. A few yards downstream from the ford, it flowed into Alder creek. They had crossed the boundary from Nevada Mining District into Fairweather Mining District, into the outskirts of Virginia City.

"Almost home," he said.

Timothy grunted.

The missionaries returned a few polite words.

The stagecoach swung into the wide turn where the main road became Wallace street, and Dan felt the uphill slant. Everything in Virginia City was either uphill or down.

"End of the line, folks," hollered the driver.

When they had said their goodbyes to the Houghs, Timothy said, "I'm livin' at Jake's house. Tell Mam I'll be to see her tomorrow." With that, he seized his valise and

25

turned away, up Wallace toward the first cross street, Jackson.

Dan arranged with the Overland agent to keep his treasure boxes safe until he could collect them. After helping the driver unload his small portmanteau, he slung his rifle over his right shoulder, tucked Martha's box under his left arm, and grasped the portmanteau in his left hand. The arrangement left his shooting arm free. He did not know if he would need the weapon, but until he knew better, he would be prepared. Virginia City had not always been so calm as it seemed now.

Late afternoon shone clear and blue; the westering sun threw his shadow before him as he walked up the street. On the corner of Wallace and Jackson, he set down the heavy portmanteau in front of the Eatery, to wait for traffic to clear. A heavy dray was unloading beer in barrels in front of a saloon, and other vehicles had to steer around it. Lighter delivery wagons, a few riders, and a mix of buggies and buckboards. All in all, they were hardly the congested traffic of Fifth Avenue, he thought. But his burdens made him slow, and he had time to wait for them to pass.

Directly across Jackson, the City Book Store shared the premises of the *Montana Post*. Catter-corner, a mix of signs on a white, one-story frame building announced "Ming's Books," a bank, a grocer, a jeweler, and a lawyer. Straight across Wallace, stood Content's Corner. Two stories and built of stone, the Gothic-inspired windows and fan lights above the doors made a decent attempt at stylish architecture. A sure sign that this rough-and-tumble town was determined to live down its crude and violent past.

When a space opened up between a fast buggy and a slow delivery wagon, he snatched up the portmanteau and hurried across. He walked in deep shadow up Jackson street along the length of Content's Corner. At the back of the building, a staircase attached to its outside wall led up to a veranda along its length.

If Sol Content remembered his promise to rent him an office, his door would open onto it, but he would see about that later. After he got squared away with Martha.

Martha. Would she be happy? She had not given him up or she would not have sent Timothy after him. Timothy who did not want him back.

His boots crunched over the boardwalk, its frozen surface pitted by hundreds of boot prints. Ahead, dark shadows cast by the sinking sun alternated with brilliant stripes of sunlit snow. Behind Content's Corner, there would be two vacant lots, and then his house. Where Martha waited for him. He had an urge to run back, catch the next stage out. Coward, he scolded himself, and put one foot in front of another. Anyway, there would be no stagecoach for three days.

Instead of vacant lots, he found the Star Restaurant and a dry goods store. A bit disoriented, he walked a few yards past his house and stopped at a pile of logs in a vacant lot.

Turning back, he looked across the street at another saloon, called the Champion Saloon, new since he'd been gone.

A dog barked. He recognized the slight up-tilted squeak at the end, that made each bark ask a question. Canary, Martha's dog, the youngsters' dog.

His house sat back from the street.

His house. He'd bought it when he first thought to persuade Martha to join him in a common-law marriage, because he knew that having her meant accepting her half-grown children, and he would not make love to her in the same room.

He walked up the path to the house and stopped, uncertain about what to say to her. He petted the dog, to give himself time. Did he want to marry her, to cut himself off from all other women? From Harriet? They could go on as they were; much of society here accepted a common-law marriage, an irregular union. Not the Houghs, of course. Or the best people, whose good opinion he would need to build a law practice, to live the life he wanted.

Home. Family. Martha.

But Harriet. Across the rough planks of his front door, a woman climbed thickly carpeted stairs; her buttocks tensed and relaxed under the soft slide of silk, and under his fingers. Harriet had led him up to her boudoir.

He knocked at his front door.

Inside the house, female voices asked each other why the dog barked so.

How could he give up Harriet? Then again, had he not already given her up by coming back? If Martha would have him, the wedding ceremony would demand promises from him, to cleave only unto her.

Till death did they part.

A young voice said, "I'll go see." Quick, light footsteps hurried to the door and opened it enough to see him. Her face, at first wary and inquiring, changed as he looked at her; her fists at her mouth stifled a scream.

"Dan'l! Mama! It's Dan'l."

Timothy's younger sister flung the door wide on a kaleidoscope of colors – red, green, purple, yellow – and a wide sweep of sun-bathed blue. Half-blinded by the rainbow swirl after walking in the shadows, his eyes took a second to adjust. The blue was the settee on the left-hand wall. The kaleidoscope came from a braided rug he'd never seen.

He took a firmer hold on Martha's box, gripped the portmanteau by its handle. Too late to leave Martha's box here and run back down the hill, too late to say it was all a mistake. Too late to go back to Harriet, unless Martha would not have him after all. Unless she thought him a murderer.

He scraped his boots on the mudsill and walked in.

The woman pushed herself up and out of her reading chair. She had been reading her Good Book, as she called it. Seeing him, she forgot the Bible, that dropped to the floor. "Dan'l?" She spoke his name in Martha's mellow tones, but if he had met her on the street he might not have recognized her. This was not the little brown sparrow of a woman he had left. She had grown obese, her cheeks were fat, purple pouches underscored her dark eyes. Her figure had changed. The deep red dress was belted beneath large breasts, the pleated skirt fell almost to the floor over a great bulge in her middle. A great bulge.

His thoughts stammered. Martha – not obese – Martha – bearing. Far gone, perhaps seven months? Eight? Swollen hands clutched her breasts, but her eyes, her luminous dark eyes, shone for him despite the circles beneath.

Martha opened her arms wide.

Somehow he set down the portmanteau, the box, the rifle, and kicked off his boots. He crossed the floor to her, but he knew nothing of that, only that he drew her to him without speaking, because he had more feeling than words could hold. Her stomach pressed against his abdomen.

Everything came clear. The swirl of colors settled. He was home. Martha welcomed him. His child was growing inside her. When he could, he whispered, "Will you marry me?"

Sobbing into his coat, she said, "Yes. Oh, yes."

Dotty danced and twirled around them, blonde curls flying. Abruptly, she stopped. "Mama, Dan'l, when are you marrying? Can – may I have a new dress for the wedding? Dan'l, what's New York City like? Can I go there sometime? Did you bring me any pretties?"

~~~

"Shall you stay here tonight?"

He had decided to find the City Bath Rooms and clean up. Sitting on the changing bench next to the door, he looked up from tightening the laces on his boot at the anxious note in Martha's voice. A little tableau opened to him: Dotty's slate, chalk, and schoolbooks lay on the oval eating table in front of the cookstove, savory aromas came from a dish baking in the oven. Mother and daughter stood together, almost shoulder to shoulder, the girl having grown so much since he'd been gone that she topped her mother by an inch. Already, at eleven years old.

And Martha? He could not mistake the anxiety in her nervous glance toward the stove that she thought he wouldn't notice. They were not prepared for him. The supper in the oven – perhaps one of Martha's excellent meat pies, the thought raising saliva in his mouth – would be only enough for two females, not considering a man's larger appetite. Especially a man fresh from a month of stage line meals, indifferent to downright bad and always insufficient, eaten on the run.

He remembered the calf's head boiling in water the color of dirty laundry.

"Why don't I stay in a hotel until the wedding?" He nodded toward the wooden box that held Martha's gift. "I'll leave that here for the time being."

"You're welcome to stay. You're home. It's just —"

"You aren't ready for me. How could you know? Even if I had written, the mails are uncertain, and the telegraph has not reached here yet, Timothy tells me." He lied about not writing. The Overland stage line was reliable.

To bridge the damning question of why he had not written once in five months, he said, "Timothy and I met at Fort Hall. He said he'd see you tomorrow."

He had not written because deep down he did not know if he would return. True, his business had proved more difficult than he'd expected, but he'd been captivated by the Gold Room. By Harriet. Almost, he had stayed in New York.

He was glad to find a room at the Planter's House, to ease himself into their lives, to become accustomed to the idea that he would be joined for life to this woman. He did not think he loved Martha now, but he owed her his duty for the sake of the child. He would begin by marrying her with all proper consideration, and he would begin now. Until after the wedding, he would not sleep over in this house. "One of the passengers mentioned the Planters House. I'll stay there for the time being. First thing in the morning, I'll talk to whoever you want to perform the ceremony, and I'll find X Beidler as soon as I can. I'll come by after that. Will that do?"

Of course. It had to be as he said. Having come back, he had taken charge. Martha told him she wanted a lay preacher named Cummings, who was the county clerk. And he'd find Deputy Beidler at the jail and courthouse, too.

"You won't be wanting to take the rifle out with you," Martha said when he would have put it under his arm.

"The Vigilantes have an ordinance agin carrying firearms in town." When he cocked his head at her, she answered his silent question. "It's to stop all the gunfights."

"Then I'll leave it here." Laying it across its pegs to the right of the door, he said, "The town has changed."

"Oh, yes," Martha said. "It's getting plumb civilized."

A bitter note in her tone made him pause, his hand on the door latch. "Is anything the matter?"

She shook her head, her lips compressed, her hands clutching bunches of her apron.

Dotty answered for her mother: "It's all the horrid gossip."

~~5~~

A bundle of clean clothes under his arm, Dan walked down Jackson to the City Bath Rooms. The sun had set, and the gloom of night spread around him. Saloon music and laughter struck his ear as false and full of sour notes, like canned milk too long on the shelf. As he passed his house, Canary barked at him, jarring his somber thoughts, and one shining idea rose in his mind to loom over all the day's events: He would be a father.

A father. His child, and Martha's. Perhaps a son. He could teach a son to hunt. To – oh, any number of things. How to grow into a man. A decent man. How to be strong, and do what was right. How to play poker.

He would teach him to be a better man than his father.

But — His steps halted. If it were a girl? A daughter? What did he know about girls? What could a father teach a daughter? How to spot a charlatan? A father could only protect his daughter. He did not know – how could he know about being a woman? Martha knew. He could trust

Martha to bring her up right. If she turned out like Martha, she would be fine.

He walked on.

Pushing open the door to the City Bath Rooms, he met an atmosphere like a hothouse that smelled of sweet hair oils and cigar smoke instead of flowers. Conversation broke off as men craned their necks to see who came in. Dan put his change of clothes on a small table and hung his coat on an empty peg. Another coat caught his attention. An officer's caped greatcoat, in the peculiar yellow-brown color called butternut, the color of faded Confederate gray. One of the sleeves was some inches shorter than the other.

Tobias Fitch. Son-of-a-bitch Fitch. Where was he?

All his happiness vanished.

He had to spot Fitch first, before Fitch saw him. His face was partly shielded by his hat, and his month-old, light brown beard and shoulder-length hair disguised him. On one side of the long narrow room, the proprietor, George Turley, and his assistant stood at two chairs backed by mirrors that reflected the line of men seated against the opposite wall. The glass behind Turley showed no one Dan recognized. Reaching for a towel on the steamer cabinet under the mirror, Turley met his eyes in the mirror, nodded to him, and picked up the towel with a pair of tongs. Dan draped the scarf over his coat. Looking into the second mirror, behind the assistant, he saw Fitch seated most of the way down the line of waiting men. He bent over a ragged copy of the *Police Gazette* taken from a pile of magazines and newspapers on a long, low table between the barbers and their customers.

"Good afternoon, Mr. Turley. Gentlemen," Dan said.

The barber laid the towel on his customer's face. "Daniel Stark, is it?" The barber finished the wrap. "Welcome back, sir. I didn't recognize you at first, what with that there beard and all."

"Thank you. It's good to be back. I'm just off the trail, and I'd appreciate a bath, a shave, and a haircut."

"Just go on back for the bath. Young Stevie will serve you with as much water as you'll need, as hot as you can stand it."

Carrying his parcel, Dan made his way toward the door at the back. A sign above it read, "Baths."

Men sitting in the line of chairs drew in their feet for him to pass. He gave them a friendly quarter-nod of thanks, all the time closing in on Fitch, who lowered his magazine to stare at him.

"Blue? Is that you under that bramble on your face? You've cost me two ounces of dust, damn you. I bet X Beidler you were gone for good, and now here you are."

Tobias Fitch. Blue, Fitch's nickname for Dan, was a sneer. It meant that Dan, though a Unionist who regarded slavery as evil, had not worn the blue uniform. His family had paid $300 to buy a substitute to fight in his place, while Fitch was a Confederate veteran who had lost his home to the Yankee 'invasion' and half of his left forearm in combat. Never mind that Dan had been obligated to the

family, that after Father's debacle they had scraped together that money for the substitute and to send him to
the gold fields to get enough gold to pay the massive debt.
Blue, indeed.

"Hello, Fitch." When Dan had first come to Alder
Gulch, Fitch scared him, because the Missourian bullied
people to get what he wanted. Yet in surveying Fitch's
claim, Dan had refused to move the boundary line to his
advantage. Last spring, Dan had lost one gold claim to his
surrogate at poker, but in the miners' court he'd saved the
Nugget claim for McDowell's family.

That fear was long gone.

The two men shook hands.

I'm not a greenhorn now, Fitch, damn you.

The barber's assistant said, "Next."

Fitch looked around Dan. "I believe it's my turn now."
The man in the assistant barber's chair waited for his gold
dust to be weighed out. "Let's have a drink sometime, and
catch up," he said.

Dan lifted the latch on the bath room door. "Any time,"
he said over his shoulder.

~~~

Soaking the dirt and chill of travel away in the tin bath-
tub, Dan fought to stay awake. Stevie, the attendant, was
johnny-on-the-spot to bring buckets of hot water from
the two stoves. There was a limit, Dan told himself, as to
how long a man could sit in a tub. Just now, though, he
couldn't say what it was.

"I gotta get more water, mister," Stevie said.

That was it. The boy would have to shovel snow in buckets to melt on the stove. Dan ducked under the surface to rinse his soapy hair and came up spluttering and shaking his head like a dog after a swim. "Not for me, Stevie. I'll get out now."

He stood up in the tub, stepped out onto the slatted platform raised a couple of inches off the floor, and reached for one of the towels stacked on a small table nearby. In spite of the fires roaring in the stoves, and the steamy air, he shivered.

The door latch lifted, and Fitch walked in.

Almost, Dan moved to cover himself, but changed the motion to dry his arms. He nodded to Fitch, who looked him over in a single swift glance that ended at the long scar around his neck. Toweling his hair, Dan thought, *I've got nothing to hide, damn you.*

"So you're back," Fitch said.

"As you see." Dan dried his torso and his back, and wrapped the towel around his waist. He plucked another towel from the pile to finish drying his legs and feet.

"How have things been here?" he asked.

"Placer gold's playing out. In July, though, they made a good strike up at Last Chance Gulch."

Dan raised a quizzical eyebrow. "That's about a hundred miles north, isn't it?"

"That's the place. I've got holdings up there now, as well as other places."

Always the cagey one, Dan said to himself. He let drop the towel around his waist and pulled on his under-pants. Fasting a button on the front closure, he heard a scrape of metal against metal. Glancing up from under clumps of his damp hair, he saw Stevie lift a bucket of melted snow onto the stove.

"How was New York?" Fitch asked. He sounded like he might have a cold, and forced the words through his clogged throat.

"Profitable." Tying the drawstring, he watched the Southerner push up the coat sleeve on his short arm and scratch around the edge of the black silk, sack-like covering over the stump. All the time, probably thinking Dan did not see him through his hanging hair, he stared as hard at Dan as at a rock to be assayed for the metal in it.

Go ahead. Try to assay my metal.

Dan fastened the pants buckle at his back and sat down on a stool to tie the strings of the legs and pull on his socks up over them. He knew he sounded abrupt, but what the hell. "The weather was as usual. Hot and sticky."

"What do you aim to do, now you're back?"

Dan put his head through the neck of his shirt. "Practice law. I've developed a taste for it, it seems. If Last Chance Gulch is as good a strike as you say it is, I might take a look up there, too. See if anyone's in need of a lawyer." To the sound of Fitch's laughter, Dan pulled his trousers on.

"Hell," Fitch said, "everybody in the damn territory needs a lawyer. Seems like somebody's always fussing about something. There'll be plenty for you to do. Here or up north, you'll always find work."

"That's reassuring." Dan pulled on his boots, tied them. "All right. I think I'm finished here. Stevie, what do I owe you?"

"Pay Mr. Turley, if you would, sir. I gets my pay from him at the end of the week."

Dan found a two-bit piece in his waistcoat pocket. "Here's a little something extra for you. Thanks for your help."

"Thank you, mister." The coin disappeared so fast Dan could not see where it went.

At the door to the barber shop, they stood aside for another bather to come in before they went through.

Fitch said, "I meant what I said. Let's have a drink. I'm heading for Deer Lodge in the morning, but I'll be back. What do you say? Con Orem has the Champion Saloon now. It's a high class gentleman's club. No women, just good liquor and beer and food."

"Sounds good to me," Dan said. "Look me up when you return." He lied, but what else could he say? Fortunately, he had no expectation that Fitch would ever seek him out. If he did, there would be something behind it. Something Fitch wanted.

~~~

Conversation died when he closed the door behind himself and Fitch. Dan found a chair among the waiting men and sat down. Crossing one ankle over the opposite knee, he waited for the talk to resume. One man leafed through a copy of the *Montana Post*, and a few men nodded to him, but no one spoke. Even the assistant barber, busy with comb and scissors on a customer's hair, was silent. That suited Dan, who preferred to think his own thoughts, about Fitch, but mostly to plan his next steps. Tomorrow morning he would arrange for the preacher and find X Beidler. Ask him to stand up with him at his wedding. His wedding.

All his life he had wanted to have a family, be a father. He hoped to God he would be a good father. Perhaps he didn't love Martha as he used to think he did, but as she was the mother of his child. He would do right by her.

Men took up their conversation where they had apparently left it, but he had a sense of much being unsaid, of men being careful of their speech. He was not accustomed to censorship in barber shops, where men felt free to speak their minds. Was it perhaps because of the unknown customer in George Turley's chair, whose face was wrapped in a hot towel?

Turley finished stropping a razor and laid it on the cabinet to pick up a shaving mug. He poured water into the mug, and dampened a shaving brush, rubbing it on the end of a stick of shaving soap. Dipping the brush into the mug, he whisked the shaving soap into a lather. With everything ready, he unwrapped his customer's face.

The man's hairline had receded halfway back on the top of his head, and he had a pendulous, over-large lower lip . Noticing Dan, he introduced himself. "I don't believe I've had the pleasure. I'm Chief Justice Hezekiah Lord Hosmer."

The man in charge of the Territory's legal system. That explained the pause in the conversation. The others waited to see how he and the judge would react to each other. All they knew of Dan was his association with Fitch, a Secessionist. For himself, Dan wanted a sense of this judge before he argued a case before him. Would he be impartial, or would a mistake here prejudice Judge Hosmer against him? "Daniel Bradford Stark, Your Honor. I'm an attorney. I've just returned from New York."

"Then I expect we shall be seeing more of each other in a professional capacity," His Honor said. "For now, perhaps you can help us with a point of discussion. I am new here myself, and I should like to gather as many opinions among people as I can."

"No talking, sir." Turley tilted Hosmer's head back and poised the razor over his throat.

The scar on Dan's neck itched. "If I can." Careful, he warned himself.

Another customer, a miner by the look of his weathered face and rough hands, spoke up. "We've just been talking about what kind of law is best for gold country."

"Hah!" snorted a man sporting a shaggy dark beard. "That's easy. The kind that don't interfere with us. We don't need laws telling us how we mark our claims. We can decide that the way we've always done. In miners meetings."

"There must be —" Hosmer's Adam's apple moved.

Turley snatched the razor into the air. "Your Honor, please!"

In the nick of time, Dan thought, surprised and pleased at his own pun.

"—uniformity," said Hosmer, "so everyone knows what's expected of him. Beg your pardon, Mr. Turley. Carry on."

"Uniformity be damned." A hoarse voice sounded from near the front door. "That's just horse feathers. I say leave us alone and we'll make things clear. We've done all right so far. Look at the Fairweather laws."

"By applying the Common law of England," said the miner.

"Yeah," said the dark beard. "Let's have the Common Law and not some foreign laws."

"Foreign?" Dan asked. "You mean like England or France?"

"No," came the hoarse voice. "Like the God-damn Idaho statutes." He sounded like Canary growling.

The Chief Justice said, "Idaho is hardly foreign. Not like China or France."

"We were part of Idaho until the end of May," Dan said.

"Damn good thing we're on our own now," said the miner. "I say, damn Idaho laws. Let us go our own way and the court can settle things if we can't agree."

"And if you don't like what the court decides?" Hosmer asked.

Knowing what might come, Dan kept silent. In New York, a defeat at court meant appealing to a higher court where different judges heard the case. With only three judges in Montana Territory, however, an appeal of one of Hosmer's cases would be heard by Hosmer and the judges of Districts Two and Three.

Turley lifted the razor and pressed his thumb on left side of the judge's jawbone to turn his face. His honor's alert brown eyes met Dan's, then slid towards the miner.

The shouter said, "The hell good appealing anything will do us here, though. You're the judge for this district court, and the Chief Justice. You decide on your own opinions ever' time they go to court. We can't get a fair trial in this Territory."

There fell a silence so heavy that Dan felt the weight of it. The fire droned in the stove. Someone chomped on his plug of tobacco. Every man seemed to hold his breath

The Territory's Chief Justice was accused of biased judgment. Short of outright criminal conduct such as bribery, prejudice was perhaps the greatest sin a judge could commit. That extended to favoring his own rulings as a sitting judge of a lower court.

Hosmer raised a hand to stop Turley.

"Your Honor," the barber protested, "the lather will dry out."

"A moment, please. This won't take long." He spoke to the shouter, but what he said was meant for everyone there. And for everyone they told. "I promise you, my colleague in Bannack and I can be impartial, even if we do sit *en banc* on our own cases. I can assure you of that."

"A Yankee judge ruling on a Southerner's case? I've seen your mudsill justice, when your God-damn Union armies invaded Missouri. You can go to hell, all of you."

From the back room a man in his bath sang a plaintive song, lamenting his lost sweetheart. Off key.

The man sitting next to Dan muttered, "Damned idiot," under his breath.

Turley wiped the razor on a towel. Hosmer's face, what Dan could see of it around the lather, flushed.

"That," Dan said, "is why damn fools need lawyers to represent them. So that when they appear before a judge they don't make more trouble for themselves." He leaned forward and pinned the shouter with a hard stare that sent a silent message: Apologize, you fool. Apologize.

The shouter's neck stiffened and his hand gripped the arms of his chair. For a moment he looked like throwing it at Dan, who met his glare with a hard scowl of his own.

From the back room, the bather declaimed The Raven:

> *From my books surcease of sorrow—sorrow for the lost
>   Lenore—*
> *For the rare and radiant maiden whom the angels
>   name Lenore—*
> *Nameless here for evermore.*

The moment broke. Men roared with laughter, Dan among them.

When the merriment faded, the shouter spoke in level tones. "I apologize, sir. I got carried away. It won't happen again."

The color of the judge's face faded from red to its normal winter pallor. Somehow, he took on dignity, as if the robes of justice settled on the shoulders of this fleshy middle-aged man in a barber's chair, one side of his face covered in lather as though someone had smashed a meringue on it.

"Apology accepted," he said. "But remember, when you insult me, you insult Lady Justice herself, whom I serve at the President's pleasure. That must stop."

The shouter exaggerated a Southern accent. "Yes, Your Honor. I do understand. I purely do."

"This war will end," said Hosmer. "I firmly believe the North will win, because God is on the side of freedom for all men. Afterwards, we must find a way to live together in peace with free black people among us. Does anyone doubt that?"

A murmur of agreement came from the other men. Apparently satisfied, he tipped his head at a convenient angle for Turley's razor.

"We've been living that way here for more than two years, your honor," Dan said. "North and South, Christian and Jew, white and black and Indian, we've mostly rubbed along pretty well, except for that gang of criminals we defeated last winter."

"Hmph." Someone let out a snort.

"All right, we don't all like each other, and what we've had is just a stop-gap, but his honor is here to regularize the law of the Territory. I think all any of us wants is to be able to manage our own affairs as we see fit in a free country."

"Hear, hear!" applauded a few of the other men, but under that chorus Dan heard a low growl: "Damn Vigilanters."

~~6~~

Inside, the courthouse smelled of cold dirt and regret. The man sitting at a table to the right of the door looked up long enough to frown at Dan when he came in, as though he resented being interrupted at his work, copying numbers from pieces of paper into a fat ledger book. He wore fingerless gloves, a brown-and-yellow checked coat, and a mustard-colored knit cap pulled down over his ears. Behind him a stove struggled against the drafts from the front door and a poorly fitted window in the wall behind him.

The clerk moved a finger to another number, dipped his pen in an ink bottle and tapped it against the rim to get rid of the excess ink. Made another entry.

As he waited, stifling his impatience, Dan looked around. Three men huddled together in a low-voiced discussion over cigars and liquids in heavy ceramic mugs. Bundles of paper tied in string lay on open shelves above them. One man jabbed his cigar toward a crude map of the Territory tacked to the wall. Dan caught the phrase, tax

49

collector. Taxes? When he left no one paid taxes. Now, apparently, they did.

"Drat." The clerk crossed out what he had entered in the ledger, moved his finger to a different place on the paper and squeezed another entry above the one he had crossed out.

Over a door in the back wall a sign read, "Jail."

If they could have jailed Slade, he might still be alive, but in February, they finished making the region safe for decent citizens, and miners would not part with their gold in a tax to pay for a jail. Without it there was only mining camp law, with three possible punishments: whipping, banishment, or hanging. After Slade, miners understood the need for a jail.

How different would it be with a Constitutional legal system that could back up its power with a jail? In another month they would see. Judge Hosmer had told Dan that court would open on December fifth.

The clerk finished his entry, set the paper on a different pile, and placed a rock on the stack to weigh it down. In the candlelight the rock sparkled. Iron pyrite. Fool's gold.

The clerk leaned to the side, and blew his nose on his fingers. When he picked up another piece of paper from a different pile, ignoring Dan, he asked, "Are you Brother Cummings?"

"Yes. I am Brother Cummings. Are you here to pay your taxes?" The clerk moved the candle closer to the ledger.

"Yes. First, though, I understand you perform marriages. I've come to inquire if you are free on Saturday afternoon."

"Did you not get a notice?"

"I returned only yesterday from an extended absence in the States."

"I can look you up in the book." Beginning the search for Dan's name, the clerk bent up some pages in the ledger.

"My name is Daniel Stark."

"Oh?" Cummings's nose twitched, and his upper lip curled. "Am I to understand that you are marrying the Widow McDowell?"

Dan used the cool glare he'd turned on competing traders in the Gold Room before he bested them in a trade and sent them sweating and shaking from the floor. Cummings' smirk vanished.

"That is correct. Mrs. Martha McDowell is a widow. She would like to be married by a man of the cloth, and she asked for you specifically." Without changing his expression, keeping the same trader's mask over his face, Dan sent a silent message: If you do not show her proper respect, you will regret it. I am a bad enemy.

Cummings swallowed. "Would you have a day and time in mind, sir?"

"Saturday next, the fifth. At two o'clock in the afternoon, if that will be convenient."

Cummings consulted a pocket diary. "That will be quite convenient." He made a note, the letters as shaky as an old man's. "You didn't ask what my fee is."

"It doesn't matter. I'll pay you now, along with my tax bill." Dan put his hand on the leather pocket attached to his belt.

The clerk riffled through a different pile of papers. When he found what he looked for, he wrote out Dan's tax bill and gave it to him. His damp fingers smudged the ink.

"Does the county take greenbacks?"

"Yes, at a discount of forty percent."

Every dollar in gold, then, was a dollar and sixty cents in greenbacks. "I'll pay in gold." He took two Double Eagles, twenty-dollar gold coins, and laid them on the table. From his trousers pocket, he brought out his poke, a deer hide pouch for holding gold dust. "I'd like the difference in dust."

The clerk's manner changed as he eyed the coins. The down-turned folds of his face smoothed out until he almost seemed to smile. He named his fee for performing the marriage ceremony. Sensing that he had doubled or tripled it, Dan made a mental note. He would not haggle over it and risk making the wedding unpleasant for Martha. He would remember, though. He would remember.

Their transaction completed, Dan held out his hand. "Thank you. Until Saturday, then."

"Yes, sir." Cummings stood up, removed his right glove. "A pleasure, sir." His handshake was as weak and moist as his lie.

~~~

The stink of night soil from an unemptied bucket made Dan's eyes water when he pulled open the jail door unto a short hallway between two cells with solid walls. Except for the barred doors, they might have been rooms in a small, deplorable hotel. By the back wall, two men played cribbage in the unsteady light of a candle impaled on a small shelf above them. One was so short his feet did not touch the floor. The other, who resembled a beached whale, wore a light logging chain around one ankle. They looked up from their game to inspect the newcomer.

"Good God," the short man said. "You."

He made a gesture like flicking away flies, and the man wearing the chain stood up. He tugged at the waistband of his trousers sagging under his belly. "Guess we finish this later." One laboring step at a time, he dragged the chain into the cell. "If I swear to come right back, can I empty the damn bucket?"

"Yeah," said the short man. "Rinse it out, too. If you're gone more than ten minutes, though, I'll charge you with attempted escape."

"Hell, I'm out there ten minutes my balls will freeze solid."

Dan waited as the prisoner took the offending bucket and went out, slamming the back door behind himself. All the time the short man stared at him, an unwelcome addition to his day.

John X Beidler. X to his friends.

They had known each other's hearts as men seldom did, except as brothers in combat. They had ridden hard snowy miles in cold saddles, swum their horses through streams where broken ice floated, risked death to bring down a gang of armed robbers and murderers. They had wept over the decision to hang a friend. Slade.

Now this? The blank unwelcoming stare through slitted eyes, the heavy drooping mustache.

Deputy Sheriff Beidler hitched himself forward until his feet touched the ground. Rising, he took hold of the double-barreled, side-by-side shotgun that leaned ready to hand against the wall and rested it in the crook of his elbow.

"Do you think you'll need that?" Dan thought of his rifle and pocket pistol at home. He had not thought he would need a firearm to visit a friend.

"That depends."

So many words crowded into his mouth: What the hell has happened to you? Why are you my enemy, when we parted as friends?

Beidler tilted his head as far back as he could to look Dan in the eye. Time was, he would have moved back a step or two to give X room to look up at him. He stood his ground, hands careful at his sides.

"I suppose you heard about Rawley." One Vigilante to another. If he could remind X of the ropes, their sworn oaths of loyalty and secrecy, he might recall their friendship.

Beidler sidled between the barrel and the wall, stood closer to the stove, perhaps to be warmer, but there he had more room to bring up the shotgun. "Yep," he said. "The boys did the right thing."

"The right thing wasn't so clear to some at first, but in the end we all voted to carry out the sentence." He was telling Beidler, *I was there, I've been in this since the beginning. Remember what we've been to each other.*

"Ah. So you were there, too."

"I was, yes."

An odor thick as mist, rancid but somehow sweet, came from the shadows behind the stove. Inside the lamp chimney, the candle flame wavered and danced. The stink became heavier; its weight bent the flame that pointed toward that darkest corner. Dan did not look. His throat closed, cutting off speech and breath.

There is no such thing as a ghost. Not since Beaverhead Rock.

The prisoner came in, went into his cell, put the bucket down, and sat on the bed.

X said, "Ain't it about time you headed over to court?" To Dan, "His trial's in the miners' court, before a justice of the peace."

"What's the charge?"

"Drunk and disorderly."

The same as for Slade.

The prisoner came out of the cell and stood by the stove warming his hands. "I'm sober now. Just let me warm up some."

Beidler's sour gesture with the muzzle of the shotgun changed his mind.

"Guess I'd better make sure I ain't late. Can't you take this damn chain off?"

"All right." X knelt with his key and unlocked the padlock.

When the prisoner had slammed the door behind him, X said, "What brings you here?"

"I came to hire Brother Cummings to perform a marriage ceremony. Mrs. McDowell has done me the honor of accepting my proposal. The ceremony will take place on Saturday afternoon." Stilted phrases, wiped bare of the joy they should have had. He could not now tell X, *I came to ask you to stand up with me.* Not as things stood. Until he knew why.

"Saturday." Beidler eyed him as a scientist might weigh methods for dissecting a specimen. He did not congratulate him, did not offer to shake his hand. The outsized mustache bristled, like the hairs on a mastiff's back. "Yeah, it's possible now, right? Sam McDowell's dead, ain't he? You'll have everything now, won't you? The lady's hand in marriage, and his gold claims. Especially the Nugget. Oh, don't look surprised, like you never thought nobody would figure it out. You killed Sam McDowell to get them, and now you're back, I don't have to go all the way to New York when I get the proof. And I aim to prove it."

He stopped, panting a bit to catch his breath, a finger raised to tell Dan to wait.

What more would he say, could he say? Dan waited, back muscles tight, braced against that more while the words already fired at him, spread and inflicted their wounds: 'You killed Sam McDowell,' 'the lady's hand in marriage,' 'get them claims.' Unsaid: 'Now that you've had your way with her.'

"If this new court don't deal with you," Beidler said, "we will. You hear that? We'll see you pay the penalty for murder."

Beidler had known him better than any man except Peter, who lay in his family's cold stone crypt in New York. Now this? Accuse him of murdering McDowell? A stab in the back? Christ. Beidler had been quicker with the rope, more willing to use it with less reason. But this? Jumping to conclusions this way?

"I did not murder McDowell. For Christ's sake, you know me better than that."

X moved toward him, the muzzle of the shotgun less than a foot from his belt buckle. "I'd arrest you, only the new Chief Justice would say there ain't enough evidence. You're too slick. Slick as shit."

Touch me with that God damn thing, and I'll grind you into pulp, damn you.

All the fibers of his body screamed to be let loose to seize the shotgun, rip it from the little man's grasp, and beat him into the hard-packed floor. Some bit of sense among the mad thoughts held him back: He must not give Beidler a reason. Through his teeth, he said, "I did not kill McDowell. How can you think I would, after – after everything? Good Christ. You know me."

"I thought I knowed Slade. No two men was ever closer'n him and me till he put that revolver in my face, and then I didn't know him at all. Not at all. So don't tell me I know you. No man knows nobody. I'll find the truth about you and McDowell. You can bet your last flake of dust."

"Go ahead, then. Look for the truth, and you'll find the real killer. You sure as hell won't find me." Half-turned to leave, Dan swung back to face him. "If you only look for something to back up your theory, God help you. You'd be hanging an innocent man."

Closing the door behind him, Dan knew at once they'd been overheard shouting through the thin walls. The three commissioners, the clerk, and a newcomer stared at him. The new man stopped brushing snow from his shoulders and stared at Dan. Good God, Chief Justice Hosmer.

"Gentlemen." Dan settled his hat on his head and marched toward the door. "Judge Hosmer." As he paused to pull on his gloves, Cummings said, "Saturday at two o'clock?" Dan wanted to ram his smirk down his throat.

His face stiffening, he said as formally as he knew how, "Quite correct. Two of the clock on Saturday next. At my house on Jackson, across from the Champion Saloon."

Outside, he trudged uphill in a roiling darkness filled with the sound of fire roaring in his ears. Beidler believed him guilty, and Hosmer had heard their every word. What did he believe? Christ, what a mess.

At the corner of Idaho and Jackson, steady hoofbeats from behind and a woman's high-pitched warning penetrated his anger as he was about to step into the street. He stopped to let the rider pass. She wore men's trousers and sat cross-saddle on a shaggy bay mule that plodded on loose reins, among the frozen ruts and piles of manure and garbage in its path. From her saddle horn dangled a lumpy, dirty burlap bag. She was bringing ore to the assay office, he realized, as he connected her with the almost-forgotten knowledge that a woman held a placer claim up near Summit City.

As she passed, he raised two fingers to his hat brim. Unsmiling, she raised two fingers from her saddle horn and rode on, leaving him startled out of his fury, his mind working again.

Beidler thought he'd murdered McDowell, did he?

He'd damn well see about that.

~~7~~

Mid-morning, Dan'l come home looking like the wrath of doom. Martha held her head bent over Timmy's sock she was darning; the needle glided up and over, dipped down and under, weaving a new heel.

Just like that McDowell would come in angered, and fling things about, stomp, swear, and shout. Dan'l, though, hung up his outdoor coat and sat on the bench to take off his boots. He reached under it and come up with his house shoes, and stayed there holding onto them like he'd forgot what they were, while his shoulders relaxed and he took a deep breath. She took that to mean the anger had seeped out of him.

Reminding herself this wasn't Sam, it was Dan'l, she asked, "When can the preacher come?"

He held the shoes up. "You kept them for me. All this time, you kept these for me."

"Yes, of course I did."

He put the shoes on, stood up, walked over to the settee, and stood looking out the window behind it. There wasn't nothing next door but a pile of logs gathering snow until spring thawed the ground enough to dig in a foundation to build on.

She asked again, "Is Brother Cummings willin'?"

"Yes." He stayed at the window, his back to her.

She nerved herself up to ask what the matter was.

"Nothing." The one word, bit off like it was, told her it was something he wasn't of a mind to talk about, maybe – oh, Lord, no – he'd changed his mind about marrying.

Even though it scared her, she asked, "Have you changed your mind?"

He swung around. "Not at all. No." But it was like he'd never seen her before, and she thought maybe he was studying on something deep inside himself.

Before he'd been gone so long, she might've knowed what that could be, but he was half a stranger to her now, and she didn't know him like she might, considering the least'un growing inside her. She would just have to wait until he come out of wherever he'd been. So as to keep some pressure on him, she folded her hands on her stomach and kept her eyes on him, while the least'un danced around inside her.

She waited so long that when at last Dan'l hunkered down beside her chair, she knew this would be a hard thing, but God willing, not too hard to bear. Waiting for it, her breathing faltered.

He stroked the back of her hand. "I have not changed my mind, but you might want to change yours when you hear this."

"Go on."

"Deputy Beidler has accused me of murdering Sam McDowell."

She couldn't take it in. "X Beidler, he thinks you, you murdered Sam?" She couldn't rightly take it in.

"He accused me of murdering him to acquire his wife and his gold."

"He thinks you– You would never." She almost laughed, the idea was so outlandish to even mention Dan'l as Sam's murderer. Or anyone's.

Then, like it was a wild hare chased by a coyote, the thought darted in a different direction, doubled back toward her, and she saw the whole animal. Not a hare at all, but the coyote itself, only not a coyote, but a wolf, teeth bared, hackles up, ready to attack and rip them to shreds.

It wouldn't matter that Beidler was wrong. All he had to do was convince enough others that Dan'l had done this thing, and they'd arrest him and try him and maybe find him guilty. And then – she couldn't think that far. She would not think that far. She would not make a picture in her mind of what could happen. That was the wolf in her thoughts. That wasn't the truth.

"You would not do that," she said.

His face lightened, his relief plain to see. "Thank you," he said. "Oh, God, thank you. I was afraid you'd believe it."

That gave her something to let her own feelings loose on. "How could you think I'd believe it? Do you think I'd give myself to a murderer? That I'm so stupid or – or blind that I'd be with a man who could commit murder? I had plenty of time to know your character when you boarded with us, and after Sam left, afore you brought me here."

The accusation – the wolf – turned around and showed itself to her from another side, so she understood what it said about her. How it made her out to be stupid or worse, that she'd knowed what she was about when she turned a blind eye to her own husband's murder.

"Does Deputy Beidler think I had no say in any of this? Like I'd have joined with you" – spreading her hands across on her stomach – "if I'd had the slightest notion? Or brought the young'uns into it?" She closed her mouth, lest she used words she'd heard from Sam. Out of breath, she sat gasping, her heart thumping faster than she'd ever knowed it to.

All in an instant he was offering her a dipper of water without her having seen him walk over to the kitchen, dip out water from the clean water bucket, and bring it to her though she'd kept her eyes on him the entire time.

She drank. Her heart slowed, and after a bit she felt steadier, like she'd slipped on a patch of ice and caught herself. When she handed back the dipper, his hand closed over hers as he took it.

"Are you all right? Should I fetch a doctor?"

"No, it was just a turn." She caught her breath. "Besides, doctors don't know nothing about women's matters."

After he'd hung the dipper on its hook, and brought a hard chair over from the oval table, she knew what else she had to tell him. The least'un moved here and there like he was trying to get comfortable. She patted him through the heavy flesh of her stomach.

"He has to have your name." As soon as she said it, she thought of all the other ideas that went with saying that. Maybe he'd take it to mean she was only marrying him to keep this one from being a bastard, or she didn't really love him, but they had to marry. Before she could explain herself, he went to pacing around the rug she'd braided in the summer to guard against drafts beneath the planks. Past the bedroom door, the kitchen, the settee, the guns on their pegs and shelves to the right of the front door. As he started on by the bench, his toe struck against that long wooden box.

"Good God Almighty. How could I forget this?" He lifted up the box.

She'd wondered about that wooden box. When she'd shook it, there had been no sound. How could something heavy like that not rattle, or shift a bit? Not liking to ask in case it was something private to him, she imagined it to be a gun, maybe, or a tool of some sort, or what-have-you.

With the box under one arm, he came back to her and sat down on the ottoman next to her feet, with the box across his knees.

"Just so we have everything straight between us," he said, "I did not court you because I wanted the gold. I wanted you. I still do. I love you. The claims were not in it then, and they are not in it now. I'm just the custodian until Timothy turns twenty-one. Then he takes control of whatever there is." He half smiled, a corner of his mouth lifting as something struck him funny. "I was a poor man then, but now I have enough gold," putting his hand on her stomach, "for all of us."

He laid the box across her knees. From his tool chest behind the stove he brought a screwdriver and chisel to remove the scarred lid that he set on the floor. Inside the wood box was another, this one covered in bottle-green padded leather, that he lifted out and gave to her to hold while he set the outer box on the floor, too.

"Open it."

She laid back the hinged lid. "Oooh." She could say nothing more.

A new mountain dulcimer.

Made all of black walnut that glowed under the lamp-light, shaped narrow in the middle like a woman in a cor-set, with S-shaped sound holes instead of simply round or long. She stroked the sound board and felt the grain run-ning just like she thought it should, like she'd tried to make on the old one. The old one. She'd put it together on the sly back home on account she loved the music and females weren't let to play. Men played music. Pap would've whupped her, and she'd kept it secret from Sam until they were packing to come here. When he wouldn't let her bring it, she hid it at the bottom of the trunk she put bed-ding in, and she'd played it ever' chance she got until, until.

She saw again his great boot stomp it, heard herself screaming, clawing at him, and that big fist coming at her.

She'd never seen him again.

Groping in her apron bodice, she found a handkerchief to wipe her eyes and blow her nose.

"Is it all right?" Dan'l sounded like he wasn't sure she'd like it.

"It's – it's beautiful. I never thought to own such a beautiful thing."

"It's a wedding present." His smile then had some fear mixed in it, that hadn't nothing to do with her liking the dulcimer.

"I don't have nothing for you."

"Yes, you do. The best present of all." He put his hand on her stomach. The least'un must've moved, on account he let out a whistle that was hardly more than a breath, and stood up to kiss her. After a bit, he said, "You give me something to fight for."

"Fight for?"

"I promise you I will find McDowell's murderer. I will clear dishonor from my name." He couldn't speak for a bit. When he did, his voice was unsteady. "I will set this straight."

She read him, and found nothing but determination – in his words, how he said them, and in his narrowed eyes, the set of his mouth. This was the man that had rode all them winter miles that ended with the deaths of two-legged varmints. He would set things straight. "I believe you will."

When he'd left to do some business before supper, she took up the dulcimer and the picks and tuned it, strummed it till it was right. At the first chord, her tears started.

Right there, in that beautiful sound, was the difference between the two men. Sam had stomped her old dulcimer. Dan'l brought her this one.

~~8~~

Like a military commander, he needed a base to mount his campaign from, away from the distractions of domestic life, and to shield Martha and Dotty from this hunt. Knowing they were safe behind the lines, so to speak, he could take necessary steps.

With no time to waste, he trotted down Jackson street, his booted feet finding their own way as he listed the tasks to be done to build that base.

Then he would begin the campaign to bring McDowell's murderer to justice.

To his relief, Solomon Content remembered his promise and rented him an office at the back of his building on the second floor. Number Five opened onto the top of the stairs leading up from the ground. Of a decent size, it was approximately ten feet by twelve, with a four-pane window in the upper half of the front door. A door in the rear wall opened onto a narrow interior hallway connecting the offices.

Having the space, he moved his boxes from the Overland office, then furnished the room with enough to get on with. Chairs, candles, the crimped-up tops of tin cans to stand them on. Extra flints and steel. He shook his head over the makeshift desk, a warped plank door laid across the boxes, but he would have time enough to find a proper desk later. After he had freed himself from the coils of suspicion.

Standing near the front door, he wrapped his scarf around his neck and put on his hat. Only one task remained to make the place habitable. Heat. A potbelly stove filled the interior corner formed by the rear wall and office Number Four. It had never had a fire. He would have to cure it, a ticklish process of warming the stove gradually, lighting ever larger fires until its iron plates locked together. If he mismanaged it, the plates might break. A lengthy process that took time he did not have right now.

He wanted to find Jacob Himmelfarb, learn Timothy's whereabouts. Martha had told him Jacob worked for a man named Lewis Hershfield in a bank in John Ming's building. Jacob, his closest friend in Alder Gulch, had come out with him from New York, and had ridden with him and the others. Would he still be a friend, particularly after Timothy told his story? He had lost one good friend already over McDowell's murder. Now to find out if he would lose another.

Then he would talk to Charles Bagg, perhaps the best lawyer he knew of in Alder Gulch. Certainly the man he trusted most.

And he sure as hell needed a lawyer.

Stepping out onto the veranda, he locked the door behind him, and clattered down the icy stairs.

~~~

Lewis Hershfield's bank was located in John Ming's squat white frame building across Jackson from Content's Corner. He stepped into a strangely musical hubbub of conversation and laughter, the low hum of men's voices punctuated here and there by women's high tones. If Sol Content had not been a man of his word, he might have been forced to rent space somewhere like this, crammed into one big room. Signs overhead or tacked to the building's outer wall helped him locate the small enterprises around the perimeter: a jeweler, a lawyer, a bank, Ming's bookstore, and a tobacconist. A fence perhaps three feet high separated the space owned by each business; most were whitewashed, but the tobacconist had painted his fence red. Occupying the center of the room, a grocer's four-sided stall advertised wholesale and retail produce.

Dan edged through the throng between the jeweler's table by the front window and the grocer's stand.

He made his way down the room's long side, between the grocer and the lawyer's booth where two men huddled in close conversation. The lawyer and his client, Dan guessed. He sidled around a clump of people watching the grocer tease three small children, two boys and a girl. Holding a large dill pickle just out of the reach, he said, "Have you been good little ones?" "Yes," they chorused. He lowered the pickle and when they held up their hands, he snatched it back out of reach. "Are you sure?" He lowered it again. "Yes," they clamored. Snatching it back, he asked, "Are you sure?" He let the pickle sink, and the girl leaped, grabbed it, and darted through the crowd, the boys following. The grocer shouted: "Stop them, the little thieves. Stop them."

No one moved. Dan laughed along with the other bystanders, who apparently thought the theft served the grocer right.

Hearing his name, he looked around. Under the bank sign, Jacob Himmelfarb waved his semaphore arm. "Daniel! Daniel Stark!"

They met in the crowded aisle, Jacob seizing Dan's hand and pumping it, welcoming him with a wide and generous smile in such a contrast with Beidler's tight-lipped animosity that Dan's vision blurred for an instant.

"Jacob, you've got fat."

Rail thin, Jacob laughed.

"No, truly, you're quite fat. You don't look starved any more." He touched his forefinger to Jacob's waistcoat. "See? Fat."

"And you? You are –" Jacob squinted at him, and his smile faded. "Are you well, Daniel? Are you quite well?"

"Weary, that's all. It's a long journey." Jacob would have heard Timothy's version of yesterday's events. What did he think? He seemed his old self, but Dan sensed a reserve in his friend underlying his enthusiasm. Timothy must have told him about Rawley. Would he also believe Dan capable of McDowell's murder? Might he believe Beidler's accusation? He felt a sour breath at the back of his neck. Just a draft, he told himself.

To turn Jacob's attention away from himself, he nodded toward a stocky, dark-haired man sitting at a desk writing a letter, who lifted the pen off the page. "So this is what you've got up to."

Jacob ushered Dan through the gate in a white picket fence that marked off the bank area. When he closed the gate, his manner changed from the deferential immigrant uncertain of his English, the Jew whose memories of Cossack raids, the pogroms, made him wary of gentiles. The yarmulke on his head might mark him out as a Jew, and the odd construction of his sentences rang with their Yiddish origins, but inside this fence he was a man among men. An equal.

The man at the desk closed his letter book, wiped the nib of the pen, put it in its holder, and corked the ink bottle. Every move was that of a man who could not be hurried. Standing up, he held out his hand. "So, Jacob, this is your friend Daniel Stark."

"Yah. Lewis Hershfield, here is Daniel Stark. Him I have maybe mentioned?"

Hershfield's eyes crinkled at the corners. "Once or twice."

"Perhaps he would also do businesses with the bank."

As the two men shook hands, the banker assayed Dan's metal with a sharp intelligence. Hershfield, it seemed, was a careful man, not to be stampeded into a hasty decision.

His bank might be a good place, Dan decided, to deposit some of his gold. Jacob would not associate himself with a fool or a thief.

"So you're the man Jacob credits with saving his life," said Hershfield. "Have a chair, if you're not in a hurry." He motioned toward the straight wooden chairs placed around the potbellied stove. A bottle of whiskey and clean glasses stood on a low table. "Would you take a drink?"

In this country refusing to drink with a man was a gross insult. "Yes, thank you."

Settled around the stove, the three men raised their glasses to each other. "Here's how."

The first small taste surprised Dan. This whiskey was no poisonous concoction of tobacco, strychnine, and watered alcohol, but a genuine single-malt scotch. Dan savored the smoky peat flavor on his palate before letting it slide down his throat. "Excellent, Mr. Hershfield. Thank you." He set the drink on a small table. "Jacob exaggerates, you know. I needed a chain man to help with surveying out here and invited him to come along. That's all."

Jacob shook his head. "Nein, nein," he said, the words sounding like "nine, nine."

"English, Jacob. You're in America now. English." Hershfield teased Jacob without looking at him. His smile was friendly, his free hand relaxed on the chair arm, while behind his affable expression he gathered information, did his sums.

Not one to make snap judgments, Dan thought.

Jacob said, "No, no. Is right, yes? So. I am just off the boat. For days at sea I have not enough to eat. Is all right because what I eat, I cannot keep. When I get off, my money is no good. I am alone in a big city, so I walk to keep warm. Then this man I meet." He tilted his head toward Dan. "In New York is crowded, not much place to walk. Everyone in such hurry. He bumps me. He knocks me over, but does he walk on? No. He gives me a hand up, dusts me off, asks am I hurt. He gives me a card and a gold coin – an Eagle, yet – and says when I have a room come see him about job." Jacob's eyes glistened; he stooped to tie a bootlace that had not come loose.

Dan said, "Hmph. Your English got better this summer, Jacob. You can now spin a yarn in three languages." As Jacob protested, he said to Hershfield, "I put it to him that the job meant moving West among wild animals and wild men, and he could take it or leave it. He took it, God knows why."

"Same reason we're all here," said Hershfield. "Opportunity. We can get rich." His smile widened. "Or go bust."

"There is that." Dan exchanged understanding smiles with him over the perils of risk in gold country. "Opportunities generally require some risk. A man who has his wits about him might take a risk or two."

"And with risk comes the possibility of failure."

"There's always another throw of the line. Even more than seven times." Dan referred to the tale of the defeated and despairing Scottish king who hid in a cave. There he watched a spider try to build a web over a large space.

Time and again she threw her web, only to come short. At last, on the seventh try, she succeeded. The king left his cave, raised his army, and went on to win his crown and free Scotland.

Recalling the story, Dan lost the thread of the conversation.

Battles. Some were fought against armies, some against shadows. An accusation. He had forgotten Beidler for a moment. Could he win his own battle? He had no choice. He must win.

Listening, he caught up with the others.

"True enough," Hershfield was saying. "Safe travel makes it a bit less risky." A smile lighted the banker's eyes. "That was well done. We are all safe now to do honest business."

Would he think the same if he knew about Beidler's accusation? Dan said, "Speaking of business, I would like to change $100 in Eagles for dust." It would not do to pay for everything he needed in coin. Not in a town quick to identify wealth. The Vigilantes had dealt with the problem of armed robbery and murder on the roads, and he had no fear of burglary here, but other forms of dishonesty could as easily part a man from his money. A slightly heavier weight on a balance scale, a thumb on a pan.

Hershfield and Jacob consulted silently with each other. Hershfield said, "We can do that. What do you say to five ounces of dust for ten Eagles?"

Gold traded here for eighteen dollars the ounce. That meant a hundred dollars in gold dust amounted to more than five and a half ounces. Five-point-fifty-six ounces, to be exact. "I think not," Dan said. "I'm looking for a trade with more parity. Perhaps five-point-six ounces." That set the upper limit of their trade.

"Five-point-three," countered Hershfield.

His pulse throbbed against his high collar. This was the excitement of the Gold Room, where fortunes were made or lost on fractions of a decimal. He had not expected to find it here, but with this banker, here it was. "Five-point-five-nine."

"Point four-seven."

Hershfield had made a bigger jump up than Dan had come down, but he had given away his willingness to meet in the middle. "Five-point-five-six." Now he would test Hershfield.

"Point four-nine."

"Point five-four." Dan lifted the whiskey glass and sipped the amber liquid. "My final offer." If Hershfield were as smart as he thought, he would give up the extra five-hundredths now; otherwise Dan would walk away, endangering further business dealings between them. Lucrative dealings, although the banker could not know that now. Not for sure.

Hershfield appraised Dan. Apparently understanding that he meant what he said, the banker raised his glass and leaned forward. "Done. Five-point-five-four ounces of dust for ten Eagles."

The two men touched glasses and drank off the whiskey.

"Shall we say this is a promise of future business between us?" Hershfield asked. "Good business. I must tell you, though, I do not make unsecured loans."

"I understand. I would not want a banker who risked my capital without security." He counted out ten Eagles, a hundred dollars, which Hershfield gave to Jacob.

Hershfield hooked both thumbs in his waistcoat pockets. "I think in the future we can do business together on mutually agreeable terms."

The two men smiled at each other, as Dan thought, in mutual understanding.

When Jacob had weighed out the dust and written a receipt, Dan read it, and folded it into his notecase. "Impressive," he said. He shook hands with Hershfield, thanked him for the scotch. "I returned late yesterday, and I have some other business to talk over with Jacob." An awkward statement, but he was not certain of Hershfield and Jacob's working relationship. Were they partners or employer and employee?

"Ah, yes." Hershfield lowered his voice so that Dan almost did not hear him. "He has been impatient for you to return so he can tell you his news." He set their glasses on the table. "Perhaps after he tells you, he may also tell me. I like hearing about opportunities."

"Perhaps so," Dan said.

As they crossed Jackson, he told Jacob about the office. "It's sparse, but we can talk freely there." There he would have to tell Jacob about Beidler's accusation. His stomach lurched and he tasted bile at the back of his throat.

~~9~~

As Dan and Jacob walked out of Ming's and paused before crossing Jackson, heavy footsteps crunched toward them from behind, along with a dog's cough-like panting.

Dan swung around.

A large black man holding a rope around the neck of a dog the size of a small bear caught up to them. The dog weighed more than a hundred pounds, Dan estimated, and he strained so forcefully at his rope that only a big man like Albert Rose could hold him.

"Mister Rose, how do you do?" Dan offered his hand to the former slave.

Albert Rose's wide bearded face split in a gleaming smile. "Mistah Stahk. Mr. Himafob." He touched his hat to both white men, his bass rumbling out of his chest. His version of English ignored the letter R. "Now, gen'men, you know it don't go over for a nigga to shake hands with a white man. Too many Secesh around here."

Secesh being short for Secessionist, a Confederate sympathizer.

"This is a free territory, Mr. Rose. Slavery is illegal here, and you're a free man."

"That's as may be, but it make me nervous, y'all talking to me like I'm white."

"All right. Have it your way. We wouldn't want you to be nervous." Dan bent down to let the dog sniff his hand. "Hello, General." The dog was about a year old, and as Dan dug his fingers into the fur, he felt the strong muscles and solid bones of a powerful creature. General wagged his tail and tilted his muzzle upward, tongue lolling in a delighted doggy grin that revealed white, sharp teeth. "I'm glad General feels friendly today. He's a big dog now."

Jacob, peering around Albert, said, "Trouble. Our way it comes."

Six or seven young boys sauntered down the boardwalk toward them, laughing and talking in a raucous mix of broken and unbroken voices. They bumped a man from the boardwalk and laughed to see him sprawl in the street. Seeing two white men standing with Albert Rose, one boy screamed, "Nigger lovers! Nigger lovers!" The other boys took up the chant: "Nigger lovers! Nigger lovers!" The first boy yelled, "Nigger, nigger, pants on fire, hang him with a telegraph wire."

Jacky Stevens. Dan might have known that misbegotten little devil would be in this. He braced himself to intercept them and demand an apology.

Albert said, "No, Marse Stahk, leave it be. Leave it be. Gen'ral and me, we cross the street. They won't —"

General lunged. The rope slid through Albert's grip. The snarling dog charged the boys, who scattered and ran.

Dashing into the street, Jacky Stevens ducked behind a horse and rider, pelted in front of a fast-moving buckboard. People on both sides of the street whistled and shouted, "Get him, dog. Get that rotten kid."

When General hesitated, blocked by the buckboard, Albert caught the end of the rope, wrapped a turn around his hand, and dragged the struggling animal back onto the boardwalk.

"General! Sit! Sit, damn you," Albert thundered. "Sit down." The dog coughed and planted his haunches on the boardwalk, facing downhill. The fur along his backbone standing stiff, he growled at Jacky, who fled down Jackson toward Daylight Gulch.

The boy stopped short. Timothy climbed up Jackson toward him. Wheeling, he bolted back to Wallace, then raced down toward Alder creek, Timothy after him.

General stood up, whining, and pulled at the rope, but Albert held him.

The thought of what had nearly happened chilled Dan. No one by himself could fight off an attack by that dog. He would have mauled Jacky Stevens to death. "That boy will come to a bad end someday."

Albert Rose scratched the dog's head between his ears. "Now, Gen'ral, y'all be a good dog, y'hear?" The dog's tail swept the boardwalk, but he watched Timothy, who had left off chasing the Stevens boy and walked toward them, head down, kicking at the piles, scattering road apples and tin cans. The dog's jaws parted in a grin. He looked up at Albert, then at Dan, a small friendly bear.

"Good afternoon, Timothy," said Dan.

"Afternoon." Timothy spoke without looking at him as he reached down to pet General. "Jacky sure set General off, didn't he, Albert?"

"Yassuh, Marse Tim. He don't like that boy at all," said Albert. "Not one bit."

"Jacky's a mean, rotten no-account, he is. He'll get his comeuppance someday."

"Gen'ral, here, though, he's a right good watch dog. Ain'tcha, General? He's suspicious of most people, but he won't hurt anyone less'n they hurts him first. Like Jacky done."

"That dog has a long memory," Dan said.

Timothy kept his eyes on the dog, spoke to Jacob, "Mam and my sister and Miz Hudson caught Jacky hurting General when he was just a little puppy. Dotty said Jacky liked it." He shook his head. "He smiled, she said, like it was fun, holding him and stabbing him with a sharp pointed stick, making him bleed, while the pup cried."

"I 'member that," Albert said. "That were Gen'ral."

Dan recalled another incident: Dotty screaming, her schoolbooks dropped in the mud, small fists flailing at a boy who backed her into a wall and pawed at her chest. It had taken all his self-restraint not to thrash him. "He's one to watch out for."

"Gen'ral? Why, he wouldn't harm nobody else," said Albert.

"Not the dog. Jacky Stevens."

~~10~~

Mounting the stairway to his office, Dan dreaded each treacherous step. Behind him, Jacob and Timothy followed, all of their boots stomping down on the treads, crushing ice. Tolling doom. It should not be this way, he thought. Damn it, he had the best possible news to tell them.

And the worst.

How to say it? Serve it like whiskey watered down? 'Your mother and I are marrying on Saturday.' Then later, 'Deputy Beidler has accused me of murdering your father.'

Or straight up? 'Beidler thinks I murdered your father and your mother has accepted my proposal of marriage.'

A wedding and a murder. They would not yoke together.

If he said nothing? If they – if Timothy – found out by other means, as he certainly would from the gossip in town, there would be hell to pay.

85

Nothing for it but he must tell them himself. It would be hell that way, too, but perhaps a lesser hell. At least no one could then accuse him of trying to hide what could not be hidden.

Dan's head rose above the steps. The breeze down the side of the building whipped his face, and tugged at his hat. Holding the brim as he stepped onto the veranda and fumbled his key into the lock, he pushed open the door and held it for them to enter. "Glad I don't have office number one. I'd hate to fight a north wind all that way."

The room smelled of cold stone. The late-afternoon sun had swung to the south at the back of the building to waste its meager light and small heat on a rock wall.

Dan waved his hand around the room. "Sol Content wants to rent this floor to the Governor if the legislature selects Virginia City as the territorial capital, so there's no point in fixing it up much. It will do as long as I need it." He'd paid three months in advance, so he had that time at least. Maybe less.

Jacob stamped his feet and flapped his elbows against his sides. "Is cold in here."

"This is a big stove." Timothy put his hand on the potbelly stove in the back inside corner. "Ain't you built the curing fires yet?"

"No, I only rented the place this afternoon."

"You have plenty of firewood." Jacob gestured toward the stove where a pile of kindling lay on the floor beside the heaping woodbox.

Another promise Content had kept. Soon the afternoon light would vanish. Dan tossed a package of candles to Timothy. "The sooner we have light and heat the better."

While the boy unwrapped the candles, Dan laid sticks of kindling on the desktop. Seeing him unfold his pocket knife, Jacob brought out his own knife and they went to work to make tinder, scraping at the bare wood rather than carving splinters.

Dan said, "Tell me your news. What did Hershfield mean, that he liked hearing about opportunities?"

Timothy set the candles on the desktop and crumpled up the wrapping paper. "Where's that go?" He tossed the paper into the stove and pointed to a door next to it that was set into the back wall.

"A hallway that connects the offices." Dan prompted Jacob: "That nugget we found last spring assayed well."

"This one?" Timothy took a pale rock the size of his thumb from a front trouser pocket and juggled it from hand to hand.

"Yes." A pretty stone, it looked dull and innocent in the dim light, a common small rock. In reality it was anything but dull, innocent, or common.

That day, rain pelting down and pooling in their saddles, they had almost given up locating the last of McDowell's claims, when Timothy found the nugget. Then, Dan had suspected it was 'salt.' A quartz nugget lying on the ground? Crooks salted claims all the time, flinging nuggets – fool's gold, mostly – on the ground to make a man think he'd struck it rich. If someone had salted this claim, they'd made a bad mistake. When the assayer said its gold was ninety-eight percent pure, they told each other the salting, if it was that, had been someone's mistake. The nugget, worth hundreds of dollars, could send a man crazy with gold fever.

If he believed in it.

Dan had not believed, then. Was not sure he'd believe now. The goose bumps on his arms rose because of the cold. Not because Jacob looked like exploding if he did not tell his news.

Jacob put down his knife. He picked it up again, put it down. Bit a fingernail.

"Please stop fidgeting and tell it, Jacob."

"Yah. So. We have a – oh, this English – we have indecision to make."

There was a snapping noise, repeated. Realizing he folded and unfolded his own knife, Dan folded it and put it in his trousers pocket. He'd caught Jacob's excitement. Was the claim rich? How rich? How could Jacob know, except by the one assay?

"You mean decisions?" Fishing out the crumpled newspaper from the firebox, he made a nest to hold the tinder of splinters and fine wood fuzz.

"Yah. Decisions. There are, what? Indications?" Jacob laid a finger across his lips. "You must keep secret." He looked toward Timothy. "Also you."

"All right. You found indications." Holding hard to his patience, Dan patted his pockets for his tinder box.

Timothy said, "For God's sake, Jake, will you get to the point?"

Ignoring Timothy, Jacob brought a candle over to the stove, standing so close that Dan smelled the whiskey on his breath.

He removed the steel and flint, held them over the tinder as Jacob prepared to give up his secret.

"Yah," Jacob whispered. "I digged a great much. Enough so people think I am desperate. So I hope." He beckoned to Timothy, who leaned against the wall between the stove and the rear door. "This is great secret. Come closer."

Dan's hand moved fast; the sound of steel against flint was snick-ick-ick-ick under Jacob's drawn-out whisper.

Timothy stood on Jacob's other side. "What did you find, Jake? Come on, tell us."

Sparks leaped onto the lint. Dan breathed on it to coax out a flame. "You don't know?" Why had Jacob not told Timothy last night?

A tiny flame leaped up. Dan set the smoldering nest of paper and tinder in the fire box. Listening for Jacob to begin, he laid most of the splinters on top of the tinder, now burning steadily, pulled one splinter out, and closed the fire door. Touching the flaming splinter to a candle, he tilted it to make a little puddles of wax on each tins.

"I don't know nothin'." Timothy tossed the nugget and caught it one-handed. All shine and glitter rising in the candlelight, it fell into shadow, to rise again. The cycle of gold mining, Dan thought.

Jacob murmured, "In summer, Tim, he cannot dig there always. He must work the Alder creek claim. Is almost played out, you see, but he works it like it has gold." He blew on his fingers.

"To fool people," Timothy chimed in. "And get what I could."

Dan lighted two more candles, pressed one each into the wax puddles, and set them on the cold cook top. The splinter burned down almost to his fingertips. He blew it out and tossed it into the firebox. The three of them held their hands over the candle flames to warm them. Candlelight wavering over their faces cast shadows under their cheekbones, hollowed their eye sockets into caves.

"Watch out for your beard, Jacob," Dan said.

Jacob pulled back, out of danger. "I dig alone mostly. Somewhat above my head, but nothing find. Then Timothy's mother, she is anxious, and he must find you. So I dig alone."

"That was dangerous, Jacob. Didn't you think of cave-ins?" Opening the fire door, he checked the fire, tossed in the remaining splinters.

"Yah, I think, but I am here, yes? No cave-in. Then four days ago, I am seven, eight feet down, and I have tunnel made. I am out maybe ten feet?" He paused, smiling. "The ground freezes above, and below is rock."

Dan shuddered. He imagined Jacob alone underground, all the weight of hundreds of cubic feet, tons of rock and dirt coming down, crushing him. "The chance you took. Promise me never again." His unspoken question was, why? Why would Jacob take such chances? He could not think of a reason.

Jacob laughed. "I find indications. Yah. Indications." His eyes held a smile, and his whole face lifted, bright with the fun of a great secret yet to be told.

Dan opened the fire door, placed enough fat splinters to strengthen the fire.

Jacob said, "A vein I find. In a wall."

"God damn." A gold seam in a wall. God damn. A wall, and gold threaded through it. His heart hammered in his ears. "Good God." He'd expected something, but this? "Good God." Flame licked his fingertips. He snatched his hands away and shut the fire door.

"Yah," Jacob said. "We have something."

Timothy said, "So? We knew it was a quartz claim already. Pap thought it was a placer claim, but the nugget, it's quartz." The nugget rose and fell as he tossed it up and down, hand to hand.

"Not like this." Dan guessed, watched Jacob to be sure he was right.

Jacob beamed. Nodding, his long thin beard patting his waistcoat, he thumped a gentle fist on Dan's chest. "You have it. Yah. You have it right. Not like this."

Dan laid the flat of his hand on the stove's side. Warm. The cold iron had warmed without cracking. "A far different proposition from a placer mine." The stove plates were warm enough to build up the fire. He laid as much kindling on the fire as he dared, while his mind ran over the complexities of quartz mining, the cost of development deep underground. How far dared they go? A hundred feet?

"How deep can a gold mine go?" he asked Jacob.

"This vein, where I find it, it is not so deep underground." Jacob lifted his shoulders almost to his ears. "Maybe ten feet. The wall goes down more. Who knows?" He dropped his shoulders. "It is the way of all gold claims. Maybe rich, more maybe no."

"Good God." Dan could not keep still. He paced the room, front door to back door, while he thought over Jacob's news. A quartz mine followed the gold lying in seams threaded through the earth's bones. To pry it out men blasted shafts and tunnels, cleared debris, loaded the ore, brought it to the surface. They would need men: miners, men to drill, set the blasting powder, shore up shafts and tunnels. They needed sledge hammers, drills, machinery, timber. Money. A payroll. The more gold, the bigger the operation, the more of everything needed.

He felt the stove, and found it not hot enough. "We can't build a bigger fire yet," he said, but he was thinking about the Nugget. So much potential, so much risk.

The greater the risk, the greater the need for capital. He had capital. But enough? How to know? So much unknown. How to determine the risk? It was like an equation, with X the unknown. In any equation, there would always be X.

X. Goddammit. What about X? Damn him and his accusation.

The unknown had the overpowering urgency of murder.

~~~

Light faded in the window, and in the corners shadows darkened. His thoughts dodged among capital, X, gold, murder. X. He could not stay with any one thought. God damn it. He should give this "indecision" careful thought, but he could not think beyond X.

A deeper shadow stirred in the corner between the back door and the outside wall, thickened into the shape of a hanged man.

Jacob's voice startled him. "We have a problem I do not tell even Tim yet."

Another unknown, Dan thought.

The nugget dropped onto the stove top, rolled to the floor. Stooping, Timothy retrieved it before it rolled under the stove. Rising, he demanded, "What problem?"

"We have not ground enough." Jacob opened his hands in front of himself.

"What do you mean, not enough ground?" Dan asked.

"This law about quartz claims, yah?" From an inside coat pocket he took a folded page from a newspaper and passed it to Dan.

Timothy pressed his hand to the stove. "It needs more wood."

"Go ahead." Unfolding it, Dan noted the masthead: *The Montana Post*, and the date, August 27, 1864. The first issue.

Jacob gestured to him to turn the page over.

On page two, a short Idaho statute was printed in full. Dan read part of it aloud: "Quartz claims shall consist of two hundred feet along the lead or lode, by one hundred feet in breadth."

He would have given the page back, but Jacob shook his head. "No, Daniel. You keep it. Is a problem, yah?"

Timothy put more sticks on the fire, one by one.

"Yes," said Dan. "It is a problem. That is not nearly enough ground. We wouldn't have enough room for a tailings pile or a stamp mill or the head frame, let alone all three." More unknowns. Did this law apply here? It had been passed while Montana Territory was still part of Idaho, but Montana had been split off from Idaho nearly six months ago, and the legislature would not meet for another month. Another unknown. Where did the vein go? What if ground were claimed on either side? Who would own the vein then?

"That's an Idaho law," Timothy said. "This is Montana. Does that even rule us?"

"I don't know. I'll have to find out, starting tomorrow, if I can." He leaned over to look through the grate on the fire door. "Or next week."

"Next week?" Jacob and Timothy spoke almost at once.

"Why wait?" Timothy demanded.

Now that the moment had come, he straightened perhaps too fast, unbalancing himself. He put his hand out to steady himself, felt a greater warmth in the stove's iron skin. "Your mother has consented to marry me. On Saturday. At two o'clock. At home."

"Daniel!" Beaming, Jacob seized Dan's right hand in both of his and pumped it. "Good news! So good. It is – so happy I am for you and your good lady."

"No!" Timothy stomped off toward the rear door. He kicked at it, his foot driving through the thickened shadow, but the specter – if it was there – made no sign. "She can't." Dry-eyed, he came into the light to face Dan. "She can't marry you. Of all people. She can't. She just can't marry you, she – she can't do this." His fist closed around the nugget. "I saw your face when Jacob talked about the Nugget. You want that claim, don't you? That's what you've been after all this time, ain't it? You hung Rawley, and you must've killed Pap. And now you think you'll have it all? Mam, and Pap's claim, both? Here, then. Take it and be damned."

He hurled the nugget at Dan, who flung his hand up to catch it before it could cut his cheekbone. Timothy wheeled for the front door.

"Wait!" Dan shouted.

The door slammed behind Timothy, rattled the window panes.

Worse than he had thought. Timothy already thinking he had murdered his father? Christ. If, after everything, the boy believed – X accused him, and now Timothy?

Jacob pulled at Dan's shoulder. "Go. Go quick after him. I tend fire. Go."

He did not – could not – move.

Jacob pushed him a step forward, but Dan stiffened his knees. "How can I? He believes I murdered McDowell."

"Then it is – you must go. Show him you did not do this evil thing."

"You don't believe it?"

"No. Is not possible."

"X Beidler thinks it is. He's accused me of – of it."

"Beidler, he is a fool. He wants easy answers, thinks only this or that, never maybe. Never he could be wrong. Now go." Jacob pushed harder. "Go. I tend fire."

Dan shoved the nugget into his waistcoat pocket and dashed out, unaware of anything except to stop Timothy until he slipped and tumbled down the last steps. He lay for a bit gathering his senses. When he regained his footing, he brushed snow from his hair, retrieved his hat, and put it on. Limping, he walked uphill to his house.

~~11~~

Tim wasn't crying, damn it, he wasn't. It was the cold making his eyes water so bad. Only babies cried. He, Tim McDowell, wasn't no baby. He didn't cry. Pap never cried. Pap was a real man. Tough. Maybe he hadn't been tough enough for Pap. Liking Dan'l better'n Pap. For a while. Not now. Nosiree. Not now.

Pap never had no use for Dan'l. Always said you couldn't never trust educated folks. Reading addled the brain. Made it so's you got so clogged up with ideas you couldn't think for yourself.

Dan'l wanted him to learn to read, write, cipher. He didn't want no education. He didn't trust Dan'l, neither.

The look on his face when he'd heard what Jake said about the Nugget. Like he'd won big at poker. The Nugget would be his once he'd married Mam. He'd have it all, then, on account what a woman owned became her husband's property when she married. Dan'l would own the Nugget when he married Mam.

He had to stop that wedding. Mam couldn't marry Dan'l. She couldn't, on account Dan'l might've, could've, prob'ly did kill Pap. For the Nugget. He didn't give a fig for them – Mam, Dotty, nor himself.

At the house, the dog set to barking, wanted him to play or rub his belly, but he didn't have no time for that foolishness. He flung open the door and shut it behind him, leaned against it, panting to get his breath.

Dresses were laid out on the settee. Laughing, Mam held one up to Dotty's shoulders. "You might try this one," she said through the laughter, turning her head toward him. One look at him, and her mouth closed, the laughter dying out of her face.

"Timmy," said Dotty, "the best news. Mama and Dan'l are getting married, and I'm the maid of honor." Taking the dress from Mam, she held it up to herself, and twirled about, as usual not seeing nobody else, not seeing him.

Dotty said, "You can be best man! Won't that be—"

All his gathered breath went into one great shout: "You can't marry him, Mam. You just can't."

Dotty stood still, holding the dress to her chest. "Don't be stupid, Timmy, Mam can so marry Dan'l." She didn't say more, didn't say Mam had to marry Dan'l, something they all knew and never said out loud, that Mam had to marry Dan'l on account she was bearing his baby.

He thought, but knew better than to say, The hell with that baby. She ought to've got rid of it when there was time. "You can't marry Dan'l. He killed Pap."

Dotty stood like she'd growed out of the rug, but Mam give him a thin-lipped look and took the dress from her, laid it on the settee, smoothed its pleats, taking a damn long time about it, too. He thought she might say something, but she went to open the oven door and poked inside with a long-handled fork.

"Mam, didn't you hear me? I'm telling you. Dan'l murdered Pap."

Mam closed the oven door and laid the fork on a platter. "I heard you." She sat down on one of the chairs at the table. "Are you staying for dinner?"

He'd choke if he had to eat a meal with Pap's killer. "No. I can't."

Dotty said, "Dan'l could never have killed Papa."

He didn't understand. How could Mam be so calm? He sat on the changing bench. "You can't marry him if'n he killed Pap."

"He did not murder your father."

"How do you know? It had to be him. There ain't nobody else could've."

Dotty sat down on the settee among the dresses. She wore a face he'd never seen afore, all serious and growed up, like the bones had set in different places, which he knew they couldn't, but – and she was quiet, too, like he'd seen her just the once after Pap knocked Mam out. He hadn't meant to do that, though, he was just upset.

Mam said, "Did you talk to Deputy Beidler? Is that what he told you?"

"What?" He couldn't grasp hold of what she was telling him.

Mam looked down at her fingers gripped together over her stomach. She spoke real soft. "He saw the deputy when he went to arrange for Brother Cummings to marry us on Saturday."

Deputy Beidler, him and Dan'l was such great pals, but he thought Dan'l killed Pap? "There. If Beidler accused Dan'l, he must've done it."

"No," screamed Dotty. "He's wrong. Dan'l wouldn't. Mama, he'd never. Never."

Ignoring her, Tim said, "He thinks Dan'l murdered Pap? And you're marrying him anyway?"

"Yes. We're tying the knot at two o'clock on Saturday afternoon."

"You know he killed Pap and you're marrying him?" He couldn't wrap his mind around those two notions. They just wouldn't fit.

"He did not kill him, Timmy."

"You can't know that."

"I do know it."

"How? How can you know it?"

"I know Dan'l. It ain't – is not in his nature to murder anyone."

"Mam, while we was in Bannack, the Vigilantes there, them and Dan'l, they hung a man, on account he come back after his sentence banished him. Mam, he had no feet."

~~~

She knew Dan'l was a Vigilante, had knowed it from the start, because someone had to rid the country of the murderers and robbers terrorizing the roads, and never mind if a body had any dust or not, he'd be as likely to be murdered for not having any money to give the road agents. They were God's thunderbolt that she'd begged for at poor Nick Tbalt's graveside, and she wasn't about to go back on them now, after they'd done the needful so's she and other honest folk could walk about town without praying a stray ball wouldn't hit them or travel without someone pointing a revolver at them.

Thinking so, she'd stopped listening to Timmy, whose voice rose, "...but Mam, that fella crawled back. He didn't have no feet on account gangrene had took them, plumb ate 'em up. They hung a man with no feet."

"Oh, no!" Pressing both hands to her mouth, Dotty jumped up and run for the slop bucket behind the stove.

~~12~~

Martha stood up as quick as she could, what with the baby's weight in her middle. Timmy clenched and unclenched his fists, his face twisted, his breath coming all raggedy, looking ready to hit someone, the spitting image of Sam in a rage.

He weren't Sam, though. He were her first, her little guardian that drew a bead on one of the outriders as found the farm and would've taken everything if'n they hadn't started in to laughing at Timmy, small as he was then and looking so much younger, sighting down the musket's long barrel.

She'd scolded him when he was small, and she could scold him now, big as he was.

"Have you no thought for other people? Look at what you done—"

Right then the front door latch lifted, and Dan'l walked in.

Everything stopped but Dotty's horrid racking noises behind the cookstove.

The lines of Dan'l's face set all downward around tight lips. It wasn't no accident he was here. He'd already had a set-to with Timmy.

Lord, Lord, please don't let this get worse, she prayed as she hurried to help Dotty.

Holding the child's forehead during the convulsions, Martha tried to listen for sounds of arguing or worse, but neither of them spoke, and somehow that scared her worse than if they'd gone to yelling at each other. When Dotty finished, Martha put her arm around her shoulders and guided her to sit at the big table. Sitting down with her, she gave Dotty mint leaves to chew so's to clean her mouth, while she wiped her face with a cloth dipped into the clean water bucket.

While Dotty recovered, Martha stole a glance at her men. Dan'l had taken off his outdoor things and put on his house shoes and sack coat. Feet wide apart, he stood in front of the guns, as silent and still as stone. Timmy sat at the end of the bench farthest from Dan'l, pretending to study his hands.

"Are you better?" Dan'l asked the child. His gentle tone sprung tears into Martha's eyes.

Dotty, chewing on the mint leaves, could only nod.

Dan'l said, "Dear child, I did not murder your father, no matter that Deputy Beidler accuses me and your brother thinks I did."

Dotty gulped. "I know that, but—" Her voice trailed off.

Dan'l waited.

"Timmy said you hung a man without– without he had feet. " She bunched up handfuls of her apron.

Dan'l's face turned a dark red that Martha had never seen. Putting her arm around the child's shoulders, she drew her close and felt the quicker rise and fall of Dotty's chest. Tensed, she waited for an explosion, from Dan'l, or Timmy.

"You told them about Rawley?"

Never imagining a near-whisper would echo like it did, Martha held her breath for fear he'd haul off and smash Timmy, like Sam would've, Sam with his loud shouting, hasty temper, and great fists.

"Yeah, I told them. I said as how you hung a man with no feet." He sprang up, took two swift strides across the room to where they sat. Dan'l put himself between them, forcing Timmy to stop so sudden he almost lost his balance.

She caught her breath for fear they'd go to fighting, but Dan'l clasped his hands behind his back, like corralling them to keep them out of trouble.

Timmy learned around Dan'l. "Mam, if he'd hang a man with no feet, he'd stab a man in the back."

Dotty let out a small cry.

"That ain't all," Timmy said. "Jake Himmelfarb says the Nugget claim is maybe rich. Don't you see? With Pap gone for good, Dan'l will have the Nugget once you're married, and – and he'll have everything."

"Timothy!" Dan'l said. "I will not own your mother's share of the Nugget when I marry her."

"But the law says you do."

"Which law? Tennessee? North Carolina? New York? This is Montana Territory. We have no Montana laws because the legislature does not meet until December twelfth. That's more than a month from now, and Idaho law does not rule here."

"So you say. I – I don't know."

"So the only law we have comes from the miners' court. Think! You were there when Judge Davis ruled that you, and your mother and sister own equal shares in the Nugget if your father died. If you don't believe me, go ask him to let you read his decision."

"You know I can't read."

"Then learn, for God's sake. Your mother and sister are learning. You could, too."

"Pap didn't know how to read, and he got along all right. What was good enough for him is good enough for me."

Dan'l gripped his hands so hard his fingers turned white and red, and trembled like they'd escape on their own, making her afraid Timmy had pushed him beyond his limits and – and what might happen then didn't bear thinking about. Dan'l hadn't never hit Timmy, though he'd had reason to more than once, but could he stop himself this time?

Between one thought and the next she knew Dan'l would not let go of his temper that way.

The least'un kicked, and she let out a squeak at the surprise of it.

Dan'l spun around. "Are you all right?"

"Yes. The least'un, he surprised me, is all." She called this baby 'he,' on account he felt more like a boy than a girl – all the time moving, kicking. Dotty had been quieter.

"Mam!" Timmy craned his shoulders toward her, like he'd use his body to block her from saying more.

"Now, you hush, you hear me? You've had your say, and Dan'l had his. I haven't changed my mind about marrying him." But when she would have said more, Dan'l said, "My dear," in a way that stopped her.

He moved in front of Dotty and hunkered down, so's he had to look up at her. "What do you think, Dorothy? Would you consent to your mother marrying me?"

The child looked from Dan'l to Timmy to her. A smile spread across her face. She'd told Martha once that she didn't like her smile on account her mouth was too big, and she showed too many teeth, but here it was, bright enough to shame the sun. "Yes. I'd like that. We'd be a proper family then."

"But why? What about Pap? The Nugget? That poor devil Rawley?" Timothy's deep bass boomed out, rough and coarse. Demanding his little sister see it his way.

"No." Dotty screamed the word at him past Dan'l. "He'd never. And I don't care about some road agent who never gave a thought to anybody else in his life. I just wish they'd do for that Jacky Stevens, too." She stopped, out of breath.

Martha soothed her, a hand on her arm, murmured, "Child, child."

Dotty shook her head so her curls brushed each shoulder in turn. "Well, I do. I purely do. He scares me. I'm scared to walk home from school by myself."

Dan'l stood up fast and said to Timmy, his voice cold as iron, "Hear me: I did not murder Sam McDowell."

Ignoring Dan'l, Timmy shouted at her and Dotty. "Mam, you can't marry him. You can't. He done it, I tell you. He —"

"No, he did not." Martha shouted at her son, her first-born turning into a stranger right in front of her.

"How do you know? How can you know?"

What could she say that would not betray Dan'l, that she knew on account she'd slept beside him night after night, and heard his nightmares, and cradled his head between her breasts when he'd come sobbing out of one. He'd said names she recognized and some she didn't, but he'd never once said 'McDowell.' Casting about for something to say, she found the dulcimer lying in its box next to her reading chair and tilted her head toward it.

"On account he brought me a dulcimer."

Timmy stared at it. "He brought you a dulcimer?"

"It's there, isn't it? Your Pap smashed up the old one, but Dan'l brought this'n." To her, the dulcimer was proof of everything. Let it be so for Timmy, she prayed. Lord, let it be so.

Timmy's ragged breathing was loud in the room.

He said, "He brings you a present, so you decide he's innocent? No, Mam. If you marry Dan'l, he's won everything. You can't marry him. If you do, you ain't my Mam no more."

"How can you do this to your mother?" Dan'l said, his voice raised.

"Stay out of it!" Timmy shouted, stamped his foot so candle flames wobbled on the table. He'd done that same thing in tantrums as a very little boy. His face turned bright red now like then, the same vein bulged over his forehead. "This don't concern you."

"It damn well does concern me. You don't see what you're doing to your mother."

Through their shouting, Martha managed to make Dan'l hear her. "Dan'l." She held out her hand, and he helped her to rise, and supported her, though she felt the tension thrum along his arm muscles. Or maybe it was her shaking. How could she choose between them, her two best loves? Why did Timmy force her to choose?

Gathering herself, she said: "Don't make me choose between you."

"You can't marry him, Mam. You just can't. Pap was our Pap." His wide eyes, his open hands, the way he bent toward her – her boy's whole being begged her to choose him. Not Dan'l. Him.

"Oh, no, stop it." Dotty sobbed, "Timmy, don't. Don't."

"Timothy," said Dan'l, "if you don't stop this right now, if you force her to choose, I'll never forgive you."

"Mam?" Timmy pleaded. "Mam."

She stiffened her back to stand a little straighter. "We are marrying on Saturday. At two o'clock. I'd like you to be there." Pressing her lips together, she said no more.

"No!" Timmy wheeled about and fled. The door slammed.

~~13~~

Fighting the urge to find Timothy and knock some sense into him, breathing as hard as a runner, Dan stood by the settee and stared at the night-black window. As awareness came back to him, the rage drained away, leaving the sound of women weeping. Mirrored in the window, multiplied and divided by the panes, Martha and Dotty huddled together in her reading chair. He did not know what to do for them, how to ease their sorrow, but he would remember how they sobbed. He would remember how dresses lay strewn about on the settee, and how their happiness – his and theirs – would be spoiled.

He would remember and never forgive.

He pulled the thick drape across the window to block out the drafts.

Martha shivered as she held Dotty, from reaction or from actual cold, he did not know, but he would build up the fires and light some candles. Lots of candles. They needed light. Standing on a kitchen chair, he held a taper to the candles in the wagon-wheel chandelier over the big table. He had made that simple arrangement before he convinced Martha to move into the house with him. Out of wedlock, McDowell absent for less than two months.

Now Beidler and (God help him) Timothy – they accused him of McDowell's murder?

Not Martha. She knew he had not done it, she knew he had not – he choked on the word, even though he did not say it aloud – debauched her to get the Nugget claim, she knew he was no Henry Plummer, no seducer. Martha knew.

Down off the chair, he crossed the room to the smaller stove in the reading corner, crouched to put wood in its firebox. The flames snatched at his fingers, but he did not feel them. Martha believed him. Martha believed in him. Martha had faith in him, the evidence of things not seen. Though she knew about Rawley, and all the others, she did not doubt that someone else had murdered Sam. Not him.

Pitch burst in a shower of sparks. He slammed the fire door and slapped the sleeves of his sack coat to quench the fires before they started. When he glanced over at Martha, she was watching him, dry-eyed, but with a sadness that accused him of everything she did not and could not know. He had seduced – no, convinced – her to live with him in this house, her and her children. He had deserted her for months while she suffered public disgrace as a pregnant unmarried woman, and worst of all, he had wronged her by his tryst with Harriet. He had told her he loved her, but now he was not sure it was true.

Yet she would marry him, she would keep faith with him, she would risk her future, her children's future on his behavior, his faithfulness.

She did not know he carried Harriet's tintype in his portmanteau.

All she wanted of him was his name, and it went without saying, to reconcile Timothy to the family they would be.

She forgave him as she wished him to forgive Timothy.

Hell. The boy could go to the devil for all he cared. He could be telling Jacob right now—

Damn.

"I'll have to go down to the office," he told Martha. "I left Jacob there, tending the curing fires."

She did not argue, but nodded her head. As he laid another quarter round in the cookstove fire box, she said, "Timmy's been upset ever since they found it – him." He knew she meant Sam's remains. "He identified it, you know, to save me seeing what was left of him. It must have been horrid." She drew her shawl around her. "I can't get warm."

"It'll be warm in here soon." Closing the fire door, he adjusted the air intake. He did not know how to comfort her. What could he say to erase what her imagination conjured? "I'd better go."

"No, wait. I want to tell you."

He wanted a drink. In the office, he had a bottle of whiskey, unopened, but Martha would have her say. Turning a wooden chair around to face her, he straddled it and waited for her to begin, tamped down his impatience.

Whatever she wanted to say, she did not want Dotty to hear it. "Child, do you go into your room and practice your reading before dinner. Then later, maybe Dan'l can hear how much you've learned while he was back East."

"I'd be happy to hear you." Dan forced a smile and hoped he looked sincere.

Even so, Dotty pouted, but Martha would have none of her complaining, said her name once more. When the door closed behind her, they were alone.

"Timmy told me it was worse than poor Nick Tbalt last winter. He hasn't been the same since." She stopped. "I'm thirsty."

Dan brought her a glass of water, took his seat again. "I know what you mean," he said. "He was only half civil all the way up from Fort Hall, and after he saw Rawley, he was not civil at all."

"He's been broody. Always thinking about who could've killed Sam. He'd hardly talk to the child and me." She shifted in the chair.

"Did you ever ask him about it?"

"Why, surely. At last he got real mad about it and said if'n he'd been a better son, none of this would've happened."

None of this. Timothy had meant him, and their coming together, and the baby. "He blames himself for his father's death?"

"So I think. He ain't to blame for it, o' course. Just try tellin' him, though."

"That does not give him the right to talk to you as he did. He's almost a man, and it is high time he learned self-control, to respect you."

The look she gave him told him plain as words that he had spoken out of turn, but he would not give in. If Timothy would be part of his family, he would apologize and never again disrespect his mother.

She held out her hand to him. "I want you to have something. Help me up." On her feet, she said, "Bring a candle, please. And a broom."

Dan did as she asked. In the bedroom, she took the broom and bent to swipe under the bed while he held the candle. "Recollect when he left, he took some things, in a burlap feed sack?" He meaning McDowell.

"Yes, I remember the youngsters saying so." Dan moved the candle for her.

"Timmy brought it all back, and I wrapped it all up in an oilcloth."

"What's in it?"

"I didn't look. I ain't sure. Timmy said there's some utensils. Our wedding picture. The clothes he was wearing. Timmy had to identify him by them."

A short sweep toward the foot of the bed brought out the bundle, and she nudged it toward Dan'l with her foot. Metal clattered against metal. "Take it away. I don't want to think about it."

"Do you want the picture?"

"No." She bit off the syllable.

Setting the candle on the chest of drawers, he took up the bulky parcel of McDowell's things. "Thank you." The words seemed meager compared to her generosity toward him. It seemed impossible that she would hear the smallest part of his meaning: Thank you for your faith in me, for choosing me over Timothy.

She put her hands under her stomach, to help carry the weight of it, he guessed. Her expression changed as though she had handed a task over to him and could rest from it. A new idea struck him.

She was a mother protecting her unborn child. He had given her this child, and now he had nothing more to do with it, except to be responsible for it, to make it and herself respectable, and for that she had to marry him to give it his name. And herself.

She hadn't chosen him over her son. She had chosen this baby over both of them.

His part in this unspoken bargain? Give it an honest name. Find McDowell's murderer.

~~14~~

Dan expected Jacob to have gone home by the time he returned to the office, but Jacob had had other ideas. Dan poured them both a generous drink of the scotch as he recounted Timothy's reaction to the forthcoming wedding.

"No one can talk to him now," Jacob said. "So much noise in his ears, he hears nothing. Like a fire, yah? It burns loud."

"And our fire?"

"Is good. Warmer. Soon, maybe we build last fire. See what you think."

Dan felt the warmth when his hand was an inch away from the stove. "Yes. We could build it now." Lifting McDowell's parcel onto the desk top, he said, "As long as you're staying, my good lady gave me McDowell's bits and pieces."

As Jacob built what they hoped would be the last curing fire, he spread the items out on the desktop.

A dead man's belongings. A pot, an iron skillet, a tin cup, a serrated knife and a two-pronged fork. A red plaid flannel shirt, a Confederate artillery officer's overcoat. Sam had been an artillery gunner, not an officer. Dan unfolded the coat, smelling of death. A pair of tall boots, corduroy trousers. No underwear. Had he been buried in it? Or had it been burned?

He and Jacob laid the coat out flat. Taking care not to drop melted tallow on it, they held the candle close to examine it until Dan saw a brown stain, dark in contrast with the coat's butternut. "Look here."

Jacob bent closer. About where McDowell's trousers waistband would have been, the stain surrounded a small slit in the cloth. Opening his penknife, Dan laid the blade against the cut. It was a little longer than his blade was wide, about three-quarters of an inch long. The size of the cut would tell no one anything. Some men, who still used quills, carried penknives to trim them, but most used them for other small tasks.

Who carried one to commit murder?

"So that's it," he said. "Clearly murder. A stab in the back."

"Foul murder," said Jacob.

"Such a small knife, and a little cut to let out so much blood." The bloodstain extended to the side, beyond the cut, indicating that the blood had flowed in a different direction than straight down. Dan turned the coat to follow it and found a larger stain on the right side.

Setting the coat aside, they smoothed the shirt over the desktop to examine it. From a small cut, blood had first run downward, perhaps into the underwear, which they did not have. "A powerful thrust, to penetrate a heavy coat, a flannel shirt, and his underwear."

"Yah. Very strong man."

"It does not make sense. A strong man uses a little knife for a murder? Why did he not shoot McDowell?"

"In the back," said Jacob. When Dan looked at him, he said, "Why this stab in the back with a little knife?"

"Yes." Dan put a hand to his own back, in the same approximate place. "The kidney is there. The murderer cut the kidney. I must talk to the doctor who examined the body, if anyone did. And the blood changed direction. Perhaps McDowell did not know he was cut." His imagination ran faster than he could say what he thought. McDowell had trudged on after the fatal blow, not knowing he bled, then after a time – how long? – perhaps grew tired and crawled into a small cave for rest and shelter. Lay down and bled to death. That explained why the bloodstain on his coat and shirt changed direction, from down his back toward his buttock when he was upright, then after he lay down, it flowed down his side where it pooled and soaked through his coat.

Jacob tilted his head toward the stove. "The plates do not lock."

Dan touched the stove. "Ouch!" He snatched back his hand. "Yes. They should have locked by now."

"So we wait." Jacob set the candle on the desk, went to the stove to warm his back.

Dan said, "I despised McDowell. He mistreated his wife and son, and he intended to sell his lovely little daughter to the highest bidder when she had budded out. The only good thing I ever knew about him was that he did not cheat at cards." He pointed to the bloodstain. "No one should die like this, by murder, alone in a dark cave."

With a scrape of iron sliding against iron and a clank, then another, the plates of the stove locked together.

~~15~~

Rounding the corner of Van Buren and Wallace, head bent to shield his face from the wind, Dan stopped short.

X Beidler barred his way. "I want to talk to you."

Dan scowled at the deputy sheriff. "We've talked enough. I have business to attend to."

"No, we damn well haven't. I've got questions. I want answers. We can talk now or in jail."

"All right. Shoot." Beidler could ask his questions right here.

"We'll freeze our asses out here." Beidler looked around. "How about there?" He pointed his chin toward the closest saloon.

"No." On the verge of telling Beidler to go to hell, Dan thought fast. Refusing to answer Beidler's questions for any reason but self-incrimination could open him up to a charge of obstructing justice. If he did invoke the Fifth Amendment, Beidler would be more certain he was guilty than he was already. Only a fool, though, would meet the deputy alone in private or where they could be overheard, and he'd be equally a fool to meet Beidler without a friendly third man to vouch for him later when words could be twisted into a confession, or misheard.

In other words, a lawyer.

"I'm on my way to find Charles Bagg."

X's laugh lifted the hairs on Dan's neck. "That's easy. I just left him at the courthouse. We can walk back together."

Nothing for it, then. Setting the pace, he climbed the slope to Idaho street, his longer stride forcing the deputy into a jogtrot. At the intersection, he waited to let X catch up before he marched past the probate court – formerly the small, one-room cabin where the McDowells had lived, past the new Union church, and down the slope to the courthouse.

On the way, he thought about Charles Bagg. Did Bagg know yet that he had returned? That friendship had been forged in the war of a trial, when they and Wilbur Sanders prosecuted George Ives for the murder of Nicholas Tbalt. Would it hold? Or would it prove as flimsy as Beidler's? Damn Beidler.

He opened the courthouse door and walked in.

Cummings stood up, offered Dan a brief nod for a greeting, but no handshake. "Have you come to cancel the wedding?" He sounded hopeful.

"No, I have not. Why do you ask?" Dan slapped his gloves into the crown of his hat.

"I'm just making sure."

"Nothing has changed since I was last here."

"Very well, then." A thought moving behind Cummings's eyes caused him to blink rapidly. He sat down at the table and fumbled his ink bottle open, spilling a few drops.

He's afraid of me, Dan said to himself. *I mean him no harm, but he's afraid of me.* He had become a man other men feared? Or does he think he'll be performing a wedding for a murderer? Neither thought gave him pleasure.

Beidler walked in, slammed the door behind him, walked toward the jail without speaking.

Following him, Dan's anger vanished in a twist of humor: It served the sanctimonious son of a bitch right to perform the wedding ceremony if he believed Dan a murderer. He would find out how wrong he'd been.

Charles Bagg sat talking with the commissioners. Noticing Dan, he rose to his feet, hand outstretched, a smile spreading across his face. "Dan Stark! I heard you were back. Good to see you. Old X here doesn't want you for anything, does he?"

Dan tried to laugh, but when Beidler went into the jail and shut the door behind him without speaking, Bagg's smile disappeared. In a glance, he summed up the situation.

"What's the difficulty between you two?"

"I was looking for you, Charles, when I ran into X. Have you got a minute?"

Bagg led Dan into the jail, and to the door of a cell. "This one's empty. Let's go in here," he muttered.

In the other cell a prisoner made grunting noises as he contributed to the jail's atmosphere.

They sat on two stools, their knees touching, and spoke in low voices.

"Shoot," Bagg said. "I gather X is looking at you for something. What is it?"

Trying to get his thoughts in order, Dan hesitated.

Bagg said, "Outside, when you said you were looking for me, you looked sick. I'm hoping it was not the thought of seeing me again."

Dan mustered a smile at the joke. "Not at all. X thinks I murdered Sam McDowell. He wants to interrogate me, and I'd like to hire you as my attorney."

"Good God. Wait. Slow down. Why should he think you'd commit murder?"

"In his view, I had two good reasons to kill McDowell. Mrs. McDowell –" His throat closed on her name. Three more days. Then Martha's name would be Martha Stark. "– and the gold claims."

"Doesn't he know you? My God, you'd think if nothing else – you saved McDowell's miserable life once."

"It goes back to Slade. Since then, he doesn't believe in anyone's friendship." Another thought occurred to him. "Besides, I'm not a Mason. He doesn't even have that to go on." Before Bagg could reply, he asked, "Fundamentally, do Masons trust anyone outside the Order?"

"Of course we do. Not as much as we trust each other, maybe, we're all human. We'll have to get you in, though. Should have done it last winter." Bagg tugged on his full, thick beard. "Let me think." He took out a pipe and tobacco. After an eternity spent on the business of lighting it, he said, "Mind if I ask you something?"

At a noise from the other cell, Dan said, "Couldn't someone take him to the outhouse?"

Bagg blew out smoke toward Dan. "Pipe smoking is an excellent fumigator."

"I believe it." Dan breathed through his mouth while he waited for the pipe smoke to do its work.

"Besides those two reasons," Bagg said between puffs at the pipe, "why else would he think you could have done this?"

"He says I had ample opportunity any time between January fourteenth and when I left for New York near the end of June."

"January fourteenth instant. It's a date that's easy to recall."

They sat silent for a moment, recollecting that day. The Vigilantes had hanged five men from the same beam in the unfinished building now occupied by the Drug Emporium.

"Where was McDowell's body found?" Bagg sat up straight, put a hand to the small of his back. "Hard to sit without a backrest."

Dan smiled. "For an old man of forty, you hold your own." He guessed at Bagg's age, but as a veteran of the Mexican War, Bagg had to be in his late thirties at least. It was an old joke; they all called him 'Old Man.' The corners of Bagg's mouth twitched. He rose to his feet, and Dan stood, too, for politeness' sake.

"Where?" Bagg referred to his question.

"In a small cave a mile or two up Daylight Gulch."

Bagg thought it over. "He didn't get very far when he left here, then, did he?"

"No, he didn't. I wonder if anyone would remember seeing him before he left."

"Did you see him?"

Dan shook his head. "No. I stayed with the McDowell family until we knew Martha – Mrs. – she would recover. When I could leave their cabin, I watched for him. I was furious about what he did to Mrs. – his – to her. If I had seen him, I'd have thrashed him within an inch of his life. But I never did. By the time I left for New York, we – the family and I – were beginning to think he might not come back, that he'd gone to California. Or maybe Texas."

"When do you think he left town?"

"I don't know." For the first time since Beidler confronted him, Dan realized he could consider his situation rationally. "While we were –"

He broke off; talking about those days raised the memory of Martha, unconscious in her bed: McDowell's sledgehammer fist had made a red swelling around her right eye and down her cheek, cut her eyebrow. Lydia Hudson and her free black servant, Tabitha Rose, had hovered around her with set and frightened faces. They held basins of blood-reddened water and cloths.

Men who hit women were scum.

"While we were busy, Tim came to fetch me." She had lain so still his heart lurched even now at the thought she might have died. The skin prickled under his beard. He cleared his throat. "I stayed with the family, on guard." He closed his hand to grip the stock of the Spencer rifle, recollected that he'd left it at home. "Until she was conscious and we knew she would recover."

"How long were you with them?"

Dan rubbed his hands over his face. "It's just a blur. A day? Two days? Three? The youngsters might recall better than I do. Or Lydia Hudson. We were all afraid for her." If he had ever been inclined to trust God again, her recovery and McDowell's death should make him believe that God balanced things out, that McDowell's death was divine retribution. But faith had not come – why not? He shook the question out of his mind.

Through the thick jail odors, he smelled something different, at once familiar and unwelcome. The stench of death. In the cell door a shadow thickened into the shape of a hanged man, iron bars running through its shoulder, a swirling fog from the knees down.

Bagg's hand on his forearm startled him. "Don't look so hopeless. We'll meet X together. I'll bring him in."

"Here? Now?"

"Why not? Now's the time to scotch this thing if we can. If not, we can at least convince X to look in another direction."

"In a moment. I have another question for you." Dan maneuvered so he faced Bagg, his back to the door. "Are you busy Saturday afternoon?"

"One or two things, but they're not important. What can I do for you?"

"Despite everything, Mrs. Mc– Mrs. –" He could not say the name.

"Your good lady," Bagg suggested.

"Yes, thank you. My good lady has agreed to join me in holy matrimony. You once offered to stand up with me. Is that offer —?"

Bagg's wide smile let his teeth show between his mustache and beard. He held out his hand. "I'd be honored." As Dan took it, the smile disappeared. "Do you know what a treasure she is?"

When he could speak, he brought out a hoarse whisper. "I know. I do know." In his normal voice, "She gave me the things McDowell had when he was found. His coat and shirt show that he was stabbed in the back just above the belt. The cut in both wasn't much. I think someone used considerable force with something like a penknife."

Bagg puffed at the pipe as he thought; small round clouds of smoke rose and vanished into the air. "I don't know of any man who does not carry a penknife, do you? But kill someone with it? That could be hard to do."

"Especially stabbing him through a heavy coat. It would take force."

"Yes." Bagg puffed at his pipe. "I can't see you stabbing a man in the back. Killing him in a fair fight, yes. But not this. Never this. This is a coward's way, and you have never been a coward." Clapping his hands to his knees, he rose. "Your good lady is right to accept you. She is very brave to do this, but she is right."

"Yes, she is. Brave, I mean." Standing, Dan found Bagg's pipe sending its clouds of smoke upward toward him, into his eyes. He blinked rapidly and moved away, toward the door. The apparition wavered, so that he thought of pulling his hand back and letting Bagg open it instead.

"Wait," Bagg said. "Another thing. I ran for the Legislature. For the Council of Senators. If I'm elected, I won't be able to help you from Bannack."

"It convenes more than a month from now, on December twelfth, am I right? I hope to have this behind me by then." He straightened his spine, threw back his shoulders. "Let's begin."

Opening the door, he called for Beidler.

~~~

"No," the deputy said. "I haven't looked at anyone else. Nobody had as good a reason to want McDowell dead as Stark does."

Vigilantes. Their alliance, their friendships had been forged in a war, not Union against Confederate, but a small band against a murderous criminal conspiracy. Judges, jury, executioners, they had done all of it. Did ghosts follow the others, too? He glanced at X, at Bagg, tried to pay attention. Anything but meet the shadow in the cell door.

"The timing is off," said Bagg. "Stark was with McDowell's family constantly for several days after he attacked his wife. That should be easy to confirm. Ask the young McDowells. Who else?" he asked Dan.

Dan mentioned Lydia Hudson and Tabby Rose. "Various other ladies brought food, but I don't remember their names."

"You see?" Bagg pointed at Beidler. "Talk to the women. And then find out when McDowell was last seen in town. He didn't go far, did he?"

X stroked his mustache. "I still say nobody had as a good reason to want McDowell dead. The lady and the gold claims."

They watched him, waiting for him to counter that truth, but they were right. He had wanted Martha. He had not thought ahead, beyond having her after McDowell left. Almost, he laughed at the irony of it. He didn't need McDowell's gold. In various New York banks he had deposited enough gold for a small city, the reward of his luck in the Gold Room. And the treasure in his office. That, too.

Last winter, however, he had not been wealthy; he'd been a poor man saddled with his father's debts. Even so the gold claims had never been part of his wanting. Only Martha. He had admired her, but so did other men.

He pictured a burly man in a Confederate cavalry officer's greatcoat. The left arm much shorter than the other. Tobias Fitch.

"What is it? Say something." That was Beidler, demanding an answer.

The man who had used the bucket was now asleep, snoring in gulps and gasps. There was no one to hear him.

"Fitch. Tobias Fitch wanted the claims. He and McDowell were partners, and when McDowell disappeared, she found their contracts, six altogether. She and her children were awarded two of them in the miners' court. I won one from McDowell at poker and lost it to Fitch's surrogate the same way. Two more that the miners' court awarded him have since proved worthless. Timothy tells me the Alder creek claim is about played out. The sixth may be just a hole in the ground." The Nugget. It was anything but a hole in the ground.

"You see?" Bagg thumped a fist on his knee. "There's someone else for you to investigate."

"I already looked at Fitch, but I'll consider him if you come up with anything new. As far as I'm concerned, this don't clear Stark. Not by a damn sight."

Dan exploded. "For Christ's sake, X."

The snoring in the other cell stopped: "Huh? What?"

Bagg put a finger to his lips.

Dan shut his jaws. His attorney warned him, anything more he said would dig him in deeper.

Bagg asked, "Will you at least consider Fitch? He and McDowell were partners."

"I said I would, didn't I? We don't know when McDowell was killed. It could have been any time between the –

what? – fifteenth or so of January and when he was found, in August. Right now, Stark, you're the best I got."

That was all they could achieve. It was not much, but they had put Beidler on notice that he was being watched. The two men strolled up Idaho as though it were a balmy spring day instead of a dull, frigid November, threatening snow. A block past Jackson, they turned downhill on Van Buren street toward Wallace. From there they walked up to Creighton's Stone Block, where Bagg shared an office with three other lawyers.

As they parted company, Dan said, "Thank you." The two simple words rang hollow in his ears. They were not enough, though he and Bagg had achieved little.

"You're welcome. When should I send you my bill?"

Dan laughed, opening his mouth wide. A few snow-flakes landed on his tongue. He felt for his poke. "I'll take care of it now."

"No, it's all right. Call it a wedding present."

"Thank you." Shaking Bagg's hand, Dan felt his eyes sting, not from cold. "Which charity do you like best?"

"Does it ever strike you that in a place with so much wealth, with millions in gold available to anyone who works hard, there are so many poor and desperate people?"

Truthfully, Dan thought, he had never considered that. He was generous to beggars, contributed to fund-raisers for the relief of a family here and there, but he had not thought in larger terms. "I've always thought that anyone could get rich here if they worked hard enough."

"You're forgetting luck, the strength of a man's constitution, and accident. You and I have had luck, and maybe we have some brains, but brains are a matter of luck, too. Many others haven't much luck at all."

Like Rawley, Dan said to himself. If he'd had more luck in the form of brains, he would have made different decisions. He would not have been hanged.

"Those of us who have had luck are responsible to the unlucky. If I do become a Councilman, I intend to support a bill to set up a relief fund. It's criminal, that you and I and other men have so much while others must beg."

This was what Bagg wanted, not a fee for himself, but a commitment to help others. Dan thought of the treasure, the result of the luck of his timing in the Gold Room. "Yes, you can count on me. But don't ask too little."

~~16~~

"I, Martha McDowell, take thee, Dan'l Bradford Stark."
Her own voice sounded far away, like it didn't come from
inside her own throat at all. She clung to his left arm,
afraid she'd drop right down if she didn't hold on tight, she
was that trembly. Under her fingertips, through the layers
of cloth, she felt the slightest tremor. He was nervy, too?
Dan'l? He wasn't the nervy sort. It must be this business
with Beidler. But she mustn't think of that. Not today. He
hadn't done what the little man said, anyways.

She should be happier than ever in her life, but she
couldn't be. Timmy was not there, though Jacob beamed
among the guests, not knowing that him being there reminded her that Timmy hadn't come with him.

Was she wrong to do this? Should she say no, right
now?

The least'un bounced, and Brother Cummings
prompted her, "To be my lawfully wedded husband."

"To be my lawfully wedded husband." She added the
rest in a rush: "To have and to hold from this day forward

till death do us part." She'd done all she could for Timmy, and this true enough love child, he hadn't done nothing to be punished for.

Then it was Dan'l's turn. "I, Daniel Bradford Stark, do take thee, Martha, for my lawfully wedded wife —"

It struck her that this was real, them marrying at last, and she was doing this for the least'un, giving him his father's name so's he wouldn't be shamed. Nor her, not no more. That shame, bearing without being married proper, melted away from her with every word as she became Miz– no, Missus– Dan'l Stark.

"...till death do us part," he said.

The unwanted thought of McDowell came to her. She'd prayed to be free of him, but not at the expense of murder. Never that. She sent up an extra prayer that somehow they would learn who really done that murder on account this man, the father of this baby that kicked so hard inside her, would never have done such a thing.

Charles Bagg, standing up with Dan'l, took something out of his pocket and gave it to Dan'l. When she saw it, she came that close to fainting away at the sight of the fat circle of gold and sparkle. Dotty, her maid of honor, took the silk nosegay from her. Dan'l held her poor, swollen left hand in his own and raised it to take the ring.

The ring would not go on. She whispered, "Screw it on."

"I'll hurt you if I force it." Speaking so all their friends could hear, he asked: "Does anyone have a ribbon?"

She wanted to melt away from sheer mortification. Was it bad luck her finger wouldn't take his ring?

"I have one." Dotty scampered into her bedroom. In a trice back she came, waving a pretty ribbon embroidered with roses.

Thanking her, Dan'l murmured, "Something borrowed," as he slid her ring onto the ribbon, and tied it around her neck so the ring laid on her bosom. Preacher Cummings said the God-given words: "I now pronounce you man and wife."

As she lifted her face for his wedding kiss, her gaze swept across the guests, and she missed Timmy so her heart felt like it froze, and then lurched as she sent up another prayer to make them a family again, all of them.

Dan'l kissed her like he'd never kissed her before, until she thought she'd faint, and his beard tickled her face, and people laughed and cheered them on. A man shouted, "Go, Dan Stark!"

When he let her go, he was a little breathless, too, and his face above the light brown beard reddened at all the laughter and clapping, but he smiled bigger than she'd ever seen on him.

She wanted to hide. Her lips felt swollen, and her face was hot. A kiss like that was properly kept for private and here he'd done it in public, like he was telling the world, Yes, this is my wife, and I put this baby in her, and I'd do it again. Her fingers went to the ring, and she glanced down at it. The most beautiful thing she'd ever thought to see – were those real diamonds? – it belonged on a rich lady's finger, her hands showed such hard work, how would it survive even one pass on the scrub board?

Thinking to tell him how beautiful it was, she surprised such a sadness in his eyes that her breath stopped.

"My dear, are you all right?" His sadness vanished like it never was. "Here, let's sit you down." He escorted her to her reading chair and steadied her into it.

Tabby Rose walked about with glasses of red wine. Mr. Bagg took two off the tray for her and Dan'l, then one for himself while Tabby stood by. She sat like a queen in her reading chair as everyone raised their glasses.

Lifting his voice to be heard over all the other voices, Mr. Bagg said, "I give you Mr. and Mrs. Daniel Bradford Stark. Long life and happiness!"

"Huzzah!" Their friends cheered and drained their wine glasses. Even Lydia Hudson, a Quaker who didn't abide liquor in any form, brought a glass close to her lips in their honor.

Dan'l stood beside her chair, his left hand on her shoulder.

Their friends grouped around, pumped Dan'l's hand, clapped him on the back. The men insisted on kissing the bride, and she gave them all her cheek and a smile.

Dan'l stepped aside for Dotty to hug her around the shoulders and kiss her. "Oh, Mama, I'm so happy."

She smelled coffee and knew they'd be expected to cut the wedding cake, but it could wait. She could contain herself no longer or she'd weep, or – or something to let out so much feeling she thought she'd burst, and the little one inside her moved around so she figured he must be dancing. She touched Dan'l's hand. When he bent to hear her, she said, "Bring me the dulcimer, please."

He raised an eyebrow, but did as she asked. Setting her wine on the reading table, it occurred to her that he'd never heard her play. Sam McDowell – she made herself add, God rest his soul.

He lifted the dulcimer out of its box and laid it across her knees. It was beautiful, not at all like the old one. Even though she'd had it just a few days, she'd played it enough to know its tone and its only flaw, the place on the sounding board where the grain went just a bit awry. To her ear that gave the instrument a personality and she treasured it for that and for what it told her about Dan'l.

Reaching around the mound of her stomach, she strummed it once, and tuned one string a mite up and another a hair down, strummed again, and found it right.

She let herself go. Her fingers knew where they belonged without her having to think, and the lamp on the table beside her broke rainbows from the ring.

Part II

~~17~~

"Timothy!"

Break it. Stomp it into the ground. Get that tintype of Mam and Pap on their wedding day and grind it to bits on account Mam, oh, Christ, Mam why'd you have to marry Dan'l and bear his get, and why hadn't he, Tim McDowell, stopped it when it started, in the winter? But he'd been happy about Dan'l taking Pap's place then, and now he wanted to puke up his insides. Pap threw him out in the blizzard, but it was his own fault on account he hadn't been the right sort of son, not the boy Pap wanted, but why not? He'd have to get the tintype back from Mam and that meant seeing her as she now was married to Dan'l and big with his bastard, always a bastard even with some words that couldn't never make it right, proof she'd betrayed Pap. So now. He'd have to do something about that, but nothing could make it right except proving Dan'l murdered Pap, and how to do that—

"Timothy!"

The damn voice. Calling him louder. Who? Leave me alone, goddammit, or I'll smash you, grind your damn face into the ground.

Jake. Jake was calling him.

He couldn't smash Jake. Jake never done nothing to him or Pap.

Tim stopped, blinking against the sunlight lancing off icy spots in the street.

"So here you are." Jake took hold of his elbow like he needed Tim's help to find his way home. "You are silly boy. You go out, no hat, no gloves, the ice grows thick on the creeks, your ears are red. We go home now and maybe you are not frostbite."

Something in Jake's voice made him want to cry, but he was a man now Pap was dead, so he cuffed a speck out of his right eye. "I couldn't sit inside. It's just eating me up." Funny how he could say that to Jake but he never could've to Pap, and as for Dan'l— He hawked and spat into the road.

They stepped aside for the stagecoach from Bannack on its way to the stable. The driver dipped the brim of his hat to them as he went by, the whole outfit all rumble, clop, and creak of wood on iron.

Jake tapped his head. "It is a plan I have. We find proof."

"Proof?" Tim asked though he knew what Jake meant. Find proof that Dan'l hadn't killed Pap. He wanted proof, too, on account nobody would take his being sure as enough to hang Dan'l.

They crossed Daylight crick and turned off Main Street, walking upstream on Cover street, to where he lived with Jake on the north bank of the crick. They'd sit on Jake's back porch in warm weather in the shade of willow saplings, but from now till spring heavy yellow curtains covered the back door and the window in front to keep out drafts. Jake liked bright colors. He said yellow made the place warmer.

While Jake lighted a couple of candles, Tim stirred up the fire, set water on the potbelly stove to boil. There wasn't but one stove that did for both cooking and heating, so they had to time meals right, exchange one pot for another on the cooktop. Jake took mugs and things from a cupboard over the wash stand, while Tim brought out a burlap sack labeled "Rio," half full of green coffee beans. Jake liked that South America coffee better than Java beans, and Rio was cheaper, too. Jake was saving his dust to go back home and find himself a wife.

He sprinkled a double handful of beans in the frying pan and set it on the stove to roast while he stood by with a fork to stir them from time to time. "What's your plan, Jake?"

"Is not much plan. Is – how to say – an idea? Yah. An idea only." Jacob set one candle on the square table and moved an old book to the side. It was printed in squiggles Jake said was Hebrew. He set the other candle on the washstand. From a shelf he brought a plate with utensils to the table, and from a closed cupboard, he brought another plate, a cup, a knife and fork. Keeping kosher, he called it, though Tim didn't see the point of having one place for some food and another place for other food and different utensils and all.

Stirring the beans, he inhaled the smell of roasting, part coffee and part heat. If he didn't like coffee so much, he wouldn't bother with all this folderol.

Jacob cut some bread and put it on their plates. "I tell you while we eat."

"No, Jake, I want to hear it now. I can listen while I do this." Even to his own ears, he sounded like a whiny baby, but damn it, first he'd waited for Pap to come back and punish them all for Mam living with Dan'l, then after Pap was found he'd waited for Dan'l to come back, and then Dan'l come back and they'd hung Rawley, and now he had to wait for X Beidler to arrest Dan'l and the court to say he'd killed Pap, and now he had to wait for goddam coffee, and the hell with it all.

And then when his arm swung wide to sweep everything off the cooktop, Jacob was there to turn him around and sit him in his chair at the table afore he could do any damage.

"I finish coffee," Jake said. "You burn yourself, maybe."

He was bigger than Jake, inches taller, and maybe twenty-five pounds heavier, but even wanting to smash something or someone, he couldn't never ever smash Jake.

By the time they finished their bread and jam and coffee, Tim could breathe regular, only he couldn't look at Jake, thinking how close he'd come to ruining the one good thing he had.

Jake said, "I tell you my idea?"

Tim managed a "Yes," and a glance at Jake from under his forelock.

"I think we look for evidence."

"You think Dan'l killed Pap?"

"No." Jake said. "Look at me." When Tim did, he said, "Daniel could never murder anyone. Why do you think this?"

"You didn't see it." Tim swallowed. He could not escape Jake's steady gaze. "On account of him being a Vigilante, and – and Rawley." When he understood that Jake didn't know what he meant, he explained it. "Him they hung over in Bannack a couple weeks ago. He'd lost his feet to gangrene. Dan'l was part of that."

"Be that as it may, hanging this man – Daniel did not do it alone, yah? There were other Vigilantes? Yah. Being a Vigilante does not a murderer make him. Some of them, maybe, yah. This I do not know. Only there is a difference between killing and murdering."

What the hell did he mean? Tim stared at Jake, who put his hand on the old book. "It is in here. Torah. What you call Old Testament? Here is origin of many things in your religion. In Christianity. Here is where Ten Commandments comes from. You understand?"

No, Tim thought, but he kept quiet.

"We – Christian and Jew – we have same laws. Ten Commandments. Given by God." He cocked his head, to Tim's mind like a bright bird, even with the long black beard and hair brushing his shoulders.

"They taught us the Ten Commandments in Sunday School."

"Do you remember?"

"Yes. Mam drilled us afore we come here. I can say them all."

"Ah. Good. What is Fifth Commandment?"

"Thou shalt not kill." Mam would've given him a hug for still remembering, and while Tim didn't expect a hug, he thought Jake would maybe nod or say that was right, or something.

"Is not right. In Hebrew, it is so." He let out sounds that made as much sense to Timothy as a cat gargling. "That means, Thou shalt not murder. Is a difference. To God is a difference. To men, also. In my country are pogroms, yah? Cossacks come and murder Jews because we are Jews. If we fight them, kill them, it is not murder. Is killing to defend ourself, save other people. Maybe we die, but that is good in sight of God. Killing, people kill for many reasons. Protect someone, defeat evil." Pausing, he sipped at his coffee, gazed at Tim over the rim of the cup, and Tim could not look away.

"Murder, ah. Is selfish." Jake put down the cup, took out his handkerchief, and dabbed a drop or two from his mustache. "Someone something has you want, and you murder him so you have it. Or he is color you don't like. Or different religion." He folded the handkerchief and laid it beside his plate.

"Pogrom," whispered Tim. Jake didn't use no fancy words, just plain talk, but something about his face, the deep black sorrow in his eyes, carried a whiff of burning, a far-off sound of screaming in the night.

"Yah. Pogrom."

They sat in silence until the wind rattled a window. For something to do, a reason to move, Tim broke the embers in the stove and laid in more wood. When he had closed the firebox door and stood the poker in its stand, he knew what to say. "So hangin' a man with no feet was killin' and stabbin' Pap in the back was murder. Right?"

"This Rawley, I do not know about murder. Your father, yes, that was murder."

"If that hangin' was murder, then Dan'l could do murder. Murderin' Pap got him the Nugget claim. And Mam."

"And you know Daniel helped that?"

"He wouldn't say." Tim sprang up, bursting invisible ropes of his own making that tied him down. "I asked, but he wouldn't tell me. I was asleep. He left before I went to bed, and was back before I woke up. It was all over then. Had to be. The body was – oh, God, it was froze solid." He knuckled his eyes, but the picture of the ragged ends of Rawley's ankle and one half of a foot would not leave him.

"Ah. This, he would not tell you." An upraised hand stopped Tim from shouting. "What he did. It is, that he could not. He has an oath sworn, yah? Nothing in meetings goes out of meetings. He protects other men. Witnesses. Vigilantes."

"Then he's protecting murderers."

"So you think." Jacob carried his plates to the separate basin he used to wash his special dishes. Instead of washing them, though, he leaned against the wash stand, his arms folded across his chest. "You and I, we have questions. We find answers, yah? In those answers I think we find your father's murderer."

"Dan'l," said Timothy. "It has to be him."

Jake shook his head. "No. Perhaps it is another man. Who?"

When Tim stood silent, surprised into a new train of thought that someone besides Dan'l might have wanted Pap's claims and Mam, Jake said, "Is not Daniel only. Your father's shares in the gold claims. Who wanted them?"

Tobias Fitch. Tim said, "Major Fitch."

"Yah," said Jake. "Also maybe someone else. So now we look?"

"No," Tim said. "It wouldn't have been Major Fitch. He was Pap's partner. He has all the claims Pap found for them except the Alder crick claim and the Nugget. Besides, he had Berry Woman, and she was bearin' his young'un."

He didn't like the pitying way Jacob said, "White men put aside their Indian wives any time they want to."

"Mam's an Indian. A quarter, anyways."

"Now Daniel has married her. Did Tobias Fitch marry Berry Woman? Marry her the white man's way?"

"No."

"Yah. So. We look about both. Or maybe someone else. Yah?"

The firm set of Jake's shoulders, the upraised chin warned Tim not to argue. Whether he wanted it or not, they would look for Pap's murderer together, and consider two men, not just one. Dan'l and Tobias Fitch.

~~18~~

Heavy footsteps stomped up the stairs to Dan's office.

Writing out a clean copy of an advertisement for the *Montana Post*, "Information Wanted About a Murdered Man," Dan lifted his pen from the paper and wiped the nib. The silhouette of a broad-shouldered man in a caped greatcoat appeared in the window. As the visitor raised a short left arm to knock, Dan corked the ink bottle.

Damn. Tobias Fitch. He'd come for that drink he'd mentioned in the City Bath Rooms. So it hadn't been just talk, after all. Dan opened the door.

Without so much as a 'How do,' Fitch walked straight to the stove and stretched his gloved right hand to the heat. "It's a cold son of a bitch out there." Icicles rattled in his beard and dripped onto the motley patches that stood out against the butternut of his coat. A battle-scarred coat, like its owner.

What was so urgent that Fitch rode far enough to freeze his beard? And came to see him before it thawed?

"Damn freezing rain." Fitch stood close to the stove, and put the fingertips of his glove between his teeth and tugged.

"I've got something to help the chill." Dan slid the desktop aside and brought out a whiskey bottle. He poured drinks for them both and handed a glass to the Southerner.

"Thanks." Fitch took a swallow and smacked his lips. His eyes widened. "That's good whiskey, by God. Damn long trip down from Deer Lodge. Cold enough to freeze my pecker." He stamped his feet. "I might've got frostbit. Crossing the Divide's a bastard, but this business won't wait." He bent over and shook his head. Droplets of melting ice from his hair and beard bounced, hissing, from the stove.

"Business?" What business was Fitch talking about and why did it concern him?

"Yeah. My business, your business." He bit off a chaw from a plug. "Gold business. You got a spittoon?"

"By the chair." Dan nodded toward the spittoon squatting by one of the chairs grouped around the stove. Other men might brook spitting tobacco on their floors, but he'd be damned if he would. He wouldn't use a tin bucket for the purpose, either. No matter how short his time in this office might be, he would have it civilized.

Opening his coat, Fitch made himself comfortable in the chair. His jaws worked the chaw between phrases as he talked. "Yes, sir. Gold business. I been up around Deer Lodge and Last Chance Gulch since you and I met at

Turley's." He spat a gob into the spittoon. "You know I lost Berry Woman. In childbirth."

"Mrs. Stark told me about that. Please accept my sympathies." There had been no salute with the first drink, no Here's how, no Happy days. Dan sat in the chair closest to his desk and took a small sip of whiskey. "Mrs. Stark esteemed her greatly." In his ears the condolence rang stiff and formal, hollow.

"Yeah, well, it happens, even to Injins, I guess. She left me a son, though. I've put him out to wet nurse. Damned if I know how I'll raise him after he's weaned." He picked at the knot tying the black satin cover over his stump. "I heard there's congratulations in order. You're a lucky man." He raised his glass. "Felicitations to you both."

As he spoke, something flared in Fitch's eyes and was gone. They touched glasses.

"Thank you." Dan set his drink on the wide arm of his chair and rose, pretending to check the fire. He opened the firebox door, and bent low enough to feel the scorching heat on his face. When they drank, there had been something – but what? He could not identify it, Fitch had smothered the flash too quickly for him to pin it down, but it had been there.

"It'll hold a while," he told Fitch, meaning the fire. He closed the door and sat down, assumed a relaxed pose in the chair. "What is your son's name?"

"Michael Berry Fitch." A twist of Fitch's lips might have been a weak attempt at a smile. "Berry. It sounds like a white man's surname, does it not?"

"It's a good name. It honors her without effeminacy for the boy." Holding up the whiskey glass, he offered a toast: "To Michael Berry Fitch."

"Yeah."

Both men drank. Dan got up, poured them each another drink, set the bottle on the desktop. He did not intend to drink his second one lest he fog his mind.

"Getting warm in here." Fitch set his drink on the floor. He shrugged out of his coat and went to hang it on the hall tree standing on the far side of the rear door. Returning, he brushed through a darker shadow that thickened as he went through it, gathered into the form of a hanged man, head lolling onto its shoulder.

Dan tensed. Did Fitch not see it, feel its dank touch, smell it? Did he alone – Daniel Bradford Stark, a man of facts and numbers – know it was there, if it was there? It wasn't, couldn't be. It did not exist.

Then what was it? A figment of his imagination? A bit of underdone potato, like Scrooge's Marley?

It was nothing. Not a ghost. I do not believe in ghosts.

He'd missed something Fitch said.

"You given any thought to moving up to Last Chance Gulch?"

"Not especially."

"I told you the gold was about played out here."

"That's true enough." What was Fitch up to? Why did he encourage Dan to leave Alder Gulch? "I grant you that with the stampede north to the new diggings, the population has declined." He touched the rim of the glass to his lips. "I think I'll hold on, though. There's talk of the Terri-torial capital moving here. That'll mean plenty of legal work." Not to mention the Nugget. If he could find McDowell's murderer.

"All right. I can work around that. You here and me up there." He eyed the whiskey in his glass. "Blue, you and me, we been through some times."

"That we have." There it was again. That old nickname, meant to get under his skin. Go to hell, Fitch, he told the other man behind his unwavering smile.

Leaning over the chair arm away from Dan, Fitch wrung out his beard onto the floor and wiped his hand on his trousers.

Dan waited.

"Like I said, I rode down here direct from Deer Lodge, and it wasn't because I needed a ride in the country. Some of us mining men, we're mighty worried. This bunch of Lincoln's toadies running Montana Territory want to ram their law down our throats."

Lincoln's toadies. Dan set the remark aside. He would not let Fitch pick a fight; he wanted to hear what Fitch wanted, why this visit. Enough of dancing around it.

"What do you have in mind?"

"I've got a promising quartz claim up in Last Chance Gulch. My partners and I did enough work that we think we have a rich one." He knocked his stump on the chair arm. "We have to make sure the legislature passes the right mining laws."

"The legislature doesn't meet for three weeks, and anyway, I'm not a legislator."

"Yeah, but you'll have friends there. Charles Bagg for one. He listens to you, and everyone listens to him. Like the Ives trial."

Dan remembered that trial: a bonfire, more than a thousand men kept at bay by other men with long guns, legal arguments that almost ended in shooting. A murderer hanged.

"We don't know if Bagg has won election yet."

"He will. Enough people like him. He's a Democrat in favor of the Union."

Knowing he was selfish to hope that Bagg lost the election, Dan prodded Fitch, "And?"

"I want to hire you."

"You? Hire me? Good God, what for?" In the shadow beyond the back door something glittered. A foul, damp odor choked off more words.

"Crazy, isn't it? You and me, we've been at loggerheads mostly. But you got justice for my boy Nick when you prosecuted his killer, and you wouldn't move a survey line in my favor and I was paying you for the damn survey."

Even if he'd wanted to speak, he could not. The dank smell knotted his throat.

"Some of us figure you for an honest man, even though you're a lawyer –" a quick lift of his mustache, perhaps a smile at the old joke "– and we, other miners and me, need someone to tell them legislators what's what." He loosened the strings fastening the black cover, pulled the cloth away.

"I can't do it. Our interests conflict. I already represent Mrs. Stark and the McDowell children."

"Oh, for Chrissakes. Your interests, their interests, my interests, every mine owner in the Territory has an interest in seeing good mining laws passed."

"True enough." Mining interests – his and the family's included – would benefit from good mining law. But join common cause with Fitch, given their history? Given what he had seen or sensed, even as quick as a snap of a whip?

Removing the black cloth revealed a wooden cover, carved from one piece and fitted to the stump. "We don't have to be pals to make common cause, you know." Fitch scratched at his arm around the edges of the cap. "About that other business. Don't pay attention to X. That damn bloodhound will find out sooner or later who really killed McDowell. Everyone knows you ain't no backstabber." He fitted the black cloth over the cap and retied it.

"What do you say?" Fitch stood up, and Dan rose with him.

If Fitch thought to shake him by talking about mutual interests and Beidler's accusation, he had failed. "The legislature doesn't convene until December twelfth."

"I'll be on my way, Blue, but I'll be back. You'll think about it, will you?" Fitch worked at buttoning his coat one-handed.

He walked Fitch to the door, took hold of the latch to open it for him. In the corner of his eye, something shivered among the shadows, and the stench of death was strong in the room. Fitch had brought up McDowell's murder. "Did you happen to see Sam McDowell after last January fourteenth?"

"What? McDowell? The fourteenth. The day we hanged the five road agents? Why?"

"That's when his family last saw him. I'm trying to track down the earliest he could have been murdered, going from the last time anyone saw him. It's a long shot, but I have to start somewhere."

Fitch ducked his head away from Dan to put on his hat. Clumps of greasy hair dangled behind and in front of his ear, flaming red, probably from the cold. "I didn't see him. I rode out with the boys next morning to finish the gang. Another goddam cold ride up to Deer Lodge."

Alone, Dan stood by the stove. It was too damn bad that Fitch had ridden out with the others on the morning of the fifteenth. He'd had the best reasons to murder McDowell. He'd been McDowell's partner, grubstaking him to do the prospecting that Fitch, having only one hand, could not do. When McDowell disappeared, Fitch had tried to take all six claims for himself without thinking that he might leave McDowell's family beggared.

Except that Dan had won the Nugget claim for Martha and her children in the miners' court, they would have had nothing from Sam's estate.

Inside the stove, burning wood shifted in a storm of small explosions, then settled into a steady muttering. Dan set himself to finish his advertisement.

~~19~~

"You've had somewhat on your mind all evenin'." Martha laid the dulcimer in its box and clasped her hands over her stomach. Dotty had gone to choir practice with friends, giving her and Dan'l a chance to be alone. He'd asked her to play for him, but he'd been so far away in his thoughts, she doubted he'd heard a note. "What has happened?"

He startled, being farther away than she thought. "Nothing. I was enjoying the music."

"Hmph." She waited a few seconds for him to confess, but he sat silent. "You're tellin' a falsehood, there."

He didn't want to talk about what bothered him, and she began to be a little scared. Did Deputy Beidler have bad news for them? Did Dan'l regret marrying her, great fat thing that she'd gotten to be? She wanted to scream at him, but she closed her teeth on her bottom lip and forced herself to wait him out.

"Tobias Fitch came to see me today."

"The Major? What on earth did he want?" McDowell's old partner had been so far from her thoughts, she'd never guessed he caused Dan'l's heavy silence.

"He said he wants to hire me to convince the legislature to write good mining law." Dan'l shifted in his reading chair so's he could face her. "He sounded like he wanted to make peace between us."

She shook her head so her back hair almost escaped its twist. "Oh, no. Don't you trust a word he says. He's after something, believe me. He's always wanted them claims, and now the Nugget is the only one left."

"Don't you think I know that? But it's safe from him. The miners' court awarded it to you and the youngsters. There is nothing he can legally do to take it from you."

"Legally? D'you think that would stop him? Tobias Fitch is a sidewinder, and he'll do anything to get what he wants." Her mending basket stood at the side of her reading chair. She laid the dulcimer in its box and took up her unfinished darning, the marble egg still in the heel, and plied her needle to weave the hole closed.

"He acted like a changed man. Perhaps losing Berry Woman has softened him. He seems genuinely to miss her."

Watching the needle, taking the smallest, finest stitches she knew, Martha said, "Maybe. At least she thought he loved her. I don't rightly know."

"Their child survived. It's a boy. He has him out to wet nurse, and he seemed genuinely worried about how to raise him after he's weaned."

Her needle caught the candlelight, as she pushed it under the thread and pulled it up, down, over, and up until she'd woven the hole together, at the same time stitching her ideas about Major Fitch together until she knew what to say. "Him raise a half-breed child? I don't know." She put everything in her basket and levered herself to her feet. "If you think you can trust him, you're wrong. You watch out for him. He's always planning some devilment or other. Now I'm going to bed. The least'un and me, we need our sleep."

"Do you need help?"

For reasons she couldn't fathom, he liked helping her out of her clothes and into her nightdress, settling her in bed. Tonight, though, he surprised her. She'd never thought any man liked a woman's body when she was bearing, but Dan'l did. The places he kissed her, touched her, even licked her made her blush even as she welcomed him, enjoyed the brush of his beard against her skin, his exploring fingers.

At last he lay beside her on his back. "I would never abandon you, or the children, any of them, yours or ours. I hope you know that."

"I know it." Unspoken, the thought of Timmy lay heavy on Martha's mind. She prayed daily to bring them two together again.

He sat up, swung his feet over the edge of the bed. "There was something off about Fitch today, though he tried to hide it." The room being chilly, he dressed himself fast to go to his room at Planters House.

"I hate to see you go out in the cold. I miss you not being here." She pulled the quilts up to her chin.

"It won't be long. And then we'll have plenty of time. All our lives together."

When he leaned down to kiss her, she put her arms around his neck and held him. "Move home. Please."

"Do you really want me to?"

"More than anything. You can't just be a visitor, coming and going."

"I thought it would be easier for you. This house is so small."

"It's a palace. It's the biggest and cleanest I ever lived in."

"It'll be crowded."

Maybe he didn't want to be here with her. "Suit yourself. If'n you don't want to be here..."

"I do. I'd rather be here with you than anywhere else."

Choosing to believe what he said, she told him, "You're the man of the house. You should be here." She released him, put her arms under the quilts, and waited for him to answer. Outlined by the unsteady light behind him, his face was not visible.

Before she could be scared that he might refuse, he touched her cheek. "All right. I'll move in tomorrow."

While he banked the fires for the night, the child came in. Dan'l asked how she liked the choir. She replied, and they talked about music, their voices sounding like music, a duet of tenor and soprano. When the door opened and closed, she woke to an unwelcome thought: All our lives together, he'd said. But Berry Woman had died, and the noose laid its shadow on Dan'l.

~~20~~

Emerging from the office of the *Montana Post,* Dan met Jacob Himmelfarb. Shaking his friend's hand, Dan saw that something was very wrong. White-faced, Jacob trembled like someone in a fever; the long hairs of his beard stirred in the still air.

"What's wrong? What is it? Not Timothy. Has something happened to Timothy?" Something like a sharp blow, that made him wonder if he'd been punched, ran through him. "Damn it, Jacob, what has happened to Timothy?"

Nein," Jacob shook his head. He followed the denial with a barrage of Yiddish words.

Dan raised both hands shoulder high. "I swear if you don't speak English – Jacob, English!" He clamped his hand around Jacob's upper arm and propelled him toward the corner, across Jackson from the Eatery. "What in God's name has happened? Christ, Jacob, answer me."

They crossed Jackson and then walked halfway across Wallace before Jacob spoke.

"Nichts. Nothing." Jacob dug his heels into the freezing mud. "Timothy is good, ja? How you say, well? Fine? Is not –" Facing down Wallace, he shouted, "Run!" Both men leaped for the boardwalk as two riders on horseback raced toward them, spurring their horses; their arms rose and fell, their quirts blurred.

Safe on the boardwalk, Jacob breathed hard as they walked along Content's Corner toward the staircase. "It is Lewis – Hershfield, Ja?" He lowered his voice, although no one was close enough to hear him. "We – Lewis – the bank, it needs dust by noon to pay back a loan. Is temporary shortfall only. Two loans from us are late, and it is that we must pay. How you say – it is obligation." He pronounced the last word syllable by syllable. Recently learned, Dan thought, but spoken without pride.

"How much do you need?"

"It is one-hundred-twenty ounces of Alder Gulch dust."

Climbing the stairs, Dan did the sums in his head and finished with a whistle. "Thirty-seven hundred dollars, depending on what gold is selling for. Is that right?"

"Yah. Is correct."

A small fortune, considering that a skilled worker earned three dollars a day. Add to that the demand for Alder Gulch dust, too, the purest gold – at .99 percent plus – mined in the Territory. "You need it by noon?"

"Yah." Jacob licked his lips. "On the dot. Hershfield says name your terms."

Jacob's breath rasped in and out of his throat; he held himself tight and still, this edgy man prone to fidgeting.

Dan did not mind taking a risk, but would Hershfield be good for it? Oddly enough, even on the basis of one meeting, he rather thought so. Besides, Jacob would not associate with anyone or anything shady. Dan unlocked his door. "Let me think."

Hearing his pocket watch chime, Dan pulled it out and pressed the stem to open it. Half past nine o'clock. He had plenty of time to decide, not about making the loan – he would always help Jacob – but to gauge the proper amount of interest, to decide on collateral. Making an unsecured loan, as Hershfield had said, was bad business, but he did not want to take advantage of Hershfield's crisis.

"You need something to steady your nerves." Taking out the whiskey bottle, he poured them both a short one. Jacob stood by the stove, while Dan paced front door to back door, carrying his whiskey glass and calculating per cents over time multiplied by the amount, compounding. How much time, how much interest? When he had the answers he stopped.

"I'll help." When Jacob's English failed under a splutter of thanks, Dan said, "Listen to my terms, though. You may not be so grateful." Jacob quieted; he held the glass in both hands. "Ten percent per month, the entire sum due by Easter. By Passover. If the bank defaults, I own a twenty-five percent share in the bank."

Jacob's mouth opened, and his eyes darkened as his face paled.

He wanted to say he was sorry. Defaulting would hurt both Jacob and Lewis, but he had to think of the family first and foremost. He had to secure them from his mistakes. If he failed to find McDowell's murderer, if worse came to worst, the family might own one-fourth of the bank.

Jacob licked his lips, stretched his fingers. "I think so, yah. I go tell Lewis and we have papers ready. You can the gold bring?" With the last sentence his English syntax broke down into Yiddish word order.

"Yes. How many ounces will you need to pay off the loan?"

"If I might use a slate?" Jacob held out his hand.

Dan stopped him. "Just tell me at what price they're buying Alder Gulch dust today." Alder creek gold dust was the most expensive. Fortunately, he had nearly a third of it already.

"Eighteen dollars and fifty cents the Troy ounce."

"And selling?"

Jacob shook his head. "I do not know. Maybe twenty dollars? Nineteen? Twenty-two?"

The numbers ran in his mind as they had in the Gold Room: the number of Troy ounces of dust needed to pay off the loan, the weight of Eagles and Double Eagles, the number of coins he would need to convert to dust in order to have enough for the loan. The amount of profit he could make just from getting the dust Jacob and Hershfield would need.

He looked at his watch. Nine forty-five. No time to lose. "I'll have it to you as soon as I can." Dan offered his hand. After a second's hesitation, Jacob took it in his own, cold and dry and rough as rusted iron.

"Thank you." Jacob said. "I go tell Lewis."

~~~

He called in at all three of Hershfield's banking competitors, and everywhere he must join them in a drink to his good health while they converted his coins to dust, while the hands of his watch ran so fast he was surprised to push open John Ming's door with twenty minutes to spare. At Hershfield and Co., he glimpsed Jacob pacing along the inside of the fence, while Hershfield at his desk gave a good imitation of a man working hard at a ledger book. Seeing Dan make his way around the grocer's stand, he spoke to Jacob, who held the gate open.

"I have what you need," Dan told them.

Hershfield patted the top of his desk. "We'll relieve you of your burden."

Dan pulled the pokes out of his pockets and set them where Hershfield indicated.

"Let's have a drink to seal our new association." The banker gestured to the chairs by the stove. "Please. Have a seat. Jacob can do the sums. We have already drawn up the agreement."

When he had poured the whiskey, the banker said, "Jacob explained your terms to me. Ten percent per month, in full by Passover. If we default, you own twenty-five percent of the bank. Do I understand correctly?"

"You do."

"I accept. It's not as steep as might be, and you're rescuing us from a tight squeeze." He reached his glass toward Dan. They touched glasses and drank. "Our note is there."

To Dan's right on a small table lay the agreement. A pen, ink, and blotter lay beside it. Hershfield, Dan saw, needed only a few lines to spell out the terms of the loan and the bank's obligation to pay. He had already signed it.

Dan added his signature to the agreement and to the fair copy. After four shots of whiskey before noon, he had to pay attention to his penmanship, but the signature was his own, and remarkably close to his sober writing. When he and the banker had initialed two copies, he folded one and tucked it into his notecase.

"Jacob, it is done." The banker gave the original and the bank copy to Jacob, who slid it under the desk blotter and continued measuring the dust. Hershfield sat back in the wing chair and watched the aisle over Dan's shoulder. "I appreciate your way of doing business. Only a fool makes an unsecured loan, even to a friend."

Somewhere behind Dan men complained: "Watch where you're going." "You can't just barge along that way." "What the hell!"

Dan turned to see for himself what the commotion was about. Fitch.

So it was Fitch who demanded repayment at twelve o'clock. Fitch who frightened Jacob.

Rising to his feet along with Hershfield, Dan murmured, "I'd rather Fitch not know I've loaned you the dust."

"I understand." Hershfield spoke without moving his lips. "Come back when you can," he said. "I think we have much to talk about, you and I." As Dan turned to leave, Hershfield stopped him with a finger on his sleeve. "This other business. If I can be of help..." He let the rest trail off.

"I'll remember that."

Fitch opened the gate and came through, ignoring Jacob, to stop at the sight of Dan and Hershfield at ease in each other's company. Plainly, he was not pleased to see them together.

"Hello, Fitch," Dan said. "I see you're still here." The drinks had given him a mad desire to laugh in Fitch's face. Whatever he had wanted from his attempt on the bank, Dan had stopped him. He wanted to gloat, to say, 'Neener, neener,' like a child, but some remaining sobriety cautioned him to check the impulse.

"I was delayed by a piece of business." Fitch smiled and offered his hand, but his eyes narrowed at Dan. "Have you thought about my offer?"

"I've thought about it, but I haven't given it the consideration it deserves." Business with Fitch. Dan wanted to laugh, to guffaw and slap his knee, shout that he'd see Fitch in hell before he'd work with him. To Hershfield he said, "It's been a pleasure."

As he left the bank, Jacob held the gate for him. "We must talk, Daniel." He mouthed Timothy's name.

"I'll be in my office."

Making his way through the crowded aisle toward Ming's bookstore, Dan touched his inside breast pocket. Another financial paper, another business deal. But no one wanted this paper badly enough to cut his throat for it. The memory of cold steel piercing his skin made him shudder, stripped all pleasure out of forestalling Fitch's attempt on Hershfield's bank.

An angry voice pierced the general talk and laughter. "You selling this filth?"

~~21~~

Inside the enclosure under the overhead sign, BOOKS, a man wearing a yellow and brown plaid overcoat brandished a thick volume at the bookseller. Concentrating on the overcoat, Dan hardly registered the other two customers, who backed as far into a corner as they could. The man had put himself in front of the woman and stood with arms spread to protect her.

John Ming held up both hands. "It's a popular novel written by our new Chief Justice."

"Well, God damn it, I guess we know what kind of justice we can expect from a mudsill judge, don't we?" Plaid Coat doubled his fist. "Guess you're a mudsill, too, then, you selling this shit." Staring fiercely around the room, daring other shoppers to interfere with him, he dashed the book to the floor, where it sprawled open, spine up. He raised his foot to stomp on it.

"No!" cried Ming.

"Stop!" Dan jumped the fence, seized the overcoat by the collar, and yanked him backward. Flailing for balance, the man brought his foot down on the floor instead of the book. Dan released him and stepped out of his way. The bastard could fall and break his neck for all he cared.

Reverend Hough stepped forward. "For shame, using that language! And with a lady present. Apologize immediately." Mrs. Hough stood behind him and to the side, her gloved fingers to her lips, her eyes round in her pale face.

Plaid Coat sneered. Dan wanted to laugh. The son of a bitch was so readable. Plain to see, he thought he could bully a preacher and destroy a book he did not like without anyone interfering. In just that way the roughs had intimidated decent people until the Vigilantes ended their reign. If he had anything to say about it, no man would make buying a book a dangerous event.

"You heard him. Apologize."

"Damned if I will."

Dan took a half step toward him.

Plaid Coat licked his lips and held up his hands. "All right. I apologize to the ladies for my language, but that book is filth and decent people oughtn't to read it." His hand went into his coat pocket. "Here. I'll buy it, so's I can burn it."

"No, you won't." Dan picked the book up, smoothed its pages, wiped his hand across the front cover. The gold-embossed title, *Adela, or the Octoroon*. The author's name: Hezekiah Lord Hosmer. "I want to buy it and read it." He knew the story from having seen the play it was taken from. A white man falls in love with a rich heiress who is exposed as one-eighth Negro before their wedding. When she is sold into slavery, and her property given to the other heirs, the heartsick fiancé follows her, eventually across the continent to San Francisco, where he persuades her again to marry him. Plaid Coat was right; in some circles the book was scandalous because it ended in an interracial marriage. Interracial marriage – miscegenation – between whites and Indians or Negroes or Chinese was illegal in most states and territories. His own marriage to Martha would be illegal in some states.

Thinking of the book, Dan's estimation of the Chief Justice rose. In this day, to write favorably of an interracial union was as courageous as writing *Uncle Tom's Cabin*.

He tucked the book under his arm. Chin raised, he said through a tight jaw, "My own dear wife is one-quarter Eastern Cherokee."

The man's face turned a deep red. He kicked aside a portion of the low fence and charged through the onlookers, yanked the door open and slammed it enough to rattle the window panes. Someone raised a cheer, and the laughter rang through the room. If some disagreed, they did not say so.

Two or three men straightened up the fence as the cheering dwindled.

Dan set the book on the sales table and offered his hand to Ming. "Hello, Ming, I see business is good."

The bookseller reached over to grasp it. "Heard you were back, but you've been mighty scarce."

"Busy getting married. Settling in. That sort of thing." Dan gave him a Double Eagle.

"I heard congratulations were in order."

"Thank you. My good lady is the former Martha McDowell, now Mrs. Daniel Stark."

"Ah, yes." The bookseller changed the subject. "Thanks for rescuing this. I thought I was out eighteen dollars. I have to give you two dollars' change in dust, though. Small coins are pretty scarce around here." He selected two thin lead wafers from a stack next to the balance scales and laid them on one pan, then dribbled gold dust onto the other.

At a touch on Dan's sleeve, he turned to find Rev. Hough smiling at him. "I'd like to shake your hand." His smile seemed as genuine as if he had forgotten how he had disapproved of Dan's Vigilante activities.

"Reverend Hough. Mrs. Hough." Removing his hat, Dan made a small bow to the lady from as great a distance as would be polite. Why had he let the bankers feed him five whiskeys this morning? His breath must reek of the stuff, and Methodists never imbibed alcohol.

"Since our journey, I've been thinking that I heard New York in your accent. And now I'm certain of it." Mrs. Hough's nose wrinkled delicately.

The room was too warm, even hot, but she kept her hands in her elegant beaver muff. He would buy one each for Dotty and Martha, to keep their hands warm as nothing made of wool could do. If, he remembered, if he– if Beidler did not find what he called evidence.

Jolted sober, he heard the echo of Mrs. Hough's question. He fumbled for the answer while a double crease formed between her brows. "Yes, Ma'am. The City." To anyone from New York or New England, New York City was always, simply, 'the City.'

"By any chance," asked Mrs. Hough, "would you – oh, how shall I put this? – be the same Daniel Bradford Stark who did so well on the Street this summer?"

Bracing himself, Dan replied, "I am." She knew his middle name? How could a missionary's wife know of his success in the Gold Room? Oh, Lord, perhaps they were acquainted with his brother-in-law, Arthur, Rector of St. David's Episcopal Church. Would she report that he had been inebriated at midday?

"My brother, Jay Gould, spoke of you as a man who understands the commodities market. He follows the financial news very closely, both in the press and among his financial friends."

Watch Mrs. Hough's tells though he might, he couldn't see a threat. "I had some luck. Doing well on the Street always requires a plenty of luck."

Hough smiled. "I would rather say that God blessed your endeavor."

"Perhaps. If that's true, He's a capricious God." He heard himself slur over 'capricious.' "Many good men lose everything on the trading floor."

"Does gold trading go on here as well?" asked Rev. Hough.

"Yes. Not on the scale of New York, of course." He wanted to leave their well-meaning chat, to be alone in his office where he could think about how to find a murderer. His thoughts ricocheted against the walls of his skull. How to get away – how cold McDowell's murderer was – he and Hershfield could do business – Martha, oh God, Martha – Hershfield understood money – Plaid Coat's wide back crashing through Ming's fence.

The ricochet stopped.

McDowell was stabbed in the back. In the back. In the back.

He wished Hough would stop talking and let him go.

McDowell had turned his back. Why? Why did he turn his back on his murderer? Think. Something lurked there, in the back of his mind. What was it? He must think.

The Reverend and his wife expected polite conversation. Damn. He could not simply walk away. They asked about gold trading here. "I have not been back long enough to know the extent of it. The bankers could tell you. Buying and selling gold and exchanging greenbacks and gold, both dust and coin, form a large part of their business."

Hough said, "It is sad when men do not understand that money is the root of all evil. So said our Lord."

"I believe He said the *love* of money is the root of all evil." Even in his fuddled state, Dan would not let anyone, not even a man of the cloth, imply that he was evil because he understood money, in gold or in paper.

Why did McDowell turn his back?

Before her husband could dispute Dan's recollection of the Gospel, Mrs. Hough said, "I shall write to my brother and let him know that I have met a men of the Street even in this rough place. And that you are not one to stand back from trouble." Mrs. Hough held out her slender, gloved hand. He held his breath as he bowed over it. "We would hope to see you at worship, Mr. Stark. Your soul would feel the blessing of our Redeemer's love." Her fingers clasped his hand and held him as she smiled into his eyes. He read nothing in hers but kindness and the glint of a dedicated Christian missionary.

Thinking of murder, he was slow to respond. "Thank you, Mrs. Hough. I expect I shall attend wherever my wife chooses." McDowell had turned his back. He had not expected his death to come from – from what? That direction? That killer? From an ambush?

Rev. Hough said, "Then we shall hope for her to prefer our new Methodist church. We shall be dedicating the sanctuary on Sunday."

They went out through the gate. Taking a step after them, he heard Ming speak his name. The book. The damned book. And the two dollars in dust remaining from his Double Eagle. Ming's scales had balanced. The little pile of gold dust on one pan was level with the two dollar weights on the other. Ming could keep the two dollars for all he cared, but that would look odd.

He gave Ming his poke. As he waited for Ming to pour the dust into it, he came within a hair of telling him to keep it, keep the book. He had to think. Get over this throbbing in his head. But Ming concentrated on pouring the dust into Dan's poke, brushing in the last few miniscule flakes with a small soft brush.

Chatting sociably, the bookseller took a cloth of oiled calico from a pile to wrap the volume in. "Durned if I know why you want it, though I do hate to see a book harmed as much as I hate for an animal to be mistreated."

Just give me the damned book and let me out of here. "I heard of it in New York."

Ming gave no sign of having heard Dan. "The very idea. A novelist as Chief Justice. A liar by avocation and a Republican in politics. It figures. Between what they say he wrote in that book and what I hear he doesn't know about gold, this territory's in trouble." Ming held onto the book, folded the cloth around it.

"Oh?" If he thought this cool response would discourage Ming's chatter, he was wrong. Ming talked on, as he wrapped the book, each fold precise, each wrinkle smoothed.

"I'm told that he thinks that gold can't be both a medium of exchange and a commodity. If that's true, he'll be in a minority around here, sure enough. Him and the Governor."

"How much would this book cost if I wanted to pay in greenbacks?"

"Twenty-eight dollars."

A dollar, then, was $1.65 in greenbacks. "Glad I'm paying in gold." Forget this. Why had McDowell turned his back on an enemy? Dan held out his hand for the book. McDowell would not have turned his back. Not if he'd had the faintest suspicion of what would come.

"That's the thing," Ming said. "If we had to use green-backs for everything we buy, inflation would send us bankrupt in no time. Nobody could afford to develop a quartz mine or start a business. Think of the jobs lost." Ming tucked in the final flap, rested his hand on the package.

"What do I owe you for the wrapping?" *Give me the God-damn book and let me go.*

Ming held the book. Was he reluctant to part with it? Did he think that if he held onto it he could get a better price in February or March? Then people would have read everything and would be desperate for something to read. "Nothing."

Smiling, Dan took the well-wrapped book out of Ming's hand, nestled the package in the crook of his left elbow. Now he could leave. At last. He made himself keep the smile, thank Ming, portray a man who had all the time in the world.

The cold breeze cleared the fug in his brain as it swept away the smoke from countless wood stoves and fire-places, leaving the air clear enough to see the five wooden crosses that marked the road agents' graves atop the hill above Daylight creek.

McDowell had turned his back because he didn't think his killer would harm him. Damn Beidler and his suspi-cions. *McDowell would never have turned his back on me. He hated me too much.*

~~22~~

He was not to be left to puzzle out McDowell's murder in peace. No sooner had he returned to his office than a woman rapped at his door. Stifling his irritation, he opened the door to admit Helen Troy, the proprietress of Fancy Annie's Saloon. And brothel.

She entered on a cloud of smells coagulated by the cold and uniquely her own. Unwashed flesh and dirty linen overlaid by cheap sweet perfume that brought memories: Joseph Slade on horseback, holding high a bottle of whiskey, singing his obscene song about then-Sheriff Fox. Slade laughing and whooping while his cronies raised hell, attacked Fancy Annie's, and raped the women. He heard again women screaming, furniture and glass breaking, gunshots in the air.

And then he defied the People's Court, the fragile instrument that the Vigilantes had established to keep order.

For all that, he gave her a drink, stood with her by the stove nursing his own drink, and did not mind his breathing.

She turned herself to the heat, so that he spoke to her face, her shoulder, her back. Her shoulder blades jutted against the flowered wool shawl wrapped around her shoulders and draped across her arms. A bedraggled red and black straw bonnet covered her ears, its small cape-like frill a pretense at protecting her neck. Festooned with a wide black bow, the brim rose high in front. Snow-clotted ostrich plumes lay on top. When she faced the stove, he talked to the hopeless feathers.

Had she no warm winter garments? Or did she wear the clothes of her trade no matter the weather?

Because of that night, he agreed to represent her in suing Slade's estate. She mentioned his fee, which he refused.

"It ain't right," she said, "you not taking pay to help me. You've a family to take care of. You gotta look out for them."

Dan called up his patience. "Slade as near as not bankrupted you. I'll represent you at the estate sale, but I won't accept a fee."

"You've earned it. I don't take no charity." She peered up at him. "I do trade, though." Her lips parted, the shawls slipped down her shoulders to show him a deep cleavage, where caked powder cracked between her breasts. The sickly sweet perfume could not stifle the odors of stale sweat and bed.

"A tempting offer. Perhaps if I were single." He let the lie dwindle, helped her adjust the shawls, though higher than before, to hide her unappetizing flesh. Nothing – no deprivation – would ever tempt him to sex with Helen Troy or any whore.

Nor accept payment to represent her.

He could not vote to hang a man, witness his execution, and profit from the sale of his estate. If the suit succeeded, the proceeds should go to the people he had ruined. "Use what you might pay me to benefit someone else."

The Troy woman turned her back to him. "Like poor Eileen?"

To his disgust, he realized he had forgotten the girl.

Miss Troy said, "Maybe there ain't nothing can benefit her no more. Rape takes some girls that way, Mr. Stark. I can hardly pry the poor child out of the kitchen to put away the plates and glasses at the bar. The girls, the customers, they all treat her like she's fine china, as gentle and kind as could be, but she's always scared. 'Specially of men."

"Maybe time will help. They say it heals all wounds." It was the best he could offer.

"It's working uncommon slow for her. Of course, having that Jacky Stevens at her constant don't help none. He caught her at the well last summer, and put his hands up her skirts. My barman heard her scream, or I don't know what more he'd've done."

Dan recalled Dotty in the livery, pinned against a stall, her school books dropped in mud and manure, as she fought Jacky's hands pawing her chest. The memory tightened Dan's jaws, swelled the veins in his temples. She had suffered no worse; thank God he had heard her scream, though nightmares troubled her sleep for weeks afterwards. Damn that misbegotten little—

Facing him, she sighed, a worried woman with an unsolvable problem. "What's to be done about the likes of him? If he's this nasty now, when he's man-grown, he'll be a monster." When he shook his head, she asked, "Ain't there nothing you-all could do?"

To cut this short, he gave a blunt answer. "Short of murdering him? Nothing. We're not murderers."

"But the law?" She cocked her head, puzzled.

"There is nothing in the law to justify punishing someone for something he might do. If we were to act before he does something, we'd be guilty of murder, and Jacky would be the victim. I can't imagine us committing murder; nothing is worth being hanged for." Moisture trickled down one of his sideburns. Especially a murder he had not done.

"Most folks wouldn't worry if something did happen to him."

"Even you say that? His mother is one of your – employees." Barely, he had caught himself in time not to say 'whores,' although he did not know why a more delicate word should matter to this jade.

"I got more right to say it than most. I'd throw them both out if I could, but she brings in custom. Somehow." When she shook her head, droplets from the plumes scattered, some landing on his waistcoat. "She's like a drug, opium or something."

Picturing Isabel Stevens's pock-marked face and small suspicious eyes, he tried to imagine what attraction she had that would bring men to her the first time, or why they might wish to repeat the experience. He failed. According to Martha, who had nursed Jacky through the typhus epidemic, she loved her son, though it was a rough love, full of harsh words and backhanded blows. He clung to the subject at hand. "We can't have people eliminating perceived threats whenever they wish. Their perceptions could be wrong."

"That ain't the case with Jacky. He's a menace."

"I know. I agree, but the law can't act until after he commits a crime." Even getting an injunction against Jacky would not stop him. It would just make him more cunning. Martha had been frightened of McDowell, certain the violence in him would erupt on her one day. She had been right, but until it happened, no one could do anything, and he had nearly lost her. "You might warn him, threaten him with a good beating, but even that is risky. He might very well view it as a challenge, and just escalate – do worse things."

"So there's nothing anybody can do? Not even the vigilanters?" She faced the front door, her back to the stove.

"Short of hanging him, no, there is no permanent solution. Besides, our time will end shortly when a court of law opens." He caught sight of a jeweled dragonfly among the recovering feathers. "Just be ready to defend yourselves. That hatpin would make a good weapon. I trust it's long enough and sharp enough to discourage unwanted advances?" Though what advances could be unwanted to a whore? Encouraging men's baser natures was their stock in trade.

Before she could say anything, he changed the subject. She wearied him; he wanted to finish their business. "Shall we discuss this lawsuit? To file on your behalf with the probate court, I need a complete list of everything you lost, with their dollar values."

"Everything?"

"Yes. Everything. Every bottle broken, every chair smashed."

"Every woman raped? What they did to Eileen?"

"I'm afraid in law there is no compensation available."

"Not for the likes of us." Her laugh was short and bitter. "Most folks think rape ain't possible with whores."

It was a saying he had heard often. Because anything he said would be useless, he kept silent. Even for Eileen, there was no redress in law for her unspeakable violation. People would think no female, even a child, in that company could be wholly innocent. Meeting Eileen that night had taught him different.

The Troy woman bent her head to study her hands in their red crocheted gloves. She shook her head, and the drying plumes scattered their last moisture across his face.

"It ain't right. My girls can't get no satisfaction from the law? And we ain't sure Eileen will ever be right inside, if you know what I mean." She gathered her shawls higher about her neck. He hoped she was about to leave.

"There should be something we could do," she said.

Thu Sep 06, 2018

(Estimated hold expiration date)

Transit Date: Tue Aug 28 2018 02:

The ghost at Beaverhead Rock /

33029062472741

Hold note:

*
*
*
*
*
*
*

Thu Sep 06, 2018

(Estimated hold expiration date)

"If we took him to court, do you think he would reform?"

"Him? Never. He's a baby rattler. Poisonous from hatching, and he'll grow up worse. "

Dan stayed silent. He could think of nothing to say that he had not already said. Those dratted plumes stank worse as they dried. He took his time putting more wood in the stove. Maybe the smell of wood burning would clean the air.

"There ain't nothing to do, then."

"I'm afraid not. Just be prepared to defend yourselves." The discussion had come full circle, and he wished she would go.

She gathered her shawls closer about her neck. "I got to get back. You'll represent me at the estate sale, then?"

"Yes, of course."

She surprised him by blinking back tears. "I'll get that list together. I'm grateful, Mr. Stark. What Slade's men done to my place and my girls, especially Eileen, why, it don't bear thinking about, but it's on the poor child's mind every day. He didn't do nothing, but he didn't stop it."

Dan followed her to the door like a gentleman, to usher her out and bring in fresh air, freezing though it was.

A pace or two from the door she paused. What could she want now? Why did she not go away, leave him to be alone, to list anyone who might know where McDowell— His thought broke off. He cursed that he'd been so slow. "You could help me if you would, Miss Troy."

Her head came up. This close to the window, her face powder emphasized the furrow between her brows, the lines from her nose to the corners of her mouth, the creases at the corners of her eyes. "Sure. Anything."

"Do you or does anyone else at your establishment recall seeing Sam McDowell after the fourteenth of January?"

"That's the day y'all hung them five boys together, ain't it?"

"Yes." He answered her without a qualm. That day harbored nothing he need apologize for.

"He was at my place for a while. I don't recollect right off how long, maybe two-three days, but I'll think on it. I'll ask around, too."

"Thank you. Your help will be payment enough for my legal services."

"Good." She tugged her shawl more tightly around her shoulders as he opened the door.

~~23~~

"Hey! Watch where you're going, dammit."

The ragged yell cut into the argument Tim was having with himself over whether to turn left, up Jackson to stop in and apologize to Mam or right and hurry on down to Jake's house.

Jacky Stevens blocked his way. Thin, round-shouldered, small for his age, he stood half sideways, eyes narrowed, ready to dodge and run any second.

Tim raised his fist to waist height, and the younger boy skipped out of the way. From that safer distance, he sneered, "So your ma married her fancy man, did she? She's no better'n a whore. She took hold of my secrets, held 'em in her hands, she did, so there."

By God, he would chase this little bastard down and smash him into the ground, grind his nasty face into the dirt. He jammed his fists into his jean pockets. Jacky wasn't worth the rope to hang his murderer. "She cleaned you up like a baby when you was sick with the typhus." What folks said then resounded in his ears: *Your mama's a saint.*

Jacky cackled. "I weren't all that sick. She liked feeling me." He eyed Tim slantways like he was calculating how far to go before he bolted. "My pecker liked it, too."

Tim's hands quivered like they would come out on their own if he didn't trap them in his pockets; he wanted to grab Jacky's scrawny throat and silence that devilish cackle forever. "She should've let you rot. My Mam's a saint."

"Yeah? She took up with that damn hypocrite Dan Stark, that fucking vigilante, and he murdered Pap, whole town knows it." Jacky snarled like a dog, something Tim had never seen in a person. His skin crawled, and he breathed, "Lord Jesus." It was not a curse.

His hands quieted as a new fear came over him. He was so much bigger and stronger than Jacky, and if he touched him, if he thrashed him, some of that evil would come off on himself, turn himself into someone he didn't like. "My mam's a saint. You, you go back to hell." Tim wheeled and walked away from Jacky's foul grin, and the mocking laugh that followed him down Jackson.

~~24~~

"I want to go to church," Martha announced as Dan and Dotty finished breakfast on Sunday morning.

Dan stared at her. "Whatever for?"

"On account I haven't been in more'n a year. You said the new Methodist church was bein' dedicated today, and the preacher and his wife invited us to come. I feel a hankering after the Word of the Lord."

Dotty wailed, "I haven't anything to wear!"

Her mother said, "Going to church ain't – isn't – for showing off your good clothes. It's for worshipping the Lord and giving thanks for His blessings."

Since he had begun living with Martha last February, Dan had not heard so much religion from her. He knew she read her Bible often, but he had thought her diligence meant she wanted to improve her reading. "Are you sure? I mean, in your condition?"

Martha did not so much as glance his way. "I feel fine. I am not such a weakling as you think." She said to Dotty, "Your great-grandmam felt your grandmam – my Mam –

coming while she was out behind the plow. She went to the house, birthed the baby, and finished plowing the field afore sundown." Her chin rose and her back straightened.

"Good God." Dan shuddered. What kind of people were these, to treat a woman in her delicate condition that way, to put her behind a plow and accept it as common-place that she finished the job after giving birth? And Martha was proud of it? The mothers of his circle, his own mother, his sister, and – yes, Harriet, if she quickened – would be brought to bed with a doctor in attendance, and a midwife, and servants to clean up afterwards.

Hearing her tell of her grandmother, he saw Martha in a different light. Those were her people? When he first loved her, he had known without grasping just how far below him on the social scale her family was, but to be proud of her grandmother who bore a child between plowing one furrow and another— It left him speechless. Did Martha not see the thing for what it was? Brave, yes, but pathetic and cruel to endanger her so.

"That's awful," said Dotty. "My great-grandmama? The poor creature. She must have been so lonely. Wasn't there anyone to help?" She looked to Dan, who nodded to her. Young as she was, the girl had taken hold of the truth of that story. She had said what he thought, near enough.

"She didn't have time to send to the neighbor's." Martha stared from her daughter to Dan. "Anyway, I'm going to get ready for church." She set her hands on the table and prepared to lift herself up. Dan pulled back her chair for her, but when he cupped his hand around her elbow, she shook it away. "I can get up and down by myself. I'm not puny."

If Martha could have looked down her nose at him, so much taller, it would have been now, as she stood with her chin up, determination clenching her fists, tightening her mouth.

Clearly, he could not prevent her from going short of tying her to a chair. He could order her to stay home, but if she defied him he would lose some of the authority he hoped to build.

"Do you realize how dangerous this is? How easily you could slip and fall?"

She shook her head.

"Mama, don't," said Dotty. "Please. Dan'l is right. You shouldn't be taking such chances what with the baby and all."

"You do not tell me what to do, you hear?"

As Dotty shrank back in her chair, her eyes filling with tears, Martha clapped her hands to her mouth. "Oh, darlin', I'm so sorry." She included them both in her next words. "The Lord has been too long absent from this house."

She held out her hand to him, and he held it, cold and trembling, in his own. "I need to know the Lord forgives my sin."

So this was what other married men meant when they referred to changes in a woman's demeanor when they were bearing. Then it hit him: 'My sin.' Not sins in general, but one great sin. What sin was great enough to drive her to risk that walk down an icy slope?

Living with him out of wedlock. Giving herself willingly to him before they could be married.

She had told him, I won't be your whore. He had replied that he wanted her for his wife, and they had come together in a common law marriage when they could not marry under statutory law, McDowell's whereabouts being unknown. Now they were lawfully married, but that yielding to him, a thing of trust and joy, was now her sin?

He could not let her attempt it with only Dotty to protect her.

He drank coffee to wet his dry mouth. "I'll walk you down."

Martha bundled up until she looked like a fat highwayman with her scarf round her face. The dog, back from his morning jaunt, barked to go along, but Dan put him on his rope to stop him from following.

"I can't see the ground," Martha said. "I can't see my feet."

"It's not too late to change your mind," he said.

"No."

"Lean on me. I'll guide you."

Her unsteady weight on his arm telegraphed every tentative step, every tiny slide as their feet broke ice-rimmed ruts and scraped frozen mounds. If he'd been on speaking terms with God, he would have prayed for their safe arrival at the church.

At the corner, Dan judged the speed of an oncoming rider and the milk delivery wagon before they crossed Wallace between them.

By the Eatery they paused for Martha to catch her breath. For a moment, he felt her quail before the long, steep slope. He put his arm around her waist and grasped her elbow. "I have you, my dear."

She took the first hesitant step, then another, and they were committed to descend.

Somewhere alongside the long wall of the Eatery, Martha slipped. "Ooh!" she cried out, going down. Himself sliding, Dan scrambled. His boot heel catching on a frozen pile held him upright. When she steadied, she leaned against him to fight for breath before they inched their way down.

"We'll be late," Martha gasped.

"We're going as fast as is safe," he said.

After a bit, a hand bell began to ring.

"We must hurry." She stepped out, trying to walk faster, but he was ready this time and held her.

"We can't hurry," he said.

"The bell is still ringing, Mama," Dotty said. "We'll be all right."

They paused on the bank of Daylight creek. Dan eyed the frozen creek, the ice-covered stepping stones, the church on the other side. The crossing was too dangerous for Martha, but the alternative was to turn around and climb back up.

Martha voiced his thought. "We're can't turn back now. If you won't help me acrost, I'll go by myself."

He could not allow that. She had not the balance to use the stepping stones, and the ice over the creek might not bear her weight. If she got wet and caught pneumonia, he would never forgive himself.

Before she could object, he swung her up in his arms and set his grip on her, and put a foot onto the ice. It broke. He sank over his boot tops in the frigid water. Unable to see his feet, he felt his way among the stones in the creek bottom, tested each step before he put weight on that foot.

Once on the north bank, he set Martha on her feet again.

Dotty held her skirts in one hand and darted across on the stepping stones, jumped up onto the bank. She smiled up at Dan. "I made it!"

"So you did." He thought he had never seen a prettier sight than his stepdaughter, golden curls flying below her knitted hat, bouncing from stone to stone. Maybe Martha carried a little girl, he thought to himself, smiling.

He and Dotty helped Martha up the steps, and the bell ringer stopped his hand bell to held the door for them.

Dan glimpsed a plain interior, bright with white paint and candles on standing candelabra, well placed to make the most of their light. In the front stood an altar draped with a white cloth where the Rev. Hough knelt in prayer in front of a plain wooden cross. The opening door caused heads to turn, frowning at the cold air.

The bell ringer murmured, "Welcome, but please close the door."

"I'm not staying," Dan said. "My dear, I'll be back for you in" – a questioning look at the bell ringer – "how long?"

"An hour and a half, but you're more than welcome to stay."

Rev. Hough rose to his feet and turned, arms high. Seeing them, he called out, "Welcome these newcomers in our midst."

Dan backed out the door, pulled it shut on the faces turned to him, on Rev. Hough's broad smile, on Martha's outstretched hand, and Dotty's low-voiced protest: "Dan'l!" Rude in the extreme, he knew, as he stumped down the steps on numb feet, but if he stayed to be polite he would be trapped for the entire service. Martha was on her own in church. She was on terms with the Almighty that he could never hope for.

He set off for Jacob's house, three or four doors downstream from the church.

If Timothy were there? Ah. He'd better mind his manners.

~~25~~

For all he could feel of his feet, he might as well have been walking on pegs by the time he knocked on Jacob's door, but he'd had wet feet and frozen socks before: *The saddle pitched like a small boat as the horse placed one hoof at a time among invisible rocks; dark icy water flowed over his stirrups.*

The door swung inward. Seeing Dan, Timothy's welcoming face settled into hard ridges and planes. "Jake, Dan'l's here."

"Hello, Timothy."

The boy turned and stalked into the room.

Damn it to hell, Dan said to himself, we were friends last spring.

Chair legs scraped against the plank floor. Quick footsteps slapped to the door. "Come in, Daniel, come in. Quick. Do not let out the heat." Jacob wore his favorite red-dyed sheepskin slippers, loose in the heels. Beaming, he held his hand out, but his eyes were anxious.

Crossing the mudsill, Dan stumbled and bumped against Jacob. "Sorry. I can't feel my feet."

"Hmph." Tim frowned at him.

Jacob took Dan's arm, guided him to a chair by the stove, asked Timothy to pour coffee for them all, built up the fire. All the time he talked, clucked over Dan's wet trousers and boots, warned him of the dangers of frostbite while Timothy grinned at him from behind Jacob.

As Dan took a drink of the hot, strong brew, Jacob said, "So. You think today is good day to wade in the creek?"

"Mrs. Stark decided to go to church. She said she felt a need to be in the Lord's house. Nothing would stop her, so I saw to it she arrived safely." Dan inhaled the steam, drank a mouthful. Warmth slid down his gullet. His trouser legs dripped as the ice melted. Soon, he thought, he would feel his feet again.

"You bring Mrs. Stark to church, but how is it you have wet trousers?"

"I carried Mrs. Stark across the creek and the ice broke."

Timothy's head came up. "You carried Mam across the creek? S'pose you'd fell in?"

A thousand needles pricked Dan's feet. "Suppose I'd let her try to cross on the icy stones and she'd fallen? She's none too steady nowadays." The pins and needles became nails and tacks jabbing his skin. He set his jaw.

The fire popped. Jacob broke up the embers and added more wood. When he had shut the door, he stayed on his feet, looked from one to the other as though ready to intervene if necessary.

A hundred hammers drove nails through Dan's feet. He could not speak, much as he wanted to yell at Timothy: You have no right to question my care of your mother. Damn you, where have you been this couple of weeks, while worry over you and this baby drain her strength? Are you afraid for her during her ordeal?

A sudden fear stabbed him: Christ, if she should die, like Berry Woman did? The coffee tasted like bile.

"I tell him." Jacob sounded stern.

"No, Jake." Timothy gulped, then tried again: "No, Jake, don't. Please."

The boy was frightened? Why? What did he not want Jacob to tell him, and why not? It would be a small thing, compared to losing Martha. He had to find competent help, a doctor, but who could that be in this godforsaken hole, where doctors patched up gunshot wounds, set broken bones, amputated limbs? Who knew about these woman things?

Except another woman. Lydia Hudson. The Quaker woman disapproved of him, but she was Martha's greatest friend. The tacks and nails dwindled to pins and needles and went away, but he was so cold; he could stand in the fire like Shadrach and not be warm.

Jacob was talking to him. Something about the murder.

"Sorry, Jacob, I was distracted." He would pay Mrs. Hudson anything she asked.

With a disgusted noise Timothy stomped to the front window. He slid the heavy curtain aside and rubbed his thumb over thick frost covering the pane.

Jacob sat sideways to the stove and laid one ankle over the other knee. That angle hid his hands from Timothy, and he held up a warning finger toward Dan, telling him plainly: Say nothing. "Timothy would learn for himself who murdered his father. I will help him."

What was this? Why would Jacob would help Timothy gather evidence to hang him? "What do you mean, Jacob?"

"We look for his father's murderer." Jacob wagged his finger side to side.

Timothy scraped at the frost, that gave off a shrill squeak, as if he scratched a blackboard.

"We look first to find where he was."

Dan said, "I've asked Helen Troy to find out how long McDowell stayed at Fancy Annie's."

"You did?" Timothy said. "How did you see her? Did you go there?"

Meaning that men went to Fancy Annie's only for immoral purposes. In effect accusing him of being the sort of man his father had been. Stung, Dan forgot the burning in his feet. The cheerful yellow curtains mocked him, the room should be gray with smoke. "No, I damn well did not go there." Lowered his voice almost to a whisper. "Damn it, she came to my office. I'm representing her *pro bono* against Slade's estate."

"Pro what? What's that mean?" Tim demanded.

"I'm taking her case for free. She said McDowell stayed there after he, uh, after. The night of the fourteenth." He could not finish the sentence, but for them he did not have to specify the month. "She didn't remember how long he was there, but she'll ask."

Tim kicked at the bottom log in the wall; the toe of his boot made a slow thumping sound. He said, "You mean he knocked Mam out and went and laid up with his poxy whore?"

How had Timothy missed knowing that? If he were just now coming to terms with what his father was, Dan could not help him. Every man had to find his place with the father he had. His own father had been a weak man, a gambler, ultimately an embezzler and a suicide. Yet he had loved him when he was small.

He said, "First, I have to know when he died. If he left the fifteenth or even the sixteenth your mother was not out of danger, and you know I could not have murdered him. I was with you. I stood guard until we knew she would recover completely." Waiting for Timothy to speak, afraid to stand up, so badly did he want to shake him, but afraid to start, he admitted the truth in a secret part of his mind: *I'd have killed McDowell if he'd come back. In a fair fight or a brawl, I'd have killed him. Even if McDowell came back to apologize it would not have mattered because he'd have struck again; his kind don't change. I would not have left him alive to hurt Martha again.*

Never, though, never in ambush. Never a knife in the back.

The silence between them thrummed in Dan's ear. Why could Timothy not see that?

Jacob said, "A bell, it rings. Is church finished."

"I have to be going." He shrank from imprisoning his feet in the damp socks and boots, and recoiled at the thought of fording the creek again. Nothing for it, though. He shoved his feet into the boots and laced them up. Putting on his coat, he said, "Thank you, Jacob. I'm grateful for the warm-up."

"Is much I owe you, Daniel. Be well, my friend."

"You can't carry Mam all the way up to the house." Timothy fetched his coat from its peg. "I'll come along and help."

"And I also," said Jacob. "Then I go to the bank. Sunday is good day for banking."

~~26~~

"Mam come down that without killin' herself?"

Weak sunlight turned the slope into a broken, icy glare. After crossing Daylight creek they had paused on the south bank.

"Yes." Dan returned the short answer Timothy's question deserved.

"I'm so sorry," Martha leaned on him. "I might could walk up it."

"No," Dan said. Because of her bulge, she would walk blind, and he would not chance that she could do it, even with himself and Timothy to support her. He bent to catch her behind the knees "Let's go."

Martha sidestepped away from him. "I can walk up."

Under his arm, she trembled. He knew she feared trusting him. He did not trust himself; he cringed from the task – if he should stumble, or fall, or drop her? Unthinkable. Yet he would trust no one else to carry her up to Wallace.

"No," he said again. "If you fell, you might injure yourself."

"Let me carry her." Timothy inched forward over the ground.

"I can walk, can't I, Mr. Himmelfarb?"

"Pardon, Madame, better it is you go on a man's big feet."

"You're outvoted, my dear. We'll be fine." He hoped he signaled confidence to her, to them all. Hoisting her into his arms, he said, "Here we go, my love."

Her lips moved against his ear. "Sweet Jesus, give him strength." She tightened her arms around his neck as he jiggled her a little to get a better grip. Would to God He was on her side. He lifted one foot, set it down, and the crust gave way under it, so that his boot found firm footing. Well begun, he said to himself, and took the next step.

At the corner of Wallace, they stopped to catch their breath and shelter from the wind against the Eatery's blank wall.

"Put me down so you can rest a bit." Martha laid her head under his hat brim.

"I'm all right," he lied.

Dotty said, "Let's stop a bit with Miz Hudson, Dan'l. Let y'all rest."

"Yes, Dan'l," Timothy said. "Mam needs to warm up."

Should they? His arms were fraying rope, and his back hurt like hell. If he yielded and set Martha down in the warmth and friendship of Mrs. Hudson's restaurant, he might not have the strength to take her up for the climb to his house. Yet they both needed a rest. He set her on her feet.

Jacob said, "Is no more I can do, I go to the bank."

"Thank you for seeing us this far, Mr. Himmelfarb." Martha held out her hand to him. "We're all obliged to you."

He bowed over her hand. "Madame Stark. You are very brave. God go with you."

~~~

"Martha, thee poor dear. Thee looks half frozen. Come, come, let's get thee warm."

Above Martha's bonnet, Dan shook his head at Lydia Hudson, contradicting her protests that she was doing well, only a little tired and they would only like to sit a minute and get warm before tackling the rest of the slope up to home.

Nothing would do then, but they must have toast and hot tea, sage tea to be sure, the best thing for them, good medicine it was, preventing scurvy and many other ills, and Mrs. Hudson would not take no for an answer.

Two long tables with benches on both sides left enough room at the ends for an aisle along each wall. Mrs. Hudson and Tabby Rose served the food from either end of the tables, setting full plates down for the customers to pass along.

They sat at the back table close to the kitchen stove, Martha and Dotty on the stove side and Dan with Timothy on the door side. Mrs. Hudson gave them sage tea and thick slabs of bread topped with her apple butter.

Timothy washed down a mouthful and asked, "Where are the Roses?"

"They bide at home on the Sabbath." Mrs. Hudson's mouth opened just enough to let the words squeeze through, as she glanced from Martha, sitting beside her, to Dan.

The woman made no attempt to hide her feelings. She disliked him as much as ever. She had disapproved of him as soon as Martha moved into his house, and seemed never to have entertained the idea that they had come together out of love. Marrying her now, doing the honorable thing as people said, cut no ice with her.

He winced as a twinge in one of his feet reminded him that if they did not get home where they could be warm and dry, they might be frostbit, or he might catch a chill.

Dotty said, "Mama wanted to attend worship, and Dan'l helped her. He carried her across the creek. Twice." She chewed her bread. "Timmy and I crossed on the stones."

Mrs. Hudson's her lips parted, so that Dan glimpsed a younger, softer woman in that unguarded moment.

"That's right, he did," said Timothy around a mouthful of bread.

Martha made a sound between a gasp and a squeak.

"My dear." Mrs. Hudson climbed out over the bench. "Thee must lie down a bit before thee starts home." She pointed her finger at Dan. "Thee, sir, should sit thyself on this side of the table, close to the stove, where thee can warm thyself. I'll be bound thy feet are frozen and thy boots are wet."

Emerging from her private room some minutes later, Mrs. Hudson carried a pair of large felt slippers and thrust them at Dan. "Put these on," she ordered Dan. "My late husband, God rest his soul, packed them in the wagon to come West before his sad accident."

"What happened to him?" Dotty moved to give Dan a place closer to the stove.

"We had hitched the horses to the wagon, and Tabby and Albert and I were waiting on him. He went into the house to take one last look around and be sure everything was shipshape for the new owners. He slipped somehow, and fell down the cellar stairs, and broke his neck." She took Dan's socks and hung them over the oven door handle, set his boots in the warming oven above the cooking surface. "Is that better?"

Dan moved his toes in the felt. "Yes. Thank you." He had expected her to let him sit with cold, wet feet the rest of the day, and he did not understand this change in a woman who hated violence, the Vigilantes, and him for their methods to establish law and order. A Quaker, she talked of turning the other cheek even at gunpoint. If 'poor Nicholas,' the young man – Fitch's foster son –

whose brutal murder had given rise to the Vigilantes, could forgive the Indians who murdered his parents, she liked to say, we can do no less to his murderers.

Remembering her words brought heat to Dan's face, and he bent over, pretended to adjust the slipper top.

"How do you think Mrs. Stark does?" he asked.

"Good, considering. This jaunt today has taken something out of her, though."

"Besides making sure she is careful," Dan asked, "what do you recommend?"

"Rest," said Mrs. Hudson. "As much rest as is possible."

"I'll make sure of that," Dan said. "I tried to talk her out of this expedition, but she would not listen."

"We both tried," Dotty said.

Mrs. Hudson smiled. "I remember how thee watched over this family after Mr. McDowell – begging thy pardon, Timothy, I hate to bring up bad memories – after he struck her and left her for dead. Thee were as much a watch dog as our General."

"Those days are rather a fog to me," Dan said. "I was so concerned that she suffer no permanent injury." He glanced sidelong at Timothy who sat rigid as stone, shoulders high, arms stiff, his hands below the table top.

"Oh, my." Mrs. Hudson shook her head. "I don't think thee moved, hardly, from the time Timothy brought thee up from the – the unfinished building, until she woke up again. We were there, thee know, Tabby and I, and three or four other women who helped Mrs. Stark and us battle the typhus epidemic. My, oh my."

From behind Dan and to the side, Timothy said, "Do you recollect when Mam woke up?"

Mrs. Hudson took a sagging Dotty on her lap, where she promptly fell asleep.

"It was daylight the next day. That would've been the fifteenth." She looked at Dan. "Thee moved around more then, spoke to her when she called thee. Went outside a few times, but thee came right back." She cocked her head to the side, her thoughts secret. "You don't remember any of this?"

"No. I've tried. It's all a blur. I remember being afraid that he'd killed her, and thinking what I would do if he showed his face around here again." He stopped short of revealing how murderous those thoughts had been.

Beyond a sharp look, and a disapproving "Mmmm," Mrs. Hudson said nothing to that. "I recollect thee were with us from when Tabby and I came to help until early the morning of the seventeenth. Then thee decided thee had to sleep some and go on thy rounds so the road agents' friends didn't get any ideas." She came as close then to a smile as he could remember from her. "I recall thee couldn't sit a horse and thee couldn't walk right with thy bullet wound, but thee did not let that stop thee from walking all around town with thy rifle. To show the roughs they'd have plenty of trouble if they started something, thee said."

Martha's voice called to him, but Mrs. Hudson's sense of propriety would not allow him to enter her private room, even to see his own wife. He smiled to himself as she woke Dotty and set her on the bench. As she went into her room, he heard Martha insist that she wanted him.

In the warm room, lighted by one candle, Martha looked worn and frail against the pillows. Dan cursed himself, fool that he was to allow her to talk him into this expedition. It had been too much for her. He bent and kissed her.

Dotty's voice carried to him from the restaurant. "Is Mama all right?"

Martha's eyes were large and dark, and her face drawn despite the puffiness. "Isn't it time we were going home?"

"Yes, my dear. Mrs. Hudson has been most hospitable, but we should be getting on if you can manage it."

"I have to, don't I?"

~~27~~

While they waited for a passing dray, Dan looked up Jackson. He could not risk it. If he tried to carry Martha any farther, he might well drop her. And yet, Timothy's frowning silence dared him to do it.

He had never been one to back off from a dare, though carrying Martha from the creek had left his arm muscles quivering. He looked down the slope. Clouds blocking the sun flattened shadows to reveal the ridges and pits left by passing horses and wagons. The sight had him marveling, *How did I do that?*

"You'll have to help with your mother," he said to Timothy. "We can make a chair and carry her that way."

If he'd had time to think, he might have wondered at the softening that changed the boy's face. "Sure thing," he said. They crossed their arms, bent together, and boosted Martha up. She put her arms around their necks and Dotty came around to tuck her cloak around her and keep her warm.

Martha said, "You-all treat me like I'm some great baby."

"Not that." He Timothy stepped off the boardwalk together. "Like the finest Ming porcelain. Fragile and priceless."

No one spoke until they came to the path. "I can walk from here," Martha said.

"No," he said.

It had never seemed narrower or icier than now, the two of them shuffling along it sideways, carrying her. Heedless of her shoes and her hem, Dotty clambered through the snowbank edging the path and ran to open the door and hold the dog, who came out from his nest to greet them.

"Put me down here," Martha ordered them, when they stood on the porch.

"No, not this time. Today I carry you over the threshold." He raised one foot, hoping it was high enough, and stepped across the mudsill.

Timothy closed the door and latched it as soon as they were all inside.

Dan set Martha on the bench and issued Gatling-gun orders to both youngsters: "Heat a rock for her feet. Build up the fire in the bedroom. Make some tea."

It surprised him how fast they hurried to do as he said.

When he had settled Martha in bed with the hot rock wrapped in flannel at her feet, he changed to his indoor clothes. Dotty took his wet socks and boots, and left a mug of hot sage tea for him on the round table between his and

Martha's chairs. Putting his feet on a footstool, he held the mug in both hands while the feeling came back. When the pins and needles faded to a bearable level, he gulped the tea down fast, to avoid it lingering on his taste buds. Horrid stuff, it was, but good for what ails you, Martha liked to say. She knew what she was talking about, being one of the town's healing women, Lydia Hudson being another.

Whyever had he yielded to her this morning? Why had he not laid down the law, protected her from this danger? If something went awry with her now, it would be his fault. His fault entirely.

At the edge of his conscious mind, pots and pans thumped, dishes rattled. The youngsters mumbled to each other.

They would need Mrs. Hudson to help Martha through the waiting, and through the lying-in. But with the Eatery to see to, she could not take care of the daily household chores. Martha must have help. But who? And live-in or daily? He must figure that out.

Hearing his name, he looked over to the big table where Dotty and Timothy sat side by side talking in low voices, their blond heads almost touching. Timothy glanced up, caught Dan's eye.

"Dan'l?"

They had left his chair vacant. Was it an invitation to sit at the head of the table? Take his rightful place?

He crossed Martha's braided rug, its multi-colored braids expanding in an ever-larger circle, until the youngsters sat beyond its farther edge as on a distant shore.

He was getting fanciful. The big room, as Martha called it, was as cramped and as filled with furniture as he thought. His damn feet forced him to an old man's pace.

Gave him time to think. It wasn't often that a person caught a change happening, like catching a ball in midair. But the way Timothy had said his name signaled him that the boy's stonewall attitude might crumble. If he were careful.

Dotty had reheated soup, a venison broth loaded with vegetables. How long had he sat thinking? His feet still tingled.

"Dan'l." Dotty's voice quavered. "You brought Mama home safe."

Pulling out his chair, he lowered himself onto it, set his elbows on the table and clasped his hands in front of him. He could not control the twitching in his biceps, a sign of their weakness. He listened to Timothy's breath rasp in his throat and knew to take care where he stepped. "Not quite, Dotty. Timothy and I brought your mother home safely."

He did not look at the boy, who breathed soundlessly. He lowered his voice, and they leaned toward him to hear better. "On no account is she to attempt anything like this again, or be challenged that way until she recovers from her lying-in." He paused, forced his hands to remain still, not to jab the air for emphasis.

They nodded, their faces solemn, their eyes big.

"Good," he told them. "She must rest and let herself be coddled. As much as we can, we must shield her from any stress." He spoke gently, softly. "If we do that, she will be all right. They will both be all right. If not ...." He left the alternative to their imaginations.

By their open mouths and rounded eyes he knew he had shocked them. Dotty lay her spoon down. Her chin quivered; tears threatened. "What do you mean?"

"Exactly what I said. Your mother may be in danger, so do not bring her any more problems than she already knows about. For God's sake don't add to them." He looked hard at Timothy. "Any more information we get about your father's last days we keep to ourselves. Is that understood?"

Timothy opened his mouth so speak. "But—"

"No. This is it. Don't let anything bother her. Get that through your heads."

He waited for them to agree.

Dotty reacted first. "I'll quit school and stay home to help her."

"No, you will not." As he expected, she did not like that. She tucked her chin, ready to fight, and he almost smiled at her pugilist pose. "It is important for you to stay in school. We do not want you to grow up ignorant."

"Mam and Pap didn't have no schoolin'." Timothy blew on his spoonful of soup.

"Your mother is learning to read and write, and cipher. She began to learn in spite of your father. Or have you forgotten?"

"No," said Timothy. "We ain't forgot that. We gave her the Good Book for Christmas, didn't we? But Pap hated educated folks. Smart people. Said they was always pulling the wool over regular people's eyes."

"And the way to prevent being cheated? Do as your mother is doing. Become educated."

Dotty waved her hand at the room. "If I'm in school, how can I keep up the house and everything here and still do my homework?"

"I will hire full-time help for her." He had an idea about this that he would tell Martha first. But there would be no discussion. He could not afford – Martha could not afford – discussion. Not about her life. She might have different ideas about the person he had in mind, but one way or another, she would have help.

He could see that neither of the youngsters liked the idea. Before they met him, they had belonged to people who hired themselves out. He watched each of them think about objecting: Timothy's eyes darted back and forth, and the corners of Dotty's mouth tucked in and down.

He waited. At last, Timothy said, "Guess so," then Dotty pouted, "All right."

Now, for the worst thing. "We can take on some chores among the three of us, don't you think?" When they did not argue, he said, to give himself time, "Dotty, think of what you can do that won't interrupt your schooling."

A few minutes later, she had staked out for herself cleaning up after meals, and ironing on Saturdays. Baking bread on weekends.

Timothy shook his head. "That's all women's work. I don't do them chores."

"All right, then." Dan braced himself. "You and I will split one chore between us. I'll do it in the morning and you'll do it in the evening."

Dotty looked from one to the other, at first puzzled, then covered her mouth to trap the laughter from spilling out.

"No," said Timothy. "That's the worst chore. I won't do it."

Dan waited. If he could bend Timothy on this – emptying the chamber pots and rinsing them out – there might be hope for later.

Timothy spluttered. "It's horrid. I won't do it."

"Argue any more and you can do it both times," Dan said. "Your mother must not chance the cold, and she must not slip and fall."

He hated the thought of it, Dan knew. Everyone hated it. Until someone thought of a better way to dispose of waste, though, they had no choice.

"All right. I'll do that." Timothy's chin jutted out at Dan. "It ain't on account of you, though. It's to help Mam. That's all."

"Good." He'd won. Hiding his triumph, Dan opened his tinder box and stood up. Pointing to the wagon wheel chandelier above the table, he said, "It's time we had more light in here, don't you think?"

~~28~~

As the echoes of Tim's battle of words with Jacky Stevens faded away, he remembered the little snake had talked about 'Pap.' Nobody called Pap that but him and Dotty. What did Jacky mean by it?

He'd have to find him and make him say.

After walking all over town, near to freezing his ass, he could not find Jacky. He stopped outside Fancy Annie's, and debated with himself until his shivering made the decision for him. He'd get warm and learn something at the same time.

Maybe Helen Troy would tell him straight up what Jacky meant.

Inside, the saloon was anything but the good time place he'd imagined. It stank of old spilled beer and old cigar smoke, and the floor was sticky under his feet. He unwound his scarf and batted snowflakes from his coat. In spite of two roaring stoves and a couple of lamps burning on the bar, it wasn't what he'd call well-lit or warm. At two of the poker tables, gamblers huddled in their coats and practiced shuffling cards. Over at the billiard table, a man running balls didn't look up.

Helen Troy sat alone at a table near the stove at the end of the bar. She dipped her pen into an ink bottle and wrote something in a notebook. As he walked toward her, she slurped from a bowl of soup and looked up. Seeing him, she laid a scrap of paper to mark her place and closed the notebook to watch him without smiling, like she couldn't tell who he was. Her face sloughed down its bones, making her look a whole lot older than Mam. Older and hard used. He hadn't seen her for months, since the last time he'd dragged Pap out. He couldn't abide her, nor the jades that laid themselves down for men like Pap. She nor Isabell Stevens had come to Pap's funeral. He'd have drove them away with a horsewhip.

When he came closer, her cheeks lifted, carrying the corners of her drooping mouth upward in something like a smile, and loosened the flowery wool shawl that hugged her shoulders so it slid back, showing most of her heavy, hanging breasts. He felt himself respond to the sliding revelation: his face heated, and his throat clogged so he couldn't speak even if he'd thought of something to say.

Her smile widened, her lips thinning, and her eyes sparkled, teasing him. She reached for a chair, brought it around, leaned way over, and patted the seat. "You're Sam's son. Take a pew." The shawl draped a little more and one shoulder lifted so the tit showed more, and he couldn't keep himself from looking at it, couldn't look away like he should on account his head wouldn't turn, and his face was hot, and the cloth slipped so he saw the whole thing, nipple and all. He could not speak, but stood trying to force words he didn't have out of his throat. He'd never seen a whole female tit before, and he wanted to – to – do things he'd only imagined, and she was telling him, showing him he could do them, looking below his belt and purring real soft, "Well, well, young fella, what do you have there? Want to follow in your daddy's footsteps?"

At that, he took his hands out of his jean pockets and closed his coat to cover what was happening. At the same time he thought, Pap. Pap? With this – with her? He coughed, turning his head away like Mam always said to do. Mam, so clean as she was. And Pap with this whore, who thought he was a chip off the old block? Shit.

She gathered her shawl up around her neck, and her face changed like she'd got old while he stood there.

Though he hadn't heard anyone walking, a little waif appeared at the other side of the table. She had a long, thin face, and the hand holding her brown shawl tight across her shoulders shook, but when she spoke, her words sounded like sweet bells. She asked, "You want more coffee, Miss Troy?"

She wrapped the shawl higher up around her neck, appearing seemly as a schoolteacher. "Yes, Eileen, dear. Young Mr. McDowell will join me. Won't you, Timothy?"

The girl kept her eyes down, like pretending she wasn't really there. Just a little thing, the top of her head wouldn't reach his shirt pocket. "Yes, Miss Troy. I'd purely relish a cup." He smiled at the little mite, thinking that from her chest, she must've been about two years older'n Dotty. She glanced up at him and shied off like a scared pony, then padded away quick.

"You can't drink coffee standing up." Miss Troy nodded toward the chair. She was composed, like tempting fellas was all in the day's work. Her stock in trade, he supposed.

Sitting down, he straightened his shoulders and stiffened his spine. "I ain't taking Pap's place. Not in nothing. Never. I just come to ask about him." He stared at her hard, like he'd sometimes stared at grown men who thought they could bump a boy off his claim. He had no axe to reach for, like at the claim, but she got the message easy.

Eileen come back looking like she'd run away if he so much as curled a finger. She changed the coffee pot for a new full one and set down a clean mug without looking at Tim. Before he could finish saying "Thank you," she scampered away. Why was she so skittish?

Miss Troy gestured toward the pot and mug. "Help yourself."

"Thanks." The mug was made of dark blue enameled tin with white speckles. Tim poured himself some coffee and tasted it. "This is good."

"Don't act so surprised. Eileen makes it." She was all business now. "What do you want to know?"

Here it was. Damned if'n he didn't want to just get up and leave, on account he suddenly thought that she might tell him things about Pap he didn't want to know. But what could be worse than what he did know? "Last winter, was Pap here much?"

"Yeah. He lived here, just about. He only went home when he wanted to get more dust. Or eat. He wouldn't eat here. Said nothing he'd ever tasted was as good as your mama's cookin'." She sipped her coffee. "Besides, his partner, Tobias Fitch, he put his feet under your Ma's table, too. Him and Daniel Stark. Both."

Mam's boarders, they was, the Major and Dan'l. Pap spent his time and his gold here when he wasn't away prospecting, and he sure as hell wouldn't be going out when the snow piled high as a ridgepole in places, and no way to see the lay of the land, or the gold in ice-covered streams. He'd knowed Pap was here mostly, but it was hard to hear, anyways. He had to study some on the steam rising from the mug before he could ask the next question. "What did he spend it on?"

She laughed. "Look around. What is there here to spend it on? Liquor, games, women. I let him run up a big bill, thinking I'd get it back, but I never did. He was a welsher, you know. He welshed on his gambling debts, too."

The shame of it. His Pap. This is what he'd have to live down his whole life, that his Pap had drunk, gambled, and whored his life away. His feet gathered under him like they'd run out of here whether he said to or not, and spare him hearing how Pap had squandered his life.

Damn good riddance.

Stocked at the thought, he sat tight, on account thinking like that was wrong. He couldn't think that way. Pap weren't much of a daddy, but he was Tim's daddy, and Dotty's, and someone murdered him.

Damn you, Pap, why did you have to be that way? Why couldn't you have done things different?

He knew the next question he should ask, but he couldn't ask it, for the shame the answer would bring, yet he had to ask it or he'd be ashamed of himself if he didn't. He braced himself for the answer. "How much did he owe you?"

"Oh, your pa owed me plenty, but don't worry about it. I ain't about to go after you and your ma for it. Your step-daddy is taking care of it by not charging me legal fees."

Stepdaddy. Dan'l, his stepdaddy? No. No. He couldn't think of him like that.

She mistook his silence for not knowing about Dan'l's pro bono legal work. "He's a lawyer, you know."

He swallowed her sarcasm like he'd swallow what else she had to say.

Gone was all the flirting, the come-hither looks, the threat of him being led into doing something dumber'n he'd ever live down. "He's helping me sue Slade's estate. I don't care what happens to the widow; that damn drunk got what was coming to him." Seeing his cup was empty, she gestured toward the pot. "Help yourself. Don't be shy. I got plenty of beans to get through the winter." She lifted her chin. "Courtesy of an admirer."

Remembering his manners, he thanked her and poured himself more of the strong brew. He hoped to hell she'd answer the question he couldn't ask so he wouldn't have to.

"He'd stay all night, Sam would. It got so we figured he thought he lived here, and no one could understand why, when he had you and your sister, and your mother being one of the prettiest, sweetest women on earth." She thought some, her eyes staring into her memories. "Your mother's a saint, you know. Me and Isabelle Stevens, we begged her to come here during the typhus epidemic, Isabelle was so scared of losing Jacky. Your ma hates what we do, most decent women do, and she knew about Sam's goings on, but she came, her and that colored gal what works for Miz Hudson. She saved Jacky's no-account life. It was mighty Christian of her."

"I know about that."

"Yeah, well, whole town knows it. Most think she had no business tending to a whore's son, especially not Jacky."

She was quiet for a bit, before she went on. "He liked Isabelle Stevens best, your pa did, seems like she caught his fancy. He laid with her most of the time. She'd of let him be with her for free, but I don't allow that. My girls have got to earn their keep. The more men they entertain, the more money we make, you know. On the other hand, how could I kick her out, her with that boy of hers that ain't right in the head?"

He didn't give a shit about Jacky Stevens's head. "Was Pap here the night they hung them five bandits?"

"You been talking to Mr. Stark?" When he shook his head, no, she said, "I already told him Sam was here, holed up with Isabelle that night. And the next." She blew on her coffee, and he made himself listen and take in her story. "Jacky, he was jealous as anything when they first got together, I remember. But after a while he warmed up to Sam, him being here so much. Started in to sorta look on him like a pappy, almost, 'stead of just one of his mother's customers."

"He coulda had him for all I cared," Tim said. "Peas in a pod, them two." He lied, on account he did care, all his life had wanted Pap to say just one word that showed he'd done good, that Pap liked him. He'd tried his damnedest to measure up, and never could get it right.

"Your daddy didn't see it that way. He'd brush Jacky off, saying what did he want with a misbegotten bastard when he had a real son." She smiled at Tim, the first genuine smile he'd seen from her. "He was proud of you. Used to brag on you all the time, and tell anyone what a great man you'd be someday."

Tim set down the cup so hard some of the coffee sloshed out onto the table. How could that be so? "All I ever got from him was a fist," he whispered, not realizing he'd spoken aloud, until she answered him.

"He'd cry about that sometimes. Yeah, weep real tears. He'd moan, 'Why am I so hard on the boy?' That came out whenever he got drunk enough." She stared into a dark corner beyond the pool tables like it had something to tell her. "I could never make out why, if he really felt what he said he felt about you and your mama, and his 'precious little flower' – your sister, you know – he'd come here.

Jacky pestered him so, it was like he wanted to take your place, but Sam wouldn't have it. There didn't seem to be no sense to him."

Tim couldn't get past what she told him. Pap had liked him? Bragged on him? Felt bad for the way he acted toward him? He'd never knowed it. She had to be wrong. To Pap he'd been a nuisance under foot or a slavey, to work the farm or dig gold for him to piss away. That didn't square with Pap bragging on him. And he'd said Dotty was his little flower? He'd gloated over the – the dowry, he'd called it – that she'd bring him someday. To his mind, calling it that made it all right, but Tim knew it for what it was. A selling price. Evil.

The Troy woman had to be wrong about Pap. Pap had hated him. He'd tried to be a good son to Pap, did his damnedest, but as far as he knew, Pap had hated him on account, on account of what? Now the Troy woman said Pap bragged on him? Had been proud of him?

God, why couldn't Pap have showed him, so's he'd know? Why'd he have to find out from a whore?

~~29~~

Dan sat by the stove in his office, elbows on his knees, his aching head resting on his hands. Hair of the dog, he told himself. Hair of the dog. Instead, he drank more water flavored with peppermint leaves to chew. Father's expert remedy for hangover and whiskey breath.

Damn, that he had been lured into celebrating Lincoln's reelection last night. And Bagg's election to the Council. The speeches, the bonfire on Wallace street, the fireworks – all glorious. Then. He'd wanted to let off steam. He'd done that, all right.

Now there could not be enough peppermint leaves in the world to stave off this hammering headache.

Someone was doing carpentry in his head. To the building? Damn them!

He set his mug aside and stood up. He'd find the blasted culprit, and show them a thing or two, whoever it was. He flung the door open.

Helen Troy shivered on his threshold.

She smelled like she'd bathed in apple perfume. Last year. Making straight for the stove, she said, "Quite a celebration y'all had last night, Old Abe getting reelected and all. Kept the whole town up most of the night." Before he could think, she winked at him. "Didn't do my business no harm, neither."

He closed the door. His brain moved with the swiftness of sludge. Then again, what was there to say?

"You Union fellas didn't cause no damage, though you-all pissed off the Secesh." She unwound her shawl, and he had a random thought that business must be good for her to afford such fine thick wool.

"I got them lists you wanted." She rummaged in her crocheted bag – a soiled, embroidered pouch that closed with a drawstring, like a poke. She handed him a wad of paper, four sheets, written in pencil, erased, and torn.

"Thank you." He tilted the papers to the candlelight on his desk, and read the list of lost property. He had not expected there to be so much. Tables, chairs, the bar mirror, beds, bedding, garments – she had even listed women's underthings such as camisoles and drawers, and shoes. By far the biggest category of losses was in the drinks, not only the liquor and beer but some 200 empty bottles. "Why 200 empty bottles?"

"They'd have been worth something to the distillery. They could wash 'em and use 'em over again. Those bastards broke ever' damn one."

If the list were all true, at a rough estimate she was due nearly $150 in damages. He folded the papers and laid them on his desk, where he settled himself to write an affidavit. "The sale will be at the front door of Rockfellow & Dennee's on the morning of December 19." He pointed the pen uphill and across Jackson before dipping it in the ink.

"When do I get my money?"

Searching for the correct legal term to use in the document, he did not answer her right away, while she breathed impatiently through her nose. "Later that day, funds will be disbursed in probate court."

"It's about time. The law don't hurry none, does it?"

"True." He wrote some more, then hoping he'd written it correctly, he took care of the pen and ink bottle and blew on the paper to dry the ink. "This needs your signature."

"What is it?" She frowned at the paper.

"It's a statement that you promise everything on the list is true to the best of your recollection."

"It's true. I'll sign it." She reached for his pen, but he set it into a holder.

"No. Take it to a notary." Giving her the document, he told her where she could find a notary, and instructed her to bring the paper back to him straightaway so that he could file it with the probate court.

Her business was finished, but he held back from easing her and her odors out of his office. They had other business, his business, to tend to though she seemed oblivious of it.

"Have you learned anything about McDowell's whereabouts after January fourteenth?"

"Oh! I plumb forgot!"

His life might depend on the answer and she had forgotten? He hoped he kept his face bland to hide his thoughts. The fool woman.

She folded the affidavit and shoved it into her bag. "I should have told you straightaway. I know you been waitin', I'm sorry. Isabelle Stevens reminded me. Sam spent the nights of the fourteenth and the fifteenth holed up with her. She recollects she kicked him out on the sixteenth, or maybe the seventeenth – she don't recollect too good because of the drink – and she ain't seen hide nor hair of him since. Nobody has."

"How could she be so certain?"

"On account she'd been sure he'd be with her permanent. She reckons that was a black day in her life."

There it was. A starting point. January sixteenth or seventeenth. Perhaps the last time anyone saw McDowell alive. "Are you sure he left then?"

"Yep. When she said that, I recollected I told him he had to pay his bill, he couldn't keep on using my place as a second home when he had a good home of his own." She brushed at something on the bag. "Too good for the likes of him." Gathering her shawl close about her neck, she rose, turned her back to the stove. "Anyways, he told me where to stuff his bill and stomped out." She lifted her shoulders and let them drop. "He never come back, neither. I been asking the customers. He was just plumb gone, they think." Looked at Dan sideways, from under her lashes. "That help any?"

"Yes, it does. Thank you. Do you know where he went from there?"

"Away, is all I know." Her mouth twisted. "You're gonna love this part. Jacky Stevens said he was going with him. Took all his plunder and followed Sam out even after Sam said he'd kill him if he did." A jagged fingernail caught on a thread in the shawl, and she jerked it free. "He come back, upset and mad as all get-out. Sam must've sent him away with a flea in his ear."

"Maybe he'd know which way Sam went."

"Hah! You try to talk to that one, you'd better carry a long, forked stick. He's a baby rattler for sure."

As she took a step toward the door, he stopped her with another question.

"How is Eileen doing?"

"She don't thrive. She don't believe none of us can keep Jacky away from her. I do my best, we all do, but a saloon, it ain't the right place for her, though she don't know no different. She thinks now she's been ruined she'll have to work upstairs. I've told her a good cook can get a respectable position, but it's like she don't hear me. I purely don't know what to do."

Dan stood up. "Perhaps I have a way to solve problems we both have."

"That so?" She cocked her head at him, arched one eyebrow.

"Yes. My dear wife could use more help around the house, and you are worried about Eileen. Would you allow her to come to us?"

Her flirtatious expression turned calculating. Her eyes narrowed, and her tongue flicked out and in, reminding him of a cat lapping milk. "I'd like to see her in a safer place, Mr. Stark, but I'd have to replace her, you know. Hire another skivvy, and maybe throw in a cot, instead of a bed-roll behind the stove."

"How much?" Dan masked his disgust. Call it what you would, the Troy woman had maneuvered him into buying the girl. If there were any other way to take her out of there, he would do it. Instead, he was reduced to an act no better than buying a slave at the auction block. Except for what came after. There was the difference.

"Will you sign an agreement?" he asked when they had agreed on a price that would not have her coming back for more.

"Sure thing. Bring it with the money when you come get her."

~~30~~

After Dan filed his petition for Helen Troy's share of Slade's estate at the probate court, he walked down Idaho street. He would find X and tell him when McDowell had left Fancy Annie's. Damn Beidler for not asking the Troy woman. He had done nothing except decide that he had murdered McDowell and leave it at that.

Seeing Beidler leave the courthouse, the shotgun in the crook of his elbow, Dan met him across from the livery stable, where he could be heard without anyone else listening. If X was going hunting, the deputy sheriff's quarry was a man, not a deer.

"I want to talk to you."

X said, "I'm on my way out."

Dan stood his ground until X said, "Have it your way, but I ain't going to stand out here and freeze my ass. You got something to say, you can say it inside."

"This is for your ears only. If we're overheard, what I have to say will be all over town in five minutes."

"Whisper then, but not out here."

Nothing for it, then. Dan followed the deputy into the courthouse, where a couple waited for the clerk to complete their certificate of union. Cigar smoke fogged the room, and conversations hummed, everyone seeming intent on his own business. Like hiding a pebble in a pile of rubble, he would hide their talk where everyone was talking. They moved to the side of a closed door, and X put his back to the wall, hiding the name plate. "Helen Troy says McDowell spent the nights of the fourteenth and fifteenth with Isabelle Stevens. He left town on the sixteenth."

"That's all you got? I talked to her, weeks ago. She told me he left on the seventeenth. It don't clear you." He squinted up at Dan.

He had talked to her? Someone was lying. "She said you never asked her when McDowell left."

"The hell I didn't. That woman's drunk most of the time. That's why she probably didn't recollect."

Dan let it go by. He had to straighten out this business of when McDowell left. "The seventeenth? Then you had better talk to her again. This morning she was certain he left on the sixteenth. Either way, it lets me out. I stood guard over the family when I wasn't patrolling the town. I hardly left their cabin. You can ask Mrs. Hudson."

"As far as I'm concerned, you're as much in the frame as ever." X stroked his mustache.

"The hell you say. You won't find a scrap of evidence against me – how many times do I have to say this? – I did not kill him."

"Then you better prove to me you didn't."

He wanted to yell at Beidler, the stubborn son of a bitch, but he reined himself in, forced a smile for the benefit of anyone who happened to notice. Almost in a whisper, he said, "Didn't you hear me? I did not kill him. You can't prove someone did not do something. You can only prove he did it. If he did it. You have to show beyond reasonable doubt that I killed McDowell, but you can't. I did not do it." He spaced the words out, as though Beidler were mentally deficient.

He stepped close to X; his coat brushed the barrel of the deputy's shotgun. "I think you decided I was guilty and quit looking."

"Get back," said the little man. "You're giving me a crick in my neck." When Dan did not move, X shifted backward until the shotgun's stock bumped the wall and tilted upward. "What do you take me for? You know I ain't the kind to grab a man and hang him on suspicion."

Dan said, "That's not how I remember it. You were always quick to vote for hanging."

"If that was true, you'd've been dead the day you come back. I looked at everyone I could think of. You and Tobias Fitch had the best reasons to kill McDowell – your missus and McDowell's gold claims. But Fitch rode with us up to Hell Gate on the fifteenth when we took care of Aleck Carter and them. Then he rode with the boys over to the Gallatin to get Ed Hunter. They didn't come back till the beginning of February.

"No, you had good reason, and you was here. McDowell was killed plenty close enough for you to've done it and come back to town. It wouldn't have took long."

"Damn it, you know I was shot during that business with the Mexican. I could not ride. Hell, I couldn't have walked that far. I hobbled around on a cane for a month."

"You looked well enough to me prosecuting them fellas in the Tribunal. And you walked up the street with the rest of us."

That agonizing walk. "Then you also remember that I defended McDowell, and we let him go. For Christ's sake, I wouldn't defend a man in court and murder him two days later."

"What he done after that, I wouldn't blame you if you'd killed him in a fair fight. Stab him in the back? That's somethin' a dirty, rotten coward would do."

"And I did not do it." Yes, he'd looked for McDowell as he limped around town. If he'd found him, he'd have fought him, leg or no leg, and McDowell would not have lived to tell about it. He'd had two ideas as his leg healed and Martha's children got used to him being around. Win them over, in order to have the mother. That was the first idea. After that, get as much gold as he could to take home and pay Father's debts.

Win over the family. Get more gold.

Was that it? People said – and Beidler thought – he'd murdered McDowell to have both McDowell's woman and his gold.

He had won Martha, and now he was a rich man. Both of those could hang him.

X seemed to read his mind. "While Fitch was out with the boys rounding up the gang, you was here seducing McDowell's wife."

The look of the thing. Dark or light. X saw it dark. How could he make him to see it light?

A hinge squeaked as the door to the office behind Beidler opened. For the first time, he noticed the small sign written in a fine copperplate hand: Chief Justice Hosmer.

How much had Judge Hosmer heard through the thin wall?

X's voice came from afar: "You're the only one that fits."

~~31~~

"As I live and breathe, look who we have here." A jovial Charles Bagg emerged from Justice Hosmer's office and closed the door behind him. "This is certainly opportune." To Beidler, "I'll take our friend away, Deputy. He and I have business."

"You can have him, Your Honor. I got business elsewhere."

Dan did not watch Beidler bull his way through the throng. "Glad to see you, too, Bagg. But 'opportune'?"

"I was coming to see you in any event, to tell you that the Chief Justice will open court Monday next. All officers of the court are to attend."

"And?"

"Think, man. You intend to practice law? Argue cases before him? That makes you an officer of his court."

"I hear an objection there, Charles." What if Beidler arrested him first?

"Yes, unfortunately. Our Bar Association president is against you becoming a member until you're proven innocent."

"Ha!" For a few seconds, Dan was speechless. He breathed deep to steady himself, and smoke catching in his throat sent him into a coughing fit. When it was over, he wiped his and blew his nose, stuffed the handkerchief into his trousers pocket. "What kind of lawyer thinks of proving innocence? At the very least he should know his logic. You can't prove a negative."

"I know, but —"

Dan charged on. "Damn it, we had better standards of proof than that." Hearing the silence in the room, he stopped, looked around. People watched him warily, as if he were a man of uncertain temper who might go off half-cocked, as the saying was. Shamefaced, he said quietly, "Sorry, Charles. This business is like grit in my shoe."

"Understandable. About the Bar president, though. He wants to be the territorial district attorney, so he's trying to show how tough he is. Just remember, no matter what they suspect, you can't be charged on suspicion alone."

"I could be held on suspicion while Beidler looked for evidence."

Behind Dan, the noise level rose. He bent closer to Bagg to hear him.

"Get hold of yourself. Believe me, not a judge in town, especially not Justice Hosmer, would issue an arrest warrant on unsupported conjecture."

He wanted to believe Charles. He wanted to believe that Justice Hosmer had brought in a new era of legal procedure and fairness. They had all feared reprisals from the road agents' friends if they tried gang members in open court, and their terrified witnesses refused to testify unless their safety were guaranteed. The only way to avoid the near chaos of the Ives trial had been the utter secrecy of the Tribunal. A violation of the outlaws' Constitutional rights. What would Justice Hosmer do about that?

Through the tightness in his chest he managed to say, "All right, I'll keep it in mind. I hope you're right."

"Yes, I am. That's why I'm the lawyer and you're the client." He smiled briefly. "Even if Beidler did arrest you, you could file a suit for wrongful arrest, which Judge Hosmer would hear."

"He might side with them."

"I don't think so. If I were you, though, I'd welcome an opportunity to speak with him yourself, informally, about something dear to him and unrelated to McDowell's murder." Bagg nodded toward the door. "He doesn't have an appointment now."

"I don't know." Dan hesitated. What plausible reason could he have for calling on Hosmer unannounced?

"Good God, man, when have you ever been shy?" Bagg asked. "Go ahead. When I told him that I represent you, he said you did him a service, and he'd like to thank you."

What service could he have done Hosmer? Dan racked his brain as he waited for an answer to his knock.

Hosmer opened the door. "Mr. Stark, is it? Come in, please. I've been wanting to speak with you."

"Yes, Your Honor." For a man suspected of murder, he received a gracious welcome. Did this judge believe that a man was innocent until proven guilty?

Walking in, he thought how Grandfather would curl his lip at this crude room. A wall of the same pine planks that made up the flooring separated it from the jail. Grandfather's opulent chambers, lost to Father's disgrace, had been paneled in mahogany and hung with original oils by modern European masters from his private collection. A solid gold desk set, big as a steamship to a small Danny, had crowned his oak desk. The only flaw had been a stain on the oceanic silk rug, where Danny had dropped the ink bottle.

Justice Hosmer's desk was a sturdy table that occupied the short inside wall next to the door. A stove, smaller than Dan's own, stood in the back corner opposite the desk. Its flue vented through a poorly fitted, drafty hole in the windowless outside wall.

Fighting an urge to break and run, Dan stood inside the doorway. He was not a little boy any more. He could not ruin this floor. Judge Hosmer had no willow switch. He took a long step into the judge's chambers.

"Come and warm yourself. It's good of you to call on me." When they stood side by side at the stove, Hosmer said, "I've been wanting to thank you."

A kerosene lamp on a small wall shelf lighted the side of the judge's face away from Dan. His shadowed expression was unreadable. "I'm not aware –"

"You rescued *Adele*."

He'd rescued a woman? When? Dan puzzled over it for a second before the penny dropped. "Ah. Yes." Hosmer referred to his novel.

"It is not a book everyone approves of." Hosmer flicked ash from his sleeve.

"Because of the miscegenation, I suppose. My own dear wife is one-quarter Eastern Cherokee. Several prominent men here have Indian wives. One has married a black woman." When Hosmer did not speak, Dan realized the man wanted him to say something about the book, but what could he say to walk the fine line between truth and seeming to curry favor with the Chief Justice of the Territory? "I bought the book, Your Honor. I've read perhaps the first seventy pages. I quite like it." So far, he spoke true.

"I hope you will let me know what you think – honestly, now – when you have read it all. Although I can imagine how you might feel that anything but praise could damage your standing in my court."

Dan suspected that Hosmer had a sense of humor, something rare in his experience of judges, beginning with Grandfather. "I'll tell the truth, Your Honor. Right now, I can say I won't dislike the politics of it. Nor the ending."

Hosmer turned his back to the stove, and in this simple act became the Chief Justice again. "I understand you had some involvement in the Vigilante organization." His tone was harder; the words had edges.

"Yes, that is true. I was one of three prosecutors."

A darker shadow quivered behind the stove. The apparition? *I do not believe in ghosts.* With Hosmer facing him, he could not turn away from it, put his shoulder toward it.

"Also, as I understand it, you are a member of its Executive Committee?"

"Yes, Your Honor. Correct."

"How do you feel about relinquishing your roles in that organization?"

The thing distracted him. He could not tell Hosmer that he had taken an oath and could not give up his role unless they disbanded. An odor of death and cigar smoke filled his nostrils. "We made the region safe for travelers and for people on the streets." A vast understatement for long, cold hours in the saddle, the constant fear that someone would waylay them, kill them. "I'm happy to have the court take over." That was the truth.

"I also understand that you were involved in that dreadful business in Bannack a few weeks ago." The judge's face set in firm judicial lines.

Tell the truth and be damned, or lie and be damned for a liar. "We discussed Rawley's fate at length that night." The secret meeting: a sharp candle flame pierced the dark, an argument no less fierce about an act that skirted the bounds of murder. "We voted to carry out the sentence imposed last spring."

"Why? Was there no disagreement?"

The oath again. He had sworn not to talk about their deliberations. Without that, he could have described the debate. He picked his way through the quagmire on words meant to keep his oath and satisfy the Chief Justice. "Our by-laws mandate that every sentence of death must be unanimous. In the end the sentence had to be carried out." With that, he damned himself in this judge's eyes, and in the eyes of the Supreme Judge.

Hosmer's lower lip pushed out and in. Waiting for him to speak, Dan avoided looking toward the corner. Damn the thing for appearing now.

Go back to hell where you came from.

"On what evidence did you convict him last spring?"

"We found no eyewitnesses willing to testify, but we traced some accounts from robbery victims to him. When we confronted him, he turned state's evidence to avoid hanging. We banished him on condition that he never return, or his life would be forfeit. We told him he could be shot on sight, and it would not be counted murder."

"Did he understand you?"

"Oh, yes. He understood us very well." Dan wanted to look away from Hosmer, but that meant looking at the shivering thing in the corner. "When he came back, he was dying. Gangrene already taken his feet."

He had not expected to have to explain himself to the Territorial Chief Justice, who regarded him with distaste. Like Grandfather after he spilled the ink. The whipping then would be welcome now, in place of Hosmer's jabbing index finger.

"Mark my words, Mr. Stark, in my court there will be no substituting of gossip for evidence, no conviction on mere supposition, no taking one man's word against another's. I will have solid corroboration, facts, material evidence. Do I make myself clear?"

"Eminently clear, Your Honor. We did the best we could, but when men fear for their lives against an enemy largely unknown, it can be impossible to persuade them to stand up in public."

"I am aware of that."

Hosmer seemed to lose himself in thought. Dan watched the flames leap and twist behind the fire door. The apparition assumed its complete form of a hanged man, the head lolling toward its shoulder, a revolver in its right hand.

Dan said, "As soon as the immediate danger from the gang had passed, we established a People's Court with Alexander Davis as judge."

"Davis is a Secessionist."

"As are the majority of men here. When the war is over we will have to live together in peace again. He was a good judge."

"You are confident the Union will win?"

"I am. I pray we will."

Hosmer scrutinized him. "What are your plans? I understand you come from a prominent legal family in New York City."

"I plan to practice law here." Did Hosmer cross-examine every lawyer this way?

"Indeed. I've also gathered that you have speculated in gold." Plainly, he disapproved.

Had he learned that from Mrs. Hough? "Begging your pardon, Your Honor, every man here speculates in gold. Buying shares in a gold claim gambles that the gold will not play out before a profit is made. Bankers speculate every time they make a loan. Merchants order goods a year in advance. They bet they will receive the goods, then gamble the gold will not play out and deplete the population before they can sell it all."

"Is that so?" After one sharp look at Dan, Hosmer changed the subject. "I shall open court Monday next, December fifth. As you wish to argue cases in my court, the law requires you to attend and swear to or affirm your loyalty to the United States. I shall administer the oath prescribed by law." He pulled in his lower lip. "In fact, if you do not attend and take the oath, you cannot be an officer of the court."

"Yes, Your Honor. I'll be there." If not, he would never practice law in Montana.

Walking up Idaho street, Dan thought over the conversation with Hosmer. There was no puzzle about requiring every lawyer to take the oath of loyalty to the Union. Except for probate court, territorial courts were both federal and territorial at the same time. That being the case, a lawyer who argued a case in territorial court also argued in federal court, and since Congress required that all federal courts – and those who did business with them – take the loyalty oath, he understood why Hosmer insisted that all lawyers attend and be sworn.

Thinking to have a convivial drink at the Champion Saloon, he turned down Jackson street.

He could not shake the feeling that Judge Hosmer had been telling him something else. Feeling his way among thoughts of guilt and innocence, he changed course and crossed over to Content's Corner. He ran up the stairs to his office, where he built up the fire. He poured himself a drink and carried it with him as he paced the room. The stove warmed his chilled body; the whiskey relaxed his mind.

What had the Chief Justice been telling him?

At an explosion behind him, he spun around. Nothing. He peered into the corners. No specter. The explosion must have been pitch.

Setting the drink on his desk, he knew what Judge Hosmer had told him.

There would be no rush to judgment in Hosmer's court. He would demand direct evidence to back up the theories. To convict him, Beidler had to find direct evidence. Eye witnesses. There could be none to a murder not done.

Except false witnesses. Someone who hated him enough to lie about his whereabouts at the time of McDowell's death – whenever he died. Or to lie about seeing him kill McDowell.

God knew he had enemies. Dozens, probably, left from his participation in the Vigilante hangings.

Who hated him enough to commit perjury in Hosmer's court?

~~32~~

Eileen was a frightened rabbit of a child. Walking home, Dan held one grubby little paw in his hand to reassure her and to keep her close in case she decided to bolt and run back to the only people she had ever known. Her other hand clutched a bundle of her few possessions wrapped in a piece of grayed calico. This terrified child differed as much as could be from lively, outgoing Dotty, who didn't seem to fear much of anything as far as Dan could tell. Except Jacky Stevens. The two girls shared that.

Turning up Jackson, Dan said, "It's not far now. Just up the hill a ways. You'll soon be warm and safe." She said nothing, but plodded on, head bent like one walking to the gallows. Her bundle slipped in her grasp, and she caught it one-handed and hitched it higher in her arm.

"Would you like me to carry your things?" he offered.

She shook her head and clutched the untidy package to her side.

Someone – Timothy? – had dug the path wider and spread ashes to prevent slipping. Expecting Canary to come out of his shelter under the porch, Dan said, "We have a dog. I hope you're not afraid of dogs."

Eileen shrank together inside her coat and stopped.

When the dog bounded out, Dan stood with her. "His name is Canary. He's a sort of yellow hound dog. He sings, or so my stepdaughter tells me. I think it's just howling. He likes people, especially young girls. When he gets to know you, he'll bite anyone who bothers you."

She lifted her head for the first time since Helen Troy had told her she was to come with him, glanced at him, then studied her feet. When Canary sniffed at her, she would not pet him, though Dan ruffled the dog's ears.

"Let's go in. You can meet my wife, and my stepdaughter. Perhaps my stepson, Timothy, will be here, too."

A shudder ran through her frame, but she marched on at his side.

Feeling unnecessary, Dan sat in his reading chair with *Adele* while Martha guided Eileen's entrance into the household with the skill of a commanding officer and a mother's sympathy. Not an easy task, he had to admit, listening to her. Eileen had never before entered a respectable home, and Martha and her youngsters had never had live-in help. From her own reading chair, Martha portioned out chores between the girls, but she had nothing for Timothy to do. In her experience, the men of the house did not do household chores. While she organized the young females, Dan turned pages.

Finished, Martha asked if Eileen had any questions. The girl nodded. In the merest of whispers she asked, "Who cleans the shit pots?"

~~~

Lying in bed that night, Martha said, "All that poor child knows is what she learned in bad houses. She'll be a fine help with kitchen chores, and she knows to wash cooking pots real clean. Tomorrow I'll find out how her cookin' is. But there's a deal besides she don't know."

"Like those pots." Dan's laughter spilled over. After a moment Martha joined in, and set the bedsprings to squeak and bounce.

"She's scared of her own shadow. Even with us." She yawned, a deep indrawn breath with a squeak at the end. "She's downright terrified of you and Timothy." Another yawn. "Stands to reason I guess. Where she's been livin' men want only one thing of women. She knows they take it how they can."

"Dear God," Dan said as a new thought struck him. Could Eileen think he had bought her out of Fancy Annie's for his own purposes?

Bile rose in his throat. Coughing, he sat up and swung his feet out of bed.

"What is it?" Martha's urgent whisper followed him.

"Something in my throat," he managed to say. When the cough subsided, he lay down again, pulled the quilts to his chin. If that was her belief, only time would convince her otherwise by proving his lack of interest.

Martha whispered, "I do hate to see you and Timmy on the outs. Can't you make it up with him?"

"No. Not after he forced you to choose between us. Not unless he apologizes. Then, maybe we'll see."

"Maybe?"

"It would depend on whether or not he decides to stop acting like his father."

"How would he do that?"

"He can start by learning to read, write, and cipher. Even those basic skills won't equip him to take over the Nugget when his time comes."

"If'n he don't?" Martha ran the words together – ifnedon. Her hill speech was more pronounced when she was upset.

"Then I'll file suit to delay him taking over until he has demonstrated his competence to manage it well."

Her breaths came short and quick. "You would do that?"

He knew she understood that he would take the Nugget away from Timothy and go on managing it himself. The idea scared her. "I can't hand over control of a gold mine to an illiterate. I have to safeguard it for you and Dotty."

"And this baby?"

"He's not in it. I will provide for the two of you separately, and you will have your share of the Nugget, but our child has no stake in this mine."

"Then I can tell Timmy that you'll forgive him if he apologizes and takes to schoolin'? He's smart enough?"

"You can tell him I'll accept his apology if he decides to go to school or let me tutor him. And yes, he is smart enough."

"But forgivin' him?"

"I don't know. It depends on how he goes." It was the best he could say.

They lay in the dark. After a bit, Dan heard Martha's breathing even out. Forgive Timothy? Didn't forgiving someone mean that he had to be able to trust him again? How could he ever trust Timothy not to turn on him? Would finding McDowell's killer restore some part of the friendship they had known in the spring? Or had he lost that forever by hanging Rawley?

He was almost asleep when she said, "I don't want no broken family. I don't want to go through life knowin' we brought this on, that our lovin' ruined my boy. You find a way to fix that, you hear? Startin' with who killed his Pap."

~~33~~

In the Planters House dining room, four tables shoved together made a platform to hold another table and a chair that would serve as the judge's bench. Eying the arrangement, Dan hoped it was sturdy enough, and that Judge Hosmer was nimble.

"All rise."

Amid the rumble and scrape of boots and chair legs, the mutterings of fifty or so men, he thought the meeting, big as it was, would be too small to contain everything Hosmer had in mind.

Standing on his right, Charles Bagg muttered, "Here comes history."

"Yes." Dan smiled to himself. Instead of arriving on a roar of cannon, history came in the person of a pudgy man who bundled the skirts of his black robe into one hand, before putting a foot on a chair. Waving off the bailiff's steadying hand, he hoisted himself up, put the other foot on the table, pushed off, and stood on the platform. The bailiff handed him his brown leather case.

"Thank you," said Chief Justice Hosmer.

Letting out his breath, Dan heard others around him begin to breathe again.

Hosmer seated himself at the table, where an inkwell, pen, blotter pad, and kerosene lamp waited for him. From his case, he brought out a gavel, a sound block, and a fat clump of papers. He fussed over the items, arranging them as he wished before lighting the kerosene lamp.

The white light, brighter than candlelight, exaggerated the sagging flesh of his cheeks, but when he raised the gavel and looked out at the assembly, the skin prickled at the back of Dan's neck. "Gentlemen, let us begin the work of the law in this new territory." He brought down the gavel, and the muttering restlessness – errant whispers, boots shuffling against the floor – dissolved into quiet.

The Chief Justice picked up a paper.

"I shall now administer the oath prescribed by law. If any man is unwilling to swear to or affirm his loyalty to the United States of America by this oath, he may leave the room." He fixed them with a hard stare over the gold rims of his spectacles.

Behind Dan someone murmured, "Get it over with. We're all tired of this damned war."

Amen to that, Dan thought. He raised his right hand and swore his oath of loyalty to the United States before God. A few necks changed color, but none of the Secessionists refused.

"Our war is over at least." There would be no more long rides that ended with men dancing on air.

On his left Wilbur Sanders replied, "Now we have to win the peace."

"Or maintain it," Bagg whispered.

Justice Hosmer wiped his spectacles, replaced them on his nose, and cleared his throat. His face settled into stern creases. What was coming now?

"I have a few words to say on the subject of voluntary tribunals previous to this time and from this time forward." He moved the lamp as though to cast more light on the top sheet of the stack before him.

Dan braced himself. He, Sanders, and Bagg were not the only Vigilantes here. Three or four others would serve on the grand and petit juries. He braced himself. From this speech there would be no going back.

"The cause of Justice," Justice Hosmer read, "hitherto deprived of the intervention of regularly organized courts, has been temporarily subserved by voluntary tribunals of the people partaking more of the nature of self-defense than the comprehensive principles of the Common law."

Dan's neck and shoulders tensed.

Bagg whispered so low Dan almost did not hear him. "It'll be all right."

Perhaps, but Dan could not relax.

"There could be but one of two courses to pursue – to hang the offenders or submit to their authority, and give the Territory over to misrule and murder. Happily, the former course prevailed, and the summary punishment visited upon a few, frightened the survivors from the Territory, and restored order and safety."

He paused, lowered the paper to regard each of the Vigilantes in turn before he went on.

"Much as we may approve the means of self-protection thus employed, and the promptitude with which they were applied, our admiration ceases, when they assert an authority defiant of law, and usurp offices which belong only to Government itself."

Led by Sanders, applause interrupted Justice Hosmer.

Bagg whispered, "I didn't think there would be trouble over what we did."

"He's apparently smarter than that," Dan said.

"Yes," murmured Bagg. "He's on the square."

Hosmer held up a hand to quiet the applause. "Let us then erect no more impromptu scaffolds. Let us inflict no more midnight executions." His stare pinned Dan like an insect to the wall. He meant Rawley.

Hosmer glanced down, turned one paper over and laid it aside.

"Let us give to every man, however aggravated his crime, the full benefit of the freeman's right – trial by jury." He looked up, found his place again on the page. "In a community restrained by the operation of good laws, any subversive organizations are criminal in themselves."

Applause broke out. One man known to be a vigorous opponent of the Vigilantes rose up, then two more, followed by every man in the room – Vigilante or not.

Bagg's mouth was so close to Dan's ear that the hairs of his shaggy beard brushed against his jaw. "If this speech isn't forgiveness, I don't know what it could be."

It was a pardon. They were safe. Safe from prosecution for everything. Including Rawley.

Hosmer's next words rang in his ears: "No more impromptu scaffolds. No more midnight executions. Any subversive organizations are criminal in themselves."

As he heard them, he recalled other words from deep in his memory: 'Go, and sin no more.' Bagg was correct. The law had forgiven them, but not if they acted again.

If Beidler took his suspicions to the Tribunal, and they acted on them, he would be liable to prosecution, and so would every man on the executive committee.

Behind him, where two of the other Vigilantes sat, one said to the other, "He'd better leave the criminal side to us. We'd do a better job."

~~~

"Do we get to eat now?" A man sitting behind them complained. "I'm so hungry my stomach thinks my throat's been cut."

Having sworn everyone in as officers of the court and made himself clear about the Vigilantes, Hosmer showed no signs of calling a recess. He excused the jurors, then signaled the Bar Association president, Harold Abbott, who called the meeting to order.

The hungry man moaned, "If I'd known lawyering could be this long-winded, I'd have taken up farming."

"Another purpose to this meeting today," Hosmer said, "is to sanction the Virginia City Bar Association. Accordingly, I want to read to you the appropriate portion of the Idaho Statutes." Taking up a thick tome, he adjusted his spectacles on his nose and opened the book to a place marked with a strip of leather.

A lawyer in front of Dan whispered, "This is sure as hell not Idaho."

His friend replied, "But until the legislature acts, there's no law in Montana."

Sanders leaned forward. "Quiet. Listen to him."

'No law in Montana,' the Chief Justice had said. By his proclamation, if the Vigilantes acted, they would be murderers. Under what law would they, or anyone, be tried? The county sheriff and the deputy sheriff were bound to enforce the law, but what law could they enforce? Idaho law did not apply to Montana any more than New York's statutes did.

Hosmer, reading from the Idaho law book, caught Dan's attention: "Every person, before receiving license to practice law, shall take the oath prescribed by law, and pay over to the territorial treasurer the sum of ten dollars for the use of the territorial library fund."

"No!" A man sitting in the front row stood up fast. "That is a tax! We cannot be taxed in order to belong to an association. It – it's unconstitutional!" By his accent, the words flowing into each other, Dan heard a Southern cadence like Martha's.

Sanders stood up. "It is most certainly constitutional. It's entirely within the right of a Legislature to pass a statute to assess a sum for building a law library. How can we defend or prosecute cases without knowing what the law is?"

A voice from the back row sounded before Sanders sat down. "I know the law of Missouri. I know it well. I can argue from Missouri precedent without referring to any book. Would Missouri law, then, pertain to Montana Territory? We all come from somewhere else." He paused to take a deep breath. "Learned counsel from New York is probably as well able to argue from his understanding of New York statutes. But should New York law or Ohio law, rule over men from Missouri or Massachusetts? I submit, gentlemen, the Idaho Statutes are no more pertinent here than are the laws of our native states."

Before he finished, men clamored to be heard.

The president shouted for order, but the Tennessean yelled over him, "We want the Common law of England."

"No!" someone shouted. "This Territory was made from Idaho, and by our Organic Act, its laws pass to us. We must use the Idaho Statutes."

The wrangle, a verbal free-for-all, went on. Dan listened and said nothing. He told himself that learning how other attorneys argued would be useful if he opposed them in court. In reality, he knew he sat silent because a man accused of murder must not call attention to himself.

As he listened, though, no one mentioned the best reason not to use the Idaho code. The *Montana Post* had printed the Idaho quartz act in late August, but no one appeared to remember that the statute allowed, what? Fifty feet in width? No. A hundred feet? Yes, that was it. The Idaho law gave quartz claims a hundred feet of ground. One hundred feet wide by two hundred feet deep.

Not nearly enough for a quartz mine, considering the complexity and workings needed by underground mining. In placer mining, one man or three crouched in a stream panned the surface gravel for color. Or dug out rocks and crushed them with a sledgehammer, then ran water through a sluice to wash away the dirt and gravel and leave the gold. Timothy had worked his father's claim that way for months. By himself.

No, a quartz mine needed much more ground for the machinery, the workings. What would be the right size for it? A thousand feet wide?

What would the Montana legislature do? Adopt Idaho law wholesale? That was the easy way. The way to disaster. It would give the Nugget or any quartz mine only a hundred feet. It would put the Nugget in danger of being jumped, on the grounds that it claimed more land than was legal, and therefore its registration would be null and void. That had to be stopped. The legislature must not adopt Idaho law wholesale. It had to write a quartz law that enlarged the ground for a quartz mine to – yes, a thousand feet. One thousand feet wide by two hundred feet long.

Only one solution was possible before the legislature could meet, haggle over, and pass a good mining law.

The Common Law of England.

Stay out of this discussion, he told himself. He had enough trouble already, he could not appear to side with the Secesh, who lobbied hard for the Common Law. He could not give anyone reason to question his loyalty to the Union.

Even as he gave himself good advice to stay out of the dispute, he was on his feet. "Mr. President. Permission to speak."

Surprised faces turned toward him. In the space before Abbott recognized him, he asked himself, *What the hell are you doing?*

Then, feeling like he'd been hunting in vain and had at last a clear shot at his quarry, he knew how to avoid branding himself a traitor to the Union by appearing to side with Johnny Reb.

Frowning, Abbott recognized him. "Mr. Stark. Go ahead."

"Gentlemen," he began, "no one knows just what the common law is, other than it would appear to leave people free to act as they see fit until someone brings suit against them. Then the court's ruling that decides the matter becomes a de facto law, although it was not written by a legislative body. In this way, local custom guides us in the absence of statutory law."

Warmed up, he let rhetorical phrases roll off his tongue. "Some of my learned colleagues suggest that the Idaho laws should rule in this territory. I regret very much that I must disagree. We are all here for one reason.

"Gold. Whether we mine it or accept it in exchange for goods and services we are all gold-seekers.

"From the first miners' meeting in June last year, sensible men in Alder Gulch have hammered out laws for themselves. They wrote new laws to fit changing conditions and had their code printed in the *Montana Post*. Being miners themselves, they know what miners need in this district, and they are perfectly able by themselves to draft laws that guide us lawyers.

"If the Idaho Statutes are adopted wholesale, they will impose laws on miners throughout the Territory that no one can work with. For example, Idaho limits the size of claims to one hundred feet wide and two hundred feet long. It is impossible to break gold out of quartz rock in such a cramped space. A quartz claim needs a minimum width of one thousand feet for its workings.

"If the Common law is adopted, each mining district could write and abide by its own rules until the territorial legislature can pass a sensible mining law."

He sat down to an applause that surprised him, although Sanders frowned. Bagg whispered to him, "Well put. We shall take up mining law as soon as possible in the Legislature."

On his other side, Sanders muttered, "What do we do between now and then, with no criminal law in force? With our hands tied and only two men to enforce the law we don't have? Some will demand that we step into that breach if the occasion arises, but we can't without incurring criminal penalties ourselves."

"God forbid we should ever ride again," Dan retorted.

"Amen to that." Bagg leaned across Dan so Sanders could hear him. "Civil and criminal codes will be our first issues." As he resettled himself in his chair, he whispered to Dan, "Let's have a drink after this. I want to talk to you before I leave for Bannack in the morning."

~~34~~

By the low rumble of men talking, and the layers of smoke from cigars and candles, it seemed most of Hosmer's audience had migrated to the Champion Saloon after the meeting. On the walls hung sporting prints of men and women riding to hounds and prints of bare-chested men with their fists up, reminding customers that Con Orem was a renowned pugilist. Dan and Charles Bagg drank to each other across a small table. "Here's to your success in the legislature."

"Thank you." Bagg smacked his lips as he set the beer stein down. "That's good beer. I was thirsty." He licked cream-colored foam from his mustache. "I think we'll need some luck and maybe a few prayers." He leaned forward, rested his elbows on the table. "I'm sorry to leave you without counsel."

A man Dan recognized from the meeting stopped by their table. "I want to shake your hand, Mr. Stark. Your speech was most impressive."

Dan stood up and took the offered hand. "Thank you, Mr. Um." The other man said his name. When he had finished with his compliments, Dan sat down.

"Where were we?"

Bagg said, "Talking about you being without counsel."

"Ah, yes. Do you know, meeting with Judge Hosmer, and attending this meeting have reassured me. I think I'll be all right. His honor won't issue an arrest warrant without concrete evidence. I think I have breathing room to find some answers."

"Any response from your advertisements?"

"None. Either no one saw McDowell, or they don't want to say they saw him, or someone who did see him has left the area."

Two other men from the meeting stopped to congratulate Dan. When they had finished, Bagg took up their conversation where it had left off. "I'm sorry you're no further along with your inquiries. Perhaps if you—" He broke off.

Harold Abbott stood by the table, his hand out. "Excellent speech, Mr. Stark. Cogent and well delivered. Your call for one thousand feet of ground for quartz mines was particularly telling. That certainly put the law into perspective."

"Thank you," Dan said. Abbott had a waxed mustache that curled at the ends, a style Dan disliked.

Abbott said, "I believe you have not been to one of our Bar Association meetings?"

Dan restrained himself. The man knew he had not attended, and what could he possibly say to that? "No, my time has been taken up with other matters."

Abbott's eyes narrowed, but he kept his insincere smile as he said, "We would welcome you to attend, and perhaps you will consider joining us."

"Thank you, I'll do that."

"Good. We meet over Kiskadden's." After telling Dan the time and date of the next meeting, Abbott strolled away.

Sitting down, Dan said, "Quick, Charles, pretend you're telling a joke. I need an excuse to laugh." Without Abbott thinking he had caused the humor.

Bagg said, "What more proof do you need? You changed what Abbott is pleased to call his mind. It was the thousand feet of ground that did it. He's not the only one, either."

"Good God, that seems obvious." Dan no longer felt like laughing.

The two men rose to put on their coats.

Bagg said, "Oh, it wasn't your brilliant logic. At least it wasn't only that."

"What else could there be?" Dan slid his right arm into his coat sleeve.

Bagg's face lighted with fun; his eyes gleamed. "He also mentioned that you don't have the physiognomy of a murderer."

"The what?" Dan forgot that his left hand groped behind his back for the other sleeve. "Physiognomy?" He tipped his head back and laughed, a great burst of merriment that Bagg joined. When their laughter subsided, he put his left arm into the coat sleeve and shrugged the garment onto his shoulders. "That does beat all. I know many believe in that phrenology drivel, but I thought sensible men knew better."

"Mmm. Sensible men?" Implying that believers in phrenology were anything but sensible. Bagg held the door for them to leave the saloon. "I heard him say it after you left."

"George Ives and Henry Plummer were two of the handsomest men in the Territory, and they were cold-blooded murderers. After them, some people still believe that nonsense? I can't credit it." Both had met their deaths on a rope.

They walked down Jackson to Wallace. Darkness had come, and stars glittered in the black sky. Dan pulled his scarf up over his nose and ears.

"I think you should come to Bannack in a couple of weeks after we've had time to organize the legislature," Bagg said. "We're bound to take up mining law among the first things, and you would be very effective arguing for that thousand feet of ground."

They walked a few more steps, heads down to watch their footing.

"I can't leave while my dear wife is in her present precarious situation. Besides, I'm certain there are others who could argue for that as well as I could."

At the corner, they came to their parting. "Keep it in mind, though," Bagg said. "We need you to persuade some of them. We've elected one or two uncommonly stubborn fools."

~~35~~

Tim being at Dan'l's house for supper was pure accident. He'd promised Jacob to meet him here on account Dan'l had something to talk to them about, some fiddle-faddle from that court meeting on Monday, and he thought they could meet and then go on down to Dan'l's office or Jacob's house to talk in private. But he'd been early and Jacob was late, and Mam wouldn't hear of him leaving without putting his feet under her table, so he was stuck. Stuck at the supper table with Mam, Dan'l, Dotty, and Eileen, the scared rabbit.

She acted like her own shadow would affright her. Or maybe it was him. Same thing. He didn't have no interest in a mousy little thing like her.

"Now you just eat, dearie," Mam said to her. "You need your vittles."

She just sat there looking like she was going to be eaten herself, instead of settling down to relish the beefsteak and taters on her plate. You'd think she'd know better, after being with them now for a couple of weeks.

"Both of you," Dan'l said. "Go ahead and eat." He didn't so much as give the little mouse the merest glance, but maybe he knowed something, on account he said, "What's on your plate is yours, Eileen. Nobody will grab it. Eat up." What struck Tim wasn't what he said, but how he said it, the kindest, gentlest way Tim had heard from him since he'd come back.

And Eileen? She turned cherry red, but she set to with her knife and fork, imitated Dotty, who kept her eyes down, eating like she was all alone at the table, instead of her usual chit-chat about school doings.

Her having to imitate Dotty told Tim she hadn't much in the way of smarts, or she'd know how to use the utensils by now. Still, all cleaned up, wearing one of Dotty's old dresses, her hair shining kind of reddish under the overhead lamps, she might get some looks once she plumped up. Nothing like Dotty, of course. Under the fear she seemed a good soul, too. Mam said she worked hard. The house smelled a deal better, on account she wasn't above scrubbing the chamber pots. He laughed inside. The scandalous words she'd used made him want to laugh out loud, but they'd want to know what —

Barking and snarling, Canary scrambled up from his rug, scratched at the door.

Outside, almost on their doorstep shrill voices yelled filthy words. A man shouted, "Away from me, away, you little demons! Help!"

Dan'l rocketed up, sent his chair crashing to the floor, Tim after him, while behind him the girls screamed and Mam shouted at them to hush up.

Dan'l grabbed his rifle off its peg and threw open the door. Scooting between his legs, Canary streaked out.

A pack of boys beat and kicked a man lying in the snow, his arms up to protect his head from one boy in particular, a skinny half-grown runt of pure meanness. Jacky Stevens.

Dan'l levered a round into the rifle's chamber. The ratchet sound splintered the air, stopping all the boys but Jacky.

"Get away or I'll shoot!" Dan'l raised the long gun to his shoulder as the dog soared off the ground at the scrawny attacker. Canary was just a snap away when Jacky pushed another boy at the dog, and pelted down the hill like the devil hisself was after him.

Tim chased him, but he'd come out in his stocking feet and couldn't get purchase on the rough ice. So he was several yards behind when Jacky ducked around the corner onto Wallace. He might have turned back, but Canary ran on, chasing him.

He had to go after the dog lest he got hurt.

When he reached the corner, Canary was already trotting back, panting, tongue hanging out. Tim figured Jacky had run into Fancy Annie's. "Good dog," he said. "You almost got him." He ruffled Canary's ears. "Race you back."

Dan'l knelt by the downed man. The rifle stood against his shoulder, and he was trying to lift the man up. "It's Jacob. Help me get him inside."

Dotty ran out to help. Dan'l gave her the rifle and told her to lay it on its pegs, careful of the round he'd chambered. Then him and Dan'l helped Jake to his feet, though he choked back a yelp, and into the house. His head bled something awful, all over Dan'l's sack coat and shirt, and even in his hair. It made Tim's stomach queasy.

Inside, Mam snapped orders to the girls to bring hot water and cloths. Quick as grasshoppers they jumped to do as she said. Dan'l used the clean rags they brought to stop the blood while he and Tim settled Jacob on the floor near the smaller stove in the reading corner. He put a folded towel under his head and felt his arms and legs for broken bones.

Jake told him to lay off. "Is nothing broken. I go home now." He tried to raise himself up, but sank back, gasping.

Dan'l laid a hand on his shoulder. "In the morning, if you're well enough. That little devil kicked you a couple of good ones in the head."

Lying back, Jake smiled. "I have Jew's head. Thick skull."

"There's nothing thick about you, Jacob," Dan'l said.

Dotty sank down on the floor beside Dan'l. "Move, please." She used a voice Tim had never heard from her before, and to his surprise, Dan'l obeyed.

He hunkered down on his heels a couple of feet away. Standing over Dotty and Jake, Mam told Dotty what to do. When she had staunched the blood, Dotty wrapped Jake's head in clean cloths so he looked kind of like a swami in a turban that Tim had seen in a picture book.

"Rest and keeping warm are best," Mam said. "Let him sleep."

"You needing rest, too, my dear." Dan'l rocked forward from his heels and stood up.

She touched his face. "You have blood in your hair."

"It's all Jacob's."

"Put your coat and shirt in cold water, or the blood will set," Mam said, but from the look she and Dan'l give each other, she was saying something more. Tim didn't fathom it, but Dan'l did, judging from the way his lips curled up at the corners. It was like they had a telegraph line strung between them.

"Everything will be all right. You get some sleep. You both need it." From the mischievous way he sounded, Tim figured he meant her and the baby. He couldn't stand to watch them so he took two buckets out to fill them with snow. The cold air felt mighty good on his hot face.

A handful of snow from somewhere else plopped into a bucket. Eileen had followed him out. She startled him; he'd clean forgot her.

"Go in the house. It's too cold out here."

She shook her head. "Mostly I'm too warm in their house. I'm used to bein' cold."

Tim recollected the little cabin up on Idaho street, how he'd always been cold and hated it. "I'd rather be warm."

The buckets full, he picked them up as she reached for one. She stammered so he hardly understood her. "He'll be back, won't he?"

He knew she meant Jacky. Did she want a lie or the truth? "Yeah. But I could come around more, and watch out for him if you don't mind."

"I don't mind. Your mama would like it if you was here more."

"Right." He nodded toward the house. "You go ahead in. I'm right behind you."

~~36~~

As Dan walked back to the house from the necessary a couple of days after the attack on Jacob, fresh snow squeaked under his boots in a pitch so high he could barely hear it. To avoid the noxious odors from the two empty chamber pots he carried, he took shallow breaths through his scarf. It didn't help. He set the things by the shovel he'd planted in a snowbank. Someone, he said to himself, should invent a better way to carry away human soil.

The shadow of a man, crisp and black in the moonlight, rounded the corner of the house. Almost as tall as himself, shoulders hunched up. Timothy. What did he want?

"This cold's enough to make a fella constipate hisself," the boy said. "Want a hand with that?"

Timothy, offering to help him? What was this about?

"Sure enough." Dan put his foot on the shovel, sank it almost to China, but when he brought up the pile of dry snow to put in the pots, much of it flew into the air. Like talking to Timothy, most of what he said would be lost between them. He shoveled more snow. No matter how careful he was, only some of it landed in a pot. Timothy thrust the flat of his gloved hand into the receptacle to pack it down. In the house it would melt and be used to scrub the things out. Working fast, they filled them both. Timothy picked them up, but instead of taking them to the house, he stopped. Cocked his head, listened.

"Somebody's coming."

The snow squeaked in a fast cadence of short steps, hurrying down the slope, unseen behind the pile of logs.

From inside the house the dog barked.

"Beidler." Dan spoke before a small man's shadow separated from the pile of logs.

"He's coming here?"

They walked to the front of the house to wait for the deputy.

"How do." Beidler stopped a few feet away. "I need to speak to Jacob Himmelfarb."

"Investigating his attack?" Dan asked. If Beidler had any other reason, he could go back where he came from.

"Yep." The deputy spat tobacco juice into the snow. The stain showed an unearthly blue in the moonlight.

"Come in, then. But leave the gun outside."

When Beidler fussed at that, Dan said, "The only guns in my house are mine."

"I ain't leavin' it where it'll get stolen."

"Then unload it and break it, before you bring it in."

They left the shovel leaning by the door, handy for more shoveling, and carried the chamber pots into the house. Setting them on the thick rush mat in front of the bench, Dan and Timothy changed into their house shoes. Beidler unloaded the shotgun, broke it, and let it rest against the wall.

Dotty sat at the table practicing her penmanship, Jacob beside her, watching. The scarlet bruise around his closed left eye, the dried cuts on his face, the bandage wrapped like a turban around his head, set Dan to cursing Jacky Stevens under his breath. From her reading chair, Martha looked up from the Good Book to greet Beidler politely, but without warmth. She did not offer him a piece of the cake sitting on the table. Peering out his right eye, the left still closed, Jacob raised a half-smile for the deputy. Dotty bent her head lower over her letters.

Sitting as close to the cookstove as possible, Eileen huddled into a shapeless gray knitted garment Martha had knitted a few years ago for herself, and pulled the sleeves over her hands.

From his stance by the door, Beidler said, "I come to see how Mr. Himmelfarb does, and to ask what everyone remembers about the attack."

Martha put a slip of paper in the Bible and closed it. "We womenfolk didn't see, only afterwards. Mr. Stark and Timmy, they ran out right away."

"All three of you?" Beidler looked at Eileen, who shied away. Trying to be invisible, Dan thought.

"All three of us." Dotty's tone of voice allowed for no questioning her, even though she was a young girl who had a smudge of chalk dust on her nose.

Beidler turned to Jacob. "So what do you remember, Mr. Himmelfarb?"

"Is not much I remember." Jacob held his hand to his jaw. It hurt him to talk; he could eat nothing but Martha's nourishing beef broth. "I am walking to this house, then boys – how you say, jump me – and there is much shouting, and punching, kicking." He touched his left cheekbone; his eye was still closed. "Maybe a cudgel they use. Next I remember, Daniel and Timothy yell, and dog bark, and Daniel stays with me while Tim and dog chase boys away. Then Timothy, he and Daniel, they lift me up and bring me in here." He attempted to smile at Martha. "This good angel, she knows how to do for hurts. See? In only three days I am better."

"You're givin' me too much credit, Mr. Himmelfarb," Martha said.

"No, dear lady. You have it in here, the knowledge." He tapped his head. "And the wish to help, in here." He put his hand over his heart.

The smile left his face as he said to the deputy, "The boys, I remember now Jacky Stevens." Shutting his uninjured eye, he said, "I see him...."

They waited for a moment or two until Jacob opened his eye. "No, is nothing more I remember. I – I did not fight back." A tear leaked out the corner of his eye and trickled down his face.

"You couldn't fight a dozen to one," Dan said. "You were lucky you weren't hurt worse. If they had attacked earlier, it might have been different." Meaning that he and Timothy would not have been home to help him.

"Why would they attack Jacob?" Dotty asked.

Dan said, "Probably because they thought you had gold, Jacob?" An uglier thought at the back of his mind would remain unspoken. There should be no pogroms in America, and if the boys had attacked Jacob for being a Jew, something nasty smoldered in the manure piles they called their minds. He glanced at Martha, whose fingertips covered her mouth. She had guessed at his meaning.

"Yah. They said, 'Give us gold, we want gold.' But we put gold in big safe at bank. I do not carry gold alone at night. Or in daylight. Is not safe." Jacob smiled at Martha. "It is only greed. Not the pogrom."

"Oh, surely not that." Martha's hands, her fingers intertwined, fell onto the Bible. "We can't be having such a thing here. Why it wouldn't be —" She broke off, looked around at them all. "It wouldn't be Christian."

"It's meanness. And greed, like Jake said. They wanted gold." Timothy sat straight, chin high, and stared at Beidler, challenging him.

How alike they were, Sam McDowell's children. In the face of Beidler's authority, they met him square, heads up, with the same determination, amounting almost to stubbornness.

For a moment no one seemed to be able to think of anything more to say about the attack. Perhaps, thought Dan, Beidler will take the hint and leave us to our evening.

Eileen, silent little creature that he thought her, surprised him by speaking up. "How's to stop 'em? Jacky an' them? What's to say they won't do it again?"

"If you want something done about him," Beidler said, "Jacob can bring a charge and I'll get a warrant for his arrest."

"No." Wincing, Jacob moved his head a little. "It makes him – what? More angry? More mean? Maybe he pays a fine. Goes to jail, a week, a month? It does not stop him. When he comes out he is worse."

"That's all you can do?" Dotty said. "Put him in jail for a while? Jacky's got nothing but meanness in him, and you can't do anything to protect us?"

Without answering the youngsters, Beidler sent Dan a silent message: Another force, the Vigilantes, could put the fear of God into Jacky, in spite of Judge Hosmer's stern warning.

Dan telegraphed back, No. Judge Hosmer had given them a chance to start over. They were in the clear. They could never go down that road again. Once that started up, he might be next.

Thinking the child deserved more of an explanation, he said, "In our law there is no way to punish a criminal before he commits a crime." He supposed that would be the end of it, but he had not reckoned on Eileen's fear.

Her voice rang out shrill as a scream. "You mean them boys could go for Mister, uh, Mister Himm another time and y'all can't stop 'em?"

"Sorry to say, that's right." Beidler scratched his ear, spoke to Jacob. "I can put those bullies in jail only if you charge them, sir. Then the law can punish them for what they did to you."

Eileen was not satisfied. "Then what good is it? The law? If it don't protect folks from the likes of him. I'm thinking the Vigilantes did better. They should be in charge."

She had revealed a fundamental flaw in the legal system, just as a grownup might, and nothing, Dan feared, would satisfy her. "The Vigilantes never hanged anyone for something they might have done. Or might be thinking of doing. That would have been murder."

The girl fixed him with an eagle's fierce stare because he had not given her the answer she wanted, and he knew she hated him for it. He could say nothing else. Nor could he, as a lawyer, ever have a different answer for any victim. On Jacky's malevolent path to whatever his end might be, there was no help for any potential target – himself or this child – until after Jacky had committed the evil deed he had in mind. Then they could punish him for it. "Under our Constitution, someone is innocent until proven guilty in a court of law."

Her shoulders sagged. "Then there's nothing to do about Jacky afore he goes and does something worse, then."

"Not in law, no. We can't do more than keep watch." He looked at the faded bloodstains on Martha's rug. Someone, probably Eileen, had scrubbed them, but the rug was ruined. Blood stains never disappeared completely. There was no comfort in law for any of them. Not for this waif, nor for the women who lived in fear, nor for himself with the responsibility to protect them. He had no illusions about what Jacky might be capable of. Not even Boone Helm, the self-proclaimed cannibal, had been so unpredictable. He would redouble his vigilance, but that was all he could do. "I won't let Jacky hurt any of you."

Timothy said, "You ain't the only one. I'll look out for them, too."

He had forgotten Timothy. "Of course. Good." They nodded to each other, perhaps in recognition – of what, he wondered.

Beidler said, "All I know, Miss, is that can't be everywhere there might be trouble." He pulled on his gloves, laid the shotgun across his arm.

After Dan had shut the door behind him and dropped the bar across it, Dotty said, "Then I guess it's up to us to protect ourselves."

Dan followed her gaze. She did not look at him, but at the guns on the rack.

~~37~~

Tim knew he shouldn't have put his coat on yet. He was all wrapped up to go out, working up a sweat doing nothin', and the silly girl wasn't ready yet. Truth to tell, it wasn't her fault. Mam had insisted he take her along, or he could've been to the Drug Emporium and back by now. But no. "Timmy, take Eileen." Mam piled wraps on her till she looked like a wooly snowman: Dotty's old, ugly brown coat, a shawl knitted from a hodgepodge of leftover yarn, and the multi-colored stocking cap in red and blue, that had a long tail Mam wrapped around her mouth and nose and tucked into her collar. If she wasn't looking at him so fierce from all those wrappings, he'd've laughed out loud.

Once they were outside, she slowed him down something awful. Either she couldn't or wouldn't move fast enough, so he had to keep stopping to let her catch up some, but not too close. He didn't want nobody to see him walking with this woolly muddle of a girl.

But looky there. Jacky Stevens – alone, for once – turned the corner by Content's and started uphill. Head down, he walked slow and careful, like he thought he'd break if he fell. Seeing him unaware, and thinking this was his chance to teach him a lesson, Tim bounded ahead. People hurrying to escape the cold, horses' hooves crushing icy ruts, a drunk singing – all masked his boots hammering on the boardwalk.

Jacky looked up, too late.

Tim caught him near the foot of the staircase to Content's second floor and cocked his fist to smash Jacky's face. "How'd you like a taste of what you give our friend?"

The little bastard dangled at the end of his arm, hands open like talons and feet kicking at him a few inches off the ground. The sight of him flailing away struck Tim so funny that he couldn't hardly keep his grip for laughing. The air bit at his lungs, and he danced a slippery quickstep to keep his own self upright. The commotion made other folks stop to laugh at Jacky, too.

Boots thundered down the staircase. Dan'l stood at his elbow. "Let him go."

Tim shook his head. "No, I've got him now."

Dan'l hand closed on his shoulder, his fingers dug in hard through the heavy wool coat. "Let him go."

Jacky writhed and snarled at the end of Tim's arm. Tim paid Dan'l no mind. He had Jacky where he wanted him, and by God he'd scare the little snake so bad he'd never make a move on them again. Just let him get a tighter grip on his collar.

"Sam weren't your pa," Jacky screamed. "He were mine. I'm his rightful son."

All he'd ever got from Pap was a fist, but by God Sam McDowell was his Pap, he'd never sired this foul by-blow of a filthy bat. Tim laughed, a sour sound in his ears, a sour taste in his mouth. "He'd never have you. Never."

Jacky stopped trying to get away, just dangled at the end of Tim's arm, crying, tears and snot sliming his face.

Dan'l let go of Tim's shoulder, and stepped back like giving him room. Good. He'd show Dan'l the way to deal with garbage like Jacky Stevens. "He weren't— I get it." Helen Troy had said, Jacky followed your pa a little way, came back a while later. "That's what happened, ain't it? You followed him, and he run you off. He wouldn't want no truck with you. That's it, ain't it? He sent you back with a flea in your ear, didn't he?"

"No. That ain't true. I come back 'cause my ma needs me."

"Like she needs a hole in her head." His arm tiring, worse than hauling on a boulder, he let go. Jacky slipped and fell splat on his ass, his feet straight out like a little kid's, to the hoots and laughter of onlookers.

"We was gonna join up later, Sam and me," he screamed. "We was gonna meet up but some son of a bitch killed him."

"You're lying. Pap didn't want you, you nasty little pest, he'd never would've met up with you." Tim shut his mouth on the rest of it, that Pap didn't want him, or Mam, or Dotty; he just wanted to be free of them all.

Jacky yelled, "I'll get you! You wait! I'll get you, you and that bitch whore with you."

"You evil-minded bastard." Tim grabbed for Jacky, but Dan'l had hold of him again, said something Tim didn't hear through the waterfall roar in his ears.

Slime freezing on his face, Jacky scrabbled to his feet, black hate spewing from his mouth at Eileen: "Which one you whoring for? Or is it both of them, you bitch? They taking turns? Or a three?"

"You disgusting little moron." Dan'l took a step toward him.

Jacky spun around and dashed away down Wallace, toward Fancy Annie's.

Some of the crowd sprinted after him, and Tim had a notion to join them, but Dan'l caught him. "Let him go."

A whimper, like a little animal being mistreated, made Tim turn to Eileen, meaning to tell her, Don't let Jacky worry you, but he lost the words at the sight of her, stuffing the woolly tail of her stocking cap into her mouth. Her eyes looked stunned, like an ox's eyes after the first blow of the sledgehammer that killed it.

He wrapped his arms around her and held her for a bit, the stiff little thing, then turned her around and walked her slowly home, murmuring to her like he would to calm a frightened horse. "It's all right, you're safe, he can't get you no more."

A man's steps followed them, and he knew without looking back that Dan'l was there. Eileen made a mouse-sound. Tim said, "Don't worry, you're safe, it's Dan'l."

~~~

As he came up to them, Dan overheard Timothy reassuring Eileen.

The small scene, those few words, stopped him. Timothy had heard him walk up to them, and did not turn around. He kept his back turned. His back. His unguarded back. He'd said to Eileen, 'You're safe. It's Dan'l.'

The little scene repeated itself in his mind: 'You're safe. It's Dan'l,' and here they were walking up the hill, and Timothy did not care that his back was turned to the man he suspected had murdered his father.

He knew Dan would not stab him in the back.

They delivered Eileen into Martha's care and walked downhill together without speaking until they reached the foot of the Content building's stairs. "Come up to my office." Dan pitched his invitation halfway to an order, leaving it for Timothy to decide which it was, whether to accept or not. "I have to talk to you."

"Don't know what about." The boy's face was sullen, but he did not bolt or offer to fight.

"Come up and get warm, damn it. I want to talk to you, and I don't want to freeze my ass out here." He put his foot on the bottom step as if it did not matter whether Timothy followed him or not.

He had reached the third step when the boy followed him. Sunlight being a cold, useless patch on the floor, they warmed themselves at the stove. Dan went at it without hesitating. Tim's temper was so uncertain, he might not have another opportunity to say this.

"You turned your back on me."

"So? What of it?" Timothy faced Dan, head thrust forward, elbows bent. He doubled his fists.

"Think about it. No one turns his back on someone he thinks might kill him. Your father turned his back on his murderer. Whom did he trust enough? He would never have turned his back on me. He didn't trust me. He hated me."

Timothy's mouth opened and closed. "What? What are you saying?"

Dan waited without speaking. Let the boy figure it out for himself, if he could.

Looking beyond Dan's shoulder, Timothy's eyes darted from side to side as he thought it through.

Dan tamped down his impatience, willed himself to stillness.

Timothy spoke as if to himself, thinking aloud about McDowell. "It weren't like he didn't trust nobody. He just figured he could beat up anyone who tried anything. Generally, he was right. He was a real hard man to sneak up on."

"Yet someone did sneak up on him. Someone stabbed him in the back."

"Yeah."

They would either get to the crux of it now, or not. Without moving, Dan gave Timothy room and time to find his way among his thoughts. He withdrew his gaze to look at the stove, so Timothy would be free to understand – oh, let him understand that McDowell would never turn his back on Dan if they had been arguing. Let him see that on his own.

"It was such a little cut," Timothy whispered.

Dan barely heard him.

"You saw it?" The horror of that sight, for a son to view his father's corpse after it had lain months in that cave. Decomposition and small creatures would have turned the body into something barely recognizable as human. Those stained and rotten clothes in one of his boxes carried the stink of death, but Timothy had seen the corpse that had worn them. His father's corpse.

"The sheriff asked me to identify the – the remains, he called it. He stripped the clothes off to show me the wound."

At last he talked about the murder. He did not exonerate Dan, but he didn't accuse him either, even as he talked about his father's ghastly remains. Dan decided not to upset him further by saying he knew this already. From Martha. "Why you?"

He swallowed. "Someone had to. It couldn't be Mam." He pinched his nose. "I still smell it."

Dan remembered the sickening, sweetish smell of Nick Tbalt's frozen corpse after it had lain a week in the open. "Yes. One does."

That stopped Timothy, who stared at him for a second or two. "You – he wouldn't have turned his back on you, would he? You're near as big as him, and he hated you, like you said." He shook his head. "But there ain't nobody else. Only you. Major Fitch rode with the posse to find the rest of the road agents after y'all hung George Ives." He fell silent, stared far off at something invisible. "When we turned him – it – the body – over. That's when I saw the cut. It was just above his belt on the right side. About this wide." He held a thumb and forefinger about half an inch apart. "The doctor said later it nicked a kidney." Turning his back to the stove, he stared out the window. "Only a nick. Just a little cut."

A little cut but enough, Dan thought. It served to bring a big man down.

After a long silence, Timothy appeared to struggle for words, before he pivoted and walked to the door. He hesitated there, and for a second or so, Dan thought he might change his mind about leaving.

Then, throwing his shoulders back, Timothy opened the door and went out.

Dan listened to his boots clatter down the stairs.

~~38~~

"Jacob! How well you look!" Lewis Hershfield welcomed Jacob and Dan with a hearty handshake. Motioning to the chairs around his stove, he offered them both a drink of whiskey. When they were seated and watching the people going about their business outside Hershfield's fence, the banker raised his glass. "Your health."

"And yours," Dan said.

Jacob said. "Yah, your health."

They drank, and Dan took a moment to appreciate the whiskey. Rolling the liquor around on his tongue, he tasted citrus and something faintly smoky.

Hershfield said, "Jacob, are you quite well? How are the ribs? Your face is healing, but your eye, that will take time, I fear."

"He insisted on going home," Dan said. "I told him he wasn't healed enough yet, but he would not stay." He wanted to make a joke about his floor being too hard, but kept silent. That might have been Jacob's idea.

"Ach, such hens you are that worry over one egg." Despite sounding like a scold, Jacob looked pleased. "Is time I come back to work. Is time to leave the lady Stark in peace. What is the saying about guests? Like fish? I have been under their feet, yah? A week already. I stink good by now."

"Not a bit of it," Dan said. "We're happy you're mending."

A silence fell between the men while they watched people pass by. Conversations swelled and faded, and laughter rolled out from the new shoe shop up toward the front of the building. Enjoying the lingering smoky aftertaste of the whiskey, Dan thought he would leave, now that he had escorted Jacob to visit Hershfield. Perhaps he would ask the grocer about his little pickle thieves.

With Hershfield's next comment, he forgot about them. "Have you considered finding investors for your quartz claim? I mean, on a limited basis, to explore further."

Heat rose into Dan's face, like sunburn where his beard did not grow. Had Jacob mentioned the Nugget to Hershfield? In his mouth, the whiskey aftertaste turned as astringent as a raw coffee bean. Not even Jacob had the right to let Hershfield in on that before they were ready.

With the next thought, he knew Jacob would not have said anything. Finding him and Hershfield regarding him oddly, Dan hid his irritation in a false laugh. "There are no secrets in this damn place, are there?"

In the dark corner between Hershfield's stove and the safe, a deeper shadow congealed into a human form. The hanged man. The hand holding a revolver quivered as if it might bring up the gun and level it at him. What was the damn thing doing here? Something sharp and cold as ice sawed across his neck.

"None at all," Hershfield said. "It's worse than before we had a newspaper, though." He tilted the bottle toward his guests' drinks. When they both refused, he set it on the low table and took up the day's *Montana Post*. "I read an interesting article, all about that legal meeting you fellows had on Monday. At first I thought it was a silly quarrel over a measly ten bucks a year. One gold Eagle. That should be mincemeat to you lawyers."

He raised his glass, noticed that it was empty, and put it down beside the bottle. "Turns out it's a fight about law, about what sort of law this territory should have." He beamed from Dan to Jacob. "A much different kettle of fish, am I correct?"

"It is," Dan agreed.

"How, Daniel?" Jacob rubbed his forehead. "Tell me. This morning you say it is small disagreement about ten dollars. Now Lewis says, it is more?"

"It is more, Jacob. I said that this morning because I don't want to bother my good lady about anything."

"Ah. That is right," Jacob said.

Hershfield murmured his agreement.

"Stop me if you know this already, but if not I have to give you some background. We have two kinds of law in this country. The Constitution says only the legislative branch can make laws. The Executive branch enforces the laws. And the courts say what the law is and decide cases brought before them." He wished now he had not turned down Hershfield's offer of another drink, although the clock on the wall said it was just mid-morning. Explaining the Constitution made him thirsty. "That's what the Constitution mandates."

After Dan explained the word, mandates, Jacob said. "Yah. This I understand. But two kinds of law?"

"The Common Law," said Hershfield. "Isn't that right?"

"Yes, that's right," Dan nodded. "Common law is a traditional kind of law people brought over from England. Instead of laws passed by a legislature, two people go to court with a dispute. In settling it, how the judge rules becomes part of the law for the next judge. That's called a precedent. The next judge rules on a similar case the way the previous judge did. In effect, that makes law.

"I think that's what Judge Hosmer is afraid of – too much law-making power in the hands of judges, rather than left to the people's representatives, the legislators."

"Wait a bit." Hershfield held out his hand to stop Dan; his eyes narrowed. "Trouble coming." Standing up, he put on a welcoming smile. "Ah. The good Major Fitch." Muttered, "Don't leave, Stark. Jacob." He reached for the gate to open it.

Rising in his wake, Dan read hot anger in Fitch's bloodshot eyes. He shook a rolled-up *Montana Post* at Dan without acknowledging the other two men and shouted over the fence. "I thought I'd find you here. Have you seen this? This travesty? Justice they call him. Ha! Chief Justice. Pah!" He spat a gob of brownish-yellow tobacco on the floor before he stepped over the fence. His coat skirt caught on the picket where the "No Spitting" sign was tacked. He yanked it free in a rip of cloth.

Hershfield dropped his hand and his smile as Fitch confronted Dan. "You know what I'm talking about? These God-damned Idaho statutes? What's this man Hosmer playing at? What, I ask you? He doesn't know his ass from a mine shaft. Someone oughta set him straight." Fitch's short left arm bent, as if to clout any lawyer he found, or any Union man. Especially a Union lawyer.

"I was there." Dan located every piece of the bank's furniture – safe, desk, lamps, chairs, side tables, whiskey bottle, glasses. The fence. In case Fitch swung at him. If Fitch started anything he would finish it.

Hershfield, standing on wide-spread legs, as immovable as his safe, blocked Fitch's way to get at Dan.

"You, you," the Southerner sputtered. He looked around for the spittoon, found it close by, and spat the rest of his chaw into it. Wiped his mouth and mustache on an unsavory handkerchief. Noticing Jacob struggling up from his chair, and Hershfield planted a few inches in front of him, some determination that braced him from inside collapsed. He stepped back from Hershfield. "You sided for the God-damn statutes, I'll bet."

"No. I ran afoul of the ironclad Unionists on that issue."

"You did?" The short arm straightened, no longer threatening anyone.

"Yes."

Hershfield said, "Shall we sit down?"

"Oh, hell," Fitch said. "You'd think I was raised in a barn. Sorry, Hershfield. Sorry, Himm – uh."

Tempers ebbing, they sat down, to all appearances four cronies settled in for a good chin-wag around the fire. Hershfield poured whiskey, and they raised their glasses in a truce: "Your health." "Here's looking at you." "Here's how."

Fitch removed his hat and folded his coat skirts over his knees to keep them off the floor. He fingered the torn lining. "How'd that happen?" he muttered.

Dan and Hershfield exchanged straight-faced looks.

Fitch sipped his drink. "Good whiskey. Y'all know how to appeal to a man's palate."

In for a penny, Dan thought. He cupped his glass in both hands. "About the Idaho statutes."

"You ain't going to tell me you think we oughta have those God-damn laws, are you?" Fitch rolled back his short sleeve and inserted his index finger under the cover of the wooden cap. "Thing itches sometimes."

In its corner the shadow vibrated.

"If I could finish my sentence," Dan snapped, "Idaho law may be all right for some things, but not quartz mining." He went on to tell about the court opening on Monday, how he had argued for a width for quartz claims of a thousand feet of ground.

The shrill Rebel yell turned all heads toward them. Major Fitch raised his right arm, an officer leading troops into combat. "I'll be damned! A Union man who sees things my way!"

Between the shadow in the corner past Hershfield's shoulder and Fitch pulling off the wooden cap over the end of his arm, Dan did not know where he could look without appearing to stare. Why did the damn thing always appear where he had no option but to see it?

Fitch set the square-bottom, wooden cap on the low table and dropped the cloth into it. The bare stump showed a sewn package of flesh; a flap of skin had been tucked over a rectangle and sewn down, leaving a white, V-shaped scar. It looked like the surgeon had wrapped the stump and made him a present of it.

"So what next? What can we do to get our thousand feet?" Fitch massaged the stump.

"First, we wait until Justice Hosmer rules for or against the Idaho laws. I think he'll go for them because he mistrusts the Common Law. It gives judges too much power to, in effect, make law." Dan waited for Fitch to ask how that would happen, but when the question did not come, he asked to look at the newspaper.

"Just a minute." Fitch smacked the back of his hand on the sheet. "For once this hare-brained Yankee editor has got something almost right." Pulling a spectacles case from an inside pocket, he threaded the bows over his ears. The decorative gold rims magnified his scowl as he read:

"The question is raised as to whether the common law of England, the Idaho code, Louisiana law, anarchy, or the old state of affairs under the rule of the Vigilantes is to be the legal status of Montana. His honor has reserved his decision and so the matter stands. There is, however a gleam of comfort in the idea that the Legislature is to meet at Bannack on Monday; when their first duty will, of course, be to settle this vexed question. As public bodies move slowly there must, however, be an interregnum, till the result of their deliberations takes the shape of an act."

"An interregnum, he calls it. Between the acts. We're still where we've been for the last eighteen months: No law of any sort until the legislature acts. Again. What do we do in the meantime?" He crumpled the newspaper and flung it at Dan, who caught it. "So much for your Union justice. Until His Honor decides," he sneered. "We're hamstrung. The Vigilantes can't keep order and there ain't no laws in force yet." Sitting back, he folded the spectacles into their case and stowed it away somewhere in his coat.

Hershfield said, "I hope the legislature acts quickly. Looks to me like we ought to send someone over there to talk to the legislators sooner rather than later, to – shall we say, act on an act – before Justice Hosmer rules for the Idaho code."

Dan smoothed out the newspaper, folded it into a tidy shape, all the while thinking that Bagg wanted him to go to Bannack. Now Fitch and Hershfield, too. Even Jacob. He could not go. He had to stay in Virginia City for Martha's sake. His sense of Judge Hosmer told him that His

Honor, feeling a distinct danger from the reign of judges under English Common Law, would rule for the Idaho code. Yet before the legislature could pass a good mining law, what were miners to do? The Nugget, like all Fair-weather District claims, was safe because of the weather. The rules provided that between October first and May first, when claim owners could not work the frozen ground and typically spent the winter in warmer places, their claims could not be jumped. But he had heard Fitch swear to be the richest man in the Territory. Fitch had wanted all of Sam McDowell's claims, and —

"Daniel, what do you think so hard? Daniel?" Jacob brought him out of the deep place his thinking had led him, before he could follow the trail to its end.

Fitch complained, "You folded that paper into a brick. How's a man to read it now?"

He was two people. One smiled at Fitch and offered him the paper, a block about an eighth its original size, apologized. The other, hiding behind the affable smile, carried on dark thoughts in secret: Had Fitch murdered McDowell? He could have got behind him, an easy thing to do, they having been friends and partners, Fitch having grubstaked McDowell to do his prospecting, a task diffi-cult or even impossible for a one-handed man.

Yet Fitch had ridden out on the fifteenth, while McDowell stayed at Fancy Annie's until the sixteenth or seventeenth. Beidler swore to it, and wrong-headed as he could be, as he was in Dan's case, he was no liar, and friendship could not stand up to his idea of justice. As Dan well knew.

Jacob said, "We talk about how someone goes to Bannack, to, to –" His voice trailed off as he hunted for an English word.

Hershfield supplied it. "To lobby the legislators. Stark, I'm thinking you're the best man for the job."

"Yah," said Jacob. "You it should be. Our emissary." He beamed at them, proud that he had found the right word in English.

Dan acknowledged his feat with a nod and a smile, at the same time that he said, "I cannot leave while Mrs. Stark is in her delicate condition."

Fitch thumped on his knee with his left arm and yelped. "Damn it to hell! I forgot I put the cap back on."

It must have been while he'd been thinking so hard, Dan realized. What else had he missed? He might ask Jacob later.

Fitch draped the cloth over the wooden cap. "I said that weeks ago. I knew it would come to this. You see, Stark? It ain't such a lunatic notion. You're the man for the job. I'll even go along. I have business with a couple of them boys elected from Deer Lodge anyway. What do you say?" Putting one end of the string between his teeth and grasping the other in his right hand, he pulled it snug.

It would be madness to travel with Fitch. "My answer is still the same. I cannot go. Besides, if someone goes running off to Bannack before His Honor renders a decision, and if he rules for the Common Law, it would be a wasted trip.

Let's wait until he rules. Then we can decide what to do."
He held the remains of his drink to his lips. Instead of the
smooth aroma of wind-swept hills and burning peat, he
smelled the stench of death.

The ghost shimmered in its corner.

I do not believe in ghosts.

Dan swallowed the whiskey; the astringent taste seared
his insides all the way down.

"Don't give us that," Fitch said. "You're the best one for
the job, even if you are a Yankee lawyer. You talk the legal
language."

"No. You'll have to get someone else. My dear wife's
health is too precarious to permit my absence." He set the
empty glass on the table and stood up, bringing the others
to their feet with him.

Hershfield said, "Keep in it mind, though. I honestly
don't know who else we might find for this."

"Trust a banker," Fitch said. "Hershfield's right. There
isn't anybody else. Nobody I'd put any dust on."

"No." Dan fired the single word at Fitch. "I cannot do
it, and you know my reasons."

A sullen cast came into Fitch's eyes. He yanked the
string on the black cover and swore when it broke.

From a thousand poker games starting with Father
teaching him to play from age three, Dan had read tells,
and now he read those that Fitch could not control, perhaps did not know he had: an eyelid drooped, his tongue
found a corner of his mouth. He gulped the last of his

drink as if the good whiskey were pig swill. When he set the glass down, his mask was in place.

They all wanted him to talk to the legislators, but Fitch had a special reason.

Jacob said, "I am weary, Daniel. You would walk home with me, yah?"

"Of course, Jacob, I'd be happy to do that."

Hershfield added some kind words to Jacob that Dan hardly heard as he helped Jacob into his coat.

All the way to down Jackson, Dan thought about Fitch's tells. Had he been wrong about them? He added them up, found the sum greater than each of them taken separately. Together, they meant that Fitch had a reason for Dan traveling with him to Bannack, and that hidden reason, whatever it might be, was extremely important, perhaps crucial.

And secret.

But why? Much as Dan felt certain that Fitch murdered McDowell, it could not be true. Fitch had ridden north with the others, hunting and hanging road agents.

Then why was the Southerner so furious at his refusal that he could not hide it? What lay behind his demand? How could he find out except by going along?

When Jacob invited him in to warm up, Dan declined. "I'll come down to see you soon, but now I have work to do."

"Yah," Jacob said. "Much work about Fitch."

"Do you read minds? I'll talk to you about it when I've sorted it out."

"Bah. Nothing to sort out. Tobias Fitch, he does not want your good."

~~39~~

"Mama!" Dotty's shout through the door of her room shattered the morning's peace. "Tell this girl she can't wear my blue gingham dress. She's a liar. She says you gave it to her."

Martha glanced at Dan'l, sitting ready for his breakfast of flapjacks and bacon. He shook his head just a bit, signaling: this was all her business, not his. Setting the bowl of batter on the table, she went to take care of the argument. Inside the girls' room, she closed the door, leaving Dan'l to sit by himself at the table.

Dotty stood at the foot of the bed, dressed for school, hands on her hips, her chin up, her face flushed and triumphant. Like she was saying, My mama will show you now.

Wearing only her shift, drawers, and stockings, Eileen huddled on her trundle bed, knees drawn up, the blue gingham dress clutched in her fists.

"I did give it to her. Eileen is telling the truth."

"You gave it to her? But it's mine!" Dotty's mouth twisted, and splotches of color painted her cheeks. "You had no call to give away what's mine. No call." Her voice rose. "It's mine. Mine. What's mine, you can't be givin' away without you ask me. You can't!"

The baby kicked. Martha let out a "Whoof!" Then, thinking she heard metal scrape against metal out in the big room, she listened, distracted: Was Dan'l cooking his own breakfast?

"Mama!" shouted Dotty. "Are you all right?"

Quick hard steps hurried toward them, and Dan'l, not bothering to knock or nothing, flung open the door, put his arms around her, and held her. His voice rumbled, but Martha couldn't hear over the noises in her own head, and she couldn't see his face, but a change came over Dotty. The child's eyes filled, her lower lip trembled, the red spots vanished from her cheeks.

When he began to walk Martha away, she had her wits about her once more, and stiffened against him. He said, "You must sit down."

"No. Wait. I have to say this." A couple deep breaths, and she had her thoughts in order. "Dorothy." The child's alarm reminded her of a deer before the rifle fired. She seldom used that name, except before a scolding. "You're right. I shouldn't be givin' away what ain't mine without I ask you first."

Triumph raised Dotty's chin; she gloated over Eileen. The poor mite was scared by the row, scared she'd have to give up the dress she'd been so happy to have. Shame on Dotty for bringing this on them all.

"You can give it to her, though. You can't wear it no more. You've growed out of it. If Eileen don't wear it, it goes in the rag bag and we'll use it to scrub with."

She could not decipher the expressions passing over Dotty's face. What did her own face show? Leaning against Dan'l, she feared something had broke between her and the child, and maybe she couldn't get it back. They could not go on as before, but she couldn't see ahead of Dotty's choice to what it would be like between them. Or what this would do to Eileen, who must be getting mighty cold in nothing but her – dear Lord, what would she think of Dan'l being in here and seeing her like this?

"You can keep the dress, Eileen," Dotty said. "I don't want the old thing."

With that, it was like a wall come down. She smelled something burning out in the big room. Dotty rushed out, Martha as close behind as Dan'l's arm allowed. "I'm all right," she snapped. "Leave me be." He stood back, but the way he watched her made her so all-fired nervous, she wanted to scream. Dotty tossed the blackened flapjacks into the slop bucket. Martha snatched the coffee pot and would have poured out the boiling coffee, except she had to sit down all of a sudden. The pot fell to the floor, Dotty springing away from the scalding liquid.

Dan'l scooped her up and carried her into the bedroom, laid her on the bed, and covered her up with the quilts. His kiss brushed her lips, and then he was gone. Through the shut door, she heard the rumble of him talking to the girls. He said 'Dorothy,' and bit off his words, but spoke soft and pleasant to Eileen. The baritone sounds soothed her, and she was warm under the eiderdown quilt. She felt her strength gathering, and peace settling around her. Dan'l was near. She'd rest a little, and then get up and tend to things. Just a bit of rest, and she'd be good as new.

~~~

Sometime later, needing to go outside, she awoke, and lay for a moment collecting her wits. When she remembered how the morning had begun, she threw off the quilts and put her feet over the side of the bed. The very idea, she scolded herself, lollygagging here in bed while there was work to be done. She opened the door, and what she saw made her gasp.

The big room was neat as a pin. Dishes had been washed and put away, the slop pail was emptied, and the frying pan, the coffee pot, and the stove glowed.

Wearing the old dress she'd brought with her, Eileen on hands and knees scrubbed at the braided rug where Dan'l and Timmy had laid Jacob Himmelfarb after those horrid boys knocked him about. That blood stain was more'n a week old, and they hadn't been able to get it out, probably wouldn't come out now. Had the young'un been working so hard all this time? The grandmother clock on its shelf said nearly noon.

"Child," she said, "leave that, please, and come help me to the necessary."

Eileen jumped, like she hadn't heard the door open over the sound of the scrub brush on the rug. Setting the brush in the bucket, she rocked to her feet. Shuffling toward Martha, her red, swollen eyes and down-dragged mouth made her the spitting image of someone expecting to be thrashed for no good reason.

The baby rolled and kicked. The need for relief became urgent. "We best hurry, dearie."

"You should use the chamber pot, Ma'am," said Eileen. "Mister said so."

"No. I want to go outside, breathe some fresh air."

Eileen helped Martha with her boots and coat. When they were both dressed for the cold, they set off down the path to the little house, where they brushed the snow off the three-hole platform. Eileen helped her with her clothes. As they perched there in the smelly cold, Eileen asked, "Missus, why do you call it the 'necessary'?"

"On account it's a politer word. Mr. Stark, he was raised different from me. His people have money, and education, and they mix with polite folks. He says 'necessary,' so I say it, too."

Telling Eileen that, Martha had to giggle. "Ain't that just the silliest thing? Calling it a politeness can't cover up this." She waved her hand around at all of it – the cold air between the wall boards and on her hinder parts, the rough gloom, the smell.

There in the cold semi-darkness, they could hardly tidy themselves for laughing. They hurried back to the house, where lamplight glowing behind a curtain welcomed them. Martha made her special sage tea, and while it steeped she sat at the table to wait for it. Eileen hovered about, bringing down cups for them as Martha asked her to do, wiping specks from the spotless table, polishing the oven handle.

"Say what's on your mind, dearie," Martha said. Not getting an answer, she added, "You're making me nervous with all that fussing." Patted the chair next to her. "Sit you down and tell me what you're bothered about. Is it Dotty?"

"No, Ma'am. Thank you. Between you and the Mister, I think that's settled." Eileen perched on the chair, all aquiver, ready to fly.

"Then why aren't you wearing the dress?"

"I can't wear that to scrub floors in. I'm saving it for special."

Martha took that in and set it aside to think on later. A dress ready for the ragbag after it had been nearly worn out, and she saved it for special? "Then what is it?"

The quivering turned into shaking, whatever bothered her was like to rattle her bones. Stammering, halting between words, whispering like she confessed a great sin, she said, "How – how long do I stay with y'all, Missus? Once the baby comes and – and you're strong again, what happens to me? D – do I go back to Miss Troy?" Having said so much, she burst out and she blurted the rest: "I can't earn my keep thataway. And that Jacky Stevens – he's always about."

The poor child. Martha took Eileen's cold hands in her own. She wanted to say, yes, you can stay here as long as you want, but how could she promise anything Dan'l hadn't said yes to? Eileen needed to know now, not after she had got Dan'l's permission, but did she dare make promises she didn't know they could afford – did Dan'l have enough dust to keep her as long as need be? Yet she shouldn't have to ever go back to Fancy Annie's or any place like it ever again. Opening her mouth to make the promise to Eileen, she had a sudden thought that almost stopped her – What if Dan'l said No anyways? Breathing a small prayer that it would be all right, she plunged.

"I been thinking after the baby comes there'll still be work for you here. Mr. Stark, he's said he'll build us a bigger house. That means more work, and a baby takes a deal of caring for. What with the baby and the bigger house, I'll need plenty of help."

"Then I wouldn't have to be on my own again? I'd be safe from – him?"

"As safe as we can do for you."

Eileen, burst into tears, with great sobs that made her whole frame shudder. Martha, rubbing the girl's back and murmuring wordless, soothing sounds, could only hope they could keep her safe enough.

~~40~~

Probate Court occupied the one-room log cabin where the McDowell family had lived. It could not hold so many people with claims against Slade's estate, so Dan and Helen Troy waited outdoors. Singly, they walked up to Van Buren street and back, one of them always staying behind in case her turn came. Moisture from their breathing condensed and froze on their scarves. When at last they could wait inside, Dan did not have room enough to lean away from the pressure of her breast against his upper arm. Even though he could not see much of it, he recalled it as it had been when he first knew the McDowells. The judge now sat where the bed had stood when he thought Martha would die. On the wall behind the claimants, she had cooked the boarders' meals kneeling at a low stove. They'd had no glass in the one window; Martha had covered it with oiled newspaper she had brought from God-knows-where.

He took shallow breaths in the close fug of unwashed bodies and Miss Troy's noxious perfume. By the time the judge awarded their claim and dismissed them, his head swam.

Maneuvering them both into the cold air, grateful to be upwind from her, he took a deep breath and said, "I wish I could have achieved a better result for you."

"It could've been worse. When it comes to handing out justice, women like me rank down at the bottom of the list." She hefted the poke of gold dust measured out to her by the probate clerk. "Fifty dollars ain't nothing to sneeze at." She cocked her head, endangering the discouraged plumes. "Maybe I'll buy me a warm coat."

He hung back to let her go ahead. She crossed Idaho and turned downhill on Jackson. Despite the slippery going she stepped along with more bounce and swing in her skirts than most people considered proper. Then again, Dan reminded himself, she was not a proper woman.

"Ain't that just like a whore," said another attorney. His Deep South accents lengthened his vowels. "You didn't even get a thank you, after you persuaded the judge to award her a small fortune."

"How did your client fare?" Dan raised his coat collar around the back of his neck. This was no weather to stand around in idle talk.

"Didn't get even a sniff." His eyes changed focus to see something farther down Idaho. "What's his hurry?"

A young man, another of the Southern lawyers, trotted up Idaho, skipping over the treacherous rough ice underfoot. As he came closer, he shouted, "It's the Idaho Statutes. His Honor has ruled for the Idaho Statutes."

"Christ," said another lawyer. "He's gone and done it now. We'll have to pay that damn tax."

"If you can't afford ten bucks a year," someone said with a laugh, "you're not much shakes as a lawyer."

The complaints mumbling in his ears, Dan joined a group walking down Jackson to the Champion Saloon. For a few steps they talked among themselves, each word carrying a little puff of breath.

One of them said, "Stark, what do you think? What can we do about this?"

"It's a travesty," someone said.

Dan said, "Until the legislature passes a law saying otherwise, there is nothing we can do. We act under Idaho law until a Montana law overrules it."

"Damn! That means we have to pay the ten dollars. That's more'n three days' pay for a skilled worker."

~~~

He'd intended to go into the saloon for a drink, to think things over, but if he did, he'd have to listen to the others complain. Breaking off from them with a wave, he ran up the stairs to his office.

Cramped as it was, the office was warm, and he had room to pace, eight steps front door to back door, ten steps side wall to wall. He seized a stick, opened his penknife, and whittled while he walked.

Assembling his problem as he would in mathematics, he constructed propositions in the form of questions.

Could Fitch realistically have murdered McDowell? Considering that he had ridden with the posse on the fifteenth of January, at least a day before McDowell left the Fancy Annie's, it was impossible. The last known sighting of McDowell was by Jacky Stevens on the sixteenth.

Despite his growing inner certainty, there was no way around that fundamental law of physics. Fitch could not be on the other side of the Divide and in Daylight Gulch murdering McDowell.

All right then. Put that aside. Was there any way to safeguard the Nugget, and therefore the family's future, without traveling to Bannack and convincing the legislators to vote for the thousand feet of ground? And why did Fitch so badly want him to go?

Granted, the legislature must give quartz mines a thousand feet of ground. To have enough space to work, but also – halting in the middle of the floor – to prevent someone, yes, why had he not thought of this? Someone could file claims on either side, thereby limiting available ground to a hundred feet. Then force the owner to sell, on the grounds that the claim would be almost useless without more ground. Not during the winter hiatus, of course, but after May first.

A cluster of wooden curls had gathered at an end of the stick. Walking again, he broke them off one by one, as his mind followed trails of its own, without his prompting.

Fitch had not filed adjacent claims because Fairweather District rules, from the beginning, had limited to two the number of claims a man could own. He wanted the Nugget. If he filed adjacent claims on either side, when it came into his possession – God forbid – he would have three claims, which was against the rules. He could not sell one before he acquired the Nugget. He was trapped. He had to have the Nugget before any adjacent claims were filed.

Would he have killed McDowell to get it? Maybe, except that it was physically impossible.

Dan stopped. He had broken off the wooden curls along the trail of his pacing. Those tells. What did they mean?

Jacob had said it: Fitch meant him no good. Never had. Never would.

For answers, he would go to Bannack. With Fitch. And watch his back.

~~41~~

From inside the house Timothy's deep bass shut off the dog's warning bark. Damn. Martha was not alone. As Dan stomped snow off his boots, the door opened, and Tim, half crouched to hold the dog back, blocked it.

"Hello, Timothy." He tried a smile, received none in return.

Swinging the door just wide enough, Timothy stepped back. "Didn't expect to see you home so early."

He felt he had walked by mistake onto a stage in the midst of a tableau: Martha's fingers lifted off the dulcimer, Timothy restrained the dog, Eileen held the flat iron over one of his shirts. Music faded into the air, and the sharp odor of sage tea was strong in the air.

"Don't let me interrupt." He spoke over his shoulder as he hung up his coat. "I had some time so I thought I'd come home." A smile for Martha who warmed him with the smile she kept for him, that began with a kissing motion of her lips.

The tableau broke.

Martha began to explain. "I was just playing my dulci-mer."

Timothy interrupted her. "Go on, Mam. You don't have to stop."

"Yes, don't stop on my account," said Dan. He would not pick up that particular gauntlet, make Martha stop her music. Other men might, but he would choose the skir-mish to fight in this war with Timothy. He had to fight a more important battle. To make them both understand why he had to leave again, to go to Bannack.

Martha's fingers descended onto the instrument.

He sat on the bench to remove his boots while the mu-sic bounded around him. As he bent over and tugged at the frozen knots in his bootlaces, Canary wriggled over to him and licked his face. Laughing, he pushed the dog away. "Get along with you." All the time he thought about why Timothy was here. Had mother and son made up? How did she expect him to treat Timothy now? She was the forgiving sort, but he had meant what he said. Timo-thy should never have forced her to choose between the two of them. He did not deserve forgiveness.

Yet Timothy would bear the brunt of protecting the three females, and Jacob, while he went to Bannack. He deserved to know what was in the wind, but first he had to speak to Martha alone. It would be cowardly to broach this while the young people were there. It would frighten Eileen, and upset Martha to have the two of them slinging words at each other.

How to separate Martha from the other two? What errand could he invent for both Eileen and Tim, seeing that he had just come in? What could he have forgotten?

He slid his boots off, put on his house shoes and his sack coat, and sat in his reading chair. Tim sat at the big table closer to Eileen than to his mother.

Eyes closed, Martha bowed over the instrument, pouring out music in a waterfall of sound, lost in a world of her own making. He thought she would have played like this even if no one heard her. After a minute or two, he realized that he listened, and this music was not as strange to him as it had been. Perhaps he was becoming used to it.

Waiting for the music to end, so as not to stare at her, he studied the guns on the gun rack. The long guns, the shotgun and his rifle, lay crosswise on their pegs: the Colt Army revolver hung in its holsters. The pocket pistol lay on a shelf. Of course. The rifle. He would send them out to buy lead and black powder so he could make more ammunition.

He leaned his elbows on his knees, thought about what he would say. How would she react?

The music ended on a satisfying resolution of a chord, and Martha sat straight and folded her hands over her stomach. He rose and applauded her, as Timothy and Eileen clapped their hands. Eileen's face lifted from wary and mouse-scared among a family of cats to joy as she laughed out loud for the first time since Dan had known her. Had she never heard music played for the pure love of it? Dan thought not. In the world she came from, music made money. The saloons and dance halls made it a prelude to sensual pleasure. Martha had shown the girl a different world, and it must be as strange to her as a fourth dimension.

By Timothy's expression of wonder, he saw that he would have no great difficulty sending them out together. Gazing at Eileen, the boy was thunderstruck, as if discovering an angel unexpected.

Dan sighed. He would have to break this up.

The time was now.

When Martha had put the dulcimer back in its box, and Eileen set the iron on the stove to heat, Dan spoke. "Timothy, I wonder if you and Eileen would mind running an errand for me. And while you're at it, there's a new chocolate shop on Van Buren." He smiled at Martha. "I think she deserves a treat for all her hard work don't you?"

What could Martha say to that but, "Yes"?

~~~

When the youngsters had left, Dan brought Martha a cup of sage tea, and one for himself. He wished he had something stronger to fortify himself against Martha's certain dislike of what he would say. He wished he could find an easy way to say it, but there was none. He could only run at it and leap. A safe landing was not guaranteed.

"I have news."

She did not answer him straightaway, but set the cup on the trivet by her Bible and laid the dulcimer in its box.

"I knew it. You didn't come home in the middle of the day just to be with us."

Her tone warned him. Hoping for the best landing, he started as far back as he could. "Justice Hosmer ruled on the Idaho statutes today."

Martha peered at him over the edge of her cup. "What on earth does that mean?"

He explained, drawing it out with an explanation of the Common law of England, while he tracked her reactions, and the pungent smell of the tea worried at his nose.

When he finished, she said, "If I have this right, the Nugget claim needs more ground for the workings, a stamp mill and such. If we buy our own stamps rather than taking the ore to another mill."

"No matter what," he said, correcting her, "we need more ground than a hundred feet." He opened his mouth to go to the next step, but she was ahead of him.

"That means the legislature has to pass a mining law that gives quartz claims enough ground for the workin's?"

"Exactly." What a woman she was. She understood the situation better on the first telling than many men directly involved in it. No matter that she dropped most of her g's, and her newly-won correct grammar sometimes failed her, this uneducated hill woman had a sharp mind. If she'd been a man she could have done anything in life that she set herself to. Like President Lincoln.

Her quick understanding, though, had brought him to the point before he was ready.

Even as he launched himself over the hurdle, he knew he had misjudged the take-off. "Jacob, Lewis Hershfield, and one or two others want me to help persuade the legislators that giving quartz claims more ground will benefit everyone."

Her hand holding the cup trembled. Using both hands, she set it on the table without spilling a drop. "That means traveling over to Bannack, don't it?"

"Yes." He wanted to hold his breath. Women in her condition were often plagued with eruptions of feeling, he reminded himself, remembering Mother when she carried his younger brothers and sister. He braced for it.

"You cain't jus' up 'n' leave us here, with that Jacky Stevens prowlin' about."

Anger and perhaps a little fear brought her accent out in full. He waited. She clearly was not finished with him. Her dark eyes smoldered, and her crossed arms rose and fell with her quickening breath. She was a volcano about to explode, while he held her gaze and waited for the eruption. All he could hope for was to come out of this unscorched, but he had made this decision for her and the youngsters. All of them, the living and the unborn.

What if he were disgraced, or tried for such a dastardly murder as stabbing a man in the back? Where would they be then? He would travel to Bannack with Fitch to make sure they – and he – were immune from Fitch's plot to take the Nugget, whatever he had in mind.

She nearly shouted. "How can you be so hardhearted?" Her fist banged the arm table. "How can you go off and leave us?"

Growling, Canary struggled to his feet; hackles rose on his spine.

Her fury rained down on him. She accused him of the worst kind of selfishness, of always looking out for himself first, of deserting them when they needed him most.

"You saw that woman in New York, didn't you? You did. I saw you looking at her picture. You keep it hid, but I found it in the summer. Do you think she's better'n what I am on account she's blonde and beautiful, and I'm fat and ugly? I'm a no-'count backwoods quarter-breed, with no book learnin', and she's your kind, ain't she, and can have her likeness taken, and I ain't never had no likeness taken, but you never wanted one of me, did you, to take back to New York? Now you're heading off to Bannack on account it's business. You won't even be home for the Lord's birthday. Why's it you can't put us first?"

She broke down and sobbed, her fists pummeled the arms of her chair, and tears streamed down her cheeks, soaked her bodice. Aghast at the wreckage he had made, at first he could not move. After a moment, he went to her, put his arms around her shoulders and held her. She fought him, screamed at him to let her go, let her be, go away. She tried to free her arms to flail at him, but strong as she was, he was far stronger, and he held her fast. He felt if he released her she might hurt herself and the baby, so he held on, murmured the only words he could think of, hoping they might break through her hysteria: "I love you. I love you. I love you."

At last, exhausted, she stopped fighting him and sank back in the chair. He held her until she seemed calmer, though she covered her face with her hands while tears leaked between her fingers.

When her sobs had dwindled away, he went to the wash stand, dipped out clean water into the wash basin, and soaked a cloth in it, cold as it was. He wrung it out and carried it to her with a clean face towel. Willing his hand to be steady, he wiped her face. All the while, she sat quietly, her passion spent, and let him care for her, whether from exhaustion or a better cause he did not know.

Before he was ready, Timothy and Eileen came through the door with Dotty, her arms full of school books. A glance at his own and Martha's faces apparently told them something dire had happened. Without changing her boots, Dotty dropped her books on the bench and ran to her mother. "Mama! What happened? Are you all right?"

Eileen cowered on the bench beside the door.

Timothy pulled off his outdoor boots and hurried over to stand uncomfortably close to Dan. "What did you do to her? What did you do?" Dan straightened, braced himself for the first blow, if he could not calm the boy.

"Judge Hosmer ruled for the Idaho Statutes this morning."

"What? He did it?"

"Yes. He did it."

"But why?"

"Oh, why bother with some old judge?" shouted Dotty. "You've upset Mama."

"I broke the news to her that I must travel to Bannack in the next few days to talk to our representatives about the mining law we need." How would Timothy react? Last week he had understood the legal problem, had thought Dan should do as Jacob and Hershfield – and God help him, Fitch – wanted, but he was capricious, apt to go off for reasons only he knew. Had he changed his mind? If he had – Dan pushed the thought away.

"You can't do that!" Dotty sprang to her feet, swung around to Dan. "How can you go and leave us alone? You're always haring off someplace, and we don't know when you'll come back or if you're dead or what's become of you." She screeched, "And now you're leaving us at the mercy of that horrible – that awful —" She bit her lip.

Her brother said, "Hush your mouth. You ain't no baby, takin' on so."

"How can you —"

"Enough!" Dan roared.

Four mouths rounded, four pairs of wide eyes stared at him as though he had fired the rifle in the house. Dorothy choked, and her unshed tears dried.

Timothy took a step backward, and on the bench Eileen tried to sink into the wall.

Dan said, "Dorothy, go and take off your wraps. You can clean up the mess your boots have made on the rug and on the floor. Your mother didn't braid that rug for you to ruin it."

"Oh, Mama, I'm sorry," Dotty said. She might have said more, but Dan looked at her in way that closed her mouth. Her face was pale as she removed her boots and carried them to the bench where she sat beside Eileen.

Easy for you, sneered a voice in Dan's mind. You can bully a child into obedience, just like Grandfather taught you.

The silence hung around them all. What did they expect? That he would act like Sam McDowell and use his fists? He said quietly, looking at Martha, "I have to do this. It's to safeguard your future, and the children's futures." As he took a breath to say more, Timothy interrupted him.

"Dan'l is right, Mam. He's got to go make sure the fool legislature don't pass a law that makes the Nugget claim useless on account there ain't room to work it." He wiped the back of his hand across his forehead, where sweat gathered.

Dan let him talk to her while the girls helped each other out of their wraps. Eileen crept to the big table and sat down, while Dotty moved closer to her mother. A big-boned girl and tall for her age, she would come into beauty early, who faced him without fear. She would be a formidable opponent for any man, Dan thought, when she got her growth.

Holding her mother's hand, she demanded, "Is this right?"

On purpose, at his driest, most lawyer-like, he explained again the Idaho laws, and finished, "We have to safeguard quartz mining in this Territory from having the Idaho Statutes forced on us."

Dotty said, "But what about that horrid, that – boy?"

From behind him, he heard a squeak. Eileen. He felt her terror as a wave in the air. And Dotty could not bring herself to speak Jacky Stevens's name.

"I can protect all of you," Timothy said. He stood slightly behind Dan's shoulder. "I done it before, remember, Mam? When they come huntin' deserters? Mam, you and me, we run 'em off, didn't we?"

"You'll have help," Dan said. "I'll speak to Beidler, and Hershfield will organize something." Albert. The name came into his mind. Would Albert be able to keep watch, too? He would go tomorrow and ask.

"I must make the trip," he said. "I don't want to. I hate leaving you in your current state of health more than anything. But I have to do this." Timothy nodded, and Dan continued, thinking how strange it felt to have the boy allied with him again. He said, "With Tim and our friends, you won't be unprotected."

Martha shook her head, a slow movement that tore at Dan's heart, it was so final. She had rendered a judgment against him. "You're leavin' me again. You're leavin' me."

~~42~~

While Dan had been with the family, a fog reeking of ashes and smoke from thousands of wood stoves descended on the town, and the mid-afternoon light dropped toward dusk, leaving everyone moving through a murky twilight. The air surrounded him like a curtain he must push through. Two men hurried by, talking; the fog muffled their voices, blurred their words into a mumble. As he walked uphill toward the Planters House to find Fitch, an unholy shriek of iron brake on iron tire over the clash of horseshoes forewarned him. Heavy horses loomed up heading downhill; the driver stood on the brake to keep the wagon from pressing on the wheel horses' tails.

When he neared the Planters House, a small man's vague shape emerged and walked toward him. Beidler. He waited until the deputy came up to him. "I have to talk to you."

"I hear there's a ruckus in Con's place. You know anything about that?"

"Not really, but I expect some lawyers are upset about Judge Hosmer's ruling."

"And you? You like it?" X kept walking.

Dan walked a few steps downhill with him. "No. I think he's wrong, but that's not what I wanted to tell you. I'm off to Bannack in a few days. With me gone, the family will need an extra watch on Jacky Stevens. Timothy will try to protect them, but he's already looking after Jacob."

X's floppy hat brim hid his face. He said nothing but forged ahead.

Dan stopped walking a few yards beyond his house and called after him. "Well?"

X walked on, fading into the fog, becoming a stocky shadow carrying a shotgun in the crook of his elbow. His voice trailed back to Dan, "Yeah. They'll be all right."

Dan retraced his steps uphill. X called after him: "You coming back?"

"Yes," he shouted. "Of course I'm coming back. My life is here."

Walking on, his anger keeping the cold at bay, he swore under his breath. The damned son of a bitch. Demand his intentions like that on a public street. Did X think he might be fleeing the scene of his crime? Did Martha think that? Or did she think he was a foul despoiler of women who would take her and desert her, seeing as how she'd lost her shape?

Women. There was no accounting for them.

"Ho, there. Stark?" A man bellowed from across the street, in front of the Champion Saloon. It could only be

Fitch – his carrying drawl, his silhouette with its uneven arms and the battered hat that rode the tilt of his head. "Hold up! I'm coming over."

Fitch strode across the street, seeming not to mind where he walked. "You're the man I've been looking for." As he stepped onto the board walk, he asked as softly as distant thunder. "Have you decided?"

"Yes," Dan said. "I'll be ready to leave by Thursday."

"Why not tomorrow?"

He would not be rushed. He would move at his own pace, not Fitch's, to have more time to reconcile Martha, if she would be reconciled. "I have arrangements to make." To ensure their safety. "What's the rush?"

"Why the delay?" Fitch's grumbling was the complaint of a man with no one's convenience to consider but his own.

Dan ignored him. "How's your son doing?"

"What? What? Oh. The boy." Fitch looked about. Did he expect to find the infant close by? "He's fine, I suppose. I'd have heard if he wasn't. Sooner we leave, sooner we return."

"I can't be ready before Thursday."

"Oh. Well. But we've no time to waste." He raised his stump. "Don't say it. I'll meet you at the Overland office on Thursday." With that, he wheeled around, peered up and down the hill. He stepped off the boardwalk, and the fog swallowed him before he had gone ten feet.

Shoulders hunched against the cold seeping through his clothes and his boots, Dan still felt unsteady, and there was a bitter taste in his mouth. His heart thudded as though to escape a tightness in his chest. Why was Fitch in such a hurry? The legislative session was sixty days, and according to the *Post*, they had wasted the first few days in wrangling about the loyalty oath.

Boots crunched over the rough ice behind him. "You're traveling to Bannack with Fitch?" Timothy's indignant cry roused Dan.

"Yes. I shall travel with Fitch. Keep your voice down. The whole town will hear?"

Timothy paid no attention. "Why? Why with him of all people? He ain't never been a friend of yours, or ours. He's after Pap's claims."

"It's too cold to stand here." Taking Timothy's elbow, he turned him downhill. As they walked, he debated with himself how much to say about his plan. He said, "Can you think of a better way to keep an eye on him?"

"You're nuts."

"Perhaps, but there's a saying: 'Keep your friends close and your enemies closer.'"

After a few steps, the boy asked, "Where are you bound for?"

"I've been making sure people watch out for Jacky. I've spoken to Beidler, who said he'll keep an eye out for him." Giving Timothy no chance to protest, he said, "Constant protection is more than one man can handle. I'm on my to call on Mrs. Hudson. Albert might look in on Jacob to give you more time to be with your mother."

"Jake's getting on right well, but I'll ask Miz Hudson."

"All right. Then you'll free me to take care of some other business." Christmas. He had shopping to do.

In full dark Dan negotiated the boardwalks along Van Buren, Wallace, and Jackson. Even in daylight he would have walked blind, loaded as his arms were with packages wrapped in brown paper printed with young fir trees and jolly men in red snowsuits. Doubt laced his satisfaction when he thought of his purchases. Would Martha approve of his presents for Eileen and Dotty? No matter, he told himself. Timothy could not be everywhere at once, and they needed protection. All in all, he thought he had done well for everyone.

At the path to his front door, he stopped. He would not be home on Sunday to see their faces when they opened their gifts.

Why in God's name had he decided to gamble everything – his life and their future – on a feeling? If it went wrong, he might never see his child.

Canary barked.

Squaring his shoulders, he walked down the path and went into the house.

Part III

~~43~~

BANNACK

If hell froze over, it wouldn't be this cold.

At every stage stop, Dan, Fitch, and the other passengers warmed themselves around the stove where the usual peculiar stew simmered over the fire. Much too soon, the driver would announce another bone-bruising leg of the journey. Or call them out to shovel through drifts.

"Overland advertisements are a joke." Fitch was a blanket-wrapped mound sitting next to him. "Virginia to Bannack in nine hours. I ask you."

"Tell that to the Almighty," another passenger said. "Maybe He'll warm this place up about seventy degrees. Get it above freezing."

Saying nothing, Dan huddled into his own Hudson's Bay blanket. The broad bright stripes did nothing to cheer him up. When they arrived in Bannack five hours late, he felt like Frankenstein's monster gone too long without oil. His joints were so stiff he expected them to squeak.

Bannack's population had shrunk since the gold strikes in Alder Gulch, but with the legislature about to meet, it "perked up" as Fitch put it. Men hurried along the boardwalks and crowded the saloons and restaurants. At Chrisman's store they asked about rooms. "Hell, boys." Chrisman's deep Southern accent rolled over them. "Every room and every bed in town is taken. Two or three times. If you want, you can roll your blankets back there, next to Plummer's old desk."

Beggars can't be choosers, Dan said to himself as he folded his blankets in half and laid them out. Despite the cold, he almost wished he had ridden over. He could have used the saddle as a pillow.

"Do you know where we can find Councilman Charles Bagg?"

"Let's see, now. Today's session adjourned an hour ago, so you'll probably find him and some others in the Gold Rush Saloon, what used to be Skinner's, you know. The Council members go there, and the House members mainly go to Blackie's." Chrisman paused, looked at the rifle slung on Dan's shoulder. "There's an ordinance against carrying firearms in town." He held out his hand. "You can leave that with me. No one will touch it."

Dan held onto the rifle. Ordinance or no ordinance, a Spencer repeating rifle was too rare and expensive a firearm to let out of his sight. He had not seen another like it in all his travels, and he would be lost without it.

Chrisman nodded, though Dan had said nothing. "Don't worry. I'll take good care of it."

"You can't be here all the time."

Chrisman said, "I'll have the boy watch it, then." Meaning his slave, also called George.

Dan would not have the black man lose sleep on his account. He gave the weapon to Chrisman, who laid it on the bottom shelf against the wall, then stacked cans of beans in front of it. "I guess that's as good a place as any."

~~~

Outside, Fitch said, "I have to see a man about a horse. You'll be at Skinner's?"

"I'll be there unless I have to track Bagg down."

Except in its clientele the Gold Rush had not changed from when Cy Skinner owned it. The rough bunch had used it as a sort of ruffians' club, a place to drink poisonous liquor and boast about their crimes. When bragging had not been enough, Skinner and a few others went out the back door one afternoon and shot at a family of Bannack Indians camped just up the hill. Among the dead had been an infant.

Looking around for Bagg, Dan said to himself, they would trouble no one again; the Vigilantes had hanged them last January up around Hell Gate. Fitch's alibi.

Bagg stood midway down the bar, his back to Dan, while a red-faced man, whose lower jaw moved sideways as he talked, jabbed a forefinger at him.

At the bar, Dan ordered a beer, and when he had it, he gulped down half of it. Edging close to Bagg, he bumped him as though by accident.

Turning to see who had jostled him, Bagg's frown changed to a smile. "Ah, Stark. I'll just be a minute." With a promise to do what he could for the red-faced man's cause, he excused himself. "You look about done in. A hellish trip, I assume?"

"We got here. Thank God it was no worse."

A cadaverous man wearing a flat-brimmed black hat approached them to demand Bagg's help in passing a law to enforce better observance of the Lord's Day. Bagg said, "I'll give your bill due consideration when it comes up in session." He tilted his head toward Dan. "Now I have to confer with this gentleman about Council Bill Twenty-two."

The fellow was too caught up in his own cause to hear Bagg. "The Lord's Day is barely observed in these parts. There's drinkin' and gamblin' and, and whorin' on the Sabbath, and it oughta stop."

"Human nature being what it is," Dan said, "you can't legislate morality. People won't behave better merely because you pass a law. They'll just sin in secret."

"Make 'em come into a church and something will rub off," he insisted.

Bagg's remained cordial. "As I said, if such a bill is introduced I'll give it due consideration. That's all I can say. Now, if you'll excuse us...." They moved to the far end of the bar away from the door, where Bagg ordered two shots of whiskey.

When the drinks came, Dan said, "Put your money away. This one's on me."

"No, I can't accept that. Someone watches our every move, ready to accuse us of taking bribes, selling out to this or that interest. If you buy the drinks, I'll be accused of being bribed to support a pet bill."

"Beer next, if you please," Dan told the bartender. "I built up a terrible thirst today."

"You want food?" the bartender asked.

"Yes, thanks. The food between here and Virginia City was inedible."

Shaking his head, the bartender went to draw their beers.

"We've drunk better whiskey than this." Bagg made a face at the shot glass. "How are things at home?"

Did he mean Virginia City as a whole, or his own situation? Dan said, "We're all hoping the Territorial capital comes to Virginia."

Before Bagg could respond, a legislator stopped to sound him out about supporting his bill to establish a fund to care for the poor. "It's criminal to have such great wealth here without making life easier for those who didn't have the luck."

Bagg assured him he would do all he could. The man went on his way with a gratified smile.

"What of your own news?" Bagg tipped his beer glass toward Dan. "Thanks."

Another bartender, a young man with pimples all over his face, set their beers down and hurried away with the empty shot glasses.

"There's not much I can tell you. Beidler sees no reason to look at anyone else for McDowell's murderer. He won't abandon his theory, but he can find no evidence for it."

The bartender returned with two plates of roast beef, eggs, and celery. "There's stew in the pot, gentlemen, if you'd like. No charge."

"Bring us two bowls, then." Dan caught the aroma of thyme. Where would a cook get thyme around here?

"I fear you will have to find the killer, truss him up like a turkey, and deliver him to our old friend." Bagg drank a swallow of beer, sucked on the hairs of his mustache to catch any remaining foam. "And the family?"

"My dear wife endures her condition bravely." Martha. How did she fare now? He should be there with her, not here. "I aim to finish my business here soonest and go home."

"If you have come about the quartz law, you may get your wish."

"That's exactly why I'm here. That and the Common Law bill. What's the latest?"

"The quartz bill was introduced this afternoon as Council Bill Twenty-two, and passed its first two readings."

"Already? Quick work." He cocked the beer mug toward Bagg. "Good going."

"Thanks. I thought that would surprise you. Would you like to see a copy?"

"Of course. How do you rate its chances of passage?" Dan's fatigue melted away. Would to God he could shorten his stay and be home before the New Year.

"Excellent, if we can resolve this dispute. Let's find a table and you can read it. I have my copy in my valise. I'll explain the issues that came up today." He nodded toward a group that stood around a table putting on their coats. "They're leaving."

When they had sat down with their food and drinks, Bagg took a sheaf of legal-sized papers from his valise and thumbed through it. "Here we are." He gave Dan a document of several pages, written in pencil. It was folded across its width in four parts with the title and date written on one part along with the bill number: "Relating to the discovery of gold and silver quartz leads, lodes, or ledges and of the manner of their location."

"We call it by its origin and number, Council Bill Twenty-two." Bagg popped a hard-boiled egg in his mouth. "Started in the Council, the twenty-second bill to be introduced in our chamber." From a small valise, he brought out some papers folded in thirds lengthwise. The bill's title and number were written on the front panel.

As Dan unfolded the bill, Bagg spoke around the mouthful of egg. "You want section two."

Section two limited claims to two-hundred feet along the vein, following all its contours and irregularities in the ground, and granted an extra fifty feet along the course of the vein for working.

Finished reading it, Dan said, "That's not nearly enough! We need a thousand feet for the workings."

"I know. That very dispute came up after the second reading this afternoon. We have argued fiercely for more ground, but some of the Councilmen fear that a thousand feet will give discoverers of leads, ledges, and lodes an unfair advantage over adjacent claims."

"Unfair advantage? What about an unfair advantage to the discoverer? Over adjacent claims?" Just what he had been worried about with the Nugget. Maybe Hershfield and Jacob were right to insist he come here. "Mining's a gamble, and hard-rock mining is the biggest gamble of all. Do these ignoramuses stop to think how much it costs to develop a mine?"

The saloon's front door crashed open, but neither man looked to see who came in.

"Calm down," Bagg said. "I tried to tell them we'd be opening the door to unending litigation if we didn't allow more ground to the discoverer, but they were adamant. They wanted to give everyone a fair shake."

Shaking his head, Dan reached for the eggs. "Damn it, veins meander wherever they will." He bit off a piece of egg. "Jacob and Timothy worked damn hard this summer, but they could lose everything if the vein crossed or came close to a vein on one side or another – which it no doubt would in two hundred feet. The owner of that claim could mine it, and they'd be out of luck."

"You're thinking of the McDowell heirs," said Bagg.

"Of course. McDowell was the original discoverer. They should not have to litigate for what is rightfully theirs."

"Doesn't Fitch say that claim is rightfully his?"

"He did until the miners' court awarded it to McDowell's heirs last spring." He looked past Bagg toward the commotion at the front door. "Here he comes."

Bagg hid a frown behind the mug's wide mouth. "Did he travel with you?"

"Yes. He's part of a group I've agreed to represent here. The others are Lewis Hershfield, Jacob, and Timothy for the family."

Tobias Fitch bulled his way through the throng, ignoring the protests in his wake. Melting snow dripped from the wide brim of his stained gray hat. Spotting Dan and Bagg, he changed course toward their table.

"What's this I hear?" Fitch demanded.

"Hello, Fitch. How was the road?" Bagg managed to sound cordial, even friendly, despite what Dan knew to be his deep dislike of the Southerner.

"What do you hear about what?" Dan asked.

"What else? The God-damned quartz law you-all have written. Two hundred feet?" Leaning across the table so his face was inches away from Bagg, he shouted, "You've fucked up mining law just about the way they did in Idaho." Transferred his glare to Dan. "You should've come when I wanted to. We'd have got here in time to stop this!"

"The quartz bill was introduced this afternoon," Dan said, "with a two-hundred-foot width for all quartz claims, but —"

"Jesus Christ!" Fitch banged his left arm down on the table, which rocked toward him. He grabbed for his beer mug; his fingers brushed the handle and toppled it over.

Dan lifted his beer mug and grabbed for the plate of food as Bagg snatched the copy of the bill out of the spreading pool and rescued his own mug.

Beer streamed onto Fitch's coat and cascaded to the floor as he grabbed at the mug and missed.

The bartender hurried to them with a large rag that he used to mop up the mess on the table. Finished, he said, "No harm done, gentlemen. Accidents happen. Can I get you all more of anything?"

"More of everything," said Fitch. "Put it on my tab. Name's Fitch." He fumbled in a pocket and came out with an Eagle that he gave the bartender.

"Yes, sir, right away, sir." The bartender hurried away.

Sitting down again, Dan avoided staring at Fitch's tight lips, the extra shine in his eyes. Fitch was humiliated, he said to himself; that would not have happened if he'd had two good hands.

Glancing around, Dan noticed grim-faced men all around glaring at them. They're waiting for something, he thought. "Apologize," he told Fitch.

"Apologize for what? Some stupid sons of —"

"Don't say it. Not another curse. Apologize for your language. You're among civilized men here." Fitch glowered at him, eyes narrowed, blood surging into his face. "Then, when you've apologized, sit down and listen." Would Fitch do it? Or would he fight? And could he win against Fitch's ruthlessness? He knew what Fitch was capable of, had seen him after they captured wanted men.

Not a word was spoken in the room, no glass chimed against another. Everyone seemed to hold their breath at once.

A cold, invisible presence shivered beyond the small, unsteady flames from candles and lanterns, but he smelled only spirits and beer and cigar smoke.

He held Fitch's gaze until Fitch broke.

"I apologize." His voice creaked, a wheel that needed grease. Rising to his feet, he spoke to the entire room. "I apologize for my language and for going off half-cocked. And I apologize to Dan Stark," a sidelong glance at Charles Bagg, "and Councilman Bagg. The best lawyers in Montana Territory."

"Hear, hear!" someone shouted, a cheer taken up by some of the other saloon patrons as Fitch yanked off his hat and bowed.

Bagg leaned toward Dan, spoke low so Fitch would not hear. "Don't believe a word he says. He's no friend of yours. Or mine. Watch your back."

"I trust him as much as I'd trust thin ice," Dan said. "Now, especially."

"Especially, what?" Sitting down, Fitch had heard the last word.

"Especially well done," Dan said. "That's what. Very handsomely done."

The bartender brought a tray loaded with food and drink. In addition to the beers, the tray held three whiskeys and three bowls of stew. "Food and drink maketh a happy heart, gentlemen." Lowering the tray, he distributed everything. "Can I get you-all anything more?"

"Not just now," Bagg said. "We'll let you know."

Dan slipped him a greenback five-dollar bill, and the man smiled as he put it in his pocket. When he walked away, Fitch said, "I apologize."

"Accepted." The three men touched their glasses together.

As they helped themselves to the food, Bagg said, "The bill sets the size of a quartz claim at two hundred feet along a lead, lode, or ledge. It also gives fifty feet on each side of those for working purposes."

"Before you go off again," said Dan, "I've already told Charles that we need a thousand feet for the workings."

"So how do we get this fixed?" Fitch turned his head toward Bagg.

"It won't be easy. When we adjourned tonight, the vote stood at four to three against amending it, but if we can persuade Milo Farnsworth, the others will follow."

Milo Farnsworth.

They had no light but starlight. Their boots crushed clumps of frozen grass. Rousted, a small animal fled, squeak-

ing. A man sobbed. Someone said: Don't drop him, for Chris-
sake. Another hissed, Shut the hell up before someone hears us.
As they lifted Rawley as high as their strength allowed, Dan
looked up into the sky. He felt someone watched, but all he saw
were stars. More stars than a man could count or even see,
flung out against the brittle black sky.

Bagg was saying, "Milo Farnsworth is the key. If you could persuade him, we'd win. He's not the Council president, but he carries weight."

"What's the sticking point?" asked Fitch.

"Some members insist that more than two hundred feet would be unfair to adjacent claim owners."

"Unfair!" Fitch's spoon clattered into the bowl. "Hell, the discoverer could claim a second claim by right of pre-emption."

'Pre-emption,' Dan knew, meant the owner or the discoverer if he still owned the quartz claim, could claim the additional ground as his by right of being there first, no matter who currently held it, unless the neighbor had been first to claim that particular ground.

"That's precisely why," Bagg said, "another sentence in the bill mandates equal ownership by all claimants when two or more veins are discovered within one hundred feet of each other."

"How much time do we have?" Dan asked. "And where can we find Farnsworth?"

"We will take the bill up again at two o'clock tomorrow afternoon. We've already argued various numbers, but so far the largest anyone will agree to is three hundred feet for the workings, besides the two-hundred feet for the claim and an additional fifty where the vein runs. They won't hear of abandoning the joint ownership clause." Chair legs screeched as he pushed back. "Sorry, I have to leave. I have a meeting about our response to the Federal government. It will probably run long." Pausing with one arm in the sleeve of his overcoat, he said, "I'll try to meet you back here."

"Wait a minute," said Fitch. "How do we find Farnsworth?"

"He lives down near where the Mexican's cabin used to be, but he sometimes comes in here with one or two of his boarders to give his wife and the girl time to tidy up the house after dinner."

"Sounds like all we have to do is wait for him here," said Dan.

"Whaddaya know about that?" Fitch said.

~~44~~

"Hell of a thing." Farnsworth stared into his whiskey.

"Yeah." Dan shuffled his feet, cold amid the drafts on the floor. Leaving him to deal with Farnsworth, Fitch played poker with a group of Secessionists. Now and then laughter burst out among them, followed by silence while they concentrated on their bids.

"Congratulations on your election." Dan lifted his glass in a toast.

Chrisman's store had been shrouded in darkness except for a single candle flame. Tin cans arranged on shelves behind the counter caught the wavering light. The argument had raged among them, Farnsworth siding with Dan.

Inhumane, Dan had said, to hang a man with gangrene so advanced.

Right, Farnsworth had said.

Inhumane, the others countered, to let a man live in certain agony when death was already on its way to take him. Humane to put him out of his misery.

We'd do the same for a horse or a dog. Why not for a man?

It's the sentence, said another.

Dan could not disagree. No one could have foreseen this.

Farnsworth gave in. If we don't show we mean what we say, the roughs will think us weak, and what chance will the new territorial government have to get started? It's like a newborn foal that can hardly stand, and the wolves are circling out there, waiting. We're the only ones strong enough to fight them off.

No one, Dan included, believed then or now that they had hanged all of the men terrorizing the region last winter, or that their friends had given up the revenge they had promised.

"Thanks. Sometimes I wonder why I bothered, though. People can be so damn stubborn."

Dan stifled a snort. From what Bagg had said, Farnsworth himself was something new in stubbornness. "Why is that?"

"Today we voted twice on a new bill to replace the quartz law Idaho put in place. I think we did a damn fine job, but some of the men just aren't satisfied. They want the moon and stars. More ground for workings. We agreed on two hundred and fifty feet, all told, but is that good enough? No. They want a thousand feet."

"I read the bill earlier this evening. It does seem to me that section two creates more problems than it solves." He raised his hand at Farnsworth's protest. "Hear me out.

Please." He knew Farnsworth was a good-humored man, a blacksmith by trade, an excellent farrier, and popular, but slow to grasp new ideas.

"All right." He sat with his arms folded across his chest, his chin down, and looked at Dan from under his heavy brows. "We've already doubled the size of a claim."

"I saw that, but the way the bill is written, I foresee a lot of business coming my way from this bill if it's passed in its current form."

"Ha!" Farnsworth smiled. He had, Dan knew, no love for lawyers, but he respected Dan for having been on the same side about Rawley.

"Of course, I should thank you gentlemen. When you make owners of two claims share ownership of crossing or parallel veins, very shortly one of them will sue the other. Suppose the owner of one claim is the original discoverer, but the owner of the other claim is a second or third owner. How's he going to like it when the discoverer claims his property by right of pre-emption?" Dan sipped his beer and waited for Farnsworth to think about that. Would he have to explain pre-emption or did the smith understand that the discoverer could claim he was entitled the second claim, having been there first?

"So it's like this." The blacksmith unfolded his arms and leaned his elbows on the table. "I buy a lot and put up my smithy and somebody comes along that says he owns the lot because he was there first?"

"Pretty much. Then what happens to your family if he's right?"

"Mmm," said Farnsworth.

"Where do you keep the iron you need for shoes and wheel rims?"

"In a shed by the smithy."

"What if you need to expand to acquire more property to keep more horses, or more iron to work?"

"I've got that covered." Farnsworth smiled. "My lot size is fifty feet wide, but I thought maybe I'd expand when I came here, so I bought two lots."

"Do you think a hundred feet is all the space you'll need?"

"No. I'm already thinking about.... Oh. You're saying I might need more than two lots, but I can't have more unless I buy more, and the businesses next to me don't want to sell out."

"That's what miners are talking about," said Dan. "I manage a quartz claim for the family of Sam McDowell."

"He was murdered, wasn't he?"

"Yes. We still don't know who did it, although I'm trying to find out."

"You married his widow, so they say."

"Yes. She expects our first child soon. I want to be home when that happens."

"Yeah, you would. I've got five of my own." Farnsworth was silent, his hands folded around the beer mug, head down. One eyebrow twitched as he thought, about what Dan couldn't say. Family responsibilities, the gossip he'd heard about Dan's liaison with Martha before they married. They had lost the thread of Bill Twenty-two when he'd mentioned McDowell. Damn. That had been a mistake.

He waited while Farnsworth stared into his beer, thought of interrupting, rejected the idea while a minute passed, then another.

He was more tired than ever before in his life. He felt his watch ticking inside his vest pocket. Or was that his heart?

Fitch, standing at the bar, took a step toward them. A sideways motion of Dan's head warned him off. The Southerner leaned his back against the bar. Stared at Farnsworth.

How long could he sit and wait without interrupting this interminable thought process? He breathed in, breathed out. Raised the beer mug to his lips. Answered his own question: As long as it took.

A candle on an empty table guttered and went out.

In the darkness a denser shadow took form, its head lolled to its shoulder, a revolver dangled in its right hand as it rested against the air.

Dan set down the mug without tasting the beer.

Go away, damn you. You do not exist. There is no such thing as a ghost.

Farnsworth stretched his fingers, straightened his back. "I ain't had a proper think about this bill. It's all been too fast. You let me think. Ain't many people do that. You're right about Twenty-two. A quartz mine's different than a placer claim. It needs more space." He smiled. "Like me. I need more time to work things out than some folks, but I get there in the end. I'll change my vote in the morning and go the way Mr. Bagg goes. There'll be a thousand feet in it for quartz claims."

"Thank you." Dan held out his hand. "I'm grateful. Not many men would change their minds on something like this."

The blacksmith shook Dan's hand. "We're having a little party tomorrow for them as can't go home. My missus and the girls have been cooking up a storm. Maybe you and your friend over there would care to join us? We'll adjourn to Chrisman's after dinner for a little poker."

~~45~~

VIRGINIA CITY

The day before Christmas, when Tim called in, thinking to catch Mam and Eileen alone, he walked in on Mam scolding Dotty, ending with, "Apologize to her this instant."

Eileen sat between the window and the stove where she could get the best light for her mending and still keep warm, but her hands rested in her lap, and she kept her head down, not even looking up to see who came in. For some reason, Tim was disappointed, not seeing her smile.

His little sister's face was set in a pouty frown. "No. I will not."

When he would have pulled his boots off, Mam said, "Timmy, when you've warmed up, go see if Mr. Gohn has any roasts. I've a hankering for a good roast beef dinner tomorrow." She cast a dark look at Dotty. "Take Eileen with you. She needs an outing."

Eileen shook her head, whispering, "Oh, no, I can't."

Mam paid her no never mind. Hauling herself out of her reading chair, she brought him a poke of dust. "Buy yourselves a hot chocolate, too. You never did get one the other time."

"Mama," Dotty whined. He could tell she was about to plead to go along with them.

Mam, her face as red as he'd ever seen, spoke like Dotty was a four-year-old. "You sit down and hush your mouth." Her voice shook just a tad when she said to Tim, "The Professor let school out early. Your sister and I have things to talk about."

He couldn't believe his luck. By its heft, the poke held more than enough dust to pay for a roast and hot chocolate with plenty left over. Whatever Mam had to say to Dotty, he sure didn't want to stay and hear.

Outside, he turned his steps toward French's Saloon.

"No!" Eileen gasped. "I can't go in one of those places." She sounded as shocked as a Methodist.

"It's all right, truly. There's a Ladies' Entrance, and they have real hot chocolate. You needn't worry."

"No, I'll go back." She planted her little boots where she stood.

"You can't go back. Mam's having a talk with Dotty, and that means we can't go back for an hour."

"An hour?"

"Yep. That's when it'll be safe. Mam will have her say by then, and Dotty will be over her fit."

When she shook her head, he said, "It's too cold to stand out here and argue about it." He must have sounded impatient, on account she flinched, but she bobbed her head up and down and followed him into the place.

When she saw ladies with gentlemen at small round tables, a barred door between the ladies' section and the men's saloon, her shoulders relaxed. This part of the saloon had been made over for ladies. Facing them, the old bar held all the equipment for making coffee, hot chocolate, and ices.

Ices. The word made him shiver.

"This all right?"

Her nose twitched like a rabbit's, and her eyes shone. "Yes."

He couldn't hear her. "Smells like heaven, don't it?" Again he thought she said yes. At any rate, she let him guide her to one of the small tables to the left of the entrance, though she kept her head down like she wanted to hide her face, bright red like it was.

"What'll it be?" He pretended to read from the chalk board on the wall behind the bar. "Coffee? Chocolate?"

Eileen mumbled something that Tim had to ask her to repeat, and then leaned toward her to hear her the third time. "Hot chocolate," she whispered.

He went to the bar to order, and while he waited for their treats, he heard an out-of-tune piano accompanied by fiddle scrapings in the saloon. Two men shouted at each other about the Union invading the South, while others took turns toasting absent friends.

"To Sam McDowell." Tim heard that plain. His earlobes tingled. A glance in the big bar mirror showed him what shock looked like – Eileen's white face and wide rounded eyes.

He paid for the chocolates and carried them to the table.

"Drink up before it gets cold," he said. "They're just being merry."

Eileen got her color back, and took her first sip. "I ain't never had this before." She had such a wonder in her eyes that he caught his breath; so this was how it felt, to make a girl happy. Her tongue came out and licked away her whipped cream mustache. "I ain't never tasted nothing so delicious."

Masking the sudden trembling in his hands, he set his own cup in its saucer. "Glad you're likin' it." Right then, he'd have given up his share of the Nugget so she would look at him like that as long as he lived.

In the saloon, a boy yelled, "You can't say that! He was my Pa. He was going to come back for me when he made his strike."

Men hooted. One jeered, "Yeah, yeah. He was your daddy, all right. We know you ain't got no Pa, a bastard like you."

The boy shrieked, "He was so my Pa! He was my real Pa, he was. He was!"

The blood left Eileen's face so fast he thought she might faint. She clutched her coat collar high around her neck and gathered her feet under her to jump up and run. Everyone in the "Ladies' Side" had gone silent.

Tim reached across the table to grasp her arm. He said nothing, only held on like she would drown if he let go.

"Yeah," said one of the men in the other room. "You're a young Sam McDowell, you are. Why ain't you with him then? He shoulda taken you along, then we'd be rid of both of you. Hey! Don't you cut me. Put it away!"

The man behind the counter hurried around to lock the connecting door. Facing his customers, he spoke over the commotion behind him: "Ladies and gentlemen, the staff will soon have everything under control." He wiped his forehead on his sleeve. "We are very, very sorry that such an outburst should put a damper on your afternoon. Please stay and have another treat, compliments of the house."

It wasn't that Tim or Eileen wanted more chocolate, but Eileen was so shaken they could not have left before the manager set two mugs, heaping with whipped cream, at Tim's elbow. "Here you are, young sir." When Tim offered him his poke, he pushed it away. "No, thank you, I said it's on the house and so it is." With a friendly pat on Tim's shoulder, the manager walked away.

"I didn't thank him proper," said Tim. "Mam would have something to say to me about that."

Eileen didn't reply. She sat like she was hiding out from something, like the whipped cream melting into her hot chocolate was the meaning of everything.

He wanted to gather her to himself, tuck her under his coat where he could protect her, like she was a baby bird or a fawn. She'd never stick it, though, she was that scared of either him or Dan'l touching her. Maybe that's what going through what she'd went through done to her.

He wished he could tell her that as long as she was with him she'd never have to worry about nothing like that. Never.

Maybe someday she'd let him hold her hand. Now she was like a wild pony that didn't trust nobody.

That was all right. He could wait.

~~46~~

BANNACK

"So you're the one." Offering his fleshy hand, the man sitting next to Dan at the poker table wore Burnside whiskers shaved to encircle jowls that quivered as he talked.

"I'm afraid I haven't had the pleasure." Dan offered his hand. He had eaten and drunk too much of Mrs. Farnsworth's Christmas feast. Eating Martha's frugal cooking, he'd grown unaccustomed to stuffing himself. The ladies had served up thick slabs of roast beef, three kinds of canned beans, and mountains of mashed potatoes with floods of salty beef gravy. To camouflage their age, he supposed. Canned peach pie topped off the meal. He'd eaten three pieces.

Thirsty from the gravy, he'd drunk prodigious amounts of the sort of wine he would normally have poured down the necessary, and his mouth felt like he'd been eating sand. Not even the walk from Farnsworth's to Chrisman's store had cleared his head. He wanted to lie down on his blankets by the stove and die.

His head felt muzzy. How could he hold his own at poker? He'd lose his shirt if he couldn't think.

"Name's Ickes," said Jowls. "You're the one who persuaded Farnsworth. He convinced me, so the amended bill passed five to two."

"Then I owe you gentlemen a debt of gratitude." To his own ears the words sounded like a mumble.

"It breezed home once Ickes came in." Farnsworth gave p-credit where credit was due. "We sent it to the House, they passed it and returned it to the Council within a couple of hours. The Governor will sign it tomorrow, and it becomes law immediately."

Ickes said, "Repeals the Idaho mining law, too." He looked toward the front door. "Are we waiting for someone?"

"Tobias Fitch." Dan stood up. "I think I'll step outside for a minute or two. Is there a bucket I can borrow to melt snow? I have a powerful thirst for water." He could not play against Fitch with a muzzy brain.

Farnsworth pointed toward a stack of new buckets. "I'm sure Chrisman won't mind if you use one of those." They would not be sold until spring, when the miners went back to work.

Wearing his coat and gloves and carrying a bucket, Dan headed for the back door. The bucket banged against a corner of the desk that had belonged to Sheriff Plummer.

A man snarled from a dark corner. "Will you cut out the damn noise? I'm trying to sleep."

"Sorry." He opened the door and faced a drop into deep snow. There was no place to stand and close the back door before he stepped down.

"Shut the door," a man shouted.

Jumping for it, Dan pulled the door shut and landed knee deep in heavy snow. Though clouds hid the moon and stars, the Plummer's empty two-room jail stood out against the snow some fifty feet from the store. The snow lay undisturbed between it and Chrisman's, but a straight path led to the necessary nearby.

Finished there, he stuffed snow into his mouth to quench his raging thirst. Cold stabbed into the top of his head, but he didn't care. He filled the bucket, packed it down, filled his mouth again, and scooped more snow into the bucket. When he could not stand the cold another instant, he went back.

As he opened the door and set the bucket inside, he thought, *Tomorrow*. He would start for home tomorrow, as soon as possible after Governor Edgerton signed the Act, and when he had a copy of it to give to the *Montana Post*. Unless a blizzard blocked the road, he could be home on Tuesday. Wednesday at the latest. Home.

He stepped up into the store, closed the door. No one awoke to complain, and he envied them their sleep.

Fitch had not returned, but a game was in progress. Jowls dealt the third up card. He leaned against Chrisman's counter to watch, the bucket by his feet. A used whiskey glass stood on the counter, and he used it to dip out melted snow to drink.

The game was five card stud; after the cards dropped, after the players assessed their hands, their calls ran around the table: "Open five bucks." "Raise five." "Call." "Fold." "Check." Chips rattled onto the table as the pot grew.

In a back corner someone snorted in his sleep.

When the game ended, a thin man sitting next to Farnsworth rose from the table. When Farnsworth had cashed him out, he pocketed his winnings. "Good night, gentlemen. A happy Christmas to you all, and thanks for the Christmas enlightening."

"Ha! We're the ones you enlightened," Ickes said. "Happy Christmas to you, too, Ben." He tilted his head to the empty chair next to him. "Here, Stark. He was just keeping your chair warm."

Dan took his seat. "Maybe it'll bring me luck, too." He could think clearly enough despite his stomach's continued revolt.

On his left sat a Councilman named Evans, who had drunk great quantities of wine and swayed in his seat. On Evans's right stood an empty chair.

"Who are we saving the chair for?" Dan asked.

"Your friend Fitch," said Evans.

Almost, Dan said that Fitch was no friend of his, but he checked the remark.

Farnsworth laughed. "Tobias Fitch is the latest man I ever knew. We were hours on the way before he joined up with us last winter."

Farnsworth was talking about the posse's ride to Deer Lodge. "Joined up with you?" He had to be sure of the timing before Fitch joined the game.

"Yeah, joined the scout. You remember. When the boys went looking for the rest of the Plummer gang. The day after the five road agents was hung over in Virginia."

"I recollect," said Dan. "That's a hard day to forget if you were there."

The front door opened and Fitch walked in.

"There you are at last," Farnsworth called to him. "I was just telling the fellows here how you're always late. You'll be late to your own funeral."

"Good evening, gentlemen. Sorry to keep you waiting. I had to stop and refresh myself."

While they waited for him take off his wraps glove, Evans asked, "How much are we discounting greenbacks?"

"I don't know about discounting, but a greenback dollar's worth sixty-five cents," said Farnsworth.

The answer came, as all mathematical answers came to Dan, without conscious adding and subtracting. "That's right. A dollar in gold buys a dollar and thirty-five cents in greenbacks."

On Evans's right sat a dark-complected man with curly black hair, name of Vincent, who looked out at them from eyes so deep set they reminded Dan of an animal in a cave. Dan glanced at Fitch, who had taken his seat. Fitch nodded to each of them, but the corners of his eyes narrowed at Vincent, who eyed his cards as if Fitch were not there.

Farnsworth said, "How about we make this a little more interesting? The game's five-card stud, high card opens, ten-dollar maximum bet, two-dollar minimum. I'll handle the table fees to Chrisman. Everybody in?"

For a friendly game of poker, the stakes were rich. Now was the time to back out, if anyone would. Around him the other players looked to find someone who would leave the game, but no one moved. In the interest of making friends, Dan decided to lose, but not so anyone would notice and be insulted. "I'm in," each man said.

"Keep the damn noise down," said another man toward the dark back corner. "Some of us need our beauty sleep."

Most of the players laughed, but neither Fitch nor Vincent so much as smiled.

They cut for the first deal, which fell to Farnsworth. He dealt the hole cards, then the first up cards. Holding his cards, Dan drew in a breath to steady himself. He either held the beginnings of a straight, or a dud hand. His hole card was a ten of spades, and the up card a nine of diamonds. He found a better fit for his bones on the chair's warped wooden seat and set himself to play.

The up cards went around. The first up card to drop in front of Ickes was an ace of clubs. No one else showed a face card. "Check" they said, one by one. Dan's second up card was an eight of clubs. Again, everyone called "Check." On the third up card, Dan received a seven of diamonds, giving him one card short of a straight. Evans now had an ace that could pair with another ace, Ickes a pair of sevens, and Fitch held one queen at least. Evans opened. "Five dollars." He tossed in a half Eagle.

Fitch said, "Call your five and raise five." An Eagle rolled to the pot.

"Call," said Evans, tossing an Eagle toward the center of the table.

"Fold," said Vincent.

"Fold," said Farnsworth.

Fold now or bet? No one appeared to notice he had most of a straight. He could lose – or win a sizeable pot – fifty-five dollars. *Do it*, said Father's silent voice. *No*, he said, *you plunged and lost.* Yet –

"Call." Dan flicked an Eagle toward the pile of gold coins.

Farnsworth dealt. Dan picked up his fourth up card, and warned himself not to fidget, to hold on, not to be too still – the hardest tell to avoid. The six of spades. He had the straight.

Ickes called.

Fitch folded.

Evans called.

Dan called.

Farnsworth folded.

Vincent folded.

They were done.

When everyone had laid down their cards, Dan waited for them to notice his hand, but they all watched Ickes and Evans.

Evans's hole card was an ace, giving him a pair of aces.

"Not good enough." Ickes gloated. His hole card was a seven for three of a kind. He stretched forward to rake in the gold.

"Not so fast," Farnsworth said to Evans.

Ickes looked past his arm. "Just a bunch of number cards."

Fitch laughed. "Is that what you think?"

"Oh, hell," Evans said. "A damn straight."

Farnsworth smiled. "I figured you might have a pair, but a straight? Never entered my mind or I'd have folded after the second up card."

"It's probably my only run of luck this week." Dan scooped up the pot as Farnsworth gathered up the cards, straightened them, and gave them to Fitch.

Fitch shuffled the cards. "Ante up, boys." He passed the deck to Evans to cut and deal.

Dan pushed his winnings toward Farnsworth. "Give this to someone who needs it."

"You don't need more money?"

"Everybody needs more money, but it's Christmas. Give it to the poor." Waiting for Evans to deal, he made a silent promise. This time he would lose.

As Evans dealt the hole cards, Farnsworth said to Dan, "Charles Bagg tells me you're looking for a murderer."

Ickes said, "I thought that was all over with. Don't we have a territorial court now?" He put a slight emphasis on the word 'that.'

"Yes, that is over." Dan echoed him. They both meant the Vigilante rule, which had ended, Dan hoped, with Judge Hosmer's speech at the opening of the court. "I'm looking for the man who murdered my wife's first husband. Sam McDowell."

"Didn't he used to be your partner, Fitch?" Evans asked.

"Yeah," said Fitch. "Are we going to play or shoot the breeze?"

Evans dealt the up cards. When his second up card landed in front of him, Dan looked at his hand. Nothing worth staying awake for. Fitch opened the betting: "Check." Everyone checked.

Farnsworth dealt the third up card.

Vincent had two kings showing. From the way he stared at his cards Dan thought he might never have held a winning hand.

"Bet, damn it," said Fitch.

"He can take all the time he wants," said Ickes.

"Mind your own business," Fitch said.

Farnsworth said, "Now, boys, like the man said, it's Christmas. Let's just play cards."

"I'm thinkin' on what to do." Vincent ran his fingers through his hair; it sprouted like a tumbleweed all over his head.

"Place your God damn bet," Fitch said.

Evans said, "Hold on there. It's Christmas. We'll not be taking the Lord's name in vain tonight of all nights."

"Right," said Farnsworth. "Besides, he's just a little late betting." He laughed to lighten the mood. "You know about being late yourself, Fitch. I was telling them we almost gave you up that day last winter."

"I wasn't late," Fitch said.

"Oh, no, only by about three hours. The scout was supposed to meet at Laurin's, and you caught up with us the other side of Lott's Bridge."

Fitch said, "Oh, that day. Now I remember. Damn horses wandered off in the night, and I had to find and then catch the sons of bitches."

Pretending to study his cards, Dan knew that no one who had been on that scout could ever forget the day, not even for an instant.

"If you insist on this profanity," Evans said, "I'm folding now."

Not hearing them, Vincent said, "I open, don't I? Fifty bucks."

"Fold," said Farnsworth.

"Fold." Dan barely heard the word echo around the table. Fitch had been late to join the other Vigilantes. Three hours. He had never mentioned that. Neither had Beidler. He had a feeling it was important, but he did not know why. He wished he could think, but his brain would not cooperate. If he weren't so damn tired.

~~47~~

VIRGINIA CITY

Playing the "Wassail" song on her dulcimer, Martha couldn't help but think how things had been last Christmas, and how they was now. McDowell drunk as always, her and the young'uns scared every minute that he'd come home and find them happy. She glanced at the reading table. With Dan'l's help, Dotty and Timmy had bought her the Bible, but she hadn't dared bring it home from Lydia Hudson's place. If McDowell had found it he'd have wrecked it, same as he'd done with the old dulcimer.

That was her last memory of him, his great boot smashing down on it.

Now she had this one. As pretty as the music it played.

Instead of a cabin with a dirt floor, they lived in a house that had a plank floor. When the baby came it would be a mite crowded, but already Dan'l had said he'd have a new one built.

Dan'l. Her fingers faltered on the strings, breaking the rhythm. Timmy and Dotty stopped singing. Trying to smile, she made some excuse about woolgathering.

When would Dan'l come home? Soon, Lord willing, soon. Please, Lord.

Scolding herself for being sad on the Lord's Birthday, she launched into the first bars of "Silent Night." Her own two sang in harmony like they'd practiced for years, which they had, in a way, singing together all their lives. Eileen, her hands tucked under her crossed arms, sat watching them with her mouth half open in wonderment.

When they stopped, Dotty said, "I think it's time we opened our presents."

"That's a good idea." Martha set the dulcimer in its box beside her chair. "What do y'all think might be under the tree for you?"

"I've been wanting new hat trimmings like I saw in John How's dry goods store." Dotty clasped her hands in front of her bosom. "The ones with silver threads worked in them."

"Eileen," Martha said, "what do you suppose there might be for you?"

Eileen crouched rather than sat on the wooden chair, her knees drawn up under her chin, her skirts wrapped around her legs. When Martha spoke to her, she raised her head. "For me?"

"Of course for you," said Timothy. "Why not?" He reached under the tree, a straggly stick of a sage hung with a chain of popped corn, and pulled out the first four packages.

Those Dan'l had bought, she could tell. They were store-wrapped in brown paper printed with pictures repeated in bright colors – cone-shaped green trees, a red-suited fat man as Saint Nick. It was a new-fangled way to disguise what was inside, but she had to admit they were pretty.

"There's one more way back there," Timmy said. "Eileen, being as how you're such a little thing, could you bring it out?"

The girl scrambled under the tree and came out with a long roll of printed paper tied by a gold ribbon. "It's for you, Missus," she said.

Martha read the card aloud: "'For Martha, with all my love, Daniel.' I think I'll save this one for last." And in spite of the young'uns clamoring – Eileen silent like usual – she held firm. Once she unrolled it, she'd be good for nothing, though she could not for the life of her think what it might be.

They unwrapped their presents from each other amid smiles and laughter. Twice Dotty jumped up to hug Timmy and her mother, and the boy smiled over a new shirt with a starched collar and cravat to go with it. "Thank you, Mam."

Shaking her head, Eileen refused to take her presents. "I ain't deservin' of nothin'," she whispered to her feet. "I couldn't get none of you nothin'."

Timothy said, "That don't matter, Eileen. It really don't."

"You give us plenty already," Dotty said. "You helping Mama keeps me in school, and it helps Timmy and me. We don't have to worry about Mama doing more than she should with you helping her. So please, open your presents. We have to do something to say thank you for everything you're doing for us."

Eileen stared at her, statue-like.

Martha caught Timmy with his mouth open, no doubt as surprised as Eileen that Dotty was being so decent to someone she hadn't wanted in the house at all. For herself, Martha smiled in secret satisfaction. That talking to she'd given Dotty the other day had sunk in, it seemed. When the child – Dotty would always be the child to her – looked over at her, Martha smiled and nodded. Blushing, she handed Eileen the present from her and Martha.

For a bit Martha wondered if it was too much. Eileen's face paled as she pulled a new dress out of the paper, like for all the world she'd seen the Lord Hisself. She sat with it in her lap, silent, only one finger stroked the fabric.

Dotty opened her mouth to speak, but Martha shook her head once, and she closed it again.

Timmy broke the silence. "I saved Dan'l's presents for last." He brought the girls each a box, and one for himself. "Shall I go first?"

Plainly, he had to be first to open his package, being so taken up with curiosity that Martha laughed. "You go right ahead. Only save the paper."

Boy-like, he saved most of it but when he saw his present, his face fell. "It's a book. He knows I can't read no book."

Dotty took it out of his hands. It was two big heavy books. "*Rob Roy* by Sir Walter Scott," she read. "Oh, that's a wonderful present. He writes such adventures. The Professor, you know he comes from part of England that's real close to Scotland – he reads to us from another book by Scott." She looked at Martha, "Mama, can I read to us this afternoon?"

What could Martha say except yes?

Then Dotty opened her present, in her usual fashion, slowly to keep them all in suspense and tease her brother about saving the paper. First she hefted the package. "It's heavy." Then she tipped it, top to bottom, side to side. "I don't hear anything. What can be heavy but you can't hear it?"

"Maybe it's another book," Timmy said.

"No, the edges are square."

"Oh, for petesake, will you open it, or do you want to save it for next Christmas?"

"A derringer!" Eileen sat staring into her box. While they'd been taken up with Dotty's little drama, she had unwrapped her present so quietly that none of them even noticed when she picked apart the knot of string and spread the paper on her lap. She held the lid to the wooden box in one hand, while with the other she steadied it on her lap so it wouldn't slide off.

Timmy went to look. "Sure enough, it's a derringer." He reached to take the little gun out of its box.

Eileen laid her hand over the small weapon to stop him. "No."

"What?" His hand stopped perhaps an inch or two above the box.

"I ain't never had nothing like this of my own afore," said Eileen. "Mr. Stark give me this? Why for you think, Missus?"

Timmy sat down by his sister. "What's yours?" he asked Dotty.

She opened her identical box. "Mine's a little gun, too. Maybe just like yours, Eileen."

Timmy leaned over to look into Dotty's box. "Looks the same to me."

Martha, thinking of peace on earth and the Prince of Peace over against defending theirselves against the likes of Jacky Stevens, spoke slowly. "I guess it's – Dan'l – Mr. Stark, he don't want you girls defenseless. If you carry them little things, and you can shoot them, ain't nobody going to harm you." She looked at the three of them. "If you've got the will for it." What a lot of meaning packed into that one little word, will, she thought: It – defending themselves. It – killing, maybe, if there weren't no other way to stop an attacker. She didn't say nothing, on account just then Canary barked just afore someone knocked on their door.

The girls closed their boxes and set them on the floor while Timothy went to open the door to a parade walking into the house. Lydia Hudson led the way, followed by the Methodist preacher, Mr. Hough, with his wife, who looked grayish and pinched with cold. Last of all came Tabby and Albert. "We've come to wish you the joy and peace of Christmas," Mr. Hough said. "And to bring you the word of our Lord."

~~48~~

BANNACK

"Governor, I have never murdered anyone, least of all Sam McDowell. I defended him last winter when he was accused of being a road agent." Dan sat forward on the wooden chair, his back straight.

On Bagg's advice he had come to pay his respects to Governor Edgerton, never thinking it would turn into an inquisition about McDowell's murder. Yet in a way he should have expected it, Wilbur Sanders being the Governor's nephew. Sanders would have written his uncle all the news from Virginia, and a suspicion of murder against the Vigilantes' prosecutor had certainly been worth relating.

In another room a baby screeched, and the smell of diapers soaking mingled with the odor of boiling cabbage. Footsteps tromped over the plank floors, accompanied by a constant hum of talk that ranged the entire tonal scale from a small child's piping to a man's deep rumble. The so-called Governor's Mansion was a log cabin that housed the Governor and his wife and a family of five children. In the midst of swirling chaos Sidney Edgerton conducted the business of establishing a new territory.

A young girl two or three years older than Dotty came in without knocking. She carried a plump baby of about five months draped over on one arm. In her free hand she brought a packet wrapped in oiled cloth. "The messenger's here, Papa, with more bills to sign. He respectfully asks did you have something for him to take back to the legislature?"

"Yes, Mattie." Governor Edgerton handed his daughter a similar parcel. "Give this to the gentleman with my thanks, and tell him I'm in conference."

"Very well, Papa." The girl dropped a short curtsy that vaguely took in Dan as well as her father, and went out.

Edgerton went to close the door behind her. His smile vanished. He fixed Dan with a fierce gaze; together with his hawk-like nose, he reminded Dan of the nation's bald eagle emblem. "You would swear to that on the Bible?"

"Yes, Governor, I would." His own stare met the Governor's challenge. Governor Edgerton might frighten some people, but he could not hold a candle to Grandfather's powers of intimidation. Over Father. *I am not Father.*

A Bible lay on a stand beside the desk. Would he be invited to put his hand on it? Swear before God that he was innocent of McDowell's murder? His word should be enough.

Edgerton asked, "Your friend Mr. Bagg recommended that I meet you. He tells me you are one of the coming men in the Territory, when you should get clear of this current–" a pause to think of a word "–entanglement. What is your opinion on Negro equality?"

Thinking of Albert Rose, Dan said, "I see no reason for black people to be considered inferior. Freedom is the first step, but I fear it will be a long way before the wounds left by slavery are healed." He thought of Tabby Rose, whose hatred of white people testified to her injuries during her years as a slave. When, if ever, would she forgive him for things he had not done?

"Ahh," said the Governor. "In that case, I am happy to have met you." He held out his hand for Dan to shake. "You may like to know that the signed Quartz Act is among the papers the messenger took with him just now."

"Thank you, sir. A pleasure to have made your acquaintance."

Feeling he had passed some sort of test, Dan left the Governor's cabin and trudged along Main Street toward the Gold Rush, where he had arranged to meet Bagg. The air felt warmer, and a few flakes of snow drifted out of the clouds on haphazard courses through the air.

It was done. He had done what he had set out to do here. The Governor had signed the Quartz Act. When a clerk had copied it for him to take back to Virginia for the *Montana Post*, he could go home. He felt lighter: almost as though he could spread his arms and let himself be wafted home. Except that the hardest part of this journey lay before him.

Last night, he had been excited to learn that Fitch arrived late to the rendezvous, but in the light of day, he had come no closer to know why that fact was as important as it felt? McDowell had stayed at Fancy Annie's until the sixteenth, so Fitch could not have murdered him. He would have been miles away with the posse by then. Dan swore and kicked apart a frozen pile of horse droppings. All he'd accomplished was to verify Fitch's story. He would arrive in Virginia City farther behind than when he'd left. If anything, he had proved his innocence.

Thinking, head bent, hat brim shielding his face from the snow, he had walked past the saloon when he realized his mistake and turned back.

He did not look up toward Hangman's Gulch, where the empty gallows waited.

~~49~~

In Skinner's old place, he put his foot on the bar rail and ordered a beer. The bartender nodded his head toward the front of the building. "It's comin' down now."

"To be sure," Dan said after a glance out the window. The snowfall thinly veiled the buildings across the street. "Damn."

"You got somewhere to go?" asked the bartender.

"Home. Virginia City. As soon as I can."

"The way this is startin', you'll be lucky to get out of here before spring." A customer down the bar called him, and he went to tend to him.

Damned if he would stay a minute longer than he had to. He'd be on his way as soon as a messenger brought a copy of the Quartz Act. Or he would leave without it. The five days he'd been gone felt like a month.

He must go home. Martha. He must go home. How was she?

When did the next stage leave? Would the Act be copied in time for him to catch that stage? God, if it didn't leave until morning, what could he do? The snow might be too deep to travel by then. Stage or no, he would leave today.

"You too good to drink with me now that you've seen the elephant?" Fitch stood at his elbow, but Dan had been so deep in thought he had not heard him come in.

"What are you talking about?"

"You've been to see that blasted Union devil."

"The Governor signed the Quartz Act. I'm leaving on the next stage."

"What about the other bills? We don't have the Common Law bill yet."

"It will be all right. They all will. Bagg tells me Anson Potter will introduce it before the New Year. They're writing it now." To soothe Fitch's ruffled feathers, he signaled the bartender for two more beers. "There's no reason for me to stay. I'm going home."

When the beers came, Dan said to Fitch, "I'll get these." He did not want Fitch to pay; after one beer to placate him, he'd buy his ticket home.

"Are you Daniel Stark?" The voice belonged to a small man only a couple of inches taller than Beidler, but much thinner. He sported neither beard nor mustache, but a dark shadow told where they might be, and his thick brown hair threatened to escape the hair oil that bound it in place.

"Yes, I am." Dan shook the hand the man offered him, without listening to his name.

"I'm looking for a good lawyer to represent my business interests, and you come highly recommended."

"Where are you located?" The little man had obviously not heard about Beidler's suspicion or he would not have approached Dan.

"Hell Gate."

"In that case, you might want to find someone else. I live in Virginia City, and I think a distance of two hundred miles is rather great for an attorney to serve his client well."

"Then I'll bid you good day, sir."

Fitch drank some of his beer. "Do you know who that is?"

"No, who is he?"

"He's rumored to be the richest man in the Territory."

Dan smiled. "I thought you had reserved that title for yourself."

"Don't laugh, damn it. I will be. I aim to be the richest man in the damn country with a mansion in your precious New York. I'll buy some lawmakers, and put my thumb in every Union eye —" A coughing fit stopped him before he could go on.

Dan had touched a nerve. He drained his beer while Fitch calmed himself and wiped his eyes, blew his nose. "I'm going to see about a ticket home."

"Might as well."

When they stepped out onto the boardwalk, the accumulation of snow muffled their steps. "It's coming down harder," said Fitch.

Dan kicked at the snow. It blew upward and scattered, caught on the wind. "It's light enough we'll make it through if we can get out of here soon."

At the Overland stage office, when they bought their tickets, the ticket agent could not promise that the next coach would leave at all. It was an extra, put on to accommodate the legislators, and Dan and Fitch would be the only passengers. "We'll put a card in the window with the time when we're ready to go. If this snow gets too deep to travel, the card will say."

As they walked across the street to Chrisman's store, Fitch said, "We won't even have to go out to see the card."

~~~

Damn this waiting.

He could settle to nothing. After eating a lunch of canned pork and beans bought from Chrisman and heated on the cook plate of his stove, Dan peered across the street at the stage office. No card stood in the window.

He lay down on his blankets and pulled his coat over himself, over his hand resting on the breech of the Spencer. Tired as he was, he knew he would not sleep. He never could sleep during the day.

They would be too late. He scrambled out of bed in his nightshirt, ran to the next room, seized Timothy by the arm, hauled him out into the knee-deep snow. Hurry! Virginia City was on fire. He dragged the boy toward the glow on the horizon. They would never get there in time. Timothy held him back. He kicked at the boy, shouted that

Martha was in Virginia City, and Timothy turned into the ghost. The solid arm he grasped turned to air, then held him and would not leave go of his nightshirt. As he fought the thing, a horseman holding a torch high galloped past them toward the burning town. That was not right. No one took a torch to a fire, even at night.

A bump at his hip jolted him awake. He sat up, grasping the rifle, before he recognized Charles Bagg and laid it on the floor.

"Don't shoot the messenger," Bagg reached a hand down and helped him to his feet. He waved folded papers at Dan. "I bring good news. Here's what you've been waiting for." As Dan took the papers, he said, "You must have impressed Farnsworth and Ickes. They have promised to vote for the Common Law bill, too. Thank you. I'm not certain we'd have the thousand feet or the Common Law bill if you hadn't been here."

The final Quartz Act. Like the others, it had been folded crossways to form three panels. The middle panel showed the title, date passed, the Governor's signature, and the date of signing. "Where is it?"

"Section Eight, on the second page."

Dan read it, but the words would not stay still. He rubbed his eyes, and saw orange snowflakes. "This will be good news indeed." He folded it, put it in his notecase, and tucked the case into his inside coat pocket. "Now to get home and take care of some other business." Virginia City was burning. "I hope the stage goes." He did not know what he would do if he had to wait another day.

"It's leaving in half an hour," said Bagg, "but I'd advise waiting. It's snowing harder, and the wind has picked up a bit."

Joining them, Fitch stood behind Bagg. "We'll chance it. Stark's determined, and I'll make sure he doesn't get into trouble." He said, "Seeing's you're in such a hell of a hurry, let's buy snowshoes. If the stage won't go past Rattlesnake, we can walk. At least from Rattlesnake to Point of Rocks."

"You're crazy," Bagg said. "In a snowstorm?"

"Hell, I know that country so well I can navigate it in the dark." He turned away. "I'll talk to Chrisman."

"I'm game," Dan called after him. He shook free of Bagg's hand grasping his sleeve. Virginia City was burning. What did that mean? Martha was in danger? He rolled up his blankets and closed the valise, snapped the latches shut.

"You're a damn fool," Bagg muttered. "Trusting your life to Fitch?"

"Do you think I'm helpless? Don't you think he could be in as much danger from me?" Dan slung the rifle onto his shoulder. "Farnsworth said he joined the posse on the fifteenth. Three hours late, but that doesn't help me any. McDowell didn't leave Fancy Annie's until the sixteenth." Yet he'd been so sure, and underneath he was even more certain. He could not rid himself of the feeling that Fitch had murdered McDowell, but he was damned if he could see how, late though he might be.

"I still think you're a damn fool, but good luck. And watch your back."

Dan paused. Something lurked in the back of his mind that he could not reach. He had forgotten something. A message for Bagg, perhaps? A present for Martha? No, neither of those. He put the blanket roll under his left arm and took the valise in his left hand.

Looking toward the door where Fitch waited with a pair of snowshoes, he said, "Thank you. I will."

When he stopped at Chrisman's scales to pay for his snowshoes, Fitch said, "I'll go tell the driver we'll only be a minute more." With that, he went out, letting the door slam shut behind him.

Waiting for Chrisman's clerk to weigh out his dust, Dan watched Fitch talking to the driver. Bagg joined him. "I wish you would reconsider. It gives me a very bad feeling to know you're doing this."

"If I could think of any other way," Dan started to say, but Bagg cut him off.

"You're aware, aren't you, that you're putting your head in the lion's mouth?"

"Can you think of a better way to find out if he bites?"

~~50~~

"So you're the damn fools rousting me out to make this trip. Get in, then. I want to be in Rattlesnake before dark." The driver squirted a plug of tobacco at a wheel horse's rump. The animal stamped a hoof and swung its tail over the place. "There ain't no other passengers, so you can toss your truck inside." Putting his foot on the front wheel hub, he growled, "Better pray we can find the road."

Dan sat in a corner of the seat facing backwards, looking at the pale shadow of Fitch's face in the dusk. Their bedrolls, Fitch's pack, and Dan's valise lay on the seats beside them, while the snowshoes stood against the empty seats. He held the rifle across his lap.

The driver shouted at the horses and cracked his whip, the coach jerked forward with a jangle of trace chains. Wind hissed through a crack in one of the leather curtains.

Fitch asked, "You ever walk that stretch of the road? Between Rattlesnake and Point of Rocks?"

"No, but I'll chance it rather than be held up at Rattle-snake."

Untying his bedroll, Fitch laughed. "Time was, we could be pretty sure of being held up almost anywhere." Tucking his blanket around himself, he said, "I'll make up my mind about walking when we know the situation. The cold in this damn country is unimaginable, even when we're in it."

Without speaking, Dan arranged his blankets around his shoulders so as to leave the rifle clear. He could not explain the sense of foreboding, this feeling that com-pelled him to go home. God, that he would be in time, but for what? Martha's delivery? That was out of his hands; the doctor, the women, would care for her. But he must be there. He must.

Fitch spoke again. "The Quartz Act is law now, is it not?"

"What? Oh, the Quartz Act. Yes. It became law when the Governor signed it this morning."

"I thought so." At bit later, "You've got the copy, don't you?"

"Yes. In my notecase."

The coach slowed to a walk. The driver shouted down, "Can't see nothin'. It's a white-out. The horses will find the road, though. They's wantin' their hay."

So much for his grumbling at the start of the trip. Dan closed his eyes. Soon he thought he heard Fitch snore. At

Rattlesnake Ranch, the driver said, "We ain't going no farther tonight. Too damn hard on the horses. Maybe in the
morning."

~~51~~

For breakfast Dan held his breath and swallowed some leftover gray stew. The driver announced, "I ain't risking the horses no farther." The ranch owner, a new man, backed him up: "You boys best lay up here. It's too chancy, ten-below and still snowing."

"I'm going," Dan told Fitch. "You do as you please."

"Hell, if you're lunatic enough to do this, I'll come along to keep you out of trouble."

As they wrapped up their heads and tucked the ends of their scarves into their coats, the ranch owner tried to talk them out of it. "You two are crazy as fleas, you think you can walk all the way to Virginia in this weather."

Fitch said, "Don't look at me. It's him wants to chance it. Me, I'd stay where it's warm, and help drink up that horse piss you call whiskey."

Dan wrapped leggings around his lower legs from boot top to knee. "I have to get home to my family. I've been gone too long."

"Pussy-whipped," sneered the driver, quietly, perhaps talking to himself.

Without thinking about it, he had the rifle in his hand, and a round jacked into the chamber. The man's face went slack, his mouth dropped open. "Say that again." As from a long way off Dan heard himself menace the driver. Astonished faces turned to him, their mouths open in a silent chorus: No, don't.

The fire chattered in the fireplace; a log broke with a thump and hiss of sparks.

The driver said, "I ain't saying nothin', mister. You go along, and good luck to you and your friend."

Dan leaned the rifle against the wall, finished wrapping the leggings. His fingers shook so that he could barely tuck in the top to stay. He had been prepared to shoot the driver. Good God. What was he turning into?

Outside, Fitch said, "Well." When Dan didn't respond, he said nothing more, but walked on ahead, setting a fast pace.

Keeping close enough to see him, yet not stepping on the tails of his snowshoes, Dan followed.

They stayed on the stage road, sometimes wind-scoured and sometimes drifted so deep the stage could not have broken through. After the first couple of miles, Dan had his rhythm with the snowshoes and found the going easier. Topping a rise, they stood to breathe through their frost-crusted scarves. Dan peered north-eastward, so he thought, looking for Beaverhead Rock, saw nothing but fog and blowing snow. Far away, he thought a faint rest-less glow separated earth from sky. He blinked the snow out of his eyes, and when he looked again the ground had merged into the sky. Remembering Genesis 1: "The world was without form and void; and darkness was upon the face of the deep," he thought white might as well be dark-ness for all he could see.

In the white-out, he knew when they walked up a rise or down by the changed angle of his snowshoes, the ache in different leg muscles. He sensed an openness when the mountains did not close in on them after a long downward trek, and reckoned they had reached the valley floor. The snow stopped.

Following Fitch, he stumped ahead, along a road he could not see. By a slight warming in the air, and a stream muttering over stones, he thought they walked along the Beaverhead River. The thought gave him heart. When they crossed the bridge, they would almost be on the Rock, and a right turn would put them a quarter mile from Point of Rocks stage station.

The wind blew snow in his face. He leaned into it, watched the toes of his snowshoes forge ahead. In front, Fitch was a dim dark shape through the wind and snow.

They crossed the bridge and turned right. They shel-tered as well as they could close to the Rock, following the folds of the bluff. The first time he saw it, he had thought erosion in the limestone resembled banks of giant organ pipes. Coming from Virginia City, he had not seen the head of a swimming beaver that the Shoshone saw.

The wind screamed, attacked from behind, then ahead, lashed at them from every direction. The temperature dropped from cold to inhuman.

Dan shouted at Fitch, walking beside him: "We have to get out of this."

"Yeah. We'll never make Point of Rocks," Fitch yelled.

~~52~~

They huddled into a fold between two of the organ pipes carved into the limestone by ages of water and wind. Dan eased back and back until he no longer felt the wind. Over his shoulder, blackness yawned. He turned, a cumbersome half step at a time on the snowshoes, and peered as far as he could beyond the hip-high scrub sage bushes. Zigzagging around them, brushing aside brittle limbs, he felt his way toward the blackness. What if that darkness turned out to be nothing? Nothingness. He had heard of people falling into caves, never to be found.

Setting the rifle down, he groped into the valise for a Lucifer match and a stub of candle, lighted it, and sheltered the flame with a cupped hand. He stood at the beginning of a darkness he had never known before. The Rock rose hundreds of feet above him.

"It's a cave," he hollered.

Fitch retorted from a few feet behind, "No need to shout."

Edging forward, hoping any hibernating rattlesnakes did not wake up, Dan shone the candle as far into the cave as he could. Beyond it, he could not tell how deep or how high the cave was. The floor was dry, fine pebbles in sand. Others had camped here and left a fire-ring of stones and a pile of sticks as thick as his forearm, enough firewood for a week.

They removed their snowshoes and set them aside.

"Might as well use some of this wood," Dan said, "we may be here a while."

"A good place to wait out the storm."

The fire going, they settled on either side of it. Dan listened to the wind blow high notes and low past the organ pipes. He lay his rifle close to hand, saying, "Varmints. They'll want out of the storm, and I don't intend us to be anything's dinner." Watching Fitch across the flames, he tried to think of how to bring up the subject of McDowell's murder. There was something wrong about Fitch's story. If he weren't so blamed tired – his thoughts ran together – but he wouldn't freeze tonight, he'd had doubts about that during the long day's hard trek on snowshoes, sagebrush burned hot, its peppery smoke drifted farther into the darkness. He thought, the trouble with a fire is that one side of a man freezes while the other side....

Footsteps rattling the gravel woke him. From behind, Fitch said, "Best not to let it burn much lower. Thought I'd put more wood on. "

Dan roused himself enough to say, "Good."

Leaves on the first branch hissed and crackled. Dan smelled a moldy, rotten odor. "What kind of wood was that? Stuff stinks."

"I don't smell anything but sage," Fitch said.

A shadow fluttered in a rocky corner just at the edge of Dan's sight. The damn ghost.

The fire made a silhouette against the cave wall, a larger shadow rising. Not the ghost.

The shadow of a man raised high his short arm, brought it down toward Dan's head. He rolled away; the clubbed stump knocked against his cranium and slid downward to strike his shoulder. Half-stunned, he scrabbled for the rifle.

Stumbling over Dan's legs, Fitch fell, twisted. To catch himself, he thrust his short arm into the fire.

Dizzy, head throbbing, blood running, Dan grabbed the rifle. Someone screamed. He pulled his feet under him, tried to rise. Fell back. His head was full of rocks, crashing against each other. He held the rifle. There was a round in the chamber.

The screams went on.

Blood ran into his eyes. Something burning. Meat.

Fitch had tried to brain him.

Something was burning. No. Someone. Fitch.

Fitch crawled out of the fire, sobbing. With his short arm he held a torch.

Not a torch. Dan's head cleared. The wooden cap was aflame. Fire burned its way up his sleeve, the flesh underneath smoldered. Setting the rifle aside, Dan grabbed

Fitch's good arm, hauled him out of the cave, threw him into the snow, rolled him in it, turned him, struggling, onto his stomach, straddled him, buried the burning arm in snow until the fire died.

He knelt straddling Fitch until his breath came in long, shuddering gasps. Stumbling off, he removed his scarf and scooped snow onto his head wound. When he pressed on the place, he nearly fainted, but nothing moved. His skull was not broken. Thank God he had not taken off his hat before he fell asleep.

He had to piss. He stumbled to his feet and walked a few feet away. The wind sliced at him.

Fitch sobbed, "Don't leave me."

"I won't." Dan shouted over the noise of the storm. The son of a bitch had too many questions to answer.

Hurry, Dan told himself. A minute more and they both might freeze to death. He buttoned his trousers, staggered back to Fitch, pulled him to his feet, hiked his shoulder under the uninjured arm, and half-dragged him into the cave.

His eyes throbbed; his vision expanded and narrowed with the damn hammer beating on his head. He lay Fitch down by the fire, in spite of his wide-eyed attempt to scramble away from it.

"Calm down. I won't burn you any more'n you've burned yourself. You have to stay warm." He rummaged through Fitch's pack, found a notebook and three canteens of whiskey. "Good thing you brought a lot of rotgut. You'll need it."

From Fitch's pack he pulled out two dirty shirts and tore them into strips for bandages. He found a spare set of woolen long johns that he ripped apart. The legs he made into pads; he'd use the arms to tie a sling around Fitch's neck.

When he had everything assembled, he rested against a rock. He must have passed out, but came awake, imagining snakes, when some gravel rattled. There were none. Fitch lay in a stupor; each breath ended in a sob.

Gritting his teeth, he nudged Fitch's boot.

"What?" Fitch rolled his head to stare at Dan, his eyes as fierce and frightened as a wild animal in a trap.

"I have to work on your arm."

"No!"

"Yes, or you could lose more of it. Don't worry. I won't cut it off. The doctor can do that if he wants to." Raising Fitch's head, he held a canteen to his lips. "Drink."

Fitch drank.

The throbbing in his eyes made it hard to see. When Fitch had drunk a few swallows, Dan took the canteen. "Mind if I help myself?"

Eyes closed, Fitch said, "You would anyway."

Dan took a healthy swallow, corked the canteen. Set it aside.

Fitch gasped, "Bowie knife. Left. Belt."

Moving Fitch to get the knife roused him to screaming again, but when it was done, Dan knew his pocket knife would not have been equal to this task.

Considering that Fitch had tried to brain him, he would not be fussy about causing him extra pain, but moving as fast as he could to get the job done and over with, he sliced away the burned parts of Fitch's coat sleeve. The blackened scraps he tossed into the fire. Taking a deep breath, he braced himself to look at what was left.

In all the black remains he could not separate flesh from the charred wood of the cap. Taking another swig of whiskey, he considered the situation. If he cut away the wood, he'd have to cut some of the burned flesh, too.

"Here." He gave the canteen to Fitch. "Drink some more. You'll need it."

He held the knife blade in the fire. When it was clean, he bent closer to see the mess better. Blinked, wished Farnsworth would stop using his head for an anvil. Holding the arm on his crossed ankles, he picked away bits of black wood and flesh with the point of the knife. Fitch clamped his jaws shut until Dan pried away a piece of the cap that had become embedded in the charred flesh.

Steeling himself to pay no attention to the screams, Dan went on with the grisly chore. The knife point nicked the end of a splinter. He poured a few drops of whiskey on it. Seizing it between his thumb and forefinger, he pulled.

Fitch screamed and fainted.

When he came to, Dan had wrapped a whiskey-soaked pad around the stump and held it in place with layers of dry shirt and long johns.

He set about heating water in a pot that reminded him of the things McDowell had carried away from the cabin.

"Damn you, Fitch, you bastard, you tried to kill me."

Fitch gasped, "Nugget claim. Belongs to me."

"Judge Bissell ruled it belongs to McDowell's family."

"That damn judge stole that claim from me." He caught his breath, and sweat broke out on his face. "Christ, this hurts."

"You've got a choice here. You can tell me what I want to know, and I'll get you to a doctor in Virginia." He raised the Bowie knife. "If you don't...." He left the rest of the sentence hanging in midair.

Fitch was not talking any more just now. He had passed out again

Forcing himself to stay awake, Dan felt a restlessness in the floor of the cave, a vibration that stirred the fine pebbles and sand. Thinking of snakes, he peered toward the back of the cave where a form shimmered, gathered darkness to itself, became the shape of a hanged man. The revolver in its hand caught points of light from the campfire, and its stench blended into the stink of burned wood and flesh. He wanted to gag, walk away from here, leave Fitch to whatever would happen. Damn the blizzard, keeping him here.

Moving to away from Fitch, he leaned his back against a boulder to rest. If he and Fitch lived through the night, he would get them both to Virginia. Then he would see.

Part IV

~~53~~

One freezing, hard-bitten step after another, every-thing they carried abandoned in the cave except the blan-kets around their shoulders and Dan's rifle, their feet encumbered by the snowshoes, they shuffled a step at a time around Beaverhead Rock. To a healthy man in clear weather, Point of Rocks stage station was no great dis-tance from the cave, but in a blizzard, more than half-carrying the delirious Fitch, Dan, whose head was bleed-ing again, lost track of time. When the low log buildings loomed out of the fog and blowing snow, Dan breathed, "Thank God."

The owner gave them food and hot tea, and rolled out their blankets in front of the fire. When Dan awoke, the man would not hear of them leaving until the stage coach arrived to take them to Virginia City.

He asked no questions, but bandaged Dan's head in clean rags. When they tried to replace the smoke-charged bandage on Fitch's arm, he screamed and fought them until they gave up.

A day later, when the weather cleared, the stage-coach to Virginia City rolled in from Rattlesnake Ranch. The driver said, "Told you boys you shoulda waited for me. Looks like you had yourselves a peck of trouble."

"Accident," Dan mumbled. He did not explain further. Even the one word set the blacksmith's hammer to work in his head. Leaving the snowshoes in the charge of the rancher, they clambered into the coach, to endure the journey over hard-packed drifts that changed a bad road to abominable.

Late in the afternoon, the sun settling behind the western mountains, the driver stopped the coach at Bob Dempsey's place on Ramshorn creek where it emptied into the Stinking Water River. A new driver with an empty coach was rolling out hours late, and in a hurry to finish the trip to Virginia in time to stable the horses and meet his lady.

Dempsey offered them food, drink, and a place to rest overnight, but Dan would not stop so close to home. "We have to find a doctor to take care of this man's arm," he told the Irishman. In the coach, he sat across from Fitch, who leaned into his corner clutching his arm and groaning. In spite of the war drums beating in Dan's head, he would not leave the coach at any of the stops along Alder Gulch. So close to the end, he would not let Fitch out of his sight.

Fitch cradled his arm in its sling. Each time he looked to be slipping into unconsciousness, Dan kicked his leg. Fitch swore at him. "Where the fuck are we?"

At last Dan could tell him, "Nevada City. Next stop Virginia."

"Good." His chin sank to his breast bone, and he seemed to sleep again, but as his hat brim dipped downward Dan caught a gleam of cunning in one eye, and knew that Fitch plotted against him, even in his agony. When the coach jerked forward and pitched across drifts and ruts to meet the road, he closed his eyes only to have his nostrils assaulted by the stench of death.

The ghost. Again.

I do not believe in ghosts.

His shout, silent though it was, rang off-key. Did he disbelieve his senses? He saw it, smelled it, felt a chilled blade against his neck, where the scar ran.

In Virginia City, the cold kept most people off the street, though lights glowing behind windows thick with ice signaled that life existed within doors. Saloon music and laughter, now and then pierced by a woman's high-pitched glee, burst out into the darkness whenever a saloon door opened.

The Overland agent came out of his office with a lantern to help the driver. "We need Dr. Glick," Dan told him. Glick was the surgeon who had fixed Henry Plummer's arm when any other doctor would have amputated it.

"You're out of luck, then." The agent raised his lantern higher. "Glick is gone. He left day before yesterday, but he said the man that bought his practice is a good surgeon."

Fitch groaned. Through his cursing, Dan asked, "Are they in Glick's old place?"

"Nope. Being as there's two of them, they're up on Van Buren, above the Virginia Hotel."

Dan flung Fitch's good arm over his shoulder. "I'll take Major Fitch to the doctor and come back for the everything else." Though there was nothing save the blankets. The rifle, as always, he slung from his right shoulder.

The agent raised the lantern higher. "Are you sure you can walk so far? You're both in bad shape. Rest inside where it's warm. When we've unloaded the mail, I can send someone to help you."

He could not wait so long. There was still much to do, and little time before his strength gave out, until the hammer in his head rang too hard on the anvil.

"Get me to the doctor," snarled Fitch.

Walking up Wallace, supporting Fitch, Dan found that some shopkeepers had sprinkled ashes over the boardwalk in front of their stores, so his halting steps did not slip. A relentless rhythm beat in his eyes. At the Eatery, he stopped, kicked the door. So close to his destination, his strength leaking fast, he would never be able to haul Fitch all the way to the doctors' office. It was past dinnertime, they should all be there cleaning up, why did someone not answer?

"We'll freeze out here," growled Fitch, in a whisper. His weight hung heavy on Dan's shoulder.

Two more kicks, and Albert's deep bass responded, "Wait a bit, I's here." Wood rasped against metal, the latch lifted in a small clatter.

Albert looked out through the crack he had made. "Mistah Stark?"

"Help me, Albert. Please. Major Fitch must get to the doctor."

Lydia Hudson called out, "Who is it, Albert?"

"It be Mistah Stark, and – and Major Fitch." The former slave's tone held a weight of fear and contempt. If he knew that Fitch had freed his inherited slaves, it made no difference to him. Fitch wore the gray.

"Help me get him to the doctor, and then find Jacob Himmelfarb." When Fitch's weight sagged toward him, Dan gasped, "Please."

From behind Albert, Lydia Hudson ordered him: "Bring them in. Do not let them stand out there in the cold."

Albert opened the door just wide enough to let them in. If he'd had his way, Dan thought he would have shut them both out: Fitch for fighting on the side of slavery, Dan for helping him now.

Dan let Fitch's arm slide off his shoulders as they collapsed onto the bench nearest the door. He longed to stretch out on it, but there was no room with Fitch sitting so close, and anyway what would happen then? He would never learn what the Fitch knew about McDowell's last day. By the stove, Mrs. Hudson conferred with the Roses in words too muffled for Dan to decipher. He longed to stay here, to be warm, to stop the knocking in his head, but he was so close, so close. He had to know what Fitch knew, get it in writing. Make him sign a relinquishment to the Nugget. If he died tonight, he must have it for Martha, the children. His child.

He struggled upright. He could not sleep now, he must see his child.

Hurry, Albert. Fetch a doctor for Fitch. Hurry.

Albert, dressed in his heavy coat, said, "I takes this one," meaning Fitch, "to the doctor. Miz Hudson, she say you stay here and she fix you up. When I come back I take you where you want to go."

He could not be separated from Fitch, not now. He was not finished yet. He had to make Fitch talk. "No. You can't." He tried to explain it, but he could not find the word he wanted. What was it? Where should he look for it?

Mrs. Hudson said, "Don't be a fool. Thee needs help."

Tabby Rose held his arm, and the women guided him in a sideways shuffle down the aisle to the kitchen where they helped him up onto the back table. When they tried to take his rifle, he would not let go. At last they covered him and the weapon with his blankets.

Somewhere far away, pots and pans scraped across metal. He smelled an unfamiliar odor, heard boiling, and remembered Mrs. Hudson was a homeopath and a healer.

They cleaned his head wound, working in efficient silence. A soapy smell in water told him they washed the blood out of his hair, and strong fingers squeezed his head around the wound. The pressure hurt, but nothing grated.

"Thy head is not broken," said Mrs. Hudson. "That is a great blessing." She held a lamp close to his head, and he shut his eyes to avoid the light. "The wound is to thy scalp only. Thee is much blessed."

They bandaged his head and let him lie on the table to get warm while the tingle in his feet grew to hammer and nails. How could anyone bear this long enough for gangrene to set in? He willed himself to think, What next?

"Wake up, Dan'l." Timothy tugged at his shoulder. "Wake up. We're taking you to Jacob's place."

Strong hands helped him to sit up, propped him upright, set his feet on the floor. He protested, "No, not to Jacob's. Where's Fitch? I have to ask him – take me there."

Mrs. Hudson, holding a lamp for the men, said, "Somebody has to watch thee. Just in case thy headache worsens. Thee must have rest."

"No. I must...." He struggled, but God, he was weak. He was a baby in their grasp, being helped into his coat, wrapped in his blankets, and set on the way. Timothy held him on one side, Albert on the other. The rising moon lighted their slow way, and the cold struck another blow to his head.

Useless to fight them. The black man and the white carried him along, a small bark on a strong current. They would not let him question Fitch. The Nugget would not be safe. He would be branded a murderer.

He had failed.

~~54~~

Perhaps he dreamed of warmth, of Jacob lapsing entirely into Yiddish. "Oy vey ist mir." They undressed him like a doll, wrapped him in blankets, dribbled hot liquid in his mouth, down his gullet, laid him warm in bed.

"Get Fitch," he said.

Sometime later, fierce whispering hissed in his ear, separated into words as he came awake. An argument flared behind him while he lay getting his bearings: he lay in a bed, peeled logs an inch from his nose, a trickle of icy air. They argued about him.

"No. That we will not do. Sleep he must." That was Jacob.

"I have to question him." Question who about what? That was X. He should question Fitch.

His temple throbbed.

X wanted to question him. He could go to hell.

"Come back later. Now he has to sleep." Timothy. Timothy here? Where was here?

437

A door opened. "I'll be back. You can bet on it." The door shut, not gently.

"Martha?"

There was no answer. He slept.

Awake again, Dan lay still. Jacob sat at the table. Elbows on the table, he held his head in his hands. His heavy book lay in front of him, and he murmured to himself, chanted ancient words. Dan stretched and yawned.

Jacob broke off his chant. "You are awake. How do you feel?"

"Yes. Albert brought me here?" He took a sort of inventory of himself. The blacksmith had taken his anvil and vacated his head, but a bass drum thumped a warning from a short distance away. "What time is it? Or – what day?"

"Past twelve of the clock. Thursday, the twenty-ninth. Are you hungry? Thirsty?"

"No, but necessity...." He tossed back the blankets and sat up, sank down again to wait for the room to stop swaying. The next attempt, Jacob helped him. Feet on the bedside rug, he sat while his head adjusted to the turning world.

The room steadied. "I just got up too fast. I'll be all right."

"I help you," Jacob said.

Sunlight on snow dazzled him. He grasped Jacob's arm, afraid to fall. He'd become an old man before he turned thirty. Returning from the privy, the sun shining on his back, he thought the temperature might have risen above zero. The air smelled smoky, but a breeze carried away the visible smoke.

Timothy met them at the door. "I went up and got provisions." He had placed a chair by the door for Dan to sit on while he knelt down to pull off Dan's boots.

"How is your mother?"

Timothy would not look him in the eye. "She's holding up. Worried about you. Sends her love."

Dan could only see the top of his blond head. "Have either of you heard about Fitch?"

Neither of them answered. Timothy said, "X is coming back pretty soon. He's got questions for you."

Dan stood up to take off his coat, grabbed for the wall to stay upright. "What now?"

Timothy steadied him, but avoided his eyes.

"Well? What is it? And where is Fitch?"

"At the Recovery," Timothy said. "The doctor's taking care of him. He says you tortured him, put his arm in the fire to make him confess to murdering Pap."

~~~

He had cleaned up as best he could at Jacob's wash basin and choked down some bread and bacon with coffee. Over his second cup, he could think more clearly. Parts of the last three days he'd lost in a fog. He recalled the fight in the cave, although he couldn't recall much of the journey after that. Except for lugging Fitch, and being afraid for Martha.

Virginia City was burning. Except it wasn't.

Hearing at last what Timothy had said, he guffawed. What an outlandish accusation: him, a torturer? First a murderer, now a torturer?

Meeting shocked stares from Jacob and Timothy, his swung to a black anger. "Christ Almighty, will this never end? Beidler thinks I could stab one man in the back, and torture another? He thinks I'm that sort of blackguard?"

Jacob shook his head, Timothy bit his fingernails.

Head thumping, Dan walked the three steps to the bed, not quite as steady as ever. He would think better when he'd had a rest. "Wake me when Beidler comes."

He was nearly asleep when Timothy spoke. "No, Dan'l, wait. You wouldn't do a thing like that. Ain't I right, Jake?"

"Yah. Daniel Stark does not hold a man's amputated arm in a fire so its cap burns into his flesh. Such – such horror? No. Never."

"Thank you." Dan kept his eyes closed, to hide the tears that threatened to leak out from under his eyelids. At least Timothy granted him that much.

Someone breathed as if he had an obstruction in his throat.

Timothy said, "He wouldn't murder Pap, neither."

~~55~~

Hearing the door open, then close, he awakened. Jacob protested: "No. We do not wake him. His head, it is not clear."

Lying still, he wanted time to come fully alert, to take stock. The drum thudded softly, more slowly than when he had lain down. He was stronger. That was unimportant, somehow. Compared to?

Timothy had said he hadn't murdered McDowell.

Tears stood at his eyelids, and he did not know if he could hold them in.

"Wake him up," said X. "I got questions that won't wait."

"I'm awake." Timothy and Jacob hurried to help him hitch himself up. He leaned against the wall. Jacob sat beside him on the narrow bed, and the boy stood at the foot. Jacob must not have felt hospitable, Dan thought. He did not offer Beidler coffee.

No remembrance of long, frigid miles, or shared grief showed in the deputy's eyes as he opened his mouth to speak.

"Do you still think I murdered Sam McDowell?" Dan said.

"I didn't come here to talk about that." X pulled out a chair and perched on the front quarter of the seat, his feet planted square on the floor, the shotgun resting across his lap. His right hand lay on the breech. "Major Fitch says you tortured him to get him to sign over the Nugget claim. "

Talking across X, Dan said, "Then we have nothing to talk about ...."

"...and then tried to kill him when he wouldn't do it."

"...Fitch is a God-damned liar."

On his right, he felt Timothy stir and put his hand out to stop him.

Jacob said, "This cannot be true. Daniel Stark murders no one, he tortures no one."

"He didn't murder Pap," said Timothy.

"Oh, yeah? How do you figure that?" Beidler sneered.

"On account Pap turned his back on whoever done it. Or the fella got behind him somehow. Pap wouldn't never let Dan'l see his back. He hated Dan'l."

Beidler's eyes were slits, and he chewed on his mustache. Looking at Dan, he said, "How'd you get him to change his story?"

Timothy shot back, "It ain't no story, and he didn't do nothin'. I figured it out while he was gone."

"Ah. As to that, Stark, what have you got to say for yourself? Don't tell me Major Fitch had anything to do with murdering this boy's father. He was with us from the fifteenth on."

Dan, his mind jogged out of its freezing fog, sorted through his options. If he told Beidler now what Farnsworth had said, or suggested any other course than his version against Fitch's, would Beidler believe him? He doubted it.

A lawyer who represents himself has a fool for a client. God, he needed Bagg's advice. As it stood now, he had one option left, and if he lost, he'd probably hang.

Oddly, he could consider that possibility as if it belonged to someone else, but he knew of an escape route. If he could make it work. If. "I demand a preliminary hearing in front of Justice Hosmer."

"Not until you answer my questions. It's the law."

"The law? You're telling me what the law is? The Idaho statutes are very plain. An accused person has the right to a preliminary examination to discover if there is any truth to an allegation." He lied, but the New York code had such a provision, and he did not doubt that Idaho had something similar as well. His head ached again, and weakness overtook him. He had not much clarity left, but he had to tell X so that Timothy and Jacob would hear. "I also reserve the right to call witnesses: Jacky Stevens, Major Tobias Fitch, and Helen Troy. To start with."

Beidler said, "Jacky Stevens don't have nothing to do with this. I don't have a reason to call him, and I can't just call a minor child into an examination on someone's say-so."

Jacob stood up, hands doubled into fists at his sides. "Then I prefer charges – that is the phrase, yes? – on Jacky Stevens. For his attack on me. He would have killed me except that Timothy chased him away."

"That's a different cause," Beidler said. "Hosmer will never go for it."

"Oh, I rather think he will." Dan crossed mental fingers that Judge Hosmer would give him the benefit of the doubt so far.

X rubbed the stock of the shotgun with his thumb. "I guess I can ask for it. Don't know what His Honor will say."

"He'll agree if he doesn't want a miscarriage of justice."

~~56~~

Again he slept, and awoke in the afternoon with a longing to see Martha so strong it amounted to necessity. When Jacob and Timothy argued against it, he said, "Whether you like it or not, I shall go. I must see her." He slid his legs into his trousers. Once upright, he willed himself to remain solid on his feet. The headache, the pulse in his eyes were gone. Was he at last on the mend? When he bent to lace up his boots, his head thudded so that he rested between one boot and the next, but he would not ask for help. If he could not dress himself, he could not fool them into thinking he was ready for the examination.

God, there was so much he did not know, could not piece together. He was six ways a fool, but what choice was there?

Climbing the slope up Jackson street would be a test, he thought, as he sought a painless position for his hat.

They insisted on ferrying him chair-style across Daylight creek, and having no faith in his balance on the icy stepping stones, he let himself be talked into it. On the trek up Jackson he had to rest more than once. Timothy and Jacob guarded him close all the way.

Jacob parted from them when they reached the path to his house.

"You are a great fool. Strong you must be for the judge. Your good lady, she would wait, yes? She would know you must defeat this business and then come to her. She is wise. She knows what comes first."

Sudden tears threatened him. Searching for a handkerchief, Dan patted his pockets. His solid slap at his breast pocket reminded him of the Act. He gave it to Jacob with a request to take it to the *Post*. "We have the thousand feet of ground."

Jacob stowed the Act away. "Is a fine thing you did, but so much risk, my friend. So much risk."

"Jacob's right," Timothy said. "We know without you, it all falls apart."

~~~

How so small a body as Martha's could grow so big without exploding, Dan did not know. In only a few days, so it seemed, her swollen cheeks almost hid her eyes, and her belly had grown even larger. He had never been much of a praying man, not at all in the last year, but the sight of her brought him to his knees beside her chair. He took her hand and kissed it, held it to his face, while one thought pulsed along his veins: Save her. Save her. If she died, how could he live?

She ran her fingers through his hair, avoiding the bandage over the place where Fitch had struck him. Silent tears flowed down her cheeks. "I was so afeared. They wouldn't tell me nothing, just that you'd got hurt and was resting."

He would not frighten her by saying how close his death had been. "I was in a hurry to get home. We walked from Rattlesnake to Beaverhead Rock. After that we caught the stage at Point of Rocks." He kissed her knuckles. "I was just worn out."

"If you hadn't come home..." She took her lower lip between her teeth. When she could speak, she said, "I prayed every day, more than once."

"I'm all right. But you?"

"I'm doing fine. I just look like a balloon, that's all. I wouldn't blame you if you'd stayed there."

"I would never have stayed. I only went for the Act. Now it appears that I still have work to do, to remove this cloud over us." He smiled at Timothy, who sat on the bench, waiting for Dan to be ready to go back to Jacob's house.

While Dotty ground roasted beans for coffee, Eileen stood behind the table cutting a sheet cake into squares. She rested the handle of the knife on the table. "Sir? Mister?"

"Yes, Eileen?" Dan had never heard her volunteer anything, even among the family. Testing the knife edge against her thumb, she whispered to the cake, "Thank you for my Christmas present."

"You're very welcome. Do you know how to use it?"

"I think so. I never shot nothing before, but I think I could. Just point it at what you want to shoot, pull back the hammer, and pull the trigger?" It was the most she had ever said to him, even though she kept her head down, hiding from him behind her curtain of hair. "I don't have to be scared no more, now, do I?"

"No," Dan said. "You don't have to be afraid of anyone ever again." Turning his head to tell Timothy they would go when they had eaten their cake, he saw the boy's face as he watched Eileen. For a moment Dan could not say what it was, so unlike his usual expressions. And then he had it. Tenderness.

Timothy said to Eileen, "I can protect you, too. Just like when Dan'l was away."

Canary stood up, barking, before Dan heard a man's boots stomp onto the porch. Timothy opened the door. "He's busy. I can give him a message," he said, and stepped outside to talk to the visitor.

Martha put her hand on his knee and pitched her voice below the voices outside, the preparations for their coffee and cake, so that he had to lean in close to hear. Her breath tickled his ear. "Please stay here tonight."

He could not stay, but how to refuse? Unsteady as he was, he had plans to make, a case to lay out in his own mind before he presented it. To Judge Hosmer, or failing that, to the Tribunal. His endurance was sliding away, and he braced himself against the oncoming weakness.

"You should not try to climb that hill again," Martha said.

Thinking of her insistence on attending church, he laughed. "Turn about, is it?" He squeezed her hand, hauled himself to his feet by the arm of her chair. "I can't stay tonight. There is much to do if what I hope for does occur."

Timothy's footsteps across the rug did not register with Dan until he touched his shoulder. "It's Deputy Beidler, come to say Judge Hosmer agreed. You got your examination. Nine o'clock tomorrow morning."

"Ah, good. Thank you, Timothy. Would you mind telling the deputy I'll be ready then?" Dan stood up, put his hand on the back of Martha's chair arm to steady himself. "We'd best make haste. There's a great deal to do."

"No," Martha said. "You can't leave before you've had some cake. Eileen baked it, her and Dotty."

~~~

Dan'l would not get off so easy, Martha promised herself. He'd want to protect her from knowing what he was about, but she couldn't have that. Maybe she couldn't get around these days like she was used to, this baby weighing on her in more ways than one, but she'd worry more not knowing about all this than she would if she knew what was this examination Timothy mentioned. She would not be fobbed off with some half-truth, either.

She waited until they were all seated around the table, herself at the warmest place in the middle with her back to the stove, Eileen nearest the washstand, Timothy and

Dotty acrost from her. Dan'l sat at the head, his back to their bedroom door.

They sat like they'd all braced themselves to ask the question: What examination? Only nobody was askin' it. Eileen tried to shrink even smaller inside the waist-length jacket Martha had knitted for her for Christmas. When Martha urged her to eat up, she jumped. "You made a delicious cake. It's a shame you don't at least taste it."

Just as Martha was about to ask, Dotty, never one to hold back when she wanted to know a thing, asked, "What examination, Daniel?"

Timothy frowned at her, probably on account she had learned how to pronounce Dan'l's name the proper way. Martha sighed to herself. Maybe her boy was right. Maybe Dotty needed taking down a peg lest she get above herself. Exceptin' that didn't mean nothin', now Dan'l and she had married, and her young'uns were his step-children. Getting above herself probably meant where he naturally was.

When Dan'l said nothing, just went on eating his cake, Martha said, "I want to know."

He laid his fork on the plate and drank some of his coffee, a special treat for him coming home safe. "Can you stand it?"

"Stand what? I've stood a heap of things this year. I've stood people sayin' you killed him, even Timmy sayin' that. I guess I can stand this, too, whatever it is." *Except if'n it's you at the end of a rope. Then I might as well die, except for this least'un you give me.*

"Timothy does not believe I murdered his father."

"He doesn't?" She stared at her boy, now near grown into his manhood, whiskers on his face.

"That's true, Mam. I been thinkin' these last few days. Pap wouldn't never turn his back on Dan'l."

Dotty said, "That ain't all, Timmy. Daniel wouldn't ever murder anybody."

"I know that. Jake says there's a difference in the Bible between killing and murder. Killing's defending yourself and murder – that's to get what you want."

He didn't look at Dan'l, but fixed his eyes on his sister, until Dan'l said, "Enough. You'll upset your mother. This is not a fit conversation for females, let alone in your mother's delicate condition."

Martha slapped her hand on the table. The cutlery jumped. "I won't have it. I won't have it, you hear? I want to know. I have to know. Or I'll worry and worry, like I did all summer, like I did while you were in Bannack. Can't you see that? I must know."

Out of breath, her heart racing, she stopped, breathing hard like she'd been running, and prayed he would mind what she'd said as they two stared at each other, like nobody else sat at their table. When he nodded, once, she braced herself: *Oh, Lord. What have I done? What if I don't want to know after all?*

He spoke to her, and her only. "I have asked Justice Hosmer for a preliminary examination into Sam McDowell's death."

If he'd set off a bomb, she might have been able to think clearer, but her brain stopped working and where it used to be was a great gaping blank place, same as the stillness in the house.

Then, laying on his rug, Canary yawned, a loud sort of Ow noise that set her laughing, all of them along with her. Timothy stopped first, then Eileen, and her and Dotty last of all, titterin' like squeaky hinges on a door someone forgot to close.

Dan'l hadn't laughed. He ate a bite of cake, put another piece in his mouth.

"What for?" Dotty asked.

He laid down his fork and finished chewing, washed it down. "I know some of the circumstances around your father's death, but I need more information to show who murdered him. This examination should yield that information."

There was more that he was not saying and far more that he would not say. By the set of his jaw, she could tell there wasn't no point asking him.

Timmy, though, he didn't pay no nevermind to Dan'l maybe not wanting to say more. "Do you think you know who did murder Pap?"

"No. Not quite. That's something I intend to dig out of the examination."

"So you'll be asking questions?" Dotty asked.

"Yes. That's what an examination is for. Asking questions, getting answers."

"Does that mean you think one of the others there knows who killed Pap?"

"I'm sure of it."

Eileen's chair scraped over the plank floor, as she got up and dashed behind the stove. What had made her sick? Martha listened, but when she didn't hear noises, she half rose from her chair.

Dan'l waved her back and followed the girl.

"Don't come no closer." Hearing the threat in her voice, Martha's breath caught in her throat. The derringer. Eileen had the derringer. If she used it....

Dan'l said, soft and quiet, "It's all right, Eileen. It's all right. No one will hurt you here. You don't need that with us."

~~57~~

To make himself as small as possible, Dan sat on his heels facing the girl crouched on the floor. Even so, he towered over her, and every flick of her eyelashes, the bulge in her apron pocket, her fist gripping the little gun, warned him of thin ice. Was it loaded? If she pulled it out, he did not know what he might do.

"You cain't make me say nothin'."

"You're right. I can't make you say or do anything you don't want to do."

"I ain't tellin'. He'd kill me sure. Just like he killt their daddy." She spoke high and shrill, words running together.

"He won't kill you, Eileen." Slowly and softly, Dan reminded himself; don't set her off. "You have your derringer, and we'll protect you, Timothy and I. Nobody will hurt you any more. Nobody."

"You ain't here all the time." Her eyes showed their whites, like a terrified horse. "He'll watch. And get me sometime."

455

"Not if we get him first."

"You might not. You might make me leave. You won't protect me then."

"I won't make you leave." He waited, let her chew on that.

"Missus said I can stay after the baby comes?" Her voice was lower in pitch.

"You may stay as long as you wish. You're free here. With us." A cramp was forming in his calf. Ignore it. He'd suffered worse than that. A cramp was not a ball in the leg.

"You paid money to bring me here."

He knew what she meant. Blacks weren't the only slaves. "Miss Troy wouldn't let you go unless I gave her money. I didn't buy you. I bought your freedom."

"So I'm free?"

"Yes."

"What if I want to go away?" Her eyes narrowed, which he read as a test, but she spoke in her normal register, though louder than usual.

"You may go if you wish, but Mrs. Stark needs a great deal of help. She has been good to you, hasn't she?"

"Oh, yes." She drew her hand out of her pocket and stretched the fingers, opened her hand, made a fist. A very small fist. "Y'all been good to me."

"We like you, and Mrs. Stark needs your help. Now and after the baby comes."

"She told me that." She looked at his shoe. "I can stay, then?"

"You can stay. I'd like for you to stay. We all want you to stay."

"Even Dotty?"

"Yes, Dotty, too. All of us."

"You won't bother me? Or Timothy?"

God, what a horrid thing for this child to ask. Before he could answer, he tamped down his indignation at the way she had grown up or she might think he was angry at her. "No, we won't bother you. We won't let anyone else bother you, either."

She thought about that, while the knot tightened in his calf muscle.

"All right, then," she murmured.

"We can't protect you if we don't know whom you're so afraid of."

Her hair flicked around her face when she shook her head. "I ain't tellin'. He'd kill me sure."

He could not speak logic to her. She was too fearful.

"I have a cramp in my leg. I have to stretch." He sat on the floor, extended the painful leg out to the side away from her, bringing himself in range to take the pistol if she went for it. Gripping his offending muscle, alert at the corner of his eye for any move she might make, he worked the calf. Echoes and shadows flashed in and out of his rec-ollection: her terror, Lydia Hudson's dog General, Jacob's beating, the kind of father McDowell had been, 'baby rat-tler.' Helen Troy had used term that about Jacky Stevens.

"It's Jacky Stevens, isn't it? He scares you so much."

Her gasp answered him. Now, could he convince her to tell him what she knew and how she knew it? "You might as well tell me the rest." On the other side of the stove, the family was silent as stone. He could not hear them breathe.

He decided to risk another question. It was the only answer that made sense of her terror and what he knew, what he surmised. "The Stevens boy managed to sneak up on McDowell?" He made himself sound disbelieving. There were stirrings from the eating table: a rustle of cloth, a gasp, and "Shhh." They might be able to hear Eileen, now that the fire in the stove burned lower.

"He did, though." Eileen pulled her feet up under her skirt. She left the derringer in her pocket to put her arms around her legs and peer at him over the barricade of her knees.

"Who did what?"

"He done knock Jacky down."

Dan guessed she meant McDowell. "That would be pretty easy to do. He hit Timothy's mother so hard she didn't wake up properly for two days afterwards."

"He didn't hit Jacky that hard."

Perhaps forgetting the others, she seemed to talk to him alone. "Jacky told me oncet he'd always wished he had a Pa, and when he and his ma first come here and he seen Timothy's pa he'd say he wished he was his daddy. He got to wishing it so hard that he started in to think it was true. One day he was saying I wish he was my daddy and then he was saying he was his daddy, and not his'n at all." She looked down, a child trying to decide what to say next.

Dan worked his way through all the masculine pronouns. Jacky had begun by saying he wished McDowell was his father, then said McDowell was his father, and not Timothy's.

In the stove, the fire coughed. An ember broke, Dan guessed.

Eileen pulled her feet under her and tucked her dress around her legs.

He kept his eyes on his calf. The knot had shrunk, though the pain had brought tears to his eyes. Or maybe it was this blasted headache.

"Then the night y'all hung them five road agents, Timothy's pa come in and got a bottle of whiskey. He drank it like he wanted to kill hisself. He spent the night...." Her face flamed more than another girl's face might, who had not grown up in a brothel, who did not know so much of that life.

To ease her way, Dan said, "With Isabelle Stevens."

She covered her face with her hands, perhaps to hide embarrassment. How must Martha feel hearing this? The man to whom she had borne two children knocked her out and went to a diseased whore in Fancy Annie's. Damn McDowell to hell, that nearly a year after he'd been killed, he could yet cause her grief.

Was McDowell the only cause of grief to her? Dan shook off the thought to tend to the business at hand.

"The next morning," Eileen almost whispered, "he et some jerky and flapjacks, and drank a little coffee. He told ever'body he was on his way to somewheres else. He said he'd killed the – the best thing ever happened to him. Isabelle Stevens come up to him about then, and he cussed at her and said, he said... said...." She stuttered to a stop.

For Martha's sake, Dan did not encourage her to say the rest of it. "It's all right, Eileen. You didn't say it, you're just telling me he said bad words. You don't have to repeat them."

She blushed from her hairline down her neck. "Yes, that's right. He called Jacky's ma names and said she was not worth a plugged nickel. Then he slapped her. Hard. Jacky saw him do that and heard what he said, and when he grabbed his coat and run out after him, he said something nasty to her, too." She paused, and Dan hoped he would not have to prompt her; she might startle, fear making her unsteady in her mind, a ropewalker crossing a chasm in a gusting wind. "No one saw neither of 'em for the rest of the day. After supper, I scrubbed down the stove top, getting' it ready for when Cook wanted to fry up breakfast. Jacky come back. I quick hid away from him in my corner. Between the stove and the wall, you know? It's warm back in there, like here, and I got my blankets there, and I'm small so's I can fit in it and nobody can find me."

"I understand." His cramp had eased. He sat cross-legged, hands folded in front of him, not looking straight at her, in a pose he hoped reassured her.

"He sat down close by the stove, and started in mumbling to hisself." Imitated the boy's voice: "'You shoulda let me come with you. I'm your true son. Not that—'" She swallowed, licked her lips. "It weren't a nice word at all."

"No, it wouldn't be."

An uncertain smile rewarded him. "'You was my Pa,' he said, 'and I killt you. You thought you was bigger'n me and I couldn't hurt you, but I'm quick, and you were going to walk away from me, but I got you how you didn't expect.' Then he started in to cry. 'Why wouldn't you be my Pa? Why wouldn't you be my daddy?'" She scrubbed her jacket sleeve across her face.

~~~

Sunlight and shadow brightened and muted the colors in the braided rug, the family swung from tears to laughter, scraps of words rang in treble and bass. In this swirl of sound and light, he stood beside Martha's, held her hand. They needed no words. She had believed him all along.

Believed in him and he had betrayed her. With Harriet. Among the roses.

Was he all that different from McDowell?

The happiness in her eyes at once rewarded and accused him, though she could not know what he thought at this moment. She tugged at his hand. Bending to hear, his balance almost slipped. He steadied himself against the table. "Bring Eileen."

He kissed her mouth before she called the girl's name.

As though it were any old day, Eileen had gathered the dishes from the table. "Yes, ma'am."

Martha gave her both hands, "Thank you, dear child."

As he moved aside to give them privacy, he saw Timothy, wearing coat and boots, take the pocket pistol off its shelf. Before he could open the door, Dan laid a hand on his arm.

"I'm going after that little bastard." Timothy spoke in a fierce whisper.

Dan answered him as quietly. "No. You can't. You must not."

"He killed Pap. He don't deserve to live."

Dotty, her teary face alight, curls bouncing, came toward them, her arms outstretched to give him a hug.

Dan put out a hand to ward her off, and she stopped a few feet away. The joy drained from her face, changed to puzzlement.

"Just a moment, while I speak to your brother."

Timothy said, "You can't stop me."

"Yes, I can, if I have to. You would be done for murder yourself. The hearing is tomorrow. Don't mess that up."

"What'll that do?"

"If Eileen will testify, I can prove at the examination that I am innocent. We have to bring it to Justice Hosmer. Let the law take care of it."

"You-all did it better. Why go to the law now when you wouldn't do it about Rawley? Why is Jacky different?"

"We're in a different time now than we've been since gold was discovered. There was no law then, and we had to step in. Now that we have the law, and a procedure for cases like this, we have to use it."

"What if it goes wrong?"

"You think we were wrong about Rawley." When Timothy's face went slack, Dan said, "Human beings aren't perfect. We can get matters wrong. Sometimes very wrong, in the law as well. Give me a chance to do what I have to do in the examination. After that, I won't interfere."

Waiting for the boy's agreement, Dan trembled inside at the chance he took. He was betting the boy's future on his skill as a lawyer, arguing his own case.

Fool, indeed.

"All right," said Timothy. "I'll wait until after the examination. Then, if'n Jacky's free, I'll get him. He ain't gettin' away with murderin' Pap."

They shook hands on it.

"Now, will you help me to convince Eileen?"

"We'll all help, Dan'l," said Dotty.

Dan had forgotten her, and she had sidled close enough to hear them.

She said, "Me, Mama, Timothy. We'll all convince her. You go along and get some rest. Leave it to us."

Fighting the sudden exhaustion that swamped him after so long braced against Eileen's determination (and her a mere slip of a girl), Dan could do nothing else. He said, "I'll just say goodbye to your mother. I need your help up to Planters House, if you will. I haven't the strength to go back to Jacob's place."

First, though, there was something he had to do.

"I'll be ready to leave in a few minutes." He limped into the bedroom. Opening the chest of drawers, the chifferobe as Martha called it, he rummaged through his underwear. Where was it? Had she moved it after she found it? The possibility made him swear. Damn fool that he was to cause her this suffering. He touched something hard. Ah. There it was.

From under his neatly folded pants he took out the tintype. Seeing the shadow of the woman's face in the dim light, he almost put it back. "Harriet," he whispered to it. "Harriet among the roses."

Out in the big room amid the activity and the girls' chatter, under Timothy's sharp gaze, he removed the picture from the frame and held it against his body to hide it, but he did not fool Martha. She knew it was the picture of Harriet, and the pain of it so unguarded on her face stung him. Prying the tintype out of the frame, he laid the frame on the table. "I've thought that we could have a family likeness taken when the weather moderates and the baby is old enough to go out. Maybe when she's christened. Or he is. You, me, Timothy, Dotty, and him. Or her. Would you like that?"

"Oh, yes." She smiled, but the hurt stayed in her eyes.

He lifted one of the burner lids on the cookstove. Flames danced gold and orange, reaching to take his offering. He thrust the portrait, face down, into the flames and snatched his hand back in time not to be burnt. For a moment he watched the fire attack the tintype. He had given

Harriet what she wanted in the summer; he had betrayed Martha and put her and her youngsters into jeopardy by staying so long in New York. True, he'd struck gold on the trading floor, yes, but also there was Harriet. He had almost stayed in New York. With Harriet.

He had betrayed them all, leaving them defenseless so long against Fitch. He had nearly remained there after that tryst, damn him. But he was here to stay now. Here to stay.

~~58~~

Candle flames wavered in the lamp chimneys. The newly lighted stove fought back the chill in Judge Hosmer's office, but Dan's damp, clammy shirt stuck to his back. Was he so weak that the walk from his office to the courthouse made him sweat?

By the outer wall, in front of the door, Tobias Fitch shot black looks at him around his attorney. Secessionists together, Dan had thought, when he exchanged polite but cool greetings with Harold Abbott. Who believed in phrenology.

Was this how soldiers felt, waiting for battle? The enemy in sight, but the general had not arrived?

Make no mistake, Grandfather had told him once, the law is war. And here he was, on the field of battle, in open war with Fitch.

Were his weapons equal to this? Could he remember everything when he needed to? Were his notes adequate? Since before Father's death he had not stood before a judge who was educated in the law. Nearly two years now.

Feigning a casual air, he sat sideways in his chair to talk to Jacob, who sat behind him. This morning he and Hershfield had escorted Dan up Jackson, Jacob carrying the bundle of Sam's belongings that he now held on his lap.

If this examination went well, Dan would ask Dobson, the three-hundred-pound court clerk, to hold that for evidence at Jacky's trial.

Hershfield, who had left the room, returned. Sitting down, he leaned forward to tell Dan, "They're not here. Should I go look for them?"

Timothy and Eileen. The boy had arranged to bring her to the hearing if she would testify, but perhaps the girl was too frightened. Damn. How could he restructure his ideas without her? "No," he said. "If she doesn't appear voluntarily, nothing can force her."

Hershfield murmured, "When you put this away, let's talk some business." He sounded as though Judge Hosmer's ruling in his favor were a foregone conclusion. Dan smiled, grateful for the encouragement, though he knew the outcome was anything but.

He removed the paper from his notecase and smoothed its folds on the broad arm of his chair.

The Chief Justice walked in, followed by Deputy Sheriff Beidler. Everyone rose without the clerk, Dobson, telling them. Hosmer hung his coat and hat on the hall tree next to his desk and put on his black robe of office. Somehow, in that cramped space he managed not to sweep any papers off his desk.

Beidler closed the door and stood with his back to it.

After the judge lead them in the pledge of allegiance to the Union, Dobson said, "You may be seated."

Hosmer fussed over the items on his desk as he had at the opening of the court: lighted his lamp, adjusted the wick, replaced the chimney. Moved the sound block. Raised the gavel – Dan thought, *Here we go* – and tapped it on the sound block, a rifle shot in his ears.

"Mr. Dobson," Hosmer said, "you may call this hearing into session, after which you may administer the oath to Mr. Stark."

Puffing, Dobson squeezed out from behind the little table between Judge Hosmer's desk and the jail wall. "District Court for Montana Territorial District Number One is now in session for the purposes of examining evidence brought by Mr. Daniel Bradford Stark, pursuant to the unlawful death of one Samuel McDowell." He held a Bible for Dan, who laid his left hand on it and raised his right hand. "Do you solemnly swear that you will tell the truth, the whole truth, and nothing but the truth, so help you God?"

"I do." Waiting for Dobson to take his seat, Dan listened to the small sounds in the room – a candle sputtered, Dobson's chair creaked under his weight, someone breathed hard through his nose.

His mind was blank.

"Mr. Stark," His Honor said, "I understand that you have asked for this examination because you believe a serious crime has been committed. A murder, in fact, that you yourself are accused of committing. Is this correct?"

He would not use his chair to brace himself. "Yes, Your Honor." The room shifted. Behind him, Jacob sucked in a breath, and Hershfield's boots scraped on the plank floor. They had each held one of his arms on the trek to the courthouse; without them he would have fallen once or twice.

"I see by the bandage that you sustained an injury to your head. Was that on your return trip from Bannack? Are you well enough to continue?"

"Yes to both, Your Honor." Would that were true, Dan said to himself. For a blessing, the drum was quieter, though he was a little dizzy.

"And you feel adequately prepared?"

"Yes, Your Honor," Dan lied. He had not had time to locate a copy of the Idaho Criminal Practice Act, much less review it. Only six copies of the Idaho statutes had come to Virginia City, and one of them lay on Hosmer's desk. Another had gone to Bannack with Charles Bagg. Whatever he or anyone else thought of Idaho law, it ruled in Hosmer's court. He would take a chance that the law regarding examinations must approximate the New York code.

"You are ready to proceed, even on such short notice?"

"I am, Your Honor."

"Good. You may be seated."

Judge Hosmer tapped his gavel once on the sound block. "This examination will now come to order." He opened the code book. "For those of you unacquainted with the Idaho Code of Criminal Practice, Mr. Daniel Bradford Stark has requested this examination under Chapter Two, Part Three, Section 102. It reads as follows:

"'When a complaint is laid before a magistrate, of the commission of a public offence, triable within the county, he must examine, on oath, the complainant or prosecutor, and any witnesses he may produce, and take their depositions in writing, and cause them to be subscribed by the parties making them.'

"Am I correct, Mr. Stark, that you have requested this examination according to this statute?"

"Yes, Your Honor." Dan rose to his feet, took a wider stance to balance himself. Hosmer had given them all a break by reading the statute, but he would be a hard man to convince with as little evidence as he had to support his theory of how Sam was murdered. He would have to be very clever to convince this intelligent and imaginative judge. *God help me.*

"What do you hope to accomplish in this examination?" The lamplight cast a shadow under Judge Hosmer's lower lip.

Dobson's pen scratched over the paper.

"If it please the court." The well-worn phrase steadied him. "I shall prove that Jacky Stevens murdered Sam McDowell. Further, I believe that a second man witnessed the murder, and can verify my version of it, though he will not wish to do so. I also—"

"Your Honor," Abbott, on his feet, interrupted. "Does Mr. Stark intend to accuse my client, Major Tobias Fitch, of being the second man?"

"Mr. Abbott." Hosmer brought down the gavel. "You will be seated and not interrupt again. Is that clear?"

"My apologies, Your Honor." Abbott frowned, muttered something to Fitch.

Hosmer banged the gavel down. "Silence in the court." He laid the gavel in its place. "Well, Mr. Stark? Have you such an intention?"

Abbott had won. The reprimand did not count.

His ears ringing, Dan could not recall the edifice of logic he had glimpsed on the long road from Beaverhead Rock and refined yesterday after talking to Eileen. He had written it down last night, rehearsed it with Jacob and Hershfield and Timothy, who had played devil's advocate. But logical as a theory might be, it did not rise to the level of direct evidence. It was not even circumstantial. It was conjecture, blocks of thought fitted together in an architecture of pure logic, and it had one great hole in it. Eileen's story was uncorroborated unless he could break Fitch.

In law, the word of a single witness to a confession she had overheard could be discounted. Abbott would challenge her on grounds of hearsay, or as being self-serving, given her long terror of Jacky, and Judge Hosmer might rule in his favor. Could he make it work here? Could it withstand Abbot's challenge? Could he recall it well enough? He could have used a large whiskey to steady his nerves, but liquor on his breath this early would prejudice any judge.

"Perhaps you would like Mr. Dobson to repeat the question." Hosmer's impatience had a sarcastic edge.

The hissing in his ears cleared. "I do not accuse Major Fitch of complicity in the murder, Your Honor. However, I believe he witnessed the crime."

"He's lying!" bellowed Fitch. "He tortured me and tried to murder me on the trip back from Bannack."

"Sit down!" Hosmer seized his gavel and hammered it on the sound block. "Deputy, quiet that man or I'll hold him in contempt."

If only Hosmer would not make so much use of the damned gavel. As he turned his head to see Fitch, the door frame wobbled. He dropped his hand to the chair arm and felt paper under his fingertips. Startled, he read the first two lines of his notes. His mind, shocked into working, sped through a reconsideration of his strategy. Damn Fitch. Damn him to eternal perdition. Accuse him of being a torturer as well as a murderer, would he? In open court. Fuck this.

Beidler said, "You heard the judge. Sit down." When Fitch did not move, the deputy said, "Now." Still pretending to read his notes, Dan heard Fitch grumble, then chair legs scrape.

The room quieted. A candle sputtered.

"Your Honor." Dan fought to hold back his anger, and knew he only partly succeeded. "I am neither a torturer nor a murderer. Major Fitch's accusation arises from pure malice and from his desire to rob my family of their rightful ownership of a promising quartz claim."

"That's a God damn lie!" Fitch, up again, shook his fist at Dan.

The gavel thundered. Judge Hosmer shouted, "Deputy, restrain that man!"

Order restored, Dan asked, "Your Honor, may I have a five-minute recess?"

Hosmer glowered at him through narrowed eyes.

Dan waited. "No, you may not." He pointed the gavel at Dan.

Dobson's pencil ceased its motion across the paper.

"I take it you have a competing account of how you sustained your head injury and Major Fitch burned his arm?"

"Yes, your honor." He wished now that he taken Hosmer up on his offer to let him sit down.

"You may be seated."

It was an order, rather than permission. Dan sank onto the chair.

Dobson struggled out of his corner and went to add more wood to the fire. When he had sat down, Hosmer raised the gavel and struck the sound block.

He did not have to call for quiet. The room had the sort of stillness Dan associated with a death watch.

"We find ourselves with an unexpected expansion of this complaint, or perhaps a counter-complaint has been lodged. After hearing Major Fitch's accusation and ascertaining that Mr. Stark has a contrary account, I have decided to separate this new allegation from the matter at hand.

"Accordingly, this examination will inquire only whether or not enough evidence exists that Mr. Daniel Bradford Stark did willfully and with malice murder Samuel McDowell."

No one stirred.

The stink of death seeped into the room. A candle guttered and went out. Hairs rose on Dan's forearms.

Go away. I do not believe in ghosts.

"As to Major Fitch's allegations," Judge Hosmer said, "we will entertain them at another time, depending on the outcome of this examination. You may continue, Mr. Stark. The witness you refer to is Major Tobias Fitch?"

Dobson's pencil sped over the paper.

"Yes, Your Honor." A sidelong glance at Fitch, who held his injured left arm upturned in its sling.

"Proceed, then," Hosmer said. "You may call your first witness."

"I call Miss Eileen."

The judge frowned. "What is her surname?"

"It is unknown, Your Honor, for reasons that will become apparent."

Dan held his breath.

Hosmer nodded to Beidler to open the door. X called, "Miss Eileen, you may come in now, please." Correct in form, Beidler's call had a grudging tone. He had refused to interview her, or to believe her, Eileen being nothing but a female, and a young one at that.

Head down, watching where she went just enough to avoid stumbling over men's boots or bumping into the judge's desk, Eileen crossed to her seat in the witness chair and sat, head down. She had borrowed Dotty's best blue wool coat, so much bigger on her that it nearly reached the ground. The right-hand pocket sagged with a heavier weight than a handkerchief.

Dan swore. Why in the name of Christ had Timothy allowed her to bring the derringer into court? Or Martha? Too late now, he thought; he only hoped no one else noticed.

"Child," said the judge, "please stand to take the oath. You must swear to tell the truth, you know."

"Yes, sir," she whispered, sliding out of her chair and standing.

"You're supposed to say 'Yes, Your Honor.'" Dobson sidled out from behind the table and held the Bible for her.

"Yes, Your Honor."

"Put your hand on the Bible, miss."

Without looking up, she laid her trembling right hand on the book.

When Dobson finished the question, she murmured something inaudible.

Dobson said, "You have to say 'I do' so we can hear you."

"Yes."

Dobson prompted her, "You're supposed to say 'I do.'"

"I do."

"You can sit down now."

Dan came forward. Looking down at her bent head, the lank, light brown hair falling past her shoulders, he began by asking how she came to live at Fancy Annie's.

She answered readily enough, though she had to be prompted to speak up so Hosmer could hear her. "I was orphaned by Indians, when I was a wee little'un. Some soldiers, they found me and took me to a town and give me to Miz Troy."

As he hoped, her voice gained some strength as she talked, but when he asked about her life with Miss Troy day-to-day, it sank to the merest whisper.

"Please speak up, child," said Hosmer. "We have to hear what you say."

She shrank away from him, although he had spoken kindly. "Yes, sir."

"Your Honor," he corrected her.

"Yes, Your Honor, sir."

Dan led her through her growing up, and without Eileen having to describe it, he made plain her constant fear that she would eventually have to make her living as the other women did in that place. He did not force her to mention the rape last March.

"You earned your keep helping in the kitchen, then?"

"Yes, sir. I got so's I could cook. I like cookin'."

Ah, he thought. She had volunteered something for the first time. Perhaps she was becoming more confident.

Abbott rose to his feet. "Your Honor, it is all very good to hear that her moral sense has triumphed over her surroundings, but it has nothing to do with why learned counsel has seen fit to put her on the stand in an examination into the circumstances of a murder."

The stench grew worse. Lamplight fluttered on Hosmer's desk.

"Your Honor," Dan said, "this will become clear soon. I'm setting background for what comes later, which is direct evidence."

"I'll allow it," said Hosmer.

Visibly pouting, Abbott reseated himself.

Where was he? What had Eileen said last? She didn't want to make her living 'thataway,' as she put it. No, she had said that at home. He could not remind Hosmer of her upbringing – upbringing, yes. Making a living. She made herself useful in the kitchen instead. The kitchen. That was it. "You worked in the kitchen of Miss Troy's various establishments for several years, am I right?"

"Yes, sir."

Could he bring in her fear of Jacky Stevens now? He asked, "You worked there all day, did you not?"

"Yes, sir." Her hands twisted in her lap.

"Where did you sleep?"

That brought her head up. "Sleep, sir?"

"Yes. Where did you sleep? Did you have a room of your own?"

"No, sir. I slept in the kitchen."

"In the kitchen?"

"Yes, sir."

"How could you sleep in the kitchen? Will you describe it for us?" She had told him, but it was important for Judge Hosmer to know how this child had lived.

"There's space between the wall and the stove, where it's warm. I had a couple o' boxes for shelves, and my bed-roll on the floor."

"It sounds like you made it very snug." The poor child, he thought. His own sisters had counted themselves abused after Father's – suicide, when the family crowded into their brother-in-law's house and they had to share a room. They had never slept on a floor or feared the men in their lives as this waif feared Jacky Stevens.

Jacob coughed. The signal. Yes, he must get on. He said, "You are acquainted with a boy named Jacky Stevens, are you not?"

Hearing the name, she doubled her hands into tight fists, the knuckles pale against the chapped red skin. "Yes," she whispered.

"He frightens you, does he not?"

"Yes." She hunched her shoulders, as though expecting a blow.

"You try to get out of his sight before he sees you, do you not?"

"Yes, sir."

"Do you remember one time in particular when that happened?" He waited while a pulse throbbed in his jaw. When at last she spoke, his teeth ached.

"Yes sir. It were the day after the Vigilantes hung them five road agents." She paused for so long that he had to prompt her.

"Yes?"

"I was scrubbing the stove top for Cook, and he – Jacky – come in the back way." Raising her head, she fixed him with a sightless stare, perhaps reliving that time.

Wishing he could spare her this ordeal, Dan prayed that no one would disturb her now, that she would go on of her own accord.

"He didn't see me a-tall, but I dropped the brush in the scrub water and crept into my space. I 'member thinking I'd just wait until he went away. I had a butcher knife in there. In case."

She paused again, so long that Abbott gathered his feet under him to stand up. Dan slapped the flat of his hand down on the air, and Abbott sank back in his chair. "Yes, and then?" He nearly whispered, and worried that she had not heard him.

"He never come after me. He just hauled up a chair by the stove and commenced to warm hisself, rockin' back and forth and mumblin'."

Dan risked a glance at Hosmer out the corner of his eye. The judge seemed absorbed in her story; he leaned toward her on one elbow, his shoulder braced to carry the entire weight of his substantial torso.

"Could you hear what he said?"

"Yes. He said he'd killt his pa."

Abbott leaped up. "Objection, Your Honor!"

Eileen shrank into herself, head down, shoulders hunched, her hair falling forward, hiding her face. The bones of her bent neck stood out, small stones under snow.

"You honor," Dan said, "on what grounds can he possibly object?" He knew perfectly well that Abbot objected on grounds of hearsay. What did Idaho law say about that?

"Well, Mr. Abbott?" Judge Hosmer asked. "Would you care to enlighten the court and Mr. Stark?"

"Hearsay, Your Honor. The witness is testifying to something she heard the young man say."

"Mr. Stark? Have you a rebuttal?"

Would Hosmer rule if he had no rebuttal? What rebuttal could he have? Wait – something – confession? Was that it? New York law was plain. "Your Honor, the witness is testifying to a confession she heard, and therefore her testimony is not hearsay."

Abbott sputtered, "But, Your Honor, where in the law is that written? Can learned counsel cite a precedent? Or the statute itself?"

"Mr. Abbott, may I remind you this is an examination and not a formal trial? Mr. Stark is perfectly correct. The witness testified to a confession she heard. I will allow it as evidence of a confession."

Still on his feet, red-faced, spittle gathered at one corner of his mouth, Abbott said, "This is grounds for appeal, Your Honor."

Hosmer regarded Abbott as though wondering, as well he might, if the man had studied law, in what state had he been licensed, or how he had passed a bar examination.

Dan braced himself by one finger on the corner of Hosmer's desk. He wanted to laugh at the change in Abbott's face when he realized that any appeal to the Territorial Supreme Court would be heard by Justice Hosmer as Chief Justice sitting *en banc*, together with his District Three colleague in Bannack. Only by appealing all the way to the United States Supreme Court, could Abbott or any lawyer in the Territory perhaps receive an impartial hearing. And that, Dan reasoned, would be subject to the Justices' own political persuasions and partialities in this time of civil war.

"Appeal if you must, Mr. Abbot. Mr. Stark, please call the next witness."

Dan tried to act as though he called an ordinary witness. "I call Major Tobias Fitch, Your Honor."

After swearing to tell the truth, Fitch sat in the witness chair, his spine straight as became a cavalry officer. Except that he had served in the wrong cavalry. He shielded his injured arm against bumps, but the set of his jaw, his tense shoulders, and the deeper lines in his face told Dan that he still suffered great pain. *Serves him damn well right.*

"Will you tell Justice Hosmer what you witnessed on the morning of January fifteenth, instant?"

"I'll tell you what I didn't see. I was looking for three cayuses, and I damn well didn't see any murders." He sent a silent threat plain for Dan to see.

"And why is that?" Dan kept his tone neutral, as if the question and answer did not matter, that his own future, the family's future did not depend on breaking Fitch's account. Here. Now.

"If you're talking about the murder of Sam McDowell, it didn't happen on the fifteenth. After I rounded up my strays, I rode past where they found the body, and there was nothing there. No tracks. Nothing."

"You say that was on the morning of the fifteenth?"

"Yeah. That's when it was. And McDowell, he was laying up with that doxy over at Fancy Annie's until the sixteenth. Ask the madam there. Ask Helen Troy. She'll tell you." Sweat broke out on his face, and he shivered and pulled the sides of his coat closer around him.

All this time, Abbott had not objected to any of Dan's questions, nor had he warned his client about providing information to the opposition. Excusing Fitch with the reminder that he was still under oath, Dan made a mental note never to engage Abbott's services.

"Thank you. You're excused," Dan said. "I shall indeed ask Miss Troy." He turned toward Beidler. "Will you call Helen Troy, please?"

As she took the witness chair, her head high, her face was set against him, as though he had never won a settlement for her against Slade's estate, or treated her with respect, even though he'd had an urge to wash his hands after she left his office. Where she had giggled and flirted with him then, she had not so much as a glance for him now. Her shoulders did not lift, her flowered wool shawl did not slip to suggest pleasures in store for him. She wore a plain gray dress under the shawl, and the ostrich-plumed hat sat straight on her piled hair. More strikingly, she had left off the paint from her face, and appeared a decade older.

The corners of his mouth felt like forming a smile. With her hostile attitude she freed him from any semblance of treating her as though she were an honest woman. She was, after all, only a lying whore, probably as diseased in mind as in body.

He began quietly, with a simple, direct question. "When did Mr. McDowell leave your establishment?"

She tried to lean around him to look at Fitch. By the expression on her face, she wanted his approval.

He blocked her view. So they were in league. Satisfaction settled on his shoulders. He could break that partnership. Would break it. Happily. With as much satisfaction as drawing a bead on fine fat buck.

She said, "Sam McDowell left my place on the morning of the seventeenth."

"Miss Eileen has testified that he left the morning of the fifteenth. The day after five men were hanged in the unfinished building now occupied by the Drug Emporium. How do you suggest we resolve this discrepancy?"

"There ain't no discrep – discrepancy that I can see. She's mixed up. She's been mixed up ever since I took her in. On account she witnessed the Indian raid that killed her folks."

"Why are you so certain Mr. McDowell left on the seventeenth?"

"I just am. It was a couple of days after that hangin'. I remember that. Old Sam, he wanted to be sure his wife would live. When he heard she'd woke up and would recover, he left. Owed me money, too."

"How much money?"

"Thirteen dollars. Give or take." She still sought eye contact with Fitch.

Behind him, the air shifted, and the stench almost made him sneeze. He wanted to swing around and shout, *Be silent!* But he held himself in check. Someone sniffed. Maybe Eileen. At the desk, Judge Hosmer's upper eyelids drooped. Did he find this questioning so tedious?

"Yet you told me that Mr. McDowell left your place on the sixteenth."

She had forgotten the date she had originally given him. Or she lied. "I don't recollect that."

"You don't?" He had her. "So you've always maintained that he left on the seventeenth?"

"Why, yeah. I never said the sixteenth. You're making that up."

Now. Do it now. "You think Miss Eileen is mistaken then."

She meant to convey a light-heartedness, he supposed, but her laugh was a mule's bray, and the plume tossing on her hat reminded him of a broken-down horse drawing a hearse. "Not only that. Why, the way that girl lies. I had to make her a kitchen helper so she wouldn't be stealing the men's money out of their trousers afterwards." She cast an inviting look over her shoulder toward Judge Hosmer. "You know."

Eileen gasped, "No. It's wrong to tell lies."

"Your Honor," Dan asked Hosmer, "could Mr. Dobson read back the portion of Miss Eileen's testimony in which she says Mr. McDowell left on the fifteenth?"

"Yes. I'd like to hear that portion again myself."

Dobson flipped back in his notes until he found the place and then read it aloud to them.

Dan said, "You tell us McDowell went away on the seventeenth, but you told McDowell's son Timothy that he left on the sixteenth. Shall we bring in young Mr. McDowell to testify to that?"

She opened her mouth, Dan supposed to deny it, but he gave her no chance. "Major Fitch also says Mr. McDowell left on the sixteenth."

She goggled at him, her mouth opening and closing as she groped for a reply.

Dan gave her time.

At last she said, "I must've been mistaken. It was the sixteenth. McDowell left on the sixteenth."

"Thank you," said Dan. "Now, Miss Troy, I only have another question for you." He moved a few inches aside, to give her space to look at Fitch.

Looking at Fitch, she preened herself, adjusted the shawl, its flowers woven in orange and blue and red.

Dan turned away, and fumbled out his handkerchief as though to catch a sneeze.

Fitch sat nursing his arm, head bowed, seeming intent on thoughts of his own.

"Sure. Anything," she said.

Wheeling to her, surprised that no dizziness threatened him, Dan asked, "Who gave you that beautiful shawl?"

"Major Fitch did. We're going to be—" Too late she stopped herself.

Fitch picked at a loose thread in the sling as his cheeks reddened.

"Ah. I see. Perhaps you can tell me," Dan paused, his words came smooth as oil. "Why did you lie?" He stood aside as far as he could, to give them a clear shot at each other.

"Me? I didn't lie." Her voice rose. "Tell them I ain't a liar. Tobias, honey. Tell them."

Fitch sat back in his chair. For all its expression, his face might have been that of a dead man. She stared at him, then at Dan. "I done it for him." She jerked a thumb in Fitch's direction.

"But why? You must have known Jacky Stevens killed Mr. McDowell. Why not tell the truth instead of maligning a young girl's character?"

"You smarmy bas —" she began.

Hosmer interrupted. "There will be no profanity in my court. If you utter one more profane word, I'll have you jailed for contempt."

"Yes, sir."

"Yes, Your Honor."

"Yes, Your Honor," she spat. After a second or two she continued her diatribe against Dan. "You think you're too good for the likes of me, you and McDowell's boy, when everyone knows you laid down with Sam McDowell's wife before they found him. Tobias Fitch is a better man than you. He'd have me, but you? And McDowell's good-for-nothing brat? You deserve to go down for murder. The Major is twice the man you are with your fancy duds and your slimy manners, and your —"

"You stupid poxy whore, you're lying now!" Fitch exploded from his chair. "You think anyone wants you?"

Her mouth dropped open, showing brown, broken teeth. "You promised me." She flung words like stones at Fitch. "You said we'd get married, you and me, as soon as this is over and you have the Nugget claim."

Fitch laughed, an ugly sound empty of merriment.

Justice Hosmer banged his gavel down. "Order! Order in the court!"

Beidler stood in front of Fitch, and though there was at least eight inches' difference in their heights, he backed Fitch against the wall. "Sit down and don't get up until you're told you can. You hear me?"

Fitch nodded. He clutched his injured arm to his body, protecting it – from whom?

Dan asked her, "When did Sam McDowell leave your establishment?"

Sobbing into a corner of her shawl, she did not answer him.

Judge Hosmer prompted her: "Miss Troy, you have committed perjury in my court when you swore to tell the truth and then lied. If you don't want to suffer more penalties, answer the question truthfully."

Sniffling, she dabbed at her eyes. "It was like Eileen said. Sam left the day after y'all hung them five boys." She gulped. "On the fifteenth. He said he'd killt the only woman ever meant anything to him, and his son would never forgive him."

In the silence, Dan and Judge Hosmer looked at each other. Someone coughed, and he heard, "Yah."

"Your Honor?" Beidler spoke to Judge Hosmer without looking at Dan. "May I testify? I think I got something to say about this."

"Mr. Stark? Do you know what Deputy Beidler would tell us?"

"No, Your Honor. But if the deputy wants to speak, I'd be happy to hear his testimony." He pointed his index finger at Helen Troy. "I think I'm finished with this witness." As she stumbled, sobbing, past him to a seat at the back of the room, he could hardly contain his satisfaction. They had tried to destroy him. They deserved what they got.

Jacob shook his head, but something told Dan he was right to trust Beidler.

After Beidler swore to tell the whole truth, he settled on the front edge of the witness chair, his feet flat on the floor. Hardly waiting for Dan to ask what he had to say, he began to tell his story to the judge. "Fitch was late on the fifteenth. He caught up with us about three hours after we'd set out to ride to Deer Lodge, over the Divide. There's maybe fifty others that know it, too. He'd been tracking stray horses, he said, and the tracks led up Daylight Gulch. He told me nobody would have to worry about Sam McDowell any more, that he'd up and left Virginia City, and he'd seen him on his way up the gulch." He faced Dan. "I'm sorry. It just didn't click for me, that he must have seen the murder until just now. I done you wrong, and you'd been nothing but friendly to me."

He could not let bygones be bygones. Beidler had known all along that McDowell had left on the fifteenth, that Dan could not have murdered him; he was watching over Martha. He could not be so quick with forgiveness, if he ever could let off this man who had once been his friend.

"This witness may be excused, Your Honor. I have no more questions of him." That was not exactly true, but he could wait until they were alone. For now, he had what he needed. "I'd like to recall Major Fitch."

"Major Fitch, you are still under oath, and I do not look favorably on perjurers." Judge Hosmer was as angry as Dan ever thought to see him.

"You may have been looking for strays, but you saw the murder, didn't you?" The leather on the seat of Fitch's trousers barely touched the chair when Dan demanded, "You've been lying because you're not satisfied that you have four of the claims that should have gone to McDowell's widow and her children, and you also have one of mine that your surrogate won in a poker game. You won't be satisfied until you have the Nugget, will you? Isn't that your motive?"

Fitch spoke in a deadly whisper. "Those claims are mine. You damn Yankees think you own the whole bloody country—" Dan lost a few words when the judge tapped the gavel on the sound block, but Fitch paid no attention, shouted louder with every word. "Your fucking Union troops invaded Missouri, and you burned down—" the gavel banged down and down again "—my plantation and run off my free blacks, but that wasn't enough for you damn mudsills—" he broke against the gavel's thunder, and regained himself to shout even louder "—you took my arm at Pea Ridge, and then—" he stood and screamed over the gavel and the judge's commands for order "—at Beaverhead Rock I had my last chance to take back the Nugget, and now you've taken that and my arm, too."

At last, whether silenced by Hosmer hammering the gavel and bellowing, "Order! Order!" or by Beidler and Abbott seizing him and forcing him into the witness chair, or by his own shortness of breath, Dan didn't know, but at last Fitch quieted. Pale and drawn, he rocked back and forth, sweat running down his temples into his beard.

Abbott pulled a flask from his coat pocket, unscrewed the cap, and gave the small flat bottle to Fitch, who tipped his head back and took a long drink.

"It's whiskey and laudanum," Abbott said. "Dulls the pain."

Hosmer had laid the gavel aside, but it still pounded in Dan's ears. He sensed the end approaching, and knew he had won. Why, then, did he feel only a great weariness along with this God-damn headache? There was still much to do. Arrest Jacky Stevens. Make Fitch confess to attempted murder. Make him tell that he saw Jacky Stevens murder Sam McDowell. Tell Timothy.

"You saw what happened to McDowell, didn't you?" Asking the question, Dan heard Dobson's pen scratch over the paper, Hosmer's hoarse breathing.

"Yeah, I saw it." He spoke as one completely defeated.

Abbot said, "You do not have to say anything that will incriminate you, although perhaps these gentlemen will look mercifully on the incident at the Rock if you come clean now."

"I'll get as much mercy from them as a Southerner has ever had from a mudsill," said Fitch. "I was out looking for strays, like I said before. I heard voices coming from a draw off Daylight Gulch. I thought it might be horse thieves, so I took a look from the lip of the draw. Jacky and Sam were going at it hammer and tongs. Jacky shouted something about him being Sam's real son. Sam yelled back that Jacky was no son of his, he had a real son that was worth a hundred Jacky's, and get the hell out of his sight. He walked off a couple of steps, and Jacky went after him and stuck him with that little knife he carries."

He raised the flask and took a swallow. "Sam didn't even turn around. He kept walking, and Jacky followed along. I stayed behind them both. Jacky was shouting at Sam to let him go with him, but Sam kept on walking, blood dripping little by little. After a while Jacky gave up and walked back toward me. I hid behind a boulder, and Jacky passed me without knowing I was there. I heard him crying, 'I killt him. I killt Pa.'"

Fitch, sinking fast under the laudanum, might have seemed pitiable to Judge Hosmer, but Dan had no pity for him. The weeks of torment when his own stepson thought he could have done this, the fear in Martha's eyes during her difficult time, this blasted headache. Damn it, the scales needed balancing. He would have every detail, every move, every conniving thought laid out for the record. He would ask Judge Hosmer to have a fair copy made of Dobson's notes, and Fitch would sign it. He would have the relinquishment. Then they would see where they were.

Right now he would have answers.

"Then what did you do?"

"I followed Sam until he crawled into a little cave. Then I caught up my saddle horse, and rode after the strays."

The door banged open. Timothy burst in, and stopped as Beidler blocked him. "You went off and let my Pap die. You helped murder him. Jacky stuck him, but you didn't do nothing for him. You're as much a murderer as – as Jacky. Why? Why'd you do it?"

Hosmer raised the gavel, but Dan forestalled him. "Your Honor, please? My stepson has not been sworn, but he asks something we would all like to know."

The judge laid the gavel down. "Then you ask the question, Mr. Stark. The witness may answer."

After Dan repeated Timothy's question, Fitch sat silent. Perhaps, Dan thought, the laudanum worked too well. Had he slipped into the semi-conscious state opium-eaters loved?

"Your Honor?"

"The witness will answer," said Judge Hosmer. "Mr. Abbott?"

"You have to answer the question, Tobias," the lawyer said.

Fitch cast a bloodshot glare at Dan. "The Nugget is rightfully mine. All six claims Sam found belonged to me, God damn it, not to his wife and children. I paid him to locate them, and once I did, he had no claim. Nobody does. They're mine." He took a deep breath and tried to shout, "The Nugget is mine."

"Calm down, Tobias," said Abbott.

Whether he heard his lawyer or not, Fitch smiled at Dan, a smile that raised the hairs on his neck. "The only thing stopping me from getting it is you, damn you. If not for you, I'd have taken possession when McDowell disappeared."

"That explains why you tried to kill me at Beaverhead Rock," Dan said.

Abbott spoke up. "Your Honor, my client invokes his right not to incriminate himself. The facts are that Major Fitch and Mr. Stark fought at Beaverhead Rock, but neither man has been charged."

"Agreed. Mr. Stark, you will confine your questions to the matter at hand."

"Yes, Your Honor," Dan said. "For the record, however, the ownership of the Nugget was settled last spring. The miners' court awarded the Nugget to the McDowell family."

From the hallway, Cummings shouted, "Miss McDowell, Miss Dorothy, you can't go in the judge's office. A hearing is in session."

Dotty stood in the open doorway, as Cummings tried to drag her away by the sleeve of her old brown coat. "Dan'l, Dan'l! It's begun. The baby's a-comin' and we need Eileen to help."

Too soon, much too soon. A month early. "Your Honor, may Miss Eileen be excused for this emergency?"

Already up, Eileen fled toward the doorway without waiting for Judge Hosmer's permission.

The gavel hammered. "Young lady! You must not disrupt this court! Dobson, make a note to write up a warrant ordering the arrest of Jacky Stevens. Deputy Beidler, you will make the arrest forthwith when you have the signed warrant from me. Mr. Abbott, you will guarantee to have your client in this office at ten of the clock on Monday morning while we consider what to do next in light of his confession. In the meantime, Mr. Stark, you are cleared of all wrongdoing in the matter of Samuel McDowell's death. We're adjourned."

He slammed the gavel down.

~~59~~

Waiting in the Champion Saloon, as close as anyone would let him come to his house, he had never felt so helpless. Just across the street, Martha labored with his child, and he must stay here. The women – Lydia Hudson – would not let him or Timothy in. No male must come among them but the doctor. He was surprised they allowed the dog, but Timothy had told him they'd taken pity on Canary and banished him to Dotty's room rather than his shelter under the porch it being so cold the mercury froze in the thermometers.

Why was he thinking about the dog? He wished he had faith; he might have spent this time in church, down on his knees, praying for her and the little one, that they'd come through this ordeal safely. At the thought of Berry Woman, fear rose up sharp and bitter in his mouth.

Someone made a joke, but he did not hear it, could not laugh at the punch line. He could only listen for sounds from his house.

He sat at a poker table by the window, watching for his front door to open. Quelling a futile impulse to yell for quiet in the saloon, he tried to listen. The other men would not be quiet, and they would forever think of him as the man who played soft while his wife fulfilled a woman's destiny.

Of all his friends at this table, only Lewis Hershfield was a married man and a father. Jacob had never been married; his turn would come to go through this. Other men heard the news from Con Orem or the bartender as they bought their drinks. They came to the table, sat down briefly, told him their wives had come through this all right. Their sisters had children, happy, healthy, running around and getting into everything. They talked about home. One or two shed tears for home 'back East,' nearly two-thousand miles away. It might as well have been the moon.

"Now is the hardest part," said Hershfield. "This is the worst, when you're waiting for someone to come and tell you everything's all right, that you have a son, or a daughter, and everyone is healthy. It will be well, you know. We all came to life this way. We all caused trouble for our mothers."

He knew all that. Yes, all people came into the world this self-same way. Had his father suffered the terror of waiting, not knowing if the outcome would be joy or an impossible grief and guilt: She might die. If she died, or the child did, he would have killed them.

He would not blame her if she never wanted him again, if she lived. Yet Mother had his older sister, then him, then the little ones. Martha already had Timothy and Dotty.

She must live, and the child, too. She must. God help her.

Timothy came in to tell him that Hosmer had deputized him to help Beidler find and arrest Jacky. "I've been waiting an almighty long time for this," he said. At the hearing, he had listened through the wall while waiting to testify before he came in to confront Fitch. His mind now was on getting Jacky Stevens, and he was pleased to be Beidler's sub-deputy. Dan wished him luck, but he could not focus on that hunt, when Martha waged her own life-and-death battle across the street.

When Dan asked what it was like when Dotty was born, Timothy shrugged. "Don't recollect."

Outside, the light failed. How much longer could this go on? Con Orem ordered more candles and lamps to be lighted. For the hundredth time, Dan thawed the ice on one of the window panes. Dotty had promised someone would come for him as soon as there was anything to tell him. He went to the door and stepped outside. Lamplight shined a slice of light between heavy winter curtains Martha had sewed. He could not see the back, where their bedroom had a window.

All was still.

"It's gone quiet over there." Shivering, he told the others.

"Sometimes they rest a little before the baby comes," Hershfield said.

Jacob said, "I would like to know about this from my own wife."

"You're not married, Jacob." Dan had to smile. "You haven't even found a woman."

"No, not here. When I get rich and go back to the Old Country, I find a bride, yah? Someone who understands how to keep a kosher house."

"Speaking of food," said Hershfield, "I'm hungry. Stark, you must be starving." He went to the bar and brought beer. "Food's coming right up."

Dan ate and drank, but the cheese and eggs and stew all tasted like brown paper. Remembering his manners, he thanked Lewis. "What do I owe you?"

"I'll take it out of your account," the banker said with a smile.

"You do that." It was Hershfield's way of telling him to forget it, but he would not.

He stepped outside again.

Two riders rode up Jackson. They rode hunched down, trusting their horses to find the way among the ruts and piles. Passing his house, the horses turned their heads toward it and pricked their ears. They stepped about restlessly, and over the clatter of iron shoes on the hard ground a woman's scream rose high and long. The riders stroked the horses' necks, and nudged them; they quickened the pace to walk faster.

Jacob brought him his coat. "It is too cold. You cannot be out here." He put the coat on, and together they walked around to the back of the building to relieve themselves.

Back inside, Jacob rubbed his hands together. "I wonder if Beidler has caught him."

"I don't know."

Hershfield said, "They should have caught him by now. It was just a matter of going to Fancy Annie's."

"Helen Troy must have warned him," Dan said. "She left the courthouse before we did. Beidler couldn't go without the warrant. She had time."

After another half hour or so, Dan heard a team and wagon rumble down the street. Iron-bound wheels, the axles rasped against the wheel hubs, the eight hooves scrabbled for purchase. The driver called out, "Easy, girls, easy does it, ladies."

He thought he heard a shriek, then silence. Grabbing his coat, he ran outside. He would have run in front of the draft horses if Hershfield had not held him back. "No. Let's go in. It was only the axle. They'll send someone to tell us. We can't go barging in there now. They won't thank us for it."

He let Hershfield bundle him into the saloon, his desire to be at home sharper than anything he had ever wanted, except perhaps Martha herself, and that wanting had led them here.

Before he had taken off his coat, another, longer, scream rose from outside. It was not Martha, but someone else. Pivoting, he raced outside in time to see a young girl backing away from – God, no!

Hunched low, Jacky Stevens stalked Eileen. She had come out of the house, a shawl around her shoulders. Moonlight glinted off a blade in the boy's hand. Dan leaped into a run. She drew out a pistol from her pocket, clutched it in both hands, raised it level with her eyes, her hands shook, the barrel wobbled; she thumbed back both hammers, pointed it at the boy – Christ, Jacky closed on her too fast.

The little gun roared, spewed flame and white smoke that blocked his view. He stumbled over Jacky's body, seized the girl. When he took the derringer from her hand, she collapsed against him, sobbing.

~~60~~

Eileen would not have hit Jacky Stevens if he had been farther away. Her hands shook too much. As it was, she had almost missed, but sometimes, Dan thought, looking down at Jacky's torn throat, the blood pumping out, almost is enough. He turned his back on the dying boy to hold the hysterical Eileen, who huddled against him, her face buried in her hands. He told her she was a brave girl, it was all right, all right, though he knew it would never be all right for her. She had killed, and even though it was self-defense and Jacky had deserved it, she would pay the price the rest of her life. He knew how it would be for her.

Then Timothy was there, reached for her, and he relinquished her to his stepson, who scooped Eileen into his arms and carried her inside.

Dan buttoned his coat, put on hat and gloves, and prepared to tend to the practical things that killing brought. He'd had experience in that.

He felt the derringer's weight in his coat pocket. He had bought it for her, and its twin for Dotty. Their protectors could not always protect them from people like Jacky. Nobody could protect her from her suffering afterwards.

A crowd came out of the nearby saloons and gathered around to gawk at the horrible sight.

Dead, Jacky Stevens still clutched his knife; its short thin blade glinted in the light from the lamps Hershfield and Con Orem brought from the saloon. He lay on his back, his mouth frozen in a snarl. A breeze stirred his hair, drifted a few flakes of snow into his wide, expressionless eyes.

"Let me through." Deputy Beidler elbowed through the crowd. He stood beside the corpse. "Can't say as I'm sorry." He stepped toward Dan, and the two of them walked a few feet closer to the house. "Self-defense, was it?"

"Yes," said Dan. "Purely. She shot him from two steps away. Look. He's still holding the knife. One more step and he'd have killed her."

"She? She shot him? She who?"

"Eileen. She was coming to tell me about my wife– dear God, what has happened?" Martha. He had heard no sounds from his house. Was Martha all right? The baby? He pivoted too fast for balance to run into the house and nearly fell.

Beidler held him by his coat sleeve. "Helen Troy warned him, you know. He was gone by the time I got to Fancy Annie's. I suppose Judge Hosmer may want to charge her with aiding and abetting a fugitive. We got no place to jail a woman, though." He glanced back toward the body, rapidly freezing. "You'd think he'd have had more sense than to tackle you."

Would Beidler never let him go? He spoke fast: "He wasn't after me. The Troy woman must have told him Eileen heard his confession and told about it. He came to kill her." He tugged against Beidler's hold on his sleeve. "I must see about my wife."

Pulling free of Beidler, he started for his front door, but the deputy would have held him. He swung around, fist cocked. Beidler let go and stepped back a pace.

"Mr. Stark?"

He swung around. The doctor walked down the path toward him. He had deep circles under his eyes, but he smiled when he saw Dan. "Congratulations, Mr. Stark. You have twin sons, and your good lady came through her ordeal very well. She may be a bit weak, but given time and rest, she will soon be completely well. She's a grand lady, very courageous, and your boys are fine little fellows."

Martha, safe. Twin boys. Everyone was safe. He wobbled, nearly sat in the snow. "Thank you, doctor." He heard himself add something about payment, as he stumbled toward his front door.

Almost there, a thought stopped him. He turned back toward Beidler. "Preserve the knife, X. Maybe we can match it to the shirt McDowell wore."

"You still have that?" Beidler blew on his hands.

"My wife—" Dan choked, tried again. "My dear wife kept them, shirt and coat both. She had faith they'd be

needed someday as evidence." He added, "Jacob Himmelfarb has them." Beyond certainty he knew that Jacky's
knife would match the cut.

~~~

Inside, Tabby Rose and Lydia Hudson bundled up
soiled linens, and Dotty thrust something into the fire.
Lydia Hudson seemed to be the honcho – well, she would
be.

Eileen sat in his reading chair, a blanket wrapped
around her. She held a mug of something hot, and Timothy sat on the arm of the chair. Neither of them spoke, but
the boy looked up at him and smiled.

"Dan'l." Dotty wore a blood-streaked coverall, and her
hair was tied up and covered with a kerchief. She held a
bundle of cloths; setting it down, she intercepted him,
drew him into the reading corner. "They're all right.
They're sleeping now. Mama and our little brothers are
just fine. Mama can be up and around as soon as she wants
to be, the doctor said."

"You stayed through it all?" How had this flibbertigib-
bet of a girl dared be present at her mother's lying-in?
How had he let her do it? Why had he not thought of
Dotty once in the last few days? The last weeks?

"I wanted to. I wanted to help, but I didn't know what
it would be like." Her eyes moved as she rearranged her
thoughts. "What happened to Eileen? She nor Timmy will
say. What was that noise?"

He brushed a lock of hair off her face to give himself time to collect his words.

Lydia Hudson, also wearing a blood-stained coverall, thrust herself between them. "You should not be here yet!" Though her face had a gray tinge, and deep lines had formed at the corners of her mouth, she had enough left to snap orders at him. "Take your dog and go away until you're told to come." She raised a bloody hand to push at him, but he blocked it before she could touch him.

"You have to know this," he said. Mrs. Hudson dropped her hand. Much as he would have liked to drop the news like a rock on Mrs. Hudson, he lowered his voice below a whisper for Eileen's sake, and to spare Dotty. "Eileen will need you both. When she came out to find me, Jacky Stevens was waiting. He attacked her with his knife, and she shot him in self-defense."

"Oh, no." One of Dotty's hands went to the sagging pocket of her overall, the other to her mouth. "Is he– is he–?"

"He's dead." How did a man comfort his stepdaughter who had grown into a young woman in the space of a few hours? He could not take her on his lap any more. "He will bother you no more."

Mrs. Hudson snapped, "You should never have given her that infernal weapon. Now she has murder on her conscience, and her soul is in danger unless she repents."

"You would rather he had murdered her? She did no murder; she killed him in self-defense, in defense of this family." About to tell her to get out, he quashed his incendiary anger. For Martha's sake, he would not forbid her the house. "I will see my wife." He walked toward the bedroom door.

Mrs. Hudson hurried after him, hissed at him, "You can't. They're sleeping!"

He put his hand on the latch and was about to say something else before he remembered that he might well owe this infernal woman Martha's life, his babies' lives. "Thank you for saving them."

~~~

He left the door open a crack behind him to give him some light without disturbing Martha or the babies. While his eyes adjusted to the dark, things emerged from the shadows: a chair newly placed near the stove, two baskets lying on his side of their bed. He took shallow breaths; the air stank of blood and sweat and excrement. Birth was a messy business, he reminded himself.

Martha slept the sleep of someone who has fought a long, hard campaign and won the last battle. He stood listening to her breathe, even and steady.

He sidled around the bed to try to see into the baskets, put a forefinger into one, touched a tiny face, wrinkled skin, a button nose. In the second basket, a tiny mouth yawned wide. Even in sleep, they squirmed and kicked. So had they done inside Martha. What kind of men would they become? How could he guide them? He was responsible for two new lives, two new human beings, and on down the generations.

God help him.

One of them hiccupped in his sleep, woke himself up, and howled.

The other baby, awakened by his brother, wailed.

Martha turned over and groped for a baby. Half asleep, she lifted him out of the basket, uncovered a breast and set the child to suck. Her head bent over the baby, she reached for the other with her free hand, touched Dan's forefinger.

"Oh!" A little time passed before she realized he was there. "Hello."

"Hello." He could not think what to say, but he had to say something. "You're beautiful." He spoke a little louder. "They are beautiful."

He leaned over to touch her cheek. Straightening, he staggered bit, dizzy. He should tell her he was clear, but that seemed a small thing now. The day held too much, was too immense to grasp, he felt he would burst from it all, and all at once he could not hold in the great booming laugh that caught Martha up with it and carried them both along.

When their laughter ebbed, he took the fed baby and put him over his shoulder to burp him.

"You know about babies?" Martha put the second baby to her breast.

"I have two younger brothers and a younger sister." His boy's tiny head fit in the palm of his hand, and he marveled that anything that small might grow as big as himself. The baby burped on his coat. He put him in the basket and wrapped the blanket around him again.

When the second baby was fed, burped, and dozing off, Dan said, "I'm clear of that other business."

"Thank God," said Martha. On her way to sleep again, she whispered, "They need names. For the christening."

"We overlooked that, didn't we? Yes, you're right. Tomorrow." He kissed her. "We'll talk about it tomorrow. Sleep well."

With that, he turned to leave. At the door he heard Martha murmur, "Build a bigger house."

"I will." He doubted she heard him as he eased out of the bedroom.

Dotty said, "Eileen went to bed, but Timmy and I waited to find out where you'll be when we need you." Everyone assumed he would not stay at home. "We're taking shifts. Where will you be?"

"I can take a watch, too," he said.

"No sir," Timothy said. "You have to get your rest. You're not so firm on your pins yet, like you should be."

"You can find me at Planters House tonight. I'll come by after breakfast." He smiled. "You're very brave, you know that? I'm proud of you both."

"Oh." Her hands went to her flaming cheeks. "I heard you tell Mama you're clear. I'm so glad."

"Thank you." Weariness threatened to swamp him. "I'd better be going."

"Yes. Don't worry about anything here." She put her hand out to hold him back. "We'll take care of Eileen, too."

"Good."

Outside, everything but the blood had been cleared away. Timothy walked with Dan up to Planters House. "Dan'l, I – I'm sorry."

"See me at the office tomorrow afternoon. About three."

"All right."

Hearing Timothy's footsteps recede downhill, he thought he should have said something, but he didn't know what it might have been, and it could not be the wrong thing. Not at this juncture. Perhaps he could think better in the morning.

~~61~~

The day felt disjointed from the moment he opened his eyes. He had given instructions that he was not to be disturbed, and the hotel staff must have taken him at his word. His pocket watch chimed twelve as he reached for it.

As he dressed, he recalled that today, Saturday, was the last day of the year. Tomorrow would begin the year of our Lord, eighteen hundred and sixty-five.

A new year, with perhaps an end to an old war.

Tying his cravat, he looked at the man in the smoky mirror. "Today's a good day to clean some slates," he told his image.

After breakfast, he negotiated terms for an indefinite stay at Planters House. The matter settled to his satisfaction more than that of the owner, Dan put on his gloves, took his walking stick, and started down the hill.

The day was not so cold as yesterday had been. Perhaps the temperature had climbed closer to zero. Heavy clouds blew across the sky, and a breeze cleared the air of wood smoke.

At home, chaos reigned. The stench of used diapers made him want to gag. Dotty argued with Lydia Hudson about how best to wash them, while Eileen stood by.

"Send them out," he ordered. "I'll not have anyone living in this stench." When Mrs. Hudson set her jaw at him, he said, "Find a washerwoman who takes in diapers and send them to her. Daily. This air is unhealthy."

In the bedroom Martha was awake but resting while the babies slept. After he kissed her, she said, "I heard you, Dan'l. Dotty and Eileen, they don't think there's another way than scrubbing up themselves." She smiled. "Thank you."

He remembered her story about her Indian grandmother plowing a field and being interrupted by the arrival of her mother. He kidded her: "Tomorrow you can shovel the path to the necessary." It took her a moment to catch the joke, but when she did, she covered her mouth to keep her laughter from waking the babies.

She asked, "What do you think about names?"

Some minutes later, as she sank toward sleep, he smiled as he left her side. They had not agreed on names, and when he had suggested No-Name 1 and No-Name 2, she had thrown a small pillow at him.

Giving a cheerful goodbye to the women, who were bundling up dirty diapers, he was struck by Eileen's wan silence. He sat down on the bench by the door to put his boots on and called her to him, patting the bench next to him. When she sat there, he said, "I know how you feel about last night."

Her muscles tensed, and he thought she might scream at him if she dared.

Across the room, Dotty and Mrs. Hudson discussed washerwomen. He did not think they could hear him, but he spoke softly. "I killed a man in self-defense this summer in New York." He had threaded a lace in his boot through the wrong holes, and pulled it out to start over. "I was also the Vigilante prosecutor. Among them, it is said truthfully that I – I pulled my own rope." Damn that lace. He'd got it wrong again. "Then in October, in Bannack, we carried out a sentence we set last spring." He ripped the lace out for the second time. "If you didn't feel like you do, I don't know how to say it, but you, we wouldn't be, I guess you wouldn't be a decent woman. There are some we dealt with, killing's nothing to them. Murder's nothing to them. Just as killing you wouldn't have been anything to Jacky. It would have just meant you couldn't talk about his confession.

"But you can't feel that way. I can't feel that way. That's a difference between him and us. Them and us. This thing, killing, hits us in our conscience."

He had never meant to say that to anyone. He hadn't even known he had it to say. But this waif needed to hear something to ease her pain, and he'd stumbled on that. It wouldn't help right away, but maybe someday she could find a way to live with what she had done.

As he had. Somewhat.

~~~

Climbing the stairs to his office, he planned his strategy with Tobias Fitch at Monday's hearing. He would write his account of what had happened at Beaverhead Rock, and a relinquishment of all interest in the Nugget mine. Fitch would sign both. Or else. With Fitch's plot exposed in the examination, Dan had no doubt Judge Hosmer would support him. He had composed the first sentences of the relinquishment as his head rose above the steps.

Timothy waited for him. "Jake took your key out of your pocket while you was out cold. We figured you'd need it now." He held out his hand. The key lay on his palm.

"I think I do." Unlocking the door, Dan ushered him in.

The room was comfortably warm. He'd thought he would have to start over with the curing fires.

Lighting two candles, he set one on his desk and the other on a trivet on the stove's cooktop. Sunlight shone bright outside, but shadows lay dense in the corners.

They sat by the stove, waiting to get warm, and he could think of nothing to say. Should he just say, I forgive you, and be done with it? If he did, would the anger disappear from them both, like a magician's abracadabra?

He opened his mouth to say it, but the words stayed inside him somewhere.

Something glimmered near the back door, no doubt a trick of candlelight reflecting on the fender. But which candle?

There was no mistaking that stink. The damned thing with its foul stench had been with him too long. Would he never get rid of it? How could he chase away this black fog, which appeared and disappeared of its own accord? It had no substance, so he could not batter it. It was dead already; he could not kill it.

He spoke of Martha. "Your mother is doing well. Have you seen your little brothers yet?" Half-brothers, but he would not quibble.

"Yeah. I guess they'll pretty up soon enough."

Dan laughed. "Yes, they will. Newborns are always red and wrinkled."

Timothy took off his gloves, held his hands to the warmth, fiddled with a button on his coat, cracked the knuckles on both hands.

Dan waited.

"I'm so damn sorry." Timothy hunched his back as he said it.

Did he expect Dan to hit him with a quarter round? Dan said nothing.

"I'm sorry," Timothy said again.

"All right, you're sorry. That's good. What do you expect to do about it?"

"Do about what?"

"About being sorry. You can't just say you're sorry and let it go at that. You have to change your ways to show you're genuinely sorry." He seemed to recollect there was something Jesus said about sinning no more. That was the promise he could not make. If he had the Vigilante business to do over again in the absence of law, he would.

"I don't know. What should I do?"

"What do you think?" Dan took up the poker and opened the fire door to poke at the fire. *I won't make this easy for him, but I can't do like he expects, hit him like McDowell would have done.* Or Grandfather, using such occasions as an excuse for more meanness.

Timothy looked down at his big callused hands, rubbed them together. Candlelight showed the stubble on his cheeks. "I can't come at it."

"All right. Then you'll have to agree to accept my direction."

"What's that?" Timothy's voice rose above his normal register.

"Go to school."

"What?" Timothy stood up. "No sir. I ain't about to sit in no school with babies learning c-a-t and d-o-g."

"Sit down." Dan's voice cracked like a whip.

Timothy sat. His jaw muscles bulged.

"Listen to me now. Let me tell you about the Nugget. You think you know mining from working a placer claim. Do you know how much dust you took out of it each week on average?"

The boy shook his head.

"A quartz mine is a hundred times more complex and you can't even give me an average of how much dust you've taken weekly out of the creek claim. You don't know how to figure averages, do you?"

Looking at the fire leaping behind the grate, Timothy muttered, "No."

"If I knew the average amount of gold that claim yielded in a week, I could say, Why don't you keep twenty percent or twenty-five percent? Or even half. For yourself." The boy's head came up, cocked to one side, listening hard.

"You have to learn, or you'll be stuck the rest of your life in backbreaking work and know nothing else. Anyone can cheat you." Dan paused for breath before he finished. "It's winter. The Alder claim, you say, is about played out, and you can't work a claim anyway until the weather warms up. You have to go to school."

"Not with all them little ones. I'd look a damn fool."

Thinking over Timothy's objection, Dan sat back, the fingers of his left hand playing the chair arm like a piano.

"You will inherit your share of the Nugget in five years."

Timothy looked up, as startled as though Dan had fired his rifle.

"Yes. Five years. What will you do, then? What will you be equipped to do?"

"I don't know. What would there be?"

"Here's what we'll be getting into if that claim proves up. In five years we might have a hundred men working for us underground. They have to be paid a good wage, all told perhaps four dollars a day each. That's four-hundred dollars a day for all of them. We'll need machinery and spare parts, and men to maintain the machines, and their wages, too. We'll need timber to shore up the tunnels and timberers to build supports for the tunnels. Tracks laid along the tunnel floors, ore cars to run on the tracks, and mules, horses, and donkeys to pull the cars to the main shaft. From there the ore will be hoisted to the surface and milled. Stamps and stamp mills to crush the ore. Mill-workers, from the foreman on down to the sweepers."

He waited, while Timothy stared at him with rounded eyes, his breathing quick and uneven.

"Complex operations. We might spend a million dollars before we make a profit. If the vein Jacob discovered doesn't peter out. If the apex, the highest point of the vein, isn't on someone else's claim. If all goes well enough to pay back our investment. We won't know until we try. It's a huge risk."

They sat in silence. Timothy knotted and unknotted his grimy handkerchief.

Dan let a minute or two go by.

"Now tell me," Dan said, "where in all that do you fit in? Digging, drilling, blasting for three, four dollars a day? Or helping to track where the vein goes?"

He stretched out his legs, thinking Timothy would go away to consider his future, but the boy's long, narrow face, that McDowell had called a donkey-face, shone. He hitched his chair closer to Dan. "With Pap, I hated mining, but this summer, on my own, I got to love it. It's the hardest work a man can do, digging and breaking rock and crushing it and washing out the gold. But I did it. I made it give up the gold. Then I got to wondering about the rock, and how the gold got in there, maybe in old streams, and where they came from and where they went. I listened to Jacob, and we talked about it down in that pit he dug at the Nugget. If we could only track the veins, make the country rock give up the gold instead of hiding it. It's a contest, me against the earth." He struck the side of his fist on his knee. "The rest is, well, it's just dust."

When Dan cocked an eyebrow at him, the boy laughed. "Yeah. Gold dust."

"Then I'll tell you what I'll do," Dan said. "I'll pay for you to go to school, as long as you earn no less than a B on everything."

Timothy's smile vanished.

"You're smart. You just don't know enough. Intelligence with ignorance is worse than useless. It guarantees failure. So learn or be like your father." And mindful of Grandfather, who had never given Father or him a choice of anything from the meat for dinner to their futures, he added, "It's your choice."

Timothy shook his head. "School's too slow. I gotta make up for lost time."

Sitting back, Dan watched the young determined face. Timothy would not yield; for pride he would make a stupid choice for his future.

"All right. Report here on Monday, after I've settled Fitch's hash, for tutoring. I'll teach you. It won't be fun; you'll work harder than you ever would in school, but when the ice melts you'll know how to read, write, and cipher. And if you study hard, when the time comes, I'll pay for you to go to college and learn to be an engineer. Or a geologist. Then the earth will keep no secrets from you. Deal?"

Timothy swallowed two or three times, but said nothing. Perhaps he could say nothing, but his face, beaming like a lantern, said everything.

Jotting a list on a piece of paper from his notecase, Dan gave it to Tim. "Go to Tilton's stationery store and get your supplies. Then on Monday we'll begin." Rising to escort Timothy to the door, Dan said, "Tell Mr. Tilton I'll be in later to settle my account." He put out his hand, and after a second's hesitation, Timothy took it.

From his trousers pocket Dan brought out the quartz nugget. "Here," he said, "Take this. It's yours."

Closing the door behind Timothy, he leaned against it. The room smelled different. Wood smoke, warm stone..

The ghost was gone.

Historical Note

I found the procedure for the "examination" scenes at the end of *The Ghost at Beaverhead Rock* in *Acts, Resolutions, and Memorials of the 1ˢᵗ Legislature of Montana Territory.* The pertinent sections of the Criminal Practice Acts occur in Chapter I, in the part titled "Arrest and Examination of Offenders," Sections 25, 36, 37, 38, 39, and 42 on pages 219 and 224-225.

In so doing, I took some historical liberties with Montana Territorial law; the First Territorial Legislature had not yet passed a Criminal Practice Act.

The *Statutes of the Territory of Idaho* contain provisions for an "examination," which is today called a "preliminary hearing," but they are less helpful to a non-lawyer because they are less detailed.

The point is that the law during the Civil War contained the same safeguards for people as the law does today, with the obvious exception that it catered to white people rather than to all people. The law was then exclusive rather than inclusive.

Yet even then white society was not monolithic. There were, as today, good-hearted white people who wanted no part of racial prejudice in any form. My main character throughout the four books of *The Vigilante Quartet,* Daniel

Bradford Stark, is an abolitionist in love with Martha (McDowell) Stark, who is one-quarter Eastern Cherokee.

Dan Stark is modeled on Wilbur Fisk Sanders, abolitionist, lawyer, and Vigilante, who became Montana Territory's first Senator. His uncle, Sidney Edgerton, was a radical abolitionist who served as both the first Chief Justice of Idaho Territory (prior to the formation of Montana Territory), and as our first Governor. Gov. Edgerton's stance on "Negro equality," as it was termed in that day, could be summed up as "Equality. Now." Edgerton was among the founders of the Republican Party.

Other historical characters are Charles S. Bagg and Hezekiah L. Hosmer. Bagg's role in *Ghost* and in *God's Thunderbolt* is consistent with his historical role. A Democrat, he was a veteran of the Mexican War who sought to find areas of agreement between Republicans and Democrats, the opponents in America's bloodiest conflict. As chairman of the Federal Relations Committee in the First Legislative Assembly, he forged a statement of cooperation between the Secessionists (Democrats) and Unionists (Republicans) and the federal government.

Hezekiah Lord Hosmer, our first Chief Justice, acted as I have portrayed him in the novel. By in effect forgiving the Vigilantes for their activities prior to December 5, 1864, the date he opened the Justice Court, he made a way for the two factions (North and South) in the Civil War to work together to write Montana law. You can find his speech reprinted in the *Montana Post* for December 10, 1864.

Another historical character is John Xavier Beidler, known as "X." His roles in all four books are historically accurate, but he puzzles me. From all I've read, including his own journal, he was capable of both great kindness and fearsome judgment. He treated a man for frostbite, and a few days later helped to hang him for murder and armed robbery.

Researching Montana's history is much easier compared to the "old days," meaning ten years ago, before the advent of digitization. The Montana Historical Society has uploaded digital copies of the *Montana Post* to the Library of Congress. Anyone can now read about Montana history as it happened from the first issue, August 27, 1864, on. Just go to http://chroniclingamerica.loc.gov/lccn/sn83025293/issues/

For more information about the era of the four books that make up *The Vigilante Quartet*, Montana Territory, 1862 – 1865, please visit my website: http://carol-buchanan.com, my blog: http://carol-buchanan.com/blog, or my Facebook page: http://facebook.com/CarolBuchananAuthor You can sign up for my Montana history newsletter at all three places, too.

ABOUT THE AUTHOR

A native Montanan, Carol Buchanan won a Spur Award
(2009), and a Spur Finalist award (2011) for her novels *God's
Thunderbolt: The Vigilantes of Montana*, and *Gold Under Ice*.
In 2016, the Whitefish (MT) Library Association honored her
with its first "Spirit of Dorothy Johnson" award for her work
telling the stories of the people of the Old West, particularly
the Montana Vigilantes.
The Ghost at Beaverhead Rock is the fourth novel in the
Vigilante Quartet.
She lives in Kalispell, Montana, with her husband of 40 years,
Richard Buchanan.
Her website is http://carol-buchanan.com

CPSIA information can be obtained
at www.ICGtesting.com
Printed in the USA
LVOW12s0125261016

510289LV00002B/375/P